LOST
BLADES

Lost Blades

Blades of the Goddess Book 1

Liz Sauco

Dark Waters Publishing

Lost Blades
Hardcover ISBN: 978-1-960723-01-7
Paperback ISBN: 978-1-960723-00-0
E-book ISBN: 978-1-960723-03-1
Audiobook ISBN: 978-1-960723-02-4

Published by Dark Waters Publishing
5600 Post Rd
Suite 114-PMB#307
East Greenwich RI 02818

First edition: September 2023
10 9 8 7 6 5 4 3 2 1

Cover design by Liz Sauco

lizsauco.com

To Mom and Dad.

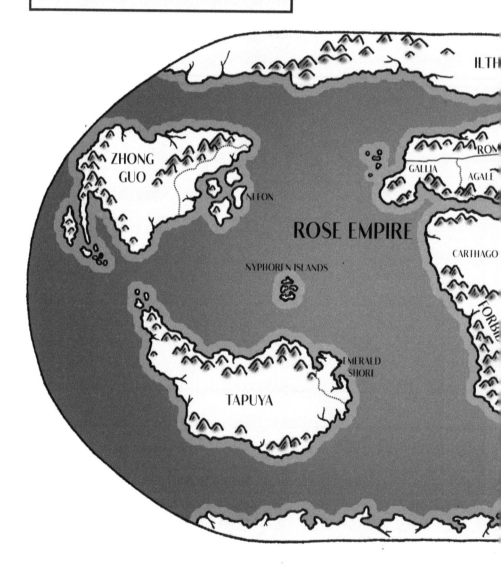

WORLD MAP
GAIA
COUNTRIES - 2026 AG

ILTH

ZHONG GUO

NEON

ROM

GALLIA

AGALE

ROSE EMPIRE

CARTHAGO

NYPHOREN ISLANDS

FORBID

EMERALD SHORE

TAPUYA

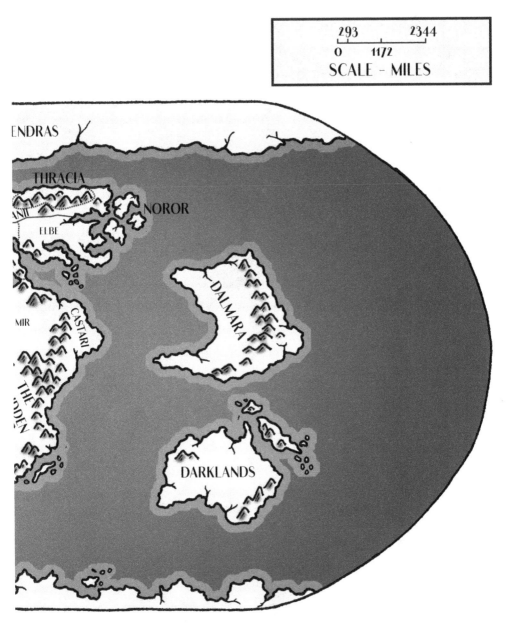

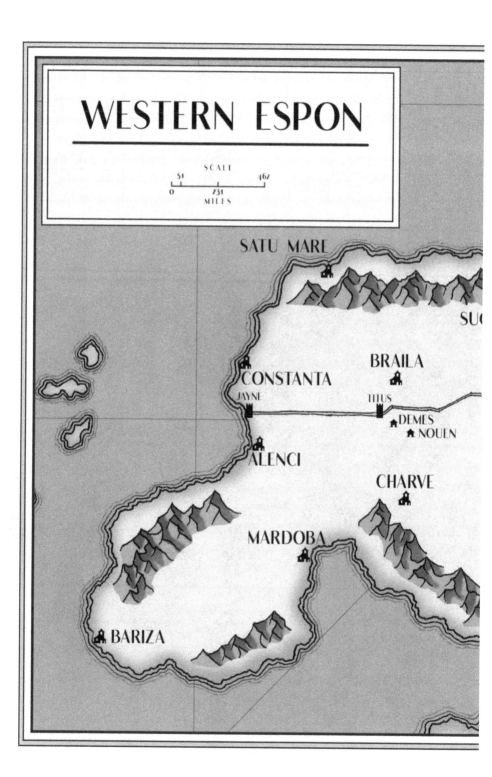

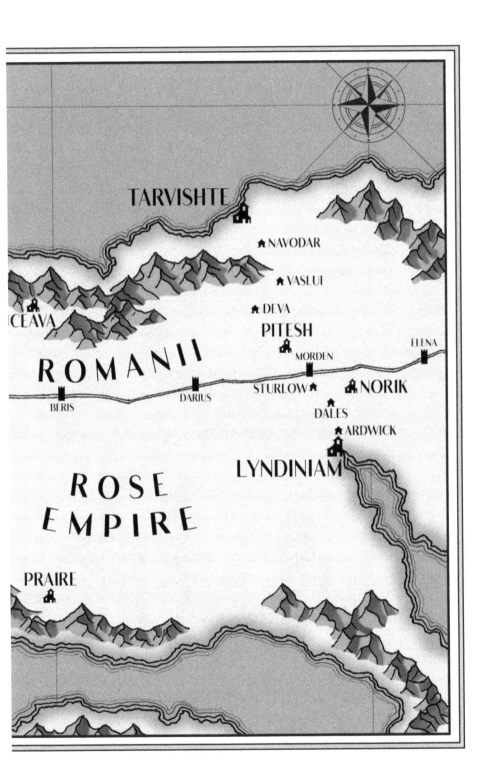

Chapter One

"**H**ey! Look at me!"

A voice cut through the surrounding haze where nothing else had. He tried to focus on it.

"Come on. You can do it."

He was trying, but he couldn't focus on the voice long enough to figure out where the sound was coming from.

"Damn; they hit you pretty badly, huh?"

He couldn't even lift his head from where it rested on his chest, a position he wasn't entirely sure how he had gotten into. He thought he heard a sigh.

"*Look at me.*"

A musical ring, almost like bells echoing, entered the voice, and he felt compelled to lift his head until he met violet eyes.

"Ah, that's it."

Immediately his head cleared and most of the pain faded, allowing him to focus on where he was.

He appeared to be in a cage, with dark metal bars and harsh lighting. It was just big enough for him, a small lumpy cot, and a waste disposal unit. The room holding the cage was gray and bare; it had only one door, with a sophisticated electronic lock, and no windows.

Wonderful. He was in jail.

There were seven other cages in the room, but only the one across from him was occupied. An Avari woman with long white hair tied up in a ponytail and curious violet eyes had somehow hooked her legs through the bars that crossed the top of her cage and was hanging upside down, long ears twitching happily. Her all-black clothing fit tightly to her body; it looked nothing like any of the local fashions. There were no guards in sight.

Then again, he was in the middle of a security station in the heart of the Empire. Of course they would have only the latest technology to keep lawbreakers in their nice cozy cages. No extra guards were required; every move they made was most likely being monitored and watched carefully for any hint of escape. Probably by more tech programmed to look for such things so no one would have to do such a dull and boring job.

She waved at him.

He stared at the woman blankly, unsure what to make of her. She was looking at him intently, but the effect was somewhat diminished by her position.

She looked ridiculous.

Then she smiled, ears perking up happily as she saw that she had his attention. "Welcome back to the land of the living," she said cheerfully. "It seems like they really don't like you, the way they just threw you in there like a sack of bricks. Are you feeling any better now?"

He ignored her, feeling his own ears drop slightly in annoyance, and brought a hand up to rub his eyes. He was not feeling quite up to speaking yet, and especially not with some weird person hanging upside down in a jail cell.

He felt a sudden spike of panic, and his hand darted down to his ankle. He touched metal and sucked in a breath in relief; his key was still tied there.

The woman seemed to take his movement as an affirmative and began to swing herself from side to side silently for a few minutes as he tried to get the last of his headache to go away. "So... what are you in here for?" she asked finally, interest clear in her voice.

He raised his eyebrows and sighed, shaking his head and letting his gaze sweep over the room again, not that there was much to look at. He didn't feel up to dealing with eccentric strangers right now. He shivered as a cold draft worked its way by him; his coat was gone. His new, warm, comfy, gray coat. It was probably considered evidence for the stolen chips, he figured glumly. Or they had wanted to make him suffer a little. Either option was a possibility.

He sighed and picked himself up off the floor to sit on the cot. It felt even lumpier than it looked, but it was better than the floor. At least everything was dry and looked clean – that was even an improvement over his normal living arrangements, where filth was practically a method of interior decorating, and the weather affected the inside of structures only marginally less than the outside. Even the fabric covering the cot was of a higher quality than he was used to.

"Well?"

He looked over at his chatty neighbor in annoyance, realizing that she was still waiting for an answer. Part of him wondered absently if she just didn't like silence. "Do you really want to know?" His voice was a little rough, but at least it didn't waver or slur. Better than he had hoped for after such a hit to the head. For that matter, he was surprised that his short ponytail was still mostly in place, just a few ruby-colored strands escaping their tie.

Her eyes widened, violet meeting silver, and she nodded earnestly at him.

He sighed again and cast his thoughts back to earlier in the day, before everything had gone to hell.

"Watch it!"

"My apologies, Miss."

The young waiter side-stepped out of the woman's way, barely missing the embroidered hem of her floor-length red gown. He took a moment to steady the drinks on his tray before continuing to thread his way through the crowd of gamblers and eye candy a little more carefully, pausing every so often to allow one of the patrons to take a full glass or place down an empty one before moving on.

There were many men and women here like the one in the red dress. Only the truly rich and influential were invited to the annual party at the Silver Ring Casino, and the truly rich of the Empire were generally also the truly snobbish. It did not matter that he had not actually made contact with the woman in any way, only that she had perceived the possibility – that something that was supposed to be a background object had intruded on her personal space and impeded her graceful movements. Or perhaps it had been his dark-red hair that had alarmed her, just a few shades too red to be Human, or the pointed ears that marked him as Avari. He didn't think she'd gotten a good look at his eyes, but the silver definitely would have given him away. Humans were always wary around the Avari these days, and such interactions were common between the two races.

He supposed it was possible that she simply hadn't expected to see an Avari at such a high-class party, but the kitchen had been understaffed for the event. A few Avari had been hired to help the regular Human workers take care of the guests, and he had joined the unfamiliar faces tonight so that he could carry out his plan.

When his tray was filled with empty glasses he made his way back to the kitchen, nodding to the security guard on the way in and ignoring the beep. Dropping the tray on a nearby counter, he quickly moved through the noise and activity until he came to a door in the back. He glanced around to make sure no one was watching as he entered the deserted room where the help changed into the provided uniforms. Approaching the place where he'd left his regular clothing, he pulled a handful of casino chips out from his pocket and hid them with the small stash that he had previously gathered. He made sure they were out of sight again before he returned to the kitchen to pick up another tray of glasses and return to the party.

Casinos such as the Silver Ring still used a chip system on the floor instead of the universal credit system that reigned outside. While credit provided the government with a clear record of purchases and sales, the chips themselves were untraceable and worth a lot of money – and thus could be sold for untraceable paper cash on the black market. Cash could only be used on the black market, but having the resources to get food for a few months was worth the risk to get it.

And there was risk. Though the chips were untraceable in an attempt to keep them as vintage as possible, the casinos did have security measures in place to keep them within their buildings. All doors leading from the floor had sensors that would beep and flash red if chips passed through them. Guards were stationed next to each sensor, and any offender was quickly escorted back to the exchange terminal.

However, though there was a sensor and a guard next to the door to the kitchen, the rules were a little different for the servers. Since they got tipped for making special trips for guests, the sensor went off nearly every time they went through. The management did not want their employees to waste time exchanging their chips every single time they got tipped, so as long as the sensor didn't flash red on their way through at the end of their shift it was ignored. He was using this to his advantage, carefully relieving the patrons of a few chips here and there and leaving them with his clothing. He was careful to bring a few back with him so the sensor would trigger on his way onto the floor, ensuring the guard wouldn't know he was leaving them in the back. This surprisingly simple plan would allow him to sell the chips on the black market later. He already had a dealer in mind who would more than appreciate the chips and pay him well.

The last few years had been difficult, and he'd been barely scraping by. He just wanted to be able to buy food. He didn't want to have to steal, or to worry about where his next meal was coming from, or if it was even coming at all. All he had to do was put up with a few rich, snobby, bigoted Humans for a few hours.

He had noticed the event two years ago as he had been wandering through the city. He hadn't paid it any mind at the time, but it wasn't long before he began to wonder how hard it would be to steal from the casino guests. They were very wealthy; surely they could stand to lose a little money that would go to a better cause. Over the course of the next few days the idea had kept coming back, until he finally considered looking into it. He began researching both the casino and the event, eventually deciding to observe the next party the casino held and hit the one after that. It had been a lot of work and a long buildup, requiring patience and dedication, but now it was all paying off. He could not have hoped for things to be going any more smoothly.

He skillfully weaved through the crowd with his tray, offering drinks as he went. Most of the conversation around him concerned the sentencing of Lady Hotaru's murderer, which was scheduled to happen within the next few days in the Ni Fon province. People seemed pretty split on whether the punishment would be death or banishment. Would the Emperor himself do the sentencing? Lady Hotaru had been the daughter of one of the seven provincial dukes, but Ni Fon was far and the Emperor rarely left Agale. He had heard a wide variety of stories surrounding the lady's death over the past eight months, and even the Avari found themselves gossiping about it. He himself did not overly care about the court drama of the Human nobles who ran the Empire, but there were many others who did. He did find it interesting that the killer had been a Human, and Hotaru's fiancé. But at least that made it not an Avari problem.

He had already amassed quite a few chips, and he was planning on making two or three more runs before leaving. He had slowed his intake to decrease the chances of getting caught, and now he was gearing up for the final part of the plan – escape.

"Excuse me?"

He blinked, ears perking up, surprised anyone would directly address him in a non-negative fashion, and turned around to see a blonde Human in a sparkly, skimpy white dress blinking large blue eyes at him. He immediately offered her the tray, thinking that she might simply want a drink, but she didn't so much as glance at it. Her eyes gained a predatory gleam and her smile widened.

Something about that set off an alarm in his head. He suddenly felt very uncomfortable, his ears dropping.

She moved closer, then followed him when he took a hasty step back. "I'm thirsty for something else, lovely. Oh, your eyes! So pretty. Silver is such a lovely color. And it goes so well with your hair! What's your name?" she cooed, reaching out as though to touch him.

He was sure that under other circumstances this would be funny, considering she looked to be about four years younger than him, maybe seventeen or eighteen, but he couldn't find it in himself to be amused. Instead he felt vaguely sick and took another step back. He tried not to think about how Avari often disappeared when they gained these sorts of attentions from Humans. It was illegal, but such trafficking did occur, especially among the rich. Why was this happening now?

"Umm..."

"Waiter."

The girl's smile slipped from her face as she looked at something over his shoulder. He stepped to the side to keep her in his line of sight and immediately saw the issue. A tall Human woman with intricately pinned-up white hair – or was it a pale blonde? She looked too young to have naturally white hair – stood a few feet behind him. Her gown was such a dark green that it was nearly black and had what looked like diamonds sparkling at the edges. A net veil covered the top half of her face, but he could still make out the sharp green eyes pinning him in place. Everything about her screamed power and wealth. "I would like a Turmoi Martini," she continued, seeing that she had his attention. "Fetch one for me."

He bowed immediately, hiding his relief as he sensed an escape from the blonde. "Of course, Miss," he murmured, careful to speak at a proper volume. "It will be a moment." He started to move away.

But before he was able to take more than a step, the blonde grabbed his arm. "Go find another one," she snapped, just barely civil. "This one's busy."

The pale-haired woman tilted her head ever so slightly to the side, taking in the situation. "Indeed; he is busy getting me my drink. I would appreciate it if you would allow him to do so." She leveled a pointed gaze at the blonde's grip on his arm.

"No he is not! I asked for his help, and he was just about to come with me." She looked at the now petrified thief and managed a sweet smile. "Were you not?" she asked almost kindly, looking at him hopefully. It was disturbing, and the sick feeling intensified as his stomach dropped.

"This is not an auction or a store for you to shop at, Ms. Kirsin. Do I have to remind you that he works here? He is not here for your entertainment, but to get the rest of us what we ask for."

The smile disappeared as the blonde snapped her gaze back to the woman. "He's mine!" she hissed, refusing to give up. "When I tell my father–"

"Yes, let us tell your father," the pale-haired woman interrupted. "You are making a scene, which I'm sure he will appreciate, and I also think that he'll be very interested in the Gallian apples, don't you?"

The woman's voice was cold as she gazed at the girl, who paled, then flushed, then paled again. She opened her mouth to speak, but nothing came out, leaving her looking rather like a fish searching for food. Her shock was palpable, and he could see it warring with the livid anger on her face.

The woman's dark-red lips turned up ever so slightly into a smile. "I didn't think so."

It was pretty clear to the thief who had won this battle. The blonde managed to pull herself together long enough to shoot a vicious glare at the woman. She snatched her hand away from him, turned on her heel, and stormed away without looking back.

He barely managed to refrain from a sigh of relief. Saved!

But then the woman turned her sharp gaze on him, pinning the thief in place before he could escape to the safety of the kitchen. She surprised him, though, when her gaze softened by a fraction.

"Now would be a good time for you to leave," she suggested coolly. "That girl is very possessive, and you do not want to end up as one of her playthings. Forget about the drink." Her gaze lingered on him for just a moment more, then she stepped back into the crowd and was gone almost immediately.

The thief stood there, frozen in shock for several long moments. Saved by a Human! But whatever her reason, she had given sound advice. He didn't trust the blonde to continue to leave him alone once she noticed that the other woman had left. It was definitely time to go; he had stolen more than enough to last him for quite some time anyway.

He quickly moved off to the side of the room, and after checking to make sure no one was looking, he dropped all the chips he had on him into the massively leafy branches of a convenient potted plant. He then put the last two drinks on his tray onto a nearby end table and headed back towards the kitchen.

When he reached the guard, he stopped. "This was my last trip," he informed the man, who nodded silently as he passed through the sensor. The light flashed green, and the guard waved him towards the kitchen. He dropped his tray on the nearest counter and headed back to the changing room. Luckily no one else was there, and within a few minutes he had changed back into his normal clothing with his precious cargo stowed in various pockets throughout his coat. He stuffed the uniform in a nearby locker and darted out the door towards freedom. He smiled as the back door to the Silver Ring closed behind him, leaving him in a side alley.

He had actually done it! He had succeeded in stealing from one of the most prestigious casinos in the entire city of Lyndiniam – no, the entire province of Agale, the very heart of the Empire!

He was going to be rich.

His mood improving considerably from the nauseating encounter with the blonde girl, he strolled out of the alley onto the main street and emerged into the bustling nightlife.

Buildings made of white lester and glass climbed in clean, straight lines all around him. Here in the center of the Empire, everything was made to be sleek, ageless, and modern. Greenery was carefully controlled. The streets were smooth, paved with a modified silvery-gray lester. The casino was the one building that stood out – in another attempt to be more traditional, the giant doors were framed in a dark-gray stone, with flourishes and decorations etched into it. Despite the late hour, the streets were crowded with people as they went along to their destinations, talking and laughing to one another as they went. Officers of the City Guard stood at attention at their posts in sharp black-and-gray uniforms, keeping a watchful eye on the populace, ready to act at the first sign of trouble.

It was nothing like the part of the city he hailed from, where Avari had to make do with whatever scraps they could get and crime ran rampant.

The cool autumn wind blew by him as he started down the street. The weather had only just started to change, but it would be cold soon enough. Winter was always difficult when you lived in buildings that were open to the elements and didn't retain heat, but this year he now had enough money to spend the cold season comfortably. His winter coat was another new thing this year; it was plain, but warm. A good steal. All in all he was looking forward to a good winter.

As he approached the front of the Silver Ring, he could hear what sounded like crying coming from within the building. The giant doors were open, and as he passed by he glanced into the lobby. He blinked in surprise as he saw the blonde girl from earlier with her white dress torn and her hair a mess. She was sobbing as she talked to several guard officers, one of which had a digital pad and stylus in hand and looked to be taking notes. Then she looked past the officer and locked eyes with him.

She screamed, backing up and pointing one damning finger at him.

The thief didn't know what exactly she had told them, but he could bet it wasn't good, and there was absolutely no one who would take an Avari's word over that of a rich, young, female Human. They wouldn't even bother asking questions. He would have no chance.

So he turned and ran.

Straight into two members of the Guard.

Luck was with him; they seemed surprised to have the blonde screaming and pointing in their direction. He dropped and spun, kicking his leg out to sweep the closer officer's legs out from beneath him. In the background, he heard a voice yell "Stop him!" and knew he had no time to get into a brawl. The other officer didn't react quickly enough, and a strong elbow to the stomach cleared an escape route, but that was when his luck ran out. The other officers had gotten close enough to join the fight, and one flying tackle landed him on the ground with the breath knocked out of him and an officer on top of him. He tried to twist and kick free but couldn't break the officer's grip. Sudden pain blossomed in his head and stars appeared as the officer slammed his head down into the ground, momentarily stunning him. This was all the opportunity the officers needed to subdue him long enough to cuff his hands behind him.

He was roughly hauled up off the ground and slammed against the hood of a nearby guard vehicle. His cheek was pressed against the hard material, and he moved just a little to rest his aching head against the cool surface. He could still hear the girl screaming in the background. "It was him!" she shrieked, over and over again. He wished she would stop as he tried to focus on what was going on around the pounding in his head. He was already being arrested; what more did she want? He felt the officer's hands begin to search him, then freeze when they encountered one of the many pockets full of stolen casino chips.

Not only was Luck no longer helping him, but she seemed to be cheering for the other side as the officer pulled out a handful of black-and-silver chips. The thief heard the officer's sharp intake of breath. Briefly he entertained the idea that the guard would let go of him in shock, but if anything the hold on him tightened. "An assailant and a thief," the guard spat in disgust.

That really didn't seem quite right to him as he tried to fight the disorientation that was steadily getting worse. He hadn't attacked any... oh. Oh. He should have figured that the blonde bitch would have told them something like that.

"What else did you expect from an Avari?" he heard another officer snort. "It's not like they know how to behave."

He reflected in a somewhat detached fashion that he was never going to see the light of day again as he felt himself being manhandled into the vehicle. He was starting to feel increasingly dizzy as he watched the lights of the city pass by in an incomprehensible blur as they drove to one of the security stations located in the city.

By the time they arrived, he had to be pulled from the vehicle and dragged into the building, as the dizziness and disorientation had increased to the point where he had to focus completely on staying awake. If he fell asleep now, he had a feeling he wouldn't be waking up again. He couldn't pay any attention to what was going on around him, where he was going, or what was happening to him. Distantly, he felt himself hit a hard surface, which knocked the breath out of him again.

"Hey! Look at me!"

Well, why not?

"I assaulted someone and stole millions from a casino."

The woman blinked, looking almost confused and a little disappointed as her ears drooped a bit. She eyed him for a moment, then raised an eyebrow skeptically.

He shrugged and decided not to explain any further. "How did you get in here, then?" he asked.

She smiled, ears perking up. "I walked."

He opened his mouth to clarify, then shut it. He wondered if she was insane, and if he should be questioning his own sanity for expecting a straight answer out of someone who had been hanging upside down for an indeterminate period of time.

"This isn't the main jail," he said instead, changing the subject and giving the room another look.

"No, it's not. You were arrested after admissions closed for the night, so we're just in Officer HQ Security Station until the morning." She began to swing herself slightly from side to side again.

Then he realized that his headache was not just better, but gone. Completely. Which was strange, as he was pretty sure that he had had a concussion. His memory was still rather fuzzy, but he could remember seeing violet eyes, and there was only one other person around.

"What did you do?" he asked suddenly, shifting to look at her.

She gave him a puzzled look. "I walked?"

"I had a concussion," he clarified. "But now I feel a lot better, and that doesn't seem possible unless you did something. What?"

She smiled and shrugged, which looked odd, given her position. "Oh, that. Magic."

He stared at her. "Crazy" was sounding like a better and better explanation. "Magic doesn't exist anymore," he reminded her slowly, wondering at the same time why he was even bothering.

"Do your concussions often heal themselves?" she asked curiously.

"What? No–"

She cut him off with a happy grin. "Of course not! Concussions don't do that. So the answer is obviously magic. Unless you have a better explanation?"

He was flabbergasted. Why was magic more likely than a self-healing concussion? He shrugged, groping for a better answer. "New technology?"

She gave him an amused look. "If you say so."

Silence fell between them for a minute or two. Maybe he had actually guessed right, since she hadn't tried to argue the point. It certainly made more sense than magic. Still, he wondered what type of tech could fix a concussion from over ten feet away.

"So... what is your name?" she asked suddenly.

He paused. "Jamirh," he finally offered.

Her eyes narrowed, and for a moment he thought he saw something dark flash in them, but it was gone so quickly he wasn't sure he had seen it at all. "I did not ask what you are called; I asked what your name is." Something in her voice changed, echoed.

He stared at her, bemused.

She stared back.

"My name is Jamirh," he finally said, ears lowering slightly. He didn't know what she was going on about, but this was ridiculous. He'd answered her; did she have to pry further?

She frowned slightly, her own ears drooping unhappily. "Stronger, this time, but whatever. I suppose you can call me Hel, then."

She was an all-around strange, annoying, invasive, insane person, and he tried to stop himself, but in the end he had to ask. "What kind of name is Hel?"

She smiled. "A very, very old one. Now, I strongly suggest you try to get some sleep. We have a big day tomorrow."

"What–"

He was cut off by a dull buzzing sound emanating from the other side of the door as the lights went out, leaving them in total darkness. Not even the emergency lights remained lit.

"Well, would you look at that." He couldn't see her, but he just knew from the tone of her voice that she had a feral grin on her face. "It's tomorrow already!"

Chapter Two

"Well, I'm sorry you didn't get any sleep, but it's time to go." Hel sounded like she could barely contain her glee.

Jamirh was trying very hard to control his temper. "What are you talking about? In case you haven't noticed, we are locked in metal cages."

"No we're not." He could hear the cheer in her voice. "Try the door."

"I can't see the door," he snapped, rapidly losing ground in his internal battle to stay calm.

A small ball of white light suddenly appeared over one of her hands, illuminating the room. Hel was grinning almost manically as she reached up to grab the bars she was hanging from so she could swing down. The little ball of light stayed where it was, hovering in place. "Can you see now?" she asked smugly as she calmly pushed open the door to her cage. Then she wobbled a bit, putting a hand to her head. "Oh, okay, that feels weird. New feeling. Not good."

He blinked and winced at the sudden brightness. Then he stared in surprise at the small flare, trying to reconcile it with logic and sense.

Perhaps she was one of those experimental bionics that the government was supposedly producing? He didn't know what the cybernetic implants were and all that they entailed, but it could explain the mental instability if her mind had been unable to cope. It was possible that she had convinced herself that she could do magic if that were the case; he had seen similar delusions in others living on the streets who had suffered traumatizing events.

He stood and walked the two steps to the door and pushed it, watching with some surprise as it opened. "More of your 'magic'?" he asked dryly, deciding to humor her.

She smiled at him. "The light, yes. The general power outage and other problems this building is suffering, no. We had outside help with that." She all but skipped over to the door, but then paused to eye Jamirh, who hadn't moved. "Aren't you coming?" she asked pleasantly. "Surely you don't want to stay arrested?"

Jamirh briefly considered his options. On the one hand, he hadn't been conscious enough to take note of how to get out of the building by himself. Also, if Hel was bionic, as he had begun to suspect, she could prove useful in escape. On the other hand, Hel was clearly unhinged, and that unstable element could land them right back behind bars. Wander around by himself and risk recapture trying to find an exit, or rely on a crazy chick. He was so stuck between a rock and a hard place.

And it was... strange, that the building had lost literally all power. Shouldn't buildings like security stations have a generator or something in the event of a power outage like this? And weren't emergency lights and systems made to be able to function despite power loss?

"Fine," he agreed. "But once we're outside, we go our separate ways."

Hel grinned triumphantly. "Stay close!" She brought the little light close to her lips as she reached out with her other hand to grab his. The woman hummed a few short, sorrowful notes, and the light flickered and died. "Remember to be quiet or they'll find us," she whispered in a sing-song tone as she squeezed his hand. "And don't let go!"

And then they were moving. Avari needed less light to see than Humans, but they did need some light. He had no idea how Hel planned to find her way in the dark, but after the first few turns were made without crashing into the walls, it was pretty clear that the lack of light was not going to be an issue. He considered as they traveled and decided that night vision was probably a pretty basic artificial enhancement.

But nothing explained what Hel was doing in an overnight cell in Officer HQ.

Suddenly Jamirh tensed as he was yanked to one side and pressed against a wall. A hand covered his mouth, stifling his instinctive grunt of surprise. "Shh," he heard Hel breathe in his ear. He nodded once to show he understood, and she removed her hand from his mouth as they both waited, listening.

After a moment, he heard the sounds of someone farther down the corridor stumbling around in the dark over the continued buzzing of the alarm, which had been getting louder as they progressed. Whoever it was did not seem to care about being heard; he was swearing and clearly having a difficult time in the dark.

"Mavin, report!" A sharp voice crackled over a transmitter, easily audible over the droning.

"It's pitch black down here, Captain. I'm about halfway to the cells. I think," he added quietly. "Whoever misplaced the glowlights is in for it."

There was a slight pause, during which Jamirh heard the guard stumble and crash to the floor amid much more cursing. Jamirh could feel the amusement pouring off Hel as she began to quietly inch them away down the hall. "Just make sure the cells are still locked." The woman's voice sounded oddly strained. "Out."

"This is ridiculous," Mavin snarled as they got farther away. "Where would he go?"

Where indeed, Jamirh thought as they moved away.

Soon they could no longer hear the unfortunate officer and were back to their original speed. Hel led him down several more hallways before a turn revealed a little pinprick of blue light indicating active tech of some sort a few feet away, barely revealing the fuzzy outline of a door. The lock was still active. Hel stopped short, allowing Jamirh to catch a glance at her face and the puzzled expression on it. Suddenly her eyes narrowed as she strode forward to the door, steps just shy of stomps, and made several short, angry clicking sounds.

The light cheerfully ignored her.

Hel dropped to one knee so she was eye level with the light, still gripping his hand. Her hiss had just as little effect as the clicks, and her expression turned just short of livid. Jamirh had just enough time to wonder what she thought she was doing before she abruptly stood and dragged him several paces away from the door.

The sound she made then was nothing like the clicks or the hiss. It was somewhere between a roar and a shriek. It was loud and piercing, and Jamirh swore at her as he tried to jerk away to cover his ears. Three things then happened all at the same time.

The door exploded.

All the lights came back on.

Alarms started to scream through the building.

Jamirh felt partially deafened by the echo of the sound ringing in his ears as Hel looked at him sheepishly, her ears lowered slightly in embarrassment.

"This may be time for speed rather than stealth. They'll have probably heard that and be on their way," she offered.

He gaped at her, his ears practically flattening in rage. "The whole *city* probably heard that! And now they have power!"

She paused for a moment, considering. "I don't think I had anything to do with the power, and I do doubt that anyone outside the building heard me. Can we go now?" The question was hopeful as her ears perked up again.

He stared at her.

"Good!" She began to pull him down the hallway. "This way!"

He reluctantly followed, having huge misgivings about going with her, but not having a choice in the matter. He consoled himself with the thought that they would be separating soon, whether or not they actually escaped.

They began to run, but as they spun around a corner, chaos ensued as they crashed into a very surprised squad of officers who had been running in their direction. Shouts erupted all around. Jamirh slammed hard into one of them, then felt his arm scream in pain as Hel continued moving without releasing the vice-like grip on it. He stumbled after her as best he could through the confused tangle, breaking into a run when they somehow reached the other side. He could hear the officers shouting for backup on transmitters as they dashed away.

They slid around another corner and burst through a door into the main lobby. Both officers and civilians were ignored as Jamirh and Hel jumped over a nearby desk, heading for the double glass doors. Suddenly Hel pulled him sharply to the left and down, just before Jamirh heard shots ring out behind them. The little light to the right of the doors blinked from green to blue.

Jamirh cringed, realizing that they were going to slam into reactive glass, but their momentum carried them through the first set before the chemical process could begin. Unfortunately, the second set was already turning from clear glass to a dull gray metal. Jamirh tried to stop, but Hel made that awful shrieking sound once more and pulled them through the resulting shards of what had been the door.

Freedom!

Hel paused, and Jamirh used the hesitation to break free from her grip before sprinting to the right through startled citizens and darting into the first alley he came across. He vaulted over a low wall and dashed across the next street and into another alley. Quickly scrambling up a pile of boxes leaning against the building to the roof, he glanced behind him – no Hel. Pursuit did not sound far behind, and he could see officers in the street below, but they did not seem to have noticed him ascend to the roofs and were pushing their way through the crowded street.

Strange. He hadn't thought it would be that easy. Why hadn't they seen him enter the alley? They hadn't been that far behind. Perhaps they had followed Hel?

He decided he wouldn't look a gift horse in the mouth.

He crossed several roofs before dropping into yet another alley. He entered the adjoining street at a brisk walk and was instantly hidden in the crowd, just one more in a sea of faces.

He shivered in the crisp air, again mourning the loss of his coat. He swiped a steaming hot beverage off a café table as he passed, its previous owner too busy digging around in her purse to notice. He took a sip: coffee, black. Acceptable, though he would have preferred it a little sweeter. Well, a lot sweeter, but this was fine. He savored the warmth as he made his way back to the Blackfields district.

Here, the buildings were far, far older, and made of stone, brick, and steel instead of the safer and more uniform lester. Often they were falling apart due to their great age. The only thing that kept them standing was that the government didn't have the money or time to tear them down and replace them with new buildings for "legitimate homes and businesses". This made them perfect for the "illegitimate" homes and businesses of the dregs of society, the vast majority of which were Avari. Whores, drug dealers, assassins, and thieves like himself all lived and worked in this neglected section of Lyndiniam, the smear on the jewel of the Empire. It was one of the few areas in the entire city where most Avari could afford to live, but everyone knew the government would wipe it out if they could. At least his ruby-colored hair and silver eyes actually blended in more here.

A group of four Avari were lurking near the entrance to one of the more central squares in this section of Blackfields. An Avari with dark-blue hair and green eyes whistled as Jamirh passed, elbowing one of his friends. "Hey, look who it is! How's it go–"

"Shut up," Jamirh snapped, not in the mood to deal with their bullshit. He knew where this was going. He continued walking, avoiding the square itself.

"Aw, come on," another Avari laughed. "Surely, the great–"

"Nope," Jamirh cut her off. "Go find someone else's night to ruin." Gods, but he missed Aether. He'd always known how to stop the badgering, had known when Jamirh just could not deal with it.

He heard their laughter fade into the distance as he continued home. He refused to let himself dwell on it as he walked through the crumbling streets. Some of the houses on the edges of the district were still structurally sound, and some were even kind of nice and well-kept, even if they were small and simple. But as Jamirh traveled deeper into Blackfields, the buildings became less sound, more decrepit. The lighting was hit or miss, but Jamirh had grown up here, and he knew his way around even in the dark. Some Avari called out to him as he passed, but he just answered with a wave and kept going. He continued through dim and narrow streets, avoiding trash, debris, and the occasional grasping hand. He wanted to collapse.

He turned down another alley, hopping the wall of almost-filled trashcans in the way and dropping the now-empty coffee cup into one. Carefully picking his way to the back of the alley and avoiding the few traps he'd set up, he shifted the large, heavy board that covered the entrance to his little hole-in-the-wall home and slipped inside. He replaced the board and took two steps to the rope ladder hanging from a hole in the ceiling. He climbed up with the ease of long practice and pulled the ladder up behind him before sealing it up with another board. He turned on the glow lamp, glancing around to make sure everything was as it should be.

The room was small and cramped, but mostly weatherproofed with the help of a number of blankets and boards Jamirh had acquired since finding this place. A pile of blankets made up his bed in one corner, and he had a small, cracked table and wobbly chair in the other. Three beat-up paperbacks lay in a neat pile on the table, a recent find he'd been very excited to stumble across. He didn't dare keep food in here, but there were a few bottles of water stashed under the table. A few other personal items and clothes were scattered about. The space was as clean as he could manage, but stains and dirt were visible on every surface.

Home.

He flopped down on his bed, taking a moment to relish the feeling of no longer being vertical and the slightly scratchy feel of his blankets. Then he reached down and untied his key from around his ankle, rubbing the worn, smooth metal between his fingers. The familiar action was soothing, and he turned the glow lamp off. He closed his eyes, feeling the cord the key hung on drape across his knuckles.

Then he slammed his fist down on the bed next to him. "Damn it," he snarled. "Damn it, damn it, damn it!" He felt sick to his stomach. Everything about tonight had turned out terribly. He was now in a worse spot than where he had started. He had lost the chips and his new coat, wasting nearly two years of planning. This winter would be just as difficult as the last few. Maybe even more difficult; he had just escaped prison. Would they come looking for him?

"Hey, it's not that bad!"

He startled, eyes snapping open at the sound of the familiar voice to see Hel looking down at him, her white hair giving her away even in the dark room.

"Holy– How the *hell* did you get in here?" He clutched the key tightly as he flung himself away from her, back pressing against the wall as his heart hammered in his chest. The worn metal pressed into his palm, grounding him.

If she was bothered by his reaction, she didn't show it, calmly turning the glow lamp back on. "I followed you," she admitted easily from where she knelt next to the bed.

"Why?!" he all but wailed, pressing his fist to his chest, trying to calm his heartbeat. "How?"

She blinked, taken aback. "I... I wanted to help you? Look, maybe just take a minute to breathe, okay? I'm sorry I scared you. I swear I didn't mean to." Her ears sank. "I forget, sometimes..." She trailed off.

He sucked in a couple of breaths before glaring at her with all the venom he could muster. "Why?" he repeated.

"Well, you helped me escape."

There was no way she'd needed him for that. But still. "No; why would I need your help?"

She shrugged. "Just because? Also, that girl you supposedly attacked has put up quite a fuss. While I was enjoying the hospitality of the nice officers currently searching for us, they were discussing how her father has proclaimed that he will not rest until justice has been served."

"So?" He raised an eyebrow, but his stomach sank. Her words echoed the direction his thoughts had been going right before she'd scared the living daylights out of him. He rubbed at his key again.

"Well, he's sort of a very powerful noble, with the time, money, and connections to ensure that you are eventually tracked down."

"Who–"

"The Duke of Agale, Stefan Belian."

Jamirh paled. "Shit." His night just kept getting worse. It figured that he would piss off one of the most important and powerful men in the country. Duke Belian governed the province of Agale, the wealthiest and most important province in the Empire, as it was the original country that the Empire had been born from. As the duke of that province, Belian would have everything and anything he needed to hunt down one escaped Avari prisoner.

Jamirh was also very lucky, however. Though he hadn't recognized her first name, both Kirsin Belian and her father were rumored to be cruel and sadistic to any Avari unlucky enough to fall into their clutches. With a shudder, he steered his thoughts away from what he had escaped earlier that night when the pale woman had saved him from Kirsin. Still...

"Why did you follow me, then? Seems to me it would be better to get away," he pointed out, slowly uncurling from his defensive position.

She shrugged. "I try not to abandon the unjustly accused. Also, like I said before, I can help you."

"Why?" he asked bitterly. "How? There won't be anywhere safe for me in the whole Empire."

Hel nodded. "Exactly. So you should leave the Empire."

Jamirh stared at her. "Are you crazy? Leave the Empire? And go where, exactly? Somehow book passage off this continent when they control all the ports?"

"Well, you wouldn't need to leave the continent, per se. Technically the true northern boundary of the Empire is the Warcross Wall," she corrected.

He wondered just how deep her mental instability ran. "You're suggesting I live in a desolate wasteland? There's nothing north of the Wall. Nothing alive, anyway."

"Wrong." She grinned. "Though that mindset does work to our advantage." She sat back on her heels. "In reality, there is an entire country north of the Wall. One that the Empire can't assimilate, so you'll be safe. I have family up there. There are some of our people down here who help people in danger cross the Wall." She paused, considering. "You definitely qualify, if you were wondering."

Clearly, the instability ran very deep. "How can the Empire – a government that controls nearly all of the world's population – have missed an entire country that shares one of their borders?"

She smiled, not unkindly. "Oh, they know about it, at the highest levels. It's just that it's easier to pretend it doesn't exist, since they can't interact with it. And as for how Romanii keeps itself separate, the answer is, of course, magic."

Jamirh opened his mouth to reply, stopped, and shut it again. He took a deep breath and counted to ten. Then he counted to ten again, and continued on to twenty for good measure. Why was he prolonging this conversation? Oh, right. Because she was in his home. Somehow. "The Empire built the Wall to keep the plague that wiped out the Gini from traveling south and wiping out the Humans and Avari. Though I suppose there was the added benefit of keeping the remaining Vampires out."

She blinked. "Where did you hear that?"

"School."

"You went to school?" She looked surprised.

"It's mandatory for all children ages five to fifteen to attend school in the mornings." He winced at the memory. "The Empire wants to be able to say that everyone has at least basic schooling, so the public schools are all free."

"Well, yes, but you actually went?"

"Free breakfast."

"Fascinating." She thought about that for a moment. "We didn't know about the free food. But I guess it's too much to ask that they would actually teach you real history and feed you. I suppose we should just be thankful that they teach reading and writing."

Taken aback, Jamirh stared at her. "What does that mean?"

"One, the Gini have not been wiped out by a plague, nor has that ever even been a worry. Two, a wall is a bad choice of barrier when the Gini are concerned, considering they have six wings and can fly. They just don't want anything to do with the Empire. And three, the Empire did not build the Wall. The short version is that when Romanii saw how the Empire was consuming everything around it, nine of their mages offered their lives to their mother-goddess, and She shaped their power into the Wall. That's what keeps Romanii safe and hidden from prying eyes." She shrugged. "More or less, anyway."

"You are not a Gini," he stated flatly.

Hel laughed. "No, no! The Gini live in the mountains. Romanii is between them and the Wall. Well, kind of around them, actually."

Jamirh shook his head. "You are so crazy."

"Well, you don't know me," she agreed. "But your choices right now are either to wait to become a Human's plaything, or trust the crazy lady and maybe have a chance of getting out of this in one piece." She looked around at the room. "They'll find this place, eventually. There's nowhere in Lyndiniam that will be safe."

He didn't respond, knowing and hating the fact that she was right. But... this was all he had ever known. Leave? How could he?

How could he not?

"I'm sorry," she said quietly. "I know I ask a lot from you. But you aren't safe here. And no one here is safe while you remain."

That point was unfortunately good; the police wouldn't hesitate to ransack Avari areas if they felt like they had a good enough reason. Raids did happen in Blackfields.

He considered her. It was still far more likely that she was a rogue bionic with a dangerous mental instability than a... something from an invisible country. That idea was ridiculous. But where did that leave him? Was it better to follow her than not, if only because he had seen that she had abilities that could come in handy later?

Then again, that could work to his advantage. If she put all her abilities towards getting him out of the Empire, did it really matter where they went, or what she thought about where they were going, or why she was doing it? As long as he was safely away, who cared that she had created a whole country and alternate history in her mind? Once he was out of Belian's reach, he could figure out what he was going to do from there. He just had to find a way to avoid the danger of her delusions.

But that meant leaving his home. His fist tightened around the key.

He could become a hermit. Actually, that was looking like a really good idea right about now. Though if Hel's insanity was catching he was going to be a crazy hermit.

That was still preferable to being dead. Or worse.

He thought back to the other Avari he had passed on the way back. Without Aether to be a buffer, the callouts and harassment had been getting worse. Maybe he should leave. Start over again somewhere else. It would be hard, sure, but would it be any worse than where he was now?

"Jamirh?"

Yeah, that was what he wanted. He closed his eyes, hugging the key tightly to his chest for a moment before pulling the cord over his head. He slid the key under his shirt to rest against his chest. He glanced around regretfully, but he really didn't have anything else worth taking. He'd lost everything he might've wanted two years ago.

"All right," he agreed. "Let's go."

Her face lit up as her ears twitched happily.

He glanced at the still-covered hole to the exit. "How did you get in here, though?"

She followed his gaze and shrugged. "Magic."

"How convenient." He frowned, but then he decided this was also some sort of bionic enhancement, even if he didn't understand what it could even be.

They descended quickly, and Jamirh disabled the traps just outside. Someone else would find this place, and maybe they'd be better off for it.

"Hmm... this way!" Hel declared, and off they went.

They passed through the decrepit streets of his home quietly, avoiding people wherever possible. It was late enough now that most people were hidden away in their homes, or what passed for them. As they passed through an old market square, one that he normally would have avoided, Hel stopped to look at a pile of stones on the ground. "Is this marble?" she asked, poking at it with her foot.

Jamirh shrugged. "The old palace used to be somewhere around here, I think. From when the Empire was still called the Rose Empire."

Hel frowned. "Didn't there used to be some very impressive statues of Ebryn Stormlight nearby?" Her eyes traveled to an old plinth that had been shoved off to the side, engraved words made illegible by weather and age.

He shrugged again, looking away. "I have no idea. For all I know you're looking at one right now." He waved a hand at the stones at her feet. "Why would you want to see a statue of him, anyway?" he asked bitterly.

She looked at him, confused. "Because he was the Hero."

"The Hero," he spat, "who brought the Empire to power so that Avari could become second-class citizens."

Hel favored him with a dry look. "He was Avari. The queen he served was Avari. The Empire was still ruled by Avari several hundred years after his death."

"Without him the Empire would not have existed and Avari would be free from Humans. Everything we suffer is because of him," he snapped back.

Hel's look turned troubled. "That's not necessarily true. Is that something you learned in school?"

Jamirh snorted. "Nope. Personal opinion."

"But then—"

He was getting fed up with the whole conversation. "It's obvious that—"

Sirens suddenly split the air, cutting Jamirh off and sounding an awful lot closer than he was perfectly comfortable with.

Shit. They had locked down the city.

"At the very least, I would suggest getting out of Lyndiniam," Hel offered. "Soon."

"Fine," he snapped again. "Every road in and out of the city is blocked off by now, so how are we going to do that?"

She shrugged. "I don't know."

Jamirh couldn't stop himself from gaping at her. "You don't know? How were you planning on getting out in the first place?"

"I didn't exactly have an escape plan," she admitted, giving him a lopsided grin.

Jamirh took a deep breath to keep from strangling her. Then he had an idea. "This way!"

He took off at a run, Hel sprinting after him. He led her deeper into the maze of Blackfields. As they ran, he noticed that the few inhabitants who had been out were now nowhere to be seen, having already fled for safer places. As they wound through the streets, Jamirh tried to pick routes that would lead them farther from the alarms. Finally they came to a small building that was partially caved in with two gaping holes in its walls. Hel followed him closely as he moved to a small grate near the back.

"They haven't filled in the old sewer system yet?" Hel asked curiously, ears twitching.

"They tried," Jamirh replied, kneeling down to start work on the grate. "Most of the tunnels are filled in, but a few were overlooked." He wrenched the grate off and then turned to Hel. "It'll be a tight fit."

She nodded. "Let's go."

He motioned for her to go first. "It's a bit of a drop, and you'll need to angle a bit to the right to land on the ledge," he warned, sweeping his eyes out over the street. The sirens were getting closer. He waited a moment for her to squeeze herself through and drop to the ledge before beginning the process himself, holding on to the grate. As he fell through, the grate caught back in its original position, and he swung himself over to the ledge. He carefully felt around for the electric glow he had hidden here previously and switched it on to see Hel just a few feet away, shielding her eyes from the sudden brightness. He held his finger to his lips to indicate silence, then grabbed her wrist as he shut off the glow and started to head down the sewer. He had noted before that both light and sound carried in these tunnels, and he had no wish to be found.

They walked for several hours, Jamirh turning on the glow every so often to check where they were. Every once in a while they could hear the sounds of sirens from up above echoing through the tunnels, but that was the only sign of pursuit. They moved silently and quickly until they started to see pale but natural light filtering in from a turn up ahead. They hurried towards it and rounded the bend, immediately seeing the large opening to the outside blocked off by thick, vertical iron bars. He realized it was just before dawn.

Jamirh pulled on the bars, but though they were rusted they were firmly embedded in the old concrete and did not budge. "Can you screech at them?" he asked Hel, who had stopped a few feet back.

"Not if I want to avoid coughing up blood for the next week or so. I'm pushing it doing it twice in one day. But don't worry, we won't need that." She stared at the bars for a few moments before gesturing one hand in a small circle just in front of the iron. Violet light followed, forming some sort of complicated circular symbol as she touched the bars carefully. The light from the symbol shattered into bright motes of glitter-like light, which disappeared when they touched the bars. Hel stared at it critically for another moment before turning to Jamirh. "Kick it really, really hard, please."

He shook his head, trying to figure out if whatever she had just done was the same as the light from the cell or something different. "I'd rather not break my foot, if it's all the same to you."

She smiled. "You won't, I promise."

He thought about it, but only for a moment. A breeze drifted into the tunnel, causing the leaves to rustle invitingly on the other side of the bars. He had never much thought about what was beyond Lyndiniam, but suddenly he wanted nothing more than to find out. He placed a hand over his key. Maybe it was time.

His foot slammed through the metal as though it were made of brittle glass. Hel eyed the destruction approvingly as she began to move the foliage aside.

"What did you do to the bars?" Jamirh asked in confusion. He had not truly expected anything to happen; he had kicked out more on a whim than anything else.

She hesitated. "It's hard to explain. The metal was already old, past its intended period of use. It was rusted and not maintained. It probably would have fallen apart on its own in about fifty years or so. Inevitable, really. So I sort of hastened the inevitable by removing what life remained in the metal, which made it brittle. So it was like you kicked metal that was much, much older than it actually was. Does that make sense?"

He just sighed. Back to the magic delusions. "Metal doesn't have life."

The look she gave him was almost affronted. "Of course it does. Everything has life of some sort."

He shook his head. "Metal is metal. It doesn't think; it doesn't live. Though just out of curiosity, when you say 'magic', do you actually mean 'very sophisticated tech that I don't want to explain to you because you won't understand'?"

Hel cocked her head to the side. "Magic is magic, tech is tech. I can't work tech. It tends to end badly. Sort of like that first door we ran into in the security station." She shuddered. "Yeah... let's never mention that again, actually."

What was wrong with this woman? She actually seemed to believe this. He still didn't. He just shrugged, giving up. "Fine, whatever."

Hel smiled a little sadly at him and turned away. "We should get moving. We have a lot of ground to cover in a short period of time." She grinned back at him wryly. "And I can't wait to see how you handle Romanii."

Chapter Three

J amirh was already tired of walking.

Hel set a brutal pace, declaring that the farther they got before they stopped, the better off they would be. The sewer had spat them out in the suburbs making up the northern part of Lyndiniam. They avoided streets as best they could, slipping through yards and the occasional park. The early hour luckily meant very few people were out and about, and Hel and Jamirh made sure to avoid anything or anyone that could mean detection.

Hel was far better at sneaking than Jamirh would have thought. For all that her personality was loud, she slipped in and out of shadows in complete silence as though born to them. Jamirh, who had been playing such games of hide-and-seek with the authorities for most of his life, found himself impressed. She seemed to have an eerie ability to know where sirens would pop up, changing their course to avoid them often before Jamirh could hear them.

Maybe her hearing had also been augmented?

Eventually, civilization began to give way to nature. Fields of wildflowers and hay dotted with trees dominated the landscape, and if nothing else, it meant that it was easy to avoid the roads.

Then they walked through more fields.

And more fields.

The life of a fugitive had so far proved to be extremely boring. At this point, Jamirh had begun to wonder if the entire world outside Lyndiniam was just the same three or four fields, endlessly repeating to the ends of the world with the occasional river or stream. At least the autumn weather was pleasant.

By noon, Jamirh had had it. He was exhausted and aching after walking and running almost non-stop since they had left the jail. His ears were in a near-permanent droop, and his feet were dragging. He had been awake for over twenty-four hours at this point. Keeping his eyes open was becoming a challenge without the adrenaline of the chase helping out. "Hey," he started, catching her attention. "We need to take a break."

Hel frowned slightly. "Do we? I'd like to be sure we are outside the city borders before we stop."

Jamirh gestured around him at the fields. "What are you hoping for? A sign? We are in the middle of nowhere! We've been in the middle of nowhere for hours!"

"Oh, this is definitely not the middle of nowhere. Like I said, we might not even be out of the city yet, technically. We are still within walking distance of civilization, which is honestly too close for my peace of mind right now."

"We are still within walking distance because we have been walking," Jamirh grit out.

"Not much we can do about that but keep walking!" Hel declared cheerfully, though she wilted slightly at the look Jamirh shot her.

"Look, I'm exhausted. I feel like I've been awake for forever. I've been arrested, concussed, un-concussed, un-arrested, scared nearly half to death in my own home, and dragged through the entire city and then through the old sewers. Everything hurts right now, and I feel like I'm going to pass out."

Hel pursed her lips as she eyed him carefully. "Maybe a short break," she conceded. "A very short break! We really do need to keep moving. It won't take them long to decide we got past the blockades in the city proper." She changed direction towards a small group of trees a short distance away.

"Is it going to be like this the entire way to the Wall? Just endless fields?" Jamirh asked tiredly, but his thoughts drifted back towards the Avari in Blackfields.

"I sincerely wish, but no," she responded dryly. "We are going to avoid the cities, but we will probably pass through some towns on the way. It is going to take over a week if we have to walk the whole way there, so I'm hoping to secure some other means of transportation at some point."

"Not walking sounds good," Jamirh agreed as they reached the trees. He allowed himself to collapse at the foot of the nearest one.

"A short break," she reminded him as she looked back the way they had come, violet eyes scanning the distance. Jamirh shut his own eyes, just to rest them for a moment.

The next thing he knew, Hel was shaking him awake. "Come on, time to go!" came the cheerful voice he was sort of coming to hate a bit. Jamirh blinked, rubbing at his eyes, and noticed that it was mid-afternoon. So, maybe three hours of sleep or so. He still felt horrible. And thirsty. He regretted not bringing the bottles of water.

"Do we have to?" he whined as she pulled him to his feet.

"Terribly sorry, but yes," came the firm answer. Her gaze swept out over the fields again. "We need to keep moving, so we can stay ahead of where they are."

Jamirh couldn't really argue with that, even if he wanted to in the name of more sleep. He quickly redid his ponytail to brush out the pieces of grass that had tried to invade and recapture the few ruby-colored strands that had escaped as he slept.

And then they were off again. Through more fields. With more trees. He wanted to ask her more about why she was doing this, but found it hard to rustle up the energy.

As the sun began to set, they finally came upon a dirt road lined with sickly-looking trees and a poorly maintained wood-and-wire fence. Hel hummed thoughtfully, looking both ways, then declared that they would follow the road for a bit. They found apples on a few of the trees as they traveled; the apples were small, but they were able to find enough to help offset a day of walking on an empty stomach. A nearby brook provided them with something to drink. They exchanged few words. Jamirh was content to stew in his misery, and Hel seemed to realize that he was not in the mood for conversation. They continued on down the road until well into the night.

Then a howl in the distance shattered the silence.

Jamirh's head snapped around. "Wolves?" he exclaimed, trying to figure out how far away they were. His hand found his key.

"Something like that," Hel agreed, and while she also appeared to be listening closely, Jamirh noticed she did not look concerned. "She's not nearby, but we should leave the road again, I think."

She? How did Hel know the wolf's gender? "How does leaving the road help us in this situation?" he asked as they climbed over a low stone wall into another field.

"She isn't hunting us, and won't bother us if we come across her. However, those who *are* hunting us will definitely be looking along the roads. We've been following this one long enough, though I think we may have been successful in hiding our direction."

"I swear, if we go over that Wall, and on the other side are more fields..."

She laughed. "You don't leave the city much, do you?"

Jamirh kicked a rock. "I've never left Lyndiniam before. Ever."

"Oh." He could hear the frown in her voice as her ears tilted down slightly. "Never? How old are you? I'd have thought people who lived in the city would at least leave it occasionally."

"Twenty-two. There was no – I never needed to leave. It was shitty, yeah, but it was what I knew." Jamirh sighed. "There weren't any wolves running around in Blackfields, at least." He considered Hel. She looked maybe late twenties, early thirties? "How old are you?"

"Why, Jamirh!" She laughed teasingly. "Don't you know you should never ask a lady her age?"

Jamirh felt himself twitch. "You asked me *my* age."

She shrugged. "You are not a lady."

Jamirh strangled down a growl, as well as the desire to strangle *her*. Why did she have to be so difficult?

There was another howl.

"Did that one sound closer?" he asked nervously, ears twitching.

"No." The answer was confident, but how could she be sure? It had sounded closer to Jamirh. "As someone who has spent a great deal of time in the wilds of not-cities, I promise you, it was not any closer."

"What if there's a pack? A hungry pack? Who are looking for a tasty Avari supper?"

She was walking ahead of him, and he could see her ears were definitely twitching in amusement. "She is alone, she is not near us, and she has no interest in eating us. We are fine. We have very different problems to worry about." Hel looked back at him over her shoulder. "Come on. A little farther, and we'll see if there is someplace to shelter for a few more hours. Maybe we can find a little more food!"

"Do you even need to eat?" Jamirh asked bitterly. They could make some sort of bionic soldier like her with all those enhancements, but they couldn't solve the food problem? Wouldn't soldiers who didn't need to eat be cheaper in the long run?

"Who doesn't like food?" Hel sounded almost offended. "I love food. Could really go for some fresh shrimp right now. With pasta. Yeah, shrimp and pasta would be good. Oh! With cheese. Warm, melty cheese."

He rolled his eyes but followed her into the darkness, stars twinkling overhead.

They did eventually find a small shed in the corner of a field that Hel deemed safe enough, and Jamirh once again got the chance to pass out for a few hours. He wasn't sure whether Hel was sleeping at all, and he didn't want to ask. He was beginning to think the only answers she had were answers he didn't want.

They found some berries growing nearby that Hel said were safe to eat for breakfast, and then they were moving again.

As they traveled, he wondered what life was going to be like after they crossed the Wall. If she was right, and there was a whole not-eaten-by-Vampires civilization there, what was it like? Were they all as crazy as she was? Was it a country of mildly crazy bionic ex-soldiers and people they had randomly adopted? That seemed unlikely, but then, everything he had lived through in the past day and a half felt unlikely, and that hadn't stopped it from happening.

And on that note, how, exactly, were they going to get past the Wall? He had heard it was something like fifty feet tall; were they somehow going to climb it? With what equipment? From what he remembered about the Wall he thought they might be heading for one of the towers; was there some secret door there only she knew about? Hel seemed to know what she was doing, but Jamirh was certain that if he asked, the answer given would be "magic" instead of a logical explanation that followed the rules of the universe.

Maybe to her it *was* magic. Maybe she legitimately did not understand the rules by which her own abilities played, and magic was the best she could come up with. Didn't really smart people sometimes say that magic was "just science we don't understand"?

The day passed much the same as the previous. Fields, scavenging food, avoiding people, more fields, the occasional stone wall, random wolf in the night, pass out in a mostly sheltered place. Jamirh found himself cursing Kirsin Belian more and more with each mile covered. He had had a good thing going before she completely ruined it.

When he woke up the next morning, Hel had somehow acquired a pair of large-brimmed straw hats. "Wear this!" she declared, plopping one on his head. "Hopefully this will help keep people from recognizing us at a glance, since we are going to hit Ardwick today."

"I can't believe I am suggesting this," Jamirh started with a sigh, "but shouldn't we just go around the town? Stick to your beloved fields?"

She shot him a disappointed look. "No need to be so dramatic about the scenery. But unfortunately, no – going around will add significant travel time, and speed is really our goal here. We need to stay in front of the search net they are probably already extending out from Lyndiniam, and going around Ardwick would work against that. So we need to go through Ardwick." As she spoke, she braided her long white ponytail and coiled it into a wide bun on top of her head, securing it with a pin she pulled from her boot and finishing the look by placing her own hat on top. "And sometimes, even very simple disguises can deceive people who are not actively looking for you." She eyed him critically for a moment. "You may want to hide your hair under the hat too, but the shadow from the brim does make your hair look a little more brownish than bright red. Excellent. Let's go!"

Begrudgingly, he tied his own hair up into a small, high bun to fit uncomfortably under the itchy hat as they started off into the field. "If only we could dye it."

"You're telling me!" she laughed. "My hair would be the perfect canvas for basically anything. Have you ever tried it?"

Jamirh winced at the memory. "Once. It was... a very weird, very gross experience." He shuddered at the memory of the dye just sliding off his hair into the sink, like some sort of oily ink monster. It had stained his hands black thoroughly, his hair not at all.

Hel nodded. "Yeah, it definitely is. Hope springs eternal though that one day they might make a formula that works."

"I doubt Humans would want us to have it," he commented dryly. "Our hair is usually the first thing they notice, and they certainly wouldn't want to accidentally think an Avari was a Human."

"I mean, if they miss the ears, I think that's on them," she laughed, twitching her ears in an exaggerated manner. "Besides, maybe I want to go full rainbow. That could be fun!"

"That isn't the direction I'd go in," he said, thinking longingly of black. Safe, solid black. A great improvement over his own gem-toned hair. Hel was probably the only Avari in the world who would want *more* colors.

They eventually found a paved road that was actually in use and wandered into town several hours later, fields melting into houses and yards. About a mile into town was a gas station that Hel insisted they stop at. She dropped Jamirh off outside at one of the umbrella-shaded tables with a warning to keep his hat as low as possible, then went in. Jamirh eyed the area, but no one seemed to be paying attention to him at all. There was a young Avari couple at a nearby table, sharing some sort of blue beverage, but their attention seemed wholly on each other. No one else appeared to be lingering nearby; most were just filling up their tanks and leaving, with a few going in and out of the store itself. It didn't look that busy.

Content that he was safe for the moment, Jamirh switched his attention to the small vid screen broadcasting the news at the corner of the store. He couldn't hear anything, but the ticker at the bottom of the screen helpfully proclaimed *Breaking news: Shuurai Takeshi banished from Ni Fon* at the bottom of the screen as the two anchors talked to each other. Jamirh snorted, unsurprised that the Human had not received the death penalty. If the murderer had been Avari, they would certainly have been put to death. He wondered fleetingly what "banishment" would look like, since Ni Fon was mostly large islands.

As he gazed at the screen, Hel returned to the table, dropping a pair of dark sunglasses and a muffin in front of him. "Luckily, the weather is sunny enough that wearing these won't look suspicious," she chirped happily. "Do I look cool?" She struck a pose, her own sunglasses already in place, another muffin held triumphantly in one hand. She had a dark canvas bag slung over one shoulder. It looked stuffed.

"I... suppose," he said hesitantly, taking the glasses and putting them on. His gaze flicked back to the vid screen, where the anchors had been replaced by a picture of a pale-skinned Human with choppy black hair and dark eyes kneeling in what looked like some sort of grand hall. He looked kind of like every Human from Ni Fon. Jamirh guessed that was Shuurai. "Another Human escapes death," he mused. "They sentenced the guy who killed the duchess's daughter to banishment."

"Eh, they were never going to kill him," she disagreed, turning to look at the screen herself. "Ni Fon has always had a really weird relationship with the assassins they cultivate. And that whole situation screams of weirdness anyway." She paused. "Though to be fair, not many of those who are banished make the crossing alive. That's a lot of ocean to cross to get to safety. It's basically a death sentence disguised as not a death sentence."

"Will he even really be safe, if he makes it?" he asked curiously. "Won't he be in danger from people who are angry he killed the girl?" He peeled the wrapper off the muffin and began to break off chunks to pop into his mouth. Corn muffins were good.

She shrugged. "Safe as anywhere else, I guess. He was a Silent One, and they have quite the skill set. He can take care of himself. Honestly, whether he dies in the crossing, or makes it to shore somewhere, my guess would be that he disappears, and no one hears from him again."

Jamirh considered the picture of the man on the screen. "Why is this guy even allowed on the continent? If Ni Fon banished him for the death of one of their nobles, shouldn't he be banished from the Empire as a whole?" Maybe he should have paid more attention to what people had been saying about the whole mess.

Hel's face twisted in a grimace. "It's a little more complicated than that. The provinces – and the dukes that control them – have a lot of influence over their own laws and whatnot, even though technically the Emperor has the final say, and Ni Fon especially takes advantage of their distance from the rest of the Empire. They have the right to punish their criminals as they see fit, but their justice ends at their own borders. It's not like here, where Elbe, Agale, and Gallia all touch each other, and so tend to act more like one state rather than three."

"Cartago-Mir connects to Agale, though."

"Yes, but just barely. The Gulf separates most of Cartago-Mir from everywhere else, so they also tend to do their own thing." She turned her gaze back towards Jamirh as the picture switched to the two anchors. "Even still, I imagine honest employment may be difficult for him to acquire, even if he's inclined to. I'm sure illegal employment might align more with his abilities anyway." She suddenly grinned slyly at him. "They use magic, you know. The Silent Ones. Shinobi. Different than what I do – they try to keep their arrays in their minds rather than manifesting them, and they call them something else – but magic nonetheless."

Jamirh shook his head. "I don't know anything about Ni Fon, really; just that it's a province across the Shae Sea, and they all kind of have that coloring." The image had changed to a rich-looking female Human, with bright-red lips and her black hair in a complicated updo, speaking into the camera. The lace-and-crystal dress she was wearing looked like it had cost enough to feed the entire town they were in for a year. Her dark eyes welled with tears, though none were actually falling. The duchess, probably. Jamirh couldn't remember her name.

"Oh." Hel's ears drooped a bit in disappointment, but she rallied quickly. "Well, they use magic. You can take my word for it!"

He could give her points for trying. "Sure," he murmured, looking back at the screen. "What's in the bag?"

"Some food for us, water bottles, and a couple of other small things that might come in handy. It's mostly different types of granola bars, though. I hope you like granola."

He shrugged. "It's fine. As long as it's edible."

Her eyebrows came together as she considered that statement. "I suppose that gas station granola bars are, at base minimum, 'edible'."

"You're the one that bought them," he pointed out. "Or stole them. Do you have money? Should we be leaving quickly?"

The look Hel gave him was clearly affronted, her ears dropping low. "I did not steal them! I bought them! Like a normal person!"

Jamirh just shrugged again. "Hey, no shade if you did. I just want to know if we need to get out of dodge." He eyed her carefully a moment. "Though, just out of curiosity, how did you pay for them? Did they lock you up with your card on you?" He'd made it through with his key; he guessed it wasn't completely outside the realm of possibility.

She glared at him, silent.

"I see." He laughed slightly. Whatever; her apparently hacking the machine was the least of his worries. He looked back at the screen with vague interest. Then he noticed something that made him freeze. "That... looks like me. In the bottom corner." The ticker displayed the words "Wanted: Avari male, dark-red hair, silver eyes, wearing..." At least the anchors still looked like they were discussing the proclamation from Ni Fon. "We might actually need to go." He didn't remember them taking that picture, but then, he'd been pretty out of it for a good portion of that night.

Hel's gaze flicked over, and her eyebrows rose in surprise before her face scrunched into a wince. "Yes, that does certainly look like you. Unfortunate, but not unexpected, I guess. Definitely time to go!" She stood up quickly, cramming the rest of her muffin in her mouth. He was pretty sure the garbled words she said translated into something like "I love these things."

He watched the screen for a moment longer before he realized what he was waiting for. "Hey," he started slowly, "why aren't you up there? Why just me?"

She blinked at him in surprise, swallowing her mouthful of food and turning to look at the vid-screen herself. They both stared at it for a few more minutes, but Jamirh's "wanted" picture was replaced by more information about the banishment, not a corresponding picture of Hel.

"I don't know." She sounded honestly surprised. "I would think I would be. We didn't exactly make it a secret that we were breaking out together."

Jamirh thought back to them crashing through two sets of glass doors with an internal wince. "No, no we did not."

"That is pretty weird. Maybe they showed it earlier?" she suggested.

"I've been sitting here for the past twenty minutes. The banishment has basically taken over the news," he countered.

They both stared at each other.

"Well," she finally stated slowly, "maybe this is a good thing. If they are not plastering my face all over everything, that means I'll have a little more freedom around other people." She looked troubled. "Or maybe they just really care about you? Since the complaint comes from the Belian family?"

"Maybe," he agreed carefully. He wasn't quite sure what to think about that, but he also wasn't sure he liked what it could imply.

As they started to head out of town, Jamirh resolved to keep a closer eye on Hel. She had been helpful so far, but overall she was a mystery to him. All he knew was that she had been in a jail cell at the same time he was and she appeared to have multiple bionic enhancements. He didn't even know why she had been in jail. If he remembered correctly, when he had asked she had simply responded with "I walked." What was her end goal, here? Was she really trying to help him? Why? What real motive did she have to haul him over four hundred miles of essentially enemy territory?

He didn't know anything about her, but she had already gotten quite a bit of information about him. And that could be dangerous.

Chapter Four

L eaving Ardwick was thankfully no more difficult than entering Ardwick. It was even easier, in fact – there was a bus heading north to the next town of Dales, and it was both cheap and mostly empty. It was also leaving in under half an hour, so they wouldn't have to stay in town for long. Hel "bought" two tickets from the nearby terminal, and they spent their half hour loitering nearby. They boarded as soon as they could, watching everyone around them warily while trying to pretend they weren't.

Jamirh felt paranoid, and he found himself playing with his key constantly. He had to keep reminding himself not to stare at people who came too close, as that would draw their attention. But if he had seen his picture on the news, that meant there was a good chance at least some of these people had seen it too. It was hard to put his faith in a straw hat, sunglasses, and the obliviousness of everyday people, no matter what Hel said. For that matter, it was hard to put his faith in Hel herself right now. He didn't know what to think.

For the entire two-and-a-half hours of their bus ride, Jamirh kept turning over possibilities in his mind as he watched the boring scenery pass by. What if Hel was working against him? But then, what would her motivation for that be? What did the authorities have to gain from Hel dragging him around the countryside for days before inevitably arresting him? But if she wasn't working with them, why wasn't she listed as wanted along with him? If she actually was helping him, what was her motivation for that? None of it made any sense, and by the time the bus pulled in to the Dales station all he had succeeded in was giving himself a headache as his questions chased themselves in circles.

Jamirh dragged himself out of his seat, wondering if his time would have been better spent napping. It almost didn't matter what the truth was; in the end, he was still reliant on Hel to get anywhere. He was under no illusions that he would do well this far outside of the city on his own. He didn't even know if he could find his way either to the Wall *or* back to Lyndiniam, though going back meant... probably death, if he were being honest. So that was out.

As they climbed down out of the bus, Jamirh touched Hel's arm to grab her attention. "By any chance, did you get anything for a headache in that bag?"

She shook her head apologetically. "No, I didn't think of it; I'm sorry. Maybe I can swing really quick into a pharmacy before we leave." They stepped out of the station. "Is there anything else–"

Hel's voice abruptly cut out as she yanked Jamirh back into the station.

"What on– what is your problem?!" he yelped in surprise, rubbing at his arm.

"*We* have a problem," she stated grimly. "Across the street."

Jamirh chanced a glance out the door and immediately saw the issue. A Human woman in a gray uniform with blue-and-red accents was walking along the sidewalk on the other side of the street. She was armed with a saber and a pistol, and a heavily embroidered strip of fabric covered her eyes. A Truth Seeker.

Truth Seekers were high-ranking officers in the Empire's military who used all kinds of cutting-edge tech to aid them in their work, which, to Jamirh's knowledge, usually ended with someone disappearing. He didn't know how they functioned with their eyes covered, but it didn't seem to bother them at all, so there was probably more tech he just didn't know about. They were not well known for having any sort of mercy or humor, and they enforced the law rigorously when they were present.

"Okay, yeah, that's bad," Jamirh agreed.

"She's almost certainly looking for us," Hel murmured. "But I think this may actually just be a stab in the dark. They do a *thing*, a sort of scan, when they are actively looking for someone, and she's not doing it. I would feel it. So they have probably sent out Truth Seekers in various directions and hoped for the best. We just got unlucky to run into one."

"Okay," Jamirh said slowly, choosing not to unpack that for now, "how do we get around her? Truth Seekers are something I have always been very happy to never deal with. Where is the bus going? Can we get out that way?"

Hel shook her head. "The bus is going on to Norik, which is extremely out of our way. We want to aim for Sturlow, and there don't seem to be any buses heading that way for a while. Since she's not actively scanning though, our best bet is just to let her walk away, and then leave as fast as we can." Hel frowned. "But even if it was a stab in the dark, I don't like that she's here."

They waited in silence for a few more minutes before Hel chanced another look outside. "She's leaving," she confirmed. "Time to get out of here."

They wasted no time in heading north-west out of the town, being sure to head in the opposite direction of the Truth Seeker. Neither of them fully relaxed until they had left the town and roads far behind them and were back to trekking through fields. Hel handed Jamirh a granola bar and a water bottle, and they ate lunch on the go.

Just as Jamirh had resigned himself again to more of the boring scenery, he noticed the landscape was actually changing. The fields had rarely been flat, but now he started to notice that the rises and falls were becoming far more pronounced. The number of trees they were seeing also started to decline. A short time after nightfall, they reached a short stone wall, and he realized that there were no more fields – just rolling hills covered in low vegetation.

They had found the moors.

"Let's not tackle this quite yet," Hel suggested. "We are seven or eight hours out of town. We can take a quick break there." She indicated one sad, lonely tree by the wall. Jamirh was quick to head in that direction. Just as they reached it, a long howl cut through the silence.

Jamirh's eyes widened. "That sounded far closer than last night."

Hel frowned slightly. "It did. But I'm sure it's fine. She's still not interested in eating two random travelers." She paused.

Another howl sounded. Jamirh was certain it was coming closer.

Hel winced. "Actually, now might be a good time to explain–"

"That howl sounded really close," Jamirh nervously interrupted, ears held low. "By what percentage, exactly, are you sure the wolves won't bother us?"

"Well," she drawled carefully, violet eyes suddenly focused on something behind him, "I am one hundred percent certain that our howling friend is not a wolf."

Jamirh froze. He very purposefully did not turn around, hand reaching up to his key. "Then what is it?"

She didn't answer right away, eyes coming back to land on Jamirh. "Have you ever heard of wargs?" she finally asked, tilting her head to the side.

"No." He was pretty sure he didn't want to, either.

"They are kind of like wolves? Like really, *really* big wolves. Very fluffy. More intelligent, too." She was looking at him apologetically. That was strange. "Maybe you should walk over to me. But, and I cannot stress this enough, there is *no reason to panic.*"

Oh. That was probably bad.

He swallowed hard. Slowly, deliberately, he took the few steps over to Hel, then turned around. He suddenly found himself unable to breathe.

It was big.

White-blonde fur covered it from head to toe. It was standing on four paws, sharp claws digging into the dirt just beyond where he had been a moment before. Its head, which was larger than his, came up to his shoulder, and he could just see a hint of what must be ridiculously large fangs. Bright-green eyes with far too much intelligence for his comfort eyed him curiously from over a wolf-like snout.

The beast made a soft whining sound and took a step in his direction. Jamirh scrambled back as Hel grabbed his arm, stretching out her other hand palm out towards the creature.

"Jeri, I am trying not to break him, please just... stay like that," Hel said desperately. "Jamirh, *breathe*. She won't hurt you."

The giant thing sat abruptly, and a thumping noise came from behind it. He realized it was the tail hitting the ground.

It was wagging its tail.

Jamirh felt faint.

"See? This is Jeri. Jeri is friendly," Hel soothed as Jamirh panicked. "Jeri won't hurt us. You could even pet her?"

He may have imagined that the beast's gaze sharpened as it turned its attention towards Hel, but the sound of its tail beat steadily.

"She's actually been with us most of the way! She's who you've been hearing at night. I've been able to keep track of where the authorities have been looking based on where she's been. She's been howling to signal to me. I've even been telling you all along that she wouldn't hurt us!"

It made a sound that was almost like a howl, but much quieter.

"See? Jeri is a good girl! I was just about to tell you about her, and maybe I procrastinated a bit too long–"

Jamirh fainted.

"This whole situation has not gone well, let me tell you."

As Jamirh slowly became aware of the world again, the first thing he heard was Hel's angry ranting.

"I'm glad you are back with us, with that Truth Seeker being so close, but we really could have workshopped this a little better." There was a lengthy pause. "Maybe I should have, but this didn't help matters!"

Jamirh blinked his eyes open.

He was lying on the ground by the sad tree, partially sheltered by the wall. Hel was kneeling close to his head, and the wolf-thing was lying about ten feet away, watching him.

Her tail started to wag when she saw him looking at her.

"Jamirh!" Hel's voice sounded relieved. "Please don't do that again. How do you feel?"

"Awful," he muttered. "It's still here."

Hel looked pained, and her ears drooped even farther than they had been. "Actually, she is likely to stay with us for the rest of our journey. I don't want her running around on her own with that Truth Seeker so close."

Privately, Jamirh thought the creature – a warg, had Hel called it? – would just eat the Truth Seeker, but what did he know? It certainly looked big enough to end any confrontation with one chomp of its jaws. Jamirh started to push himself up.

"Oh, no! No no no! We are taking our break here, remember?" Hel pushed him back down again. "You should just lie there and rest a bit. Or... or I'll have Jeri sit on you!"

Jamirh looked at Hel with horror. Jeri's ears went flat to her head.

"She'd squish me," Jamirh squeaked out.

"Ah, maybe not, that's a bad – never mind, pretend I didn't say that." Hel's ears were completely sunk at this point; she looked miserable. "Please don't pass out again."

Jeri snorted.

Hel sent a hurt look the warg's way. "Don't be like that," she muttered. She curled back against the tree.

Jamirh wondered if this was how the insanity started.

They stayed at the little tree for several hours. Jamirh managed to doze a bit, despite the large predator lying only several feet away. It was still well before dawn when Jeri made a huffing sound and hauled herself to her feet.

"Yeah, we should probably get moving," Hel sighed. "We have a ways to go before we reach Sturlow." She dug around in the bag before handing Jamirh a granola bar. "And now, instead of fields, we have the moors!"

So they set out again, this time with a wolf the size of a small pony accompanying them. The warg didn't exactly follow them closely; she wandered in and out, and sometimes Jamirh could see her looking around on top of the hills quite a bit away.

Their luck with the weather also broke; it started to drizzle, then rain around noon. By the time they stopped again for the night by some large rocks protruding out of the ground, everyone was wet, cold, and miserable. Even Hel didn't seem able to rustle up her usual cheer, and between the cold and the wet Jamirh was barely able to rest for the duration of their stop. By the time they dragged themselves back into movement, he felt like he was actually worse off than when they had stopped.

And so it was in this frame of mind that they came upon Sturlow.

Sturlow was smaller than either Ardwick or Dales, and Hel seemed to be considering whether she wanted to try going around instead of through. In the end, she decided that they would try to get some sort of rain gear at one of the small stores in the town. Jeri peeled off from them when they found the road, heading farther into the moors, and Hel said they'd meet up with her later. Jamirh breathed a sigh of relief.

It was still drizzling as they entered town, hats firmly in place. Hel was determined to find a convenience store quickly and then get out. Jamirh got the impression that the near encounter with the Truth Seeker in Dales had spooked her far more than she let on.

In some ways, Sturlow reminded Jamirh of Blackfields more than anywhere else they had been since leaving Lyndiniam. The town was grungy. The roads were less maintained than in the other towns, and there were multiple buildings that looked like they needed repairs. There were barely any people out and about. The gray cast to the sky and persistent drizzle did not improve the overall look of the place.

They found a small store fairly quickly. Jamirh followed Hel into the store, where she found an aisle full of random outdoor gear. He looked around as she considered the products on display, regretting that his pockets were only big enough for a package of fish hooks he thought could be useful and a small spool of fishing line. They had passed a few lakes; perhaps they could try to catch some fish? Aside from the cashier they were the only two people in the store. Even here, there were signs of mild neglect.

Finally having made her selection, Hel brought it up to the cashier. Jamirh was wondering how, exactly, this was going to work when a now-familiar howl echoed from somewhere outside the building.

Jamirh froze. Jeri had never signaled them during the day. Where even *was* she?

Hel didn't hesitate. "We need to go. NOW." She grabbed his arm and pulled him out the door, abandoning the ponchos on the counter, stopping abruptly as they hit the damp air outside.

Not even fifteen feet away, paused looking out towards the moors with a puzzled look on her face, was a Truth Seeker. Her head turned slowly and unerringly in their direction. Even though her eyes were covered, Jamirh could not help but feel the weight of her gaze on him. He felt a chill travel down his spine like a pulse.

"Ah," she said, voice distant. "I see."

A brilliant flash of violet light, and a large circle made of lines and symbols appeared in front of Hel. It reminded Jamirh of the very small circle he had seen when she weakened the bars back in the sewer, but five feet across, and more complex.

"You don't want to do this," Hel warned, voice dark. "You can't win. Not against me."

The Truth Seeker cocked her head to the side, considering. "Nothing is determined until action is taken. The Avari behind you is Wanted. Give him to me." Jamirh did not like the way she had said "Wanted." Everything about her was creepy.

"No," Hel said flatly.

Something skittered across the ground towards the woman–

Jamirh did not understand what happened next.

It was as if a cloud of shadow suddenly erupted from around her feet in large, tentacle-like shapes surrounding the Truth Seeker. Bright-green eyes glittered angrily from somewhere in its depths as a portion of the shadow coalesced into the form of a woman in black, long white-blonde hair in a braid. She was holding two narrow, slightly curved short swords, one in each hand.

The Truth Seeker's head hit the ground separately from her body.

"What in the actual–"

"And we're out!" Hel interrupted him, starting to move. "The short, short version is that's Jeri–"

"WHAT?!?"

"–and that was almost certainly too late, so we need to go!" Hel was running, pulling Jamirh with her; a large, white-blonde wolf ran with them. The few people they saw got out of their way quickly.

They didn't stop running until they were well out of the town, by which point Jamirh was seriously out of breath. The past couple of days of being on the run in near-constant motion with little sleep were starting to catch up with him. He nearly collapsed when Hel finally slowed to a stop, Jeri circling back to them.

"We can take a minute, I think, but really not much more than that. Our plan now is basically to rush our way to the Wall, and pray we get there before they can catch us." She sighed.

Jamirh wheezed for a moment, trying to catch his breath. "What was that?!" he finally exclaimed, staring at Jeri. She whined slightly.

Hel sighed again. "This is not Jeri's native form. That would be the humanoid form you saw back in the town. But it is hard for her to be out during the day; she's old enough where she can be, but not old enough to do so comfortably. Her warg form protects her from the UV rays, mostly." Hel tilted her head slightly to the side. "We should probably be thankful for the rain, honestly."

"Why didn't you tell me this earlier?" Jamirh was flabbergasted.

Hel winced. "I've been trying not to overwhelm you. You don't really seem to take to new things well. I thought we could explain more once we were safely on the other side of the Wall."

Jeri whined, clearly unhappy.

"Jeri disagrees; she thinks I've been doing you a disservice."

Jamirh stared at her, something niggling at the back of his mind. He poked at it a bit and came to a realization. "Were you the woman from the casino?"

Jeri nodded.

"Jeri is the one who first alerted me that you were in trouble, actually. She didn't really believe that Belian would let you go so easily." Hel's eyes flickered down briefly, then back up. "We should get moving. We can talk and walk."

"But if you killed the Truth Seeker, doesn't that buy us time? Not lose it? It didn't even look like Jeri had any problems killing her, so why can't you just... do the same if any more come after us?" Jamirh was confused. "How did she do that, anyway?"

Hel shook her head. "As soon as she saw you, that Truth Seeker alerted every other Truth Seeker as to where you were. They are all connected. Unfortunately, that means that the military now knows where we are and can make a very good guess where we are headed. And while Jeri made it look easy, that was not an easy or safe thing to pull off." Jeri's tail wagged happily, as her mouth opened in something like the dog version of a grin. "It only worked because, for a moment, the Truth Seeker's attention was entirely on the two of us. Which was an indicator she might not have been very good at her job; she heard Jeri's warning and probably should have guessed there was a third threat, even if she didn't know who or what it was."

"What was the purple... thing?" he asked.

"A shield array. I am very good at them." A hint of pride entered Hel's voice.

"What is an array?" That answer had cleared up nothing.

She sighed. "I am still not sure that now is the time for this, but the short version is that an array is the catalyst for most spell casting. Choose glyphs based on the effect you want, arrange them into the circle, add the bridging lines to balance them, supply the array with energy, and there you go – a functioning spell. The bigger the array, the more glyphs you can use, the more complex the spell, and the more energy it takes."

Jamirh's head hurt. "I didn't see any magic circles when Jeri did... whatever it was she did."

"Jeri's shadow abilities are innate, so she doesn't need an array to use them. Same with her ability to shift into a warg."

"I see." He did not see. How did anyone ever keep any of this straight? None of this made sense to him.

They lapsed into silence as Jamirh thought that over. If it were true, that would mean that a fundamental belief of the Empire – that magic had died out long ago

– was false. Supposedly, Avari had been better at magic than Humans. Was that why? Otherwise, why try to suppress magic?

The little group trudged along. As they crested a hill near dusk, Jamirh noticed something strange about the landscape in the distance. It looked like the land had been flattened.

"What is that?" he asked, squinting ahead.

"That is the Waste. Or the start of it, at least," Hel answered. "It means we are almost there. The Waste stretches about thirty miles out from the Wall."

"It looks unnatural," Jamirh commented.

"It is. It was created when the Wall was."

"Through some sort of magical sacrifice ritual." He was pretty sure he was remembering that correctly.

"Yes. There is great power in such things," she said softly, ears lowering.

Jeri whimpered.

"I know," Hel murmured softly. "I sense it too."

Jamirh frowned. "Sense what?"

"We are being followed," Hel sighed. She looked at Jeri. "You need to get him to the Wall."

Jeri's form suddenly shifted into shadow, and when it receded it was the Human woman who stood there. She glanced quickly at Jamirh, who was staring at her in surprise, then turned her attention back to Hel. "That is an *awful* idea. And you have had some pretty choice ones on this little jaunt."

"It will catch up to us long before we can reach the Wall otherwise. I can buy you the time you need. Besides, I wonder – can I win like this, do you think?" Hel's voice was wry.

"Your body won't be able to handle the stress of that! Ander said–"

"Eh, I think it'll be okay." Hel shrugged. "Besides, what's the worst that could happen?"

Jeri stared at her. Jamirh was totally lost.

Hel smiled at him. "Well, it's been fun! Five days of intense bonding while on the run from evil people makes us friends at least, right?"

"Does it?" he asked weakly, as Jeri slowly put her face in her hands.

"I think it does!" she chirped cheerfully, ears twitching up. "Think of all the good times we had!"

"You're leaving?" he asked, suddenly realizing what was happening. He gripped his key tightly. He hadn't known her very long at all; he hadn't thought it would hit like this. This was why he stuck to himself.

"Well, I'm staying, to be more precise. You two are leaving. The country, if all goes well." She smiled at him. "Don't worry! I'll catch up when I can. Tell Vlad I was right!"

"Who...?"

"Don't worry, I know who he is," Jeri sighed. She looked at Hel. "Are you sure?"

Hel met her gaze evenly. Something in her eyes gleamed. "Positive."

Jeri looked down for a long minute. When she looked up again, she nodded firmly at Hel, then touched Jamirh's arm. "Come on. We still have a ways to go."

"But, Hel—"

"Is for better or worse an adult who makes her own – often very bad – decisions."

Hel sat down. "I'm just going to wait here. You two go – if you stay here for much longer there won't be any point to this."

Jamirh stared at her, conflicted. For all that she had been an annoying, confusing, and miserable pain for the vast majority of their journey, she had been there. Even though he had his doubts about her, doubts that were beginning to look more and more foolish, she had still tried to help. Maybe in a completely nonsensical way, but the intent had been there. Even now, she was trying to help get him to safety by putting herself in danger.

And now she was leaving.

Everyone left.

Jeri tugged on his arm.

"Yeah," he said quietly. "I guess we are friends."

She beamed at him.

He followed Jeri into the Waste.

It was just before dawn when the Wall came into view.

It was tall and gray. A large round tower stuck out of it.

"That is the Tower of Morden. It is where we need to go," Jeri commented. It was the first either of them had spoken since leaving Hel behind. "Morden was the mage who died in this spot. The towers are all named for their mages."

Jamirh hummed in acknowledgement.

"I'm going to shift back into warg form before the sun comes up," she continued. "But don't worry – I'll still be able to guide you, and I'll still be able to understand anything you say. Once we are in the tower, I can shift back and we can talk about our next steps."

He nodded.

"Don't worry!" she exclaimed suddenly. "Hel may seem a little flighty and have no idea how people should interact with each other, but she is a very capable... mage. She'll be fine. She knows how to cross the Wall. She'll follow in her own time." It sounded a bit forced.

Jamirh appreciated that Jeri was trying to make him feel better, but nothing about this whole situation was sitting well with him anymore. "We should get going, then?" he suggested tiredly. Maybe they would be able to sleep for longer than a few hours at a time once they crossed. That would be a positive. He stared at the distant tower numbly, rubbing his key between his fingers.

When he glanced back at Jeri, she was already a warg. She woofed softly at him and nudged him towards the Wall.

"Yeah, yeah, I'm going," he sighed, forcing his aching body to move.

"Colonel Rhode, sir." A woman in full military dress with short, wavy black hair approached the colonel as he eyed the large crater.

"Report, Major." Aven Rhode ran a hand over his close-shaven brown hair, wondering what the hell had happened here to cause this much destruction. He hoped there had been some sort of recording equipment somewhere that might have picked up the event.

"We have completely lost our asset. It is basically in pieces scattered over a fifty-square-foot area."

Well, that was unfortunate.

"Farah thinks we might be able to reclaim some of the implants, but I personally don't hold out much hope for that." Major Cole adjusted her glasses as she continued. "And the likelihood of the criminal having successfully crossed the Wall is high by now. We've probably lost him."

Lovely. Belian was going to throw a fit.

"However," she continued, "we did get one of theirs."

Rhode perked up at that. "Really?"

"Yes. We found her unconscious in the middle of that." She indicated the crater.

He stroked his goatee, considering. They had never managed to capture one of Romanii's agents before. Something might yet be gained from this, even though it came with an expensive loss.

"Secure the prisoner," he finally commanded. "Prepare transport to the Charve facility. If she was capable of this, then we take no chances. Have a Truth Seeker monitor her at all times. Keep her unconscious."

"Yes, sir!" Cole snapped a smart salute.

"Let us see what this brings," he mused, eying the crater one last time. "Perhaps this will be the edge we need."

Chapter Five

"Shuurai Takeshi."

He knelt before the throne of the puppet Empress he had served loyally for the entirety of his three-and-a-half decades of life with his hands bound behind him and twin glaives crossed at his throat.

"You have been found guilty of assassinating the Princess and attempting to assassinate the Empress. The penalty is death."

He closed his eyes.

"However, due to your service to the throne, our beloved Empress is inclined to be merciful and has spared your life."

This was the path he had chosen. There would be no turning back.

"Therefore, you are instead hereby stripped of your rank as Captain of the Imperial Guard and are henceforth banished from Ni Fon."

Well, it could have been worse. They could have taken his name. Or limbs.

"You will be escorted to the border immediately following the end of this hearing. You will be allowed to keep the clothing you are wearing. Your katana will be returned to you at the border."

In other words, after he was securely on a boat, since the border was several miles offshore.

"Any attempt to return to Ni Fon will result in a swift death. Your exile is eternal."

He opened his eyes and looked at the Empress. She stared back at him, face unreadable.

"No true citizen of Ni Fon will give you aid or shelter. Neither look for it nor ask for it."

His gaze flickered to the herald reading the sentence from the judgment scroll. Immediately after the sentencing, copies of the scroll would be sent to every city, town, and village to be displayed for three weeks, and the original would be placed in the Hall of Records for public viewing.

"Be gone from this place. Never return."

Ceremonial banishing ritual over, Takeshi was pulled to his feet. The Hall of Justice, filled with members of the noble houses and the Imperial families, was silent as he was led through the great doors.

He did not even glance back as he was led into the sunlight, where the crowds of people who had shown up to witness the sentencing were clamoring to know the verdict. He ignored them as he was led to a group of eight mounted shinobi and helped onto a free horse. He didn't find it comforting that he knew each member of his "escort." Nearby, another herald began to recite the sentence again. Takeshi looked down to see Morita approach and swing up behind him in the saddle.

Morita used to be part of his command. When he had one.

The herald finished speaking, and the crowd roared and surged forward, only to be held back by shields created by shinobi standing at fixed distances from each other. Takeshi could feel the weave from where he sat, recognizing those individuals who had joined to create–

"Shield up!" Morita's command brought Takeshi's attention back to him. Another shield formed around the party, which had formed a circle around Takeshi and Morita. "Forward!" Morita barked, and the group began to force their way through the throngs of people, who were all very intent on ripping Takeshi limb from limb, but the shield was doing its job well. As a result, their progress was slow, but they eventually came upon the great gates of Edo. They passed through unchallenged, then broke into a gallop once they were free of the crowds.

They traveled through the countryside, pausing only to tend to the horses. Just after the sun set they turned off the road. Morita swung down, leaving Takeshi sitting on the horse as a camp sprung up around him.

A small, lithe woman appeared next to him, standing silently as she waited for him to dismount. Like Morita and the other members of the escort, the bottom half of Satomi's face was covered by the customary black mask of a shinobi. He glanced at it longingly as he stood in the stirrups and swung his right leg up and over the horse's back, dropping as gracefully to the ground as he could with his hands still tied behind his back. She made no move to help him; when he had steadied himself she led him to a very small tent ringed by protective glyph patterns etched into the dirt. He put up no resistance as she ushered him in. He was forced to drop to his knees instantly; the tent was not tall enough for him to stand. A swift knife cut freed his hands, and the door flap was closed a second later. The only two things in the tent besides himself were a thin blanket and a bowl of thin-looking rice gruel. The blanket was too thin for the chill in the air and the gruel was likely drugged. He had seen Kawano in the escort, and since his only real skill was in poisons and drugs it made sense to suspect any food offered.

Another shield surrounded the tent – he felt Morita, Satomi, and Hara in the weave – and he understood that they would give him no opportunities to flee.

He didn't really feel like being drugged, but he dared not starve himself. At the end of this ride he was going to be put on a tiny boat and pushed out to sea, and if he wanted to survive the experience and make it to Espon he could not afford to turn down food. He also had little doubt that his escort was prepared to force-feed him if need be. The laws regarding banishment were rather strict. No harm, whether self-inflicted or other, was to befall him for the short time he remained in Ni Fon, and part of his escort's job was to prevent self-harm or neglect.

As he sat there, contemplating which drug might be in the gruel, he reflected that "no harm" might be a slightly subjective concept. He rubbed his wrists and shifted to ease the soreness of being in a saddle for nearly six hours after weeks of stillness in a dungeon. He was not even sure how much time had passed while he was kept under arrest; it had been impossible to keep track of the days while under the influence of the drugs used to keep him from using his magic.

After a moment he sighed and picked up the bowl. The gruel was tasteless, but he forced himself to swallow it all before placing it next to the tent door. Maybe this drug would keep him from dreaming, as he had in the dungeons. He grabbed the blanket and wrapped it around himself. Thin though it was, it still offered more protection against the cold air than the sleeveless shirt and loose pants he was wearing. He lay down, exhausted by the day's events, and allowed himself to be dragged into oblivion.

When he woke up the next morning, he was still groggy from the effects of the drug. It allowed Morita to easily bind his hands behind him again and put him back on the horse while the camp disappeared. Takeshi did not fully wake up until they had been on the road for nearly an hour. He was offered no food, and any personal business had to wait for the next stop.

The next two days continued in much the same manner.

They tied his hands behind him every morning, but they needn't have bothered. Takeshi would not attack those who had served in his command, and he had no desire to cause them trouble, either. He continued to be drugged every night, but overall he was treated with watchful indifference.

They avoided people as much as they could. Though the laws regarding those banished protected Takeshi, there were always those who felt that there could be no sentence other than death, even if they had to carry it out with their own hands. When they passed people on the road, Takeshi was stared at with accusing eyes, and whispers followed them. Even as far out from the capital as they were, people still knew about his crimes and the trial. Shuurai Takeshi was the most despised person in the entire country. Still, the journey was uneventful; most civilians acknowledged that attacking shinobi was suicide.

At the end of the third day of travel, as Morita watched Takeshi dismount, he finally broke the silence. "We reach the coast tomorrow," he stated coolly. It was the first thing someone had said directly to him since his sentencing. Takeshi nodded once, understanding that this would be his last night in Ni Fon. He was led to his tent. Once alone and secure inside a shield, he stared at the bowl for a long moment – this was the last meal he would be given; he could very well starve to death after this if he was unable to find food. He picked up the bowl with a sigh.

"Captain Shuurai."

He blinked and put the bowl down, not entirely sure if he had really heard someone whisper his name. He waited.

"Captain Shuurai!"

"Not Captain anymore, Satomi," he murmured back, shocked that she would risk this. "And you really shouldn't be speaking to me."

"This is your last night in Ni Fon," she stated, ignoring him. "We... cannot forgive your actions, but you were a much-loved captain by us all. We are willing to grant you a request, if it lies within reason."

Now he was even more surprised. "Why? I killed her."

Princess Hotaru, beloved by the people.

Satomi spoke slowly, as though she were not entirely sure of her own answer. "There is something wrong with this whole situation. Your actions make no sense to we who have worked with you–"

"Satomi Natsuko, do not pry into my reasons," he snapped, cutting her off as his grief threatened to break free. They couldn't know. "None of you would be able to understand them."

There was a short silence, and he regretted snapping at her, but it was for the best.

"You are not yourself any longer. We don't know what to think." She sounded sad. "But if your position were switched with any of ours, you would do the same."

He sighed heavily. He hadn't expected this level of loyalty. But if they were offering, there was really only one thing he wanted. "A mask."

Another pause. "Is that all?"

"It is more than enough, Satomi."

He could sense her regarding him through the tent, perhaps trying to determine his truthfulness. "You will receive it tomorrow with your katana," she finally agreed.

"Thank you."

When he received no answer, he picked the bowl back up, considering the gruel for a moment. Everything would be different starting tomorrow. This would be his last night home, and he would spend it in a drugged sleep. With a look of distaste he lifted it to his lips, swallowing it as quickly as possible before lying down. He sat back up again when he was still awake nearly ten minutes later.

They hadn't drugged the gruel.

Takeshi smiled slightly. He wasn't sure why he was being given this small, undeserved mercy, but it was kind of them regardless.

He thanked them silently and decided to settle into a light meditation. He could use this time to restore some strength and energy for the sea voyage he would soon be embarking upon. It did surprise him that they would take this chance. He knew he wasn't going to make a run for it, but they couldn't be sure of the same. Granted, in his current condition he would almost certainly lose a fight against all of them – he doubted he could even break through the three-shield, though he could definitely destroy the tent – so perhaps they simply felt secure enough to allow it.

He finally broke out of his trance when the shield fell early the next morning. He felt stronger and more rested than he had in a while, and he smoothly moved so he was kneeling with his back to the tent door with his wrists crossed behind him. A moment passed before the tent flap was pulled aside and his hands were bound behind him. He carefully rolled to his feet and backed out of the tent. The group mounted as the last of the camp was dismantled, and then they were off.

They only rode for about an hour before they came upon the sea. Takeshi had been able to smell the salt water for quite some time now, but he began to feel dread at the sight of the blue waves. It continued to grow as they rode into the small fishing village he was to depart from.

The villagers stared at him as the group rode past, eyes accusing. Takeshi ignored them as he had the crowds in Edo, pushing away the flare of pain, secure in the knowledge that very soon the only beings anywhere near him would be fish. Banishments weren't terribly common nowadays, but he idly wondered what the villagers thought about living in the last place where an exile would step foot in Ni Fon, if they thought about it at all.

The horses slowed to a walk. The former captain was glad he had been able to meditate in an attempt to stabilize himself the night before; he doubted he would have been as calm if he had had to deal with the aftereffects of the drug, the staring villagers, and the fact that he was being thrown out of his country. As it was, he was having trouble ignoring the pain and grief that were fighting to rise as he looked at the beloved country he was leaving.

He had known he would have to do this, but he hadn't expected it to hurt so much.

As they approached the shore, Takeshi saw a single villager waiting beside a small, beached fishing boat, which did not look like it was going to be able to make the trip across the ocean. It was floating and it didn't look damaged; it was just too small. He had his work cut out for him.

The shinobi dismounted, and Morita paid the villager for the boat. No one expected to ever see it again, and no one wanted to penalize the village. Satisfied, the villager left as the boat was pushed into the water. Takeshi dismounted and was led over, feeling nervous apprehension as he waded a few feet into the water. He almost couldn't make himself get into the boat, but the eyes of his former shinobi on him helped him make the jump into the tiny craft.

It was one of the hardest things he had ever done.

But not *the* hardest; that title went to the death of a princess who had looked at him with complete and utter trust in her eyes even as he killed her.

Takeshi's hands were suddenly free again as he sat down carefully in the rocking boat. All nine shinobi arranged themselves to be standing in a half-circle around him, staring at him silently for several long moments.

A portion of his mind pointed out that according to custom and law, nine katana should have been pointing at him as well, but the only weapon immediately in sight was the familiar katana belonging to him in Morita's hands.

"Have you any last words before you leave Ni Fon forever?" Morita asked. Takeshi couldn't read his face due to the mask, but he noted the somewhat resigned tone that had entered the previously cool voice.

He thought for a moment, before simply stating, "Thank You."

Even through the masks, he could see confusion milling in the gathered shinobi. They waited for an explanation of some sort, but he remained silent, and after a few minutes Morita continued with the ceremony. He moved forward through the water and held out the katana for Takeshi to take. "Shuurai Takeshi, you are no longer welcome in this land. You have been cast out, and you will never be allowed to return. Go. We wish you no luck in your crossing."

Hara and Satomi let go of the ropes they had been holding to keep the boat in place and gave it a push to send him out to the open ocean. Takeshi found himself fighting down a wave of panic as he began moving away from the only place he had ever known. It hurt, to be cast out of his home, but he knew that it was necessary. He stared bleakly at the circle of people he would never see again as he drifted slowly out of sight. Eventually even the land was no longer visible on the horizon, and he was alone in the middle of a blue expanse of water.

He put his head in his hands then and allowed himself to give into self-pity now that he was finally able to drop the carefully constructed mask. Only after he had pulled himself together again did he turn his attention to his new boat and its contents. While it was technically supposed to have nothing in it, the rules seemed to have been stretched yet again – he had a net, a harpoon, the ropes Satomi and Hara had been holding, and two oars. He also had his katana. This was good; it gave a slight increase to his chances of survival on this trip. He switched his attention to his sword, smiling weakly as he unwrapped black cloth from around the hilt. Satomi had kept her promise to give him a mask. Takeshi wasted no time in putting it on, feeling comfort with the familiar black fabric hiding the bottom half of his face, even if no one was around to see.

Misery quickly returned, though, as he glanced around himself again. He briefly considered what to do next before deciding on more meditation in the hopes that he would be able to re-center himself. He settled into a comfortable position, purposefully ignoring the rocking of the boat as he turned his attention inward–

/*You must be strong, Takeshi.*/

His eyes flew open at the sound of the familiar voice in his mind. Sitting comfortably in the boat facing him, regal finery out of place in the given surroundings, was the Empress herself. Sorrow and grief threatened to break from his control at the sight of the woman he had served for so long, but he controlled it quickly as he fluidly knelt before her, gaze to the bottom of the boat. "Empress," he breathed respectfully. He had not expected this.

"I see you are wearing your mask again," she murmured, reaching down to tilt his face up towards her as she studied it.

"The others... they gave it to me with my katana," he admitted slowly.

"I am glad." She smiled at him. "You have looked wrong to me these past weeks without it." The Empress paused, looking thoughtful. "I don't think I had ever seen your face before the first day of the trial. I nearly didn't recognize you."

He hid a wince at the memory. "The other shinobi seem to suspect something strange about the whole situation," he warned her, trying to change the topic.

She nodded. "This is understandable, and not entirely unexpected. You were much loved by those under your command, and even with my testimony to your crimes they still hold doubt in their hearts that you could even do such a thing. Their loyalty to you is commendable, to still have even a little faith in you after all that has passed."

He twisted out of her grasp, angry – she was, after all, part of the reason for the events that had led to him sitting on a boat floating in the middle of the ocean. Memories assaulted him and threatened to overwhelm him. "Do you regret it?" he asked harshly.

He wished he could take the question back instantly. There was a long, cold silence as he gazed out over the calm waves, and he wondered if she would leave for his insolence. He both dreaded it and wished for it.

"It was necessary." The words were clipped and cool. "We all knew it; have you forgotten?"

He didn't answer.

"Times are changing for the Rose Empire and there is now talk of rebellion on the continent. Ni Fon may be able to use this to regain our autonomy. So I need a spy, and you are the best option. You now have a way to leave Ni Fon without the Rose Empire watching your every move. The Rose Empire will never expect that the very person who killed the Imperial princess will be spying on them for the throne he betrayed. They will see you as a pitiful figure not worth their attention."

Something in him was horrified by how little her only daughter's life had meant to her. How could she be so unaffected, when he was tortured by the memory of what he had done?

She paused, and her voice softened. "Do you fear that we do not recognize your service to our throne? Or that we do not recognize your sacrifice?"

He could not answer.

She continued, voice soothing. "I know the truth, as do you. Am I not the only one who matters? I recognize the truth behind what you have done. I ask that you do this last thing for us: help me set our beloved Ni Fon free." Once again she made him look at her. "After that, your life will be your own. Ni Fon will ask no more of you, you will have our eternal gratitude, and we will send you funds or whatever you might wish so you may live in comfort. Is that not appropriate compensation?"

He could not understand how she truly seemed to believe that that was enough; that the loss of his home and friends meant so little to him.

Suddenly she began to fade, losing opacity. "You are at the edge of my range, Takeshi. Be strong, and remember that our love goes with you, wherever you are."

Takeshi jolted awake, off balance as his mind tried to re-stabilize from the invasion. His head ached; he never had been able to adjust to the Empress's preferred method of private communication. He wondered vaguely how they were going to communicate with him in the future; the one time he had asked they told him not to worry about it.

She was right in that he had agreed to this exile; his loyalty and devotion to his rulers as well as his abilities made him the perfect choice for this assignment and he knew it. In the end, they probably would not have trusted any other to do what he had done.

But he wished that he didn't feel like he had torn his soul apart in order to do so.

Chapter Six

It was storms like this, Takeshi figured, that played a large part in keeping people from sailing across the ocean in dinghies.

For the past two days the banished shinobi had been involved in an intense battle to keep his little craft afloat amidst fierce winds, torrential downpours, and waves higher than most buildings. He combined shields and carefully controlled blasts of air to keep from being crushed under the walls of water surrounding him and to retain heat, attempting to use his energy as efficiently as possible. Still, after two days without rest he was beginning to flag, exhaustion starting to take its toll. He would not be able to keep this up for much longer.

He wished that lightning would dance. That would, at the very least, provide a means to replenish his energy, if an unsafe one. He'd be willing to attempt just about anything at this point. Otherwise, there was going to be a wave he didn't see, and it was going to put him under. He doubted he would be able to come up again.

Water rose high to his right, threatening to crush the little boat to splinters. Takeshi spun and *pushed*, calling on his limited reserves...

...and broke through to the other side. The wave collapsed, having been denied its prize. Another wave rose up beneath him, carrying him up, and he took a moment to look around. There was nothing but water, wind, and rain in any direction, and he felt the beginnings of despair.

The wave brought him back down. He quickly double-checked that his few belongings were still secured in the bottom of the boat, eyes lingering for a brief moment on his sword. Everything was soaked, but still there.

To the left...

Takeshi took a deep breath as he broke through yet another mountain of water. How much longer could one storm last? Surely the weather would calm soon. At the very least it could drop a fish or something else edible into his boat; he couldn't remember the last time he had eaten due to trying to keep himself afloat.

Takeshi called the necessary pattern to mind and briefly wove a shield with threads of power as a thin sheet of water broke over his head. He wondered where he was. There was no way to tell where the storm was bringing him. Hopefully it wasn't back to Ni Fon.

Several more waves threatened the fishing boat in quick succession, and he focused on the movements necessary to save his vessel. He quickly lost track of how long he spent spinning the air as his reserves dropped further. The storm was getting worse, not better.

Then he heard it. Music to his ears, a deep rumbling audible over the crashing waves and howling winds.

Thunder.

Where there was thunder, there was lightning.

Takeshi would have only one chance at this.

He spun his magic into another shield quickly to give himself a few moments. Dropping to the bottom of the boat, his fingers quickly found his katana and untied it. With the familiar feel of the hilt in his hand, Takeshi stood as the shield dissipated, leaving him open to the elements once more.

Listening intently, he tried to gauge where the thunder was coming from. Using the last dregs of his energy, he wove the winds into the necessary patterns to bring himself closer. Patiently, he waited to get close enough. He could pull the lightning towards him to some degree with his blade, but he would have to be closer to the strike than this.

A wave of dizziness assaulted him; he shook his head quickly to clear it. Now would be a bad time to collapse in exhaustion, especially when he was so close to an energy boost. A wave of water nearly unbalanced him; he fought to keep right side up.

The lightning was close. Was it close enough? He supposed that he really had no choice. If he tried and failed he would die; if he did not try, he would die.

A large wave swelled beneath the boat, raising it up. Takeshi could feel the lightning building in the air, charging, about to strike. He raised his katana just as the wave reached its peak, calling the pattern in his mind to life...

...and slammed into a hard, unyielding surface. The pattern he had been weaving unraveled; the lightning struck elsewhere. He gasped as he smashed into the bottom of his boat, accidentally inhaling a lungful of water as the wave crashed on top of him. Suddenly the pressure lessened, and he forced himself up into clear air, ripping his mask down and coughing up water.

Belatedly he realized that he had crashed into the metal deck of another ship. A much larger ship with crew running around and shouting to each other. He wiped his mouth with the back of his hand before pulling his mask back up. Everyone seemed to be ignoring him. His hand was still locked tightly around his sword; nothing else appeared to have been lost. Suddenly his senses screamed *danger*, and his head snapped up to see another wave bearing down on him. He spun—

Nothing.

His eyes widened in panic as another wave of dizziness caused him to stagger and spots to dance across his vision. He had used everything up in that last gamble. Even the warmth-pattern he had been trying to hold was shattered into nothing. His knees buckled underneath him as he tried to brace himself for the impact—

Which never came, as he was yanked backward by a huge hand on his arm. He looked up to see a mountain of a man looking down at him with a huge grin on his face.

"Ahoy there, li'l wizard," the gigantic man greeted in a booming voice. "Don't quite 'ave yer sea legs yet, aye?"

Takeshi blinked. He spoke several languages, including that of the Rose Empire, but he didn't think he had ever heard the words "ahoy" or "yer" before, and he was uncertain what "sea" and "legs" meant when put together like that.

Legs made out of seawater? What did that mean? "Uh... sorry?" he offered after a moment when it became clear that the huge man was not going to continue.

The big man laughed. "Come! The deck be no place fer ye right now." He turned and started to walk away.

Takeshi still didn't know what he was saying. "W-wait!" he sputtered, his head snapping back to his surprisingly still intact dinghy. "My boat, I can't leave..." He trailed off, stumbling over the unfamiliar word order.

The other shook his head in bemusement but turned back towards the boat. "Yer boat'll be safe enough wit' th' rest," he stated, lifting it with one hand and carrying it to a rack of similarly sized boats. Takeshi watched, feeling rather lost, as the man fastened it to the others. "It seems that we should be gettin' ye int' th' warm, wizard," the man observed as he took another look at Takeshi, who wondered just how bad he looked, standing there clutching his sword with numb fingers. "This way!"

One of his giant hands came down on Takeshi's shoulder and all but hauled him across the slippery deck of the ship. It wasn't long before Takeshi found himself being propelled into a warm, dry space, followed by the huge man. There was a large window on one wall, showing the storm raging outside in all its glory, and another door on the wall opposite it. Several terminals stood at various places throughout the room, though only two had people standing at them. The shinobi just stood there, shivering, as the man pulled off an equally large raincoat and strode farther into the room to join the others.

"Cap'n!" the young woman exclaimed, sounding rather annoyed. "Where'd ya go? Ya can't just wander off like that when we're sail'n a god storm!"

Oh gods, they all spoke like that. He was never going to understand anything said to him on this ship.

The big man laughed again. "Marjori, ye always be worry'n too much. Besides, now we have a guest! The storm threw us a wizard an' 'is fishin' boat." He gestured back to where Takeshi had been trying to disappear into the wall.

"Hello?" he offered into the ensuing awkward silence as three heads turned to look at him.

The girl – Avari, if her bright-blue hair was anything to go by – twitched, pointed ears jerking down.

"No. Absolutely not. March right back out there an' throw 'im o'erboard if ya have to, but we are not takin' in another o' yer strays!"

"What?" Takeshi was trying really hard to follow the conversation, but whether it was the past two days without sleep or the strange dialect, he just couldn't make it make sense. All he could gather was that it seemed to be about him and it wasn't looking good.

"Now, Marjori..." the man – Cap'n? – tried to break in with a placating tone, but the girl refused to be interrupted.

"Four o' the last five have tried to rob us, an' two o' the last seven tried t' feed us t' th' fish! It be dangerous enough t' sail th' sea without worry'n 'bout strange people bein' thrown on deck. Ya be addled?"

Takeshi began to wonder if it would be safer back outside as he looked from one to the other in confusion.

"But–"

"No buts! Ya called 'im a wizard; ya know what that means? A wizard be far more likely, an' able, t' kill us 'n 'th' crew than all yer other strays combined! I. Will. Not. Have it!"

The other man in the cabin, a Human, though of a more normal size than the other one, shook his head with a sigh and, ignoring the argument going on next to him, turned to Takeshi. "You are from Ni Fon, correct?"

It was, perhaps, a result of how tired Takeshi was that all he could say was, "You speak normally."

The man smiled at him wryly. "Indeed I do."

"I can't understand them," he blurted out desperately.

"It takes some practice," the other man admitted. "My name is Benjen. I'm the first mate on this ship, the *Sea Spirit*. The man who brought you inside is our captain. His name is Caron, and the lady he's arguing with is our navigator, Marjori."

"Shuurai Takeshi," he responded.

Benjen eyed him critically. "Mask and sword – one of their Silent Ones. In a fishing boat halfway to the Nyphoren Islands." He paused for a second. "You've been banished."

Takeshi looked away, his silence answer enough.

"May I ask why?"

Takeshi paused, choosing his words carefully. "I killed someone. Someone very important."

He could not deny it, after all. Her eyes–

"See? SEE? This be exactly what I be sayin'." Marjori had apparently heard his answer. "Ya bring a murderer on th' ship–"

"Enough!"

Silence settled over the room at the captain's exclamation.

"I be th' captain o' this ship still, 'less there be a mutiny o'er the horizon?"

Marjori stared at him wordlessly.

"Good. Then on this ship me word be law. The wizard didn't stow away on th' ship, didn't decide t' come aboard at all. He be a gift o' th' sea, an' only a true fool would throw such a thing back." He turned to look at Takeshi and smiled. "Do ye plan on cutting our throats while we be sleepin' in the wee hours o' th' night?"

Takeshi looked to Benjen for help. "What?"

"He wants to know if you have any plans to kill us," the first mate translated helpfully.

"What? No!" Takeshi wasn't any less confused. Was this normal behavior outside of Ni Fon? And even if he were, why would he ever answer "yes"?

"Good! Then th' wizard stays wit' us fer now, an' that be all," Caron declared.

"Fine, on yer head be it," Marjori muttered, ears very low. "Though ya might be lookin t' get 'im t' th' infirmary. He be listin t' one side, an' he be shiverin' something fierce. He don't look all that well, either."

Interesting. He had not noticed he was shivering until she pointed it out.

"I'll take him, Captain," Benjen offered. "Now that you're back, you and Marjori should be able to handle the helm."

"Aye, make sure he doesn't keel o'er in th' hallways," Caron ordered. "See 'im safe t' Ashi, won't ye?"

"Aye aye, Captain," Benjen responded with a lazy salute. He turned back to Takeshi. "Come on, this way." He opened the door on the back wall of the room and ushered the shinobi through to a short hallway leading to another door. Takeshi closed his eyes for a moment while Benjen closed the door they had just come through and went to open the next one.

"'Eye, eye'? What do eyes have to do with anything?" he asked after a moment.

"Ah, wrong kind of 'aye'," Benjen laughed. "It has nothing to do with seeing; around here it just means 'yes'." Benjen guided him down through a nearby hatch.

Takeshi was already done with this whole language thing. This was not what he had signed up for...

He supposed an argument could be made that this was, in fact, exactly what he had signed up for.

Takeshi sighed and resigned himself to learning this disaster of a language variant as Benjen led him down another level. Though, perhaps, it could wait until after he had passed out for a bit.

At the bottom of the narrow staircase, Benjen opened a door into a brightly lit room. There were several unoccupied med-berths and holo screens, and a woman with forest-green hair in a low bun whose pointed ears were raising slightly in interest as they came through. She cocked her head to the side as she studied them.

"Benjen, why does it look like ye brought me a half-drown'd shadow?"

Takeshi frowned – he wasn't sure that black hair and black clothing made him particularly shadow-like – but allowed the Avari to guide him over to sit on one of the med-berths. At least he could mostly understand her, and the soft lilt to her voice made it pleasant to listen to.

"Your husband would say that the sea gave him to you, Doctor. Shuurai, this is Dr. Ashi. Ashi, Shuurai."

"He certainly looks like the sea cough'd 'im up." She frowned, grabbing a large towel from a nearby cabinet and wrapping it around Takeshi like a blanket. "Ye think ye can rustle up some dry clothes for 'im? Somethin' with actual sleeves."

Another towel dropped onto his head. "Start drying off with those, hun. And put that sword down. Benjen, clothes. Now."

Benjen shot Takeshi a wry smile as he obediently put his katana on the berth next to him. "Are you able to understand her well enough?"

Takeshi nodded as the doctor frowned, ears snapping down in displeasure.

"That sounds like *something I should know*," she started dangerously, turning back towards Takeshi quickly, but Benjen cut in before she could truly go off.

"No, it's the sea-speak. He's not familiar with the lingo and such."

Her bright copper eyes widened as Takeshi nodded. "I do not understand the way your captain speaks. At all." He paused slightly. "Or the other one."

"Marjori," Benjen clarified as the woman frowned again at him.

"This is still something I should know! *Communication*, Benjen! Is there anything else immediately relevant concernin' our guest?"

Benjen winced slightly and shot an apologetic look to Takeshi. "Not that I'm aware of. I'll be back shortly. She doesn't bite. Good luck!" And with that, he made a quick exit from the room.

Takeshi was fairly certain that Benjen must have been able to feel the glare the doctor sent after him. Then she turned back to him, eyeing his wet form quizzically.

"Where did ye come from, anyway? I don't remember ye gettin' on at the last port."

"Ah... I accidentally crashed my boat onto your boat in the storm."

She stared at him. "I didn't notice a collision. How bad is the damage?"

He shrugged. "It didn't really look like there was any. I have a very small boat."

"A small enough boat to not cause any damage would be somethin' like a wherry... and ye were out in this storm in it? We're miles from the nearest shore." She raised an eyebrow at him. "How were ye stayin' afloat?"

"By weaving the wind and water very carefully," he answered, rubbing the towel against his head to dry his hair. "With greater or lesser success."

She hummed thoughtfully, taking a blanket down from a high shelf and bringing it over to one of the tech stations, fiddling with the controls. "Useful skill to have, out on the sea. But what were ye doin' out there in the first place?"

Takeshi sighed, wondering if he was going to have to say it to literally everyone he met. "I have been banished. That is the law. To be sent out with katana and boat, from one shore to hopefully another."

"Hopefully for who, I wonder?" Ashi mused. "Seems a little stack'd against ye, no?"

"The hope is certainly that the one banished does not make it across," he admitted easily. "But, if you do..." He trailed off, shrugging.

"Freedom." She finished with a nod. Copper eyes peered at him with interest. "It was ye who killed that girl – Kobayashi's daughter? That's why ye're banish'd?"

He nodded. He supposed Hotaru had not been a princess to the Rose Empire at large, just the daughter of one of the provincial dukes.

The doctor shrugged slightly "Good for ye. Unfortunate ye couldn't get the mother, too."

Takeshi started slightly in surprise. That was not a reaction he had expected. But then... she was Avari, and the princess had been Human, so he supposed it made some sort of sense? He had supposedly done it for political reasons, after all – that they were relics of an old system that was long gone, and someone else from new blood should rule the Ni Fon province. Though most people in Ni Fon would assume he had been hired, and then lied to protect his employer.

Shinobi had started out as assassins, after all. And it wasn't like they were completely incorrect with that assumption, either.

It still hurt, to think that this would be the legacy of the princess's sacrifice. That some would think that she had deserved to die. Hotaru had never disliked anyone to his knowledge, had certainly never hurt anyone. Above all, if he had to choose one word to describe her, Takeshi would choose "gentle." He'd had a lot of time to get to know her, considering he had spent the better part of the last year of her life engaged to her.

He hadn't truly loved her like that, but he had loved her. They had been friends, certainly. The match had been considered advantageous for all parties. And now, it looked like he had agreed to it purely to get close enough to strike.

So many lies.

Ashi must have seen his surprise. "Don't worry. Ye won't find many pirates who hold much love for those allowin' the Empire to keep on turnin'. Definitely none on this ship. Ye'll be safe enough here, as long as ye don't try to kill or steal from us." She smiled.

He recognized the threat for what it was. Honestly, he had asked for this. "I really do not intend to." He allowed his eyes to slide down and away. "I'm just... tired."

"Well, if ye were using magic to keep yeself afloat in this monster of a storm in a wherry, I can understand that." Her tone was firm. "Ye're still wet. Do ye feel the cold? Ye're still shakin' a bit?"

He nodded. "I was trying to keep myself warm with another spell-pattern, but it collapsed when I hit your boat. It is not so bad now, though, with the towels."

"We should be aiming for 'warm', not 'not so bad,'" she scolded gently. She took the blanket off the station and wrapped it around him over the towels.

Gods, but it was *warm*, even through the towels. "Oh," he breathed out, as the heat slowly began to seep into his skin. He didn't actually remember the last time he had been warm. Before everything, maybe? This was wonderful. And he had thought the towels were nice. His pattern couldn't compare to this. Nothing could compare to this. He was never going to move again.

Ashi smiled, amused. "It will be even better with dry clothes."

"This is fine," he assured her quickly. This was far more than he had hoped for, he didn't need more. His clothing would surely dry anyway in this heat.

Her ears twitched down slightly, which he took as a warning. "No, it's not. My sick bay, my rules. When Benjen comes back, ye'll change out of those wet rags."

He thought that was a little harsh. His clothing wasn't in the best of shape, but "rags" felt a little strong. It had been through a lot with him. He gripped the blanket a bit tighter.

She eyed him for a moment longer but seemed satisfied with his lack of dissent. She went back to the computer she had been sitting at when he had come in, and he settled himself to wait for Benjen's return, soaking up as much warmth as he could.

Had she said "pirates"?

Takeshi forced his mind to go back over the conversation and decided that, yes, Ashi had at the very least strongly implied that this was a pirate ship. That could be a good thing? He was technically fleeing the law, and pirates weren't generally known for their adherence to law, so that could work out in his favor.

Takeshi decided this was a problem to consider later. Of the four people he had met so far, only one seemed to take issue with his presence. Benjen had even noticed and remarked that Takeshi was shinobi, so they knew what he was, and for the most part they were unconcerned by it. From Ashi's reaction, he could even assume that killing Hotaru and being subsequently banished worked in his favor.

But pirates.

He did not particularly care for pirates. Their loose interpretation of laws and rules made him twitchy, especially when they were explaining how *technically* they did not break any laws because of some strange reading where they completely ignored the entire point of the law in question. They also caused problems for imports and exports, and sometimes the small coastal villages. He'd never really met any pirates before now, though, and these seemed to be decent so far? At least they hadn't thrown him back overboard when they found him on their ship, though he conceded that he couldn't know what they were really like after only twenty minutes of interaction. He supposed that going forward he was going to have to interact with people he normally wouldn't, both because they would be more willing to work with him than regular law-abiding citizens, and because it would help his appearance as an exile.

Takeshi sighed. He had known doing this would mean sacrifices and concessions. He was going to have to be willing to make them. Arguably, he had already made the biggest one. He was going to have to remember that.

Not that he would ever forget the way she—

Takeshi was startled out of his thoughts when the door to the sick bay opened again, and Benjen entered holding a large cardboard box with fabric sticking out of it. It might have been a sleeve.

"Doctor, I found some stuff I think would probably fit our guest here," Benjen said as he set the box down on the berth next to Takeshi's.

Ashi nodded, getting up to come over. "Excellent. Let's see about getting' ye in some better clothin', then."

Takeshi sighed again and turned his attention towards the first of many small concessions.

Chapter Seven

T akeshi did feel much better after some sleep. He was pretty sure it was the first real, uninterrupted sleep he had gotten since before Hotaru's death months ago. As a result, he was unsurprised when Dr. Ashi told him he had slept for over sixteen hours. Unfortunately, this apparently signaled to his body that it was now allowed to make him aware of everything he had been trying to ignore, and so Takeshi's *everything* was sore.

He had known he would pay for that kind of prolonged weaving, especially since he had started with low energy reserves and then used basically all of his strength in the attempt. His reserves were still much lower than he would prefer, and he was still exhausted, so the persistent ache just felt unnecessary on top of everything else.

It had been a rough couple of months.

At least the new clothing was comfortable, even if not what he was used to. He had picked the most neutral color palette that he could find in Benjen's box of odd clothing – mostly blacks and dark grays, with a blue scarf he had liked. He could move in it, and it pleased him that it looked like it all went together. Finding a pair of boots that fit had been exceptionally lucky, as there hadn't been many options.

He was also wearing his mask, and had tucked his katana through the sash at his waist. He was not going to give up the last remnants of home he had.

When Ashi had finally determined that Takeshi wasn't going to keel over in the immediate future, she brought him up a ladder to "the mess" for some food. There was one long wooden table in the center of the room with benches on either side. Two long but narrow windows stretched on either side of the room overlooking the ocean to the sides of the ship. There was a door centered on one wall that he thought might lead out to the deck, and another door on the wall opposite – the kitchen, maybe? The walls were covered in a warm wood paneling, and the sun streaming through the windows gave the place a cozy glow. As it was just before dinner, several members of the crew were hanging around, waiting to be fed. Three Humans – a pair of blonde, green-eyed women in their mid-thirties who looked enough alike to be twins, and a kid who looked to be about seventeen with dark skin and hair and an annoyed look on his face – were playing a card game at one end of the large table, but they turned their attention to Takeshi as soon as Ashi led him in.

"Oooh, is this the wizard Cap'n keeps talking about?" one of the women asked. "The one that killed the Kobayashi girl?" If Takeshi had to describe her tone, he would go with "aggressively curious."

"Who else would it be?" the boy muttered as he stared angrily back at his cards. "How many people do ye think there are on this ship that we don't know? It's not that big."

"Don't be rude, Don," the other woman said playfully. "It's nice t' ask first, before making assumptions."

"He's got a point, though," Ashi noted. "Unless my dear sweet husband's been hidin' other wizards on board I don't know about. Is he almost done with dinner?"

Takeshi blinked. Something Benjen had said last night ran along the same lines, but he thought he'd misunderstood. Was Ashi married to the captain? A Human and an Avari? That was... not something he'd ever seen before.

The first woman shrugged. "Yer guess is as good as mine. Ye know he doesn't let us in the kitchen when he's cooking." She switched her attention back to Takeshi. "So, then – ye be Shuurai Takeshi. Made quite a name for yerself, eh?"

Takeshi suddenly realized that Benjen had to have known – or at least have had a very good guess – who he was as soon as he saw him. Everyone on this ship so far was well aware of Hotaru's death, if not the particulars. Why ask then for his name and why he had been banished? A test of some sort?

"I suppose." At least speaking a bit more with Ashi was allowing him to pick up on some of their speech patterns, as well, though none of those present seemed to have it quite as strongly as the captain. "I'd rather not discuss it, if you don't mind."

"Yeah, I guess it didn't really work out for ye, though ye kind o' succeeded." The second woman laughed, tucking a loose strand of hair behind her ear. "My name is Desha, and that lovely lady over there is my sister, Salisha."

Salisha waved at him cheerfully as Ashi pushed Takeshi down onto the nearest bench. His muscles protested loudly at the forced movement.

"And this is Don. Don't let him fool ye; he's just upset that he's losing at cards."

Don just grunted at them.

"I'm going t' go check on Caron. Please don't eat the wizard while I'm gone," Ashi drawled as she disappeared through the rear door, throwing one last warning look over her shoulder. Takeshi narrowed his eyes after her, confused. And he had thought he'd been doing well with the language so far.

"Wizard, ye play Brigand's Bluff?" the second woman – Desha – asked.

He shook his head. "I don't know any card games, I'm afraid."

"Lucky for ye." Don's voice was bitter. "I'm pretty sure they cheat."

"Don! We would never cheat in a game with ye," Salisha gasped, sounding hurt. "We only cheat with non-crewmembers!"

"Like me," Takeshi interjected dryly.

"Exactly!" Desha grinned, predatory.

"Forgive me, then, if I choose to sit this out."

The sisters laughed at him. "No magic t' help ye out with a card game?" Salisha purred. He wondered if they always spoke like this, alternating between sisters.

"No, it doesn't work that way." Takeshi had always found it amusing how people without magic thought magic worked. "And besides – that would be cheating."

Desha's eyes sparkled in amusement. "But ye'd be cheating cheaters, no? Surely that's fair!"

"Perhaps it would be justified, but I prefer to avoid it entirely whenever possible," he stated firmly.

"Aw, that's no fun!" The whine in Salisha's voice was mildly grating.

Don snorted. "Ye just want more people to torture."

The women looked at each other, then shrugged simultaneously, big grins on their faces. "Maybe!" they chorused.

Takeshi just shook his head slightly.

Desha eyed him. "Must say, yer not what we thought ye'd be." She knelt on the bench opposite him and leaned over the table as though inspecting him.

Takeshi's eyebrows rose, and he leaned back slightly. "Oh?"

"We'd thought ye'd be..." Salisha's voice trailed off as she gestured wildly around her, as though that would make her point. Takeshi stared. "...More," she finished lamely.

Takeshi dared a glance at Don, who nodded at him tiredly. "Yeah, they're always like this."

"What does 'more' mean?" he asked after a moment.

"Well, yer not very interesting, t' be honest," Desha suggested apologetically. "Kinda thought ye'd talk a bigger game. Fer a revolutionary, yer not very revolutionary. Yer not even very wizard-ly."

He blinked at her. "You've known me for five minutes," he protested, realizing that yes, they were absolutely going to discuss this, no matter what he requested.

"And in those minutes, ye've not done *any* magic for us, or even talked anything about those awful people!" Salisha's gaze sharpened. "Unless ye killed the girl for more... personal reasons? Ye were t' be married, no?" She slid closer to him on the bench. He was beginning to feel a bit cornered.

"Oh!" Desha's eyes widened comically as she practically climbed onto the table. "A love triangle gone wrong, maybe?"

What? "My reasons are my own. I prefer *not* to discuss them," he rebuked coolly, emphasizing the "not" as he leaned farther away from the sisters.

"Okay, the mysterious thing ye got going is kinda working for me," Salisha laughed. "Ye be sure ye don't want t' share? We're great listeners, ye know."

Takeshi could see Don slowly burying his face in his hands behind the girls. He looked mortified and miserable. Takeshi could relate.

"I just spent a significant period of time thinking about it in jail. Is it any surprise that I wouldn't want to discuss it now that I'm out?" he suggested.

"Oh yeah, they certainly took their time figuring out what they were going t' do, hmm? I'd 've thought the death o' such an important person would've sped the process up, not slowed it down," Desha said thoughtfully.

Takeshi cocked his head to the side slightly, a bit confused. "How do you mean?" He thought it had taken a long time, but he had also been the one in jail. It was bound to feel longer to him. He hadn't thought it had actually taken longer than normal.

"Well, ye killed the little lady way back in February, no? But they waited a whole eight months t' sentence ye. Seems a bit excessive t' me." Salisha shrugged. "Ye don't get such lengthy waits for justice on the sea, I can assure ye," she declared firmly.

"Eight months?" Takeshi said uneasily. That didn't sound right; he had thought it had been closer to two. He hadn't had the best grasp of time while he had been incarcerated due to the drugs they had used to sedate him, but surely he wasn't *that* far off.

"Well, yes? Since it's late October now." Desha eyed him strangely.

Takeshi thought back to the ceremonial ride through the Ni Fon countryside to bring him to the shore. He realized that he hadn't really paid any attention to his surroundings and had been so caught up in his own thoughts that he had completely failed to notice whether it was an entirely different season than he thought it should be. It explained the chill in the air, he supposed, but he had chalked that up to being on the ocean. It was actually a bit embarrassing, if it were true, though the sisters had no reason he could think of to lie to him. They were weird, certainly, and a bit invasive, but he couldn't think of a reasonable motive for them to purposefully deceive him over the date.

But it did beg the question – how was he missing six months of time? He had been drugged, yes, but he hadn't thought it had been that severe. It shouldn't have been, according to protocol. Had he really been drugged so thoroughly that he had been completely unaware for six whole months? Why? That was not standard protocol, even with a prisoner as skilled in weaving as he was. Such an order would have had to come from the Empress herself, but she knew he wasn't going to try to escape, so why the excessive force? And if the trial was going to take that long, why hide it from him at all?

"Ah, yes. Of course," he murmured, realizing that he had been silent a bit too long. He wasn't sure he wanted to advertise that he had no idea what month it was. He had no intention of making himself look even weaker in front of these pirates than he already had. That felt like a poor idea.

The door Ashi had disappeared into opened once again. "How's the harassing goin'?" the doctor asked dryly as she swept back into the room.

"It's going." Don's words were muffled from where he had buried his head under his arms on the table, but his voice sounded pained.

One of Ashi's ears twitched slightly as she took in the scene, with Desha almost on the table and Salisha sitting very close to Takeshi while Don tried to melt into oblivion. "I see." A pause. "I said *not t'* eat him. Food'll be out shortly."

That worked to take their attention more or less off Takeshi as they started pelting Ashi with questions about what and when dinner was going to be. He appreciated the rescue, but he also found himself wondering what, exactly, he was missing. Was it time, or something else?

***

Caron turned out to be not just the captain of the ship, but also its cook – and yes, married to Ashi. Dinner was a perfectly acceptable meal of rice and chicken drenched in a sweet sauce with a yellow squash and rolls on the side. Ashi made it very clear Takeshi was to eat his entire portion; apparently he hadn't been eating enough lately. He decided not to tell her just how little it had actually been.

Besides the sisters and Don, they were joined by Benjen, who said Marjori would eat later. Watching the group interact as food was dished out, Takeshi realized that they functioned more like a family than a hierarchy. Conversation was animated. Food was enjoyed. Rolls were thrown.

He stayed silent through most of it, answering the occasional question with short, quiet answers. This was despite Desha and Salisha's numerous attempts to draw him into conversation, prompting Benjen to remind the annoyed sisters that he was, in fact, a *Silent* One, emphasis on the 'silent'. Takeshi was relieved by the support, as the sisters made him vaguely uncomfortable with their intense desire to pry. He supposed their curiosity was natural, but having all of their focus on him was extremely unpleasant. As it was, they made little cooing sounds when he pulled down his mask to eat, only stopping when Benjen gave them a warning look. They still stared at him for most of the meal.

After the crew had finished eating and Takeshi had eaten enough to satisfy Ashi, most of the crew dispersed. Ashi and Takeshi stayed behind to help Caron clean up, though all Takeshi really did was wipe down the table, unfamiliar as he was with everything on the ship. He moved fairly slowly, as his body was still protesting movement. He hoped more rest would allow him to heal. He still felt weak, energy-wise and physically. Perhaps he could find somewhere to nap?

He didn't need to wonder about it for long, as Ashi guided him to the lowest deck, pointing out various parts of the ship as they went. Below were several small cabins tucked in the front half of the boat. The green-haired Avari told him Marjori, the sisters, and Don all had rooms down here, but that four were empty and he could stay in one of them while he was on the ship. Ashi let him into one, revealing a cramped space painted stark white, just big enough for a berth, a small chest, and a sink with a mirror and a small digital clock hanging next to it. She showed him how to lock the door, which eased his mind slightly about being so close to the sisters, and then left, telling him to get some sleep. He collapsed onto the small berth and was almost instantly asleep.

When he woke up again, some of the pain had receded, and he felt like he might be able to light a candle with magic if asked. After he had found his way back up to the main deck, he discovered that he had slept through both the night and breakfast. Caron had been kind enough to save him some scrambled eggs and toast, which he scarfed down quickly. Food was definitely something that he needed to help him recover, physically and magically.

Then he found himself without any real direction. The crew seemed to be doing their own things around the ship, content to let him wander, though he noticed that someone was always nearby. That was wise. He purposefully did not touch anything. They seemed content with him onboard for now, but he preferred not to give them a reason to throw him overboard.

He went on deck and checked on his little fishing boat, which had been secured to a rack next to another, larger boat that made his look quite shabby. His harpoon, net, and oars were all still where they belonged as well. He wondered how long he could stay here before he needed to set out again on his own – though if by chance the pirates were going to Gallia, maybe he wouldn't need to worry about it at all? That would be a much safer plan than the fishing boat, especially since he wasn't actually sure where they were anymore. Perhaps at a minimum he could convince them to drop him off near Gallia? He had managed to survive several days in the little boat on his own before; if he had to do it for a few more days he was sure he would be fine.

He looked around the deck, noticing that the front section was raised and had what looked like a small room built into it. Two sets of stairs, one on either side, led up to the level with the door, and then two more sets of stairs continued up to a narrow deck around the room. He wandered up the stairs curiously, noting the strange triangular shape of the structure, though he supposed it made sense based on the pointed shape of the bow of the ship. Some sort of storage, maybe? He wasn't overly familiar with ships of this sort, but the placement seemed a little strange to him. Hadn't Ashi also mentioned that there was room for cargo down below?

Don was nearby, checking over what looked like a gun structure on the right side of the boat. Takeshi shot him a quick glance, and without looking at him Don called out that it was fine for him to go in there, if he wanted to. Takeshi pushed the door open.

It was, to his surprise, a shrine.

A small table draped in a deep-blue cloth stood in the middle of the small room. Centered on the table was a copper-colored metal bowl, half-filled with water. Takeshi could see what looked like small blue stones sitting at the bottom of the bowl. On the cloth, embroidered in a lighter blue thread, was a circle over an inverted triangle, capped at the top and bottom with smaller circles. Two curved shapes, thick where they started about midway up the triangle, tapered to points as they curved around the center pieces to form a teardrop shape, almost meeting above the highest circle.

The symbol of the Nyphoren.

The twin gods of the ocean, of water and storms; the patron deities of the Veren and the islands they hailed from. Nyphore and Nyphora.

Takeshi didn't think of himself as particularly religious, though he occasionally gave offerings to Taijin and Kijin, the goddesses of combat and magic. Generally, he preferred to deal with his problems himself rather than ask for help from a higher being that may or may not decide to lend its aid. There were certainly those in Ni Fon who worshiped one or more sets of the elemental twin deities, but Takeshi himself had never given them much thought. Most people chose one or two gods who were important to them, and Takeshi was no different.

He eyed the small shrine carefully. He wondered if he should be thanking the Nyphoren now, though he thought that it was even more unlikely after all that had happened that a god would take an interest in helping him. His landing on the *Sea Spirit* was strange, but not so strange as to be the result of the divine.

Just very lucky.

"Ye be thinking o' making an offering, li'l wizard?"

The booming voice came from behind him, and Takeshi spun around in surprise to see Caron grinning at him cheerfully, hazel eyes twinkling. His large form filled the entire doorway. "Might not be a bad idea, considering they saw fit t' drop ye here instead o' the bottom o' the ocean!"

Takeshi hummed and turned back to the small shrine. Practice listening to the rest of the crew was making it easier to understand their captain. "I was surprised to see a shrine on a ship."

"Eh, we may not have ourselves a priest onboard, but we make do. They may not've called me t' their service in that way, but the sea did choose me, and I remember that, always." He eyed Takeshi. "It's not often wise t' ignore gifts o' the Twins."

Takeshi inclined his head slightly. Even if he wasn't perfectly onboard with divine intervention having saved him, it was very clear Caron was. "All I have to offer them for now is my thanks, unfortunately. Perhaps when I finally reach the Espon mainland I will be able to arrange a better offering for them."

Caron frowned. "Ye be really going t' aim for Gallia? Ye'd be better off elsewhere – the Nyphoren Islands, or the Emerald Shore. They're Empire, but they tend more t' their own devices." He paused for a moment. "It'd be easier for ye t' make a life in those places."

Takeshi's eyes dropped to the ground. His life still wasn't his own, not really. Everyone on this ship was free, and they thought he was too. They couldn't understand that his ghosts would haunt him always, no matter where he went. And he still didn't know how Ni Fon was planning on collecting the information he was supposed to gather. "I have to go to Gallia," he said after a moment. "It is what it is."

"It don't really seem that ye have t' do anything anymore, li'l wizard. Yer out o' their waters; isn't that enough, according t' yer own laws?"

"The letter of the law, perhaps; but the spirit of it is that I go to Espon. It is probably because I am more likely to die that way."

"I'll never understand yer laws, wizard. They seem strange, and unnecessary." Caron sounded confused. "If they want ye t' die, why not just kill ye? Why make it the Twins' problem?"

Takeshi smiled wryly. "According to my culture, I am so dishonored that I am not worthy of being killed by one of my own people. So they hope the elements will do it."

A frown overtook the captain's face. "That sounds cowardly, t' hope that yer dirty work be done by someone else."

He shrugged. "So it has been for hundreds of years."

"That... is not often a good reason t' do a thing," Caron said slowly. "'Tis a good thing ye were brought t' us. Lucky, even."

Takeshi could not argue with that. "It is, yes." He frowned to himself. He had accepted that this plan would be phenomenally risky, but Caron was right – he had survived completely by luck.

The risk of failure was high, but it had been made clear to him that they simply could not afford for him to fail. He was skilled, yes – one of the best of his generation – but he knew he was not immortal or invulnerable. His death was a possibility, even if failure would be unacceptable to his Empress.

He was beginning to think he should have asked more questions. Then again, the Empress usually did not react well to excessive digging into her plans, and the horror of the plan itself had left him mostly numb and not-thinking in the days leading up to Hotaru's death.

After all, shinobi were weapons, wielded by their rulers. What else was there to understand?

Chapter Eight

Takeshi spent a while more wandering about the ship before returning below for a nap. He woke up in time for dinner, joining the crew for some sort of fish stew. He helped Caron clean up after the crew dispersed again, then climbed to the ship's top deck, where he morosely watched the sun set over the waves. He tried to put his thoughts into some sort of order, but they chased themselves round in circles until he gave up. Too much just didn't make sense. He decided there would be time to dwell on the past after he succeeded, if he even survived that long. He needed to focus on what he was doing now. Namely, what his next immediate step should be.

The actual goal was obvious – get to Gallia. The question was *how*. He decided he could afford to take some time to figure that out, and take advantage of having a relatively safe place to rest and recuperate. That way, when he finally reached the continent he would be in a better position to achieve his next goal – determining how best to make contact with the rebellion forming against the Rose.

Small steps.

Feeling marginally better that he now had the vague outline of a plan, he retreated back below for more sleep.

When Takeshi woke the next morning, he was pleased to find that his body was merely sore instead of actually aching. He wandered up to the mess to discover that breakfast was more of a grab-and-go affair on the *Sea Spirit*, with a small selection of things laid out on the large table. He passed Benjen and Don, who both wished him a good morning, as did Ashi and Caron, who were sitting and eating their breakfast next to the windows. He refused to stare. He took a plain bagel and a cup of coffee, silently mourning the lack of tea, then went and found himself an out-of-the-way place to eat in peace. He tried to meditate for a while but ended up dozing instead.

He roused himself for lunch, deciding that a bagel had not really been a sufficient breakfast considering where his reserves were, and headed back to the mess. Caron was setting up another buffet-style meal, this time with various sandwiches and some sort of salad made of thinly cut ingredients. It reminded him of a cabbage salad but tasted different than what he expected. Caron insisted he take an extra sandwich, explaining that Ashi had apparently not been impressed with Takeshi's scant breakfast and demanded that her husband make sure Takeshi ate more for lunch. Thanking him, Takeshi again took his food elsewhere, deciding to sit in the sun above deck for a bit.

When he went back to the mess to return his plate, the sisters appeared to be doing the same. He winced internally as they lit up upon seeing him.

"Wizard!" one of them cooed happily. "There ye are! Where've ye been all day?"

"Around?" he suggested weakly. It wasn't really like he could go very far; he was stuck on this boat with them.

"Well, we're glad we found ye," the other chirped. He wondered if there was an accurate way to tell them apart. "We have a question for ye!"

"Oh?" An intense sensation of dread settled over Takeshi. He was certain he would not like this question.

"Who's cuter? Me or Desha?"

"You are both very lovely," he stated flatly, trying to avoid the trap he sensed closing in. At least now he knew who was who for the rest of this conversation, which with any luck would be short.

"Aww, come on! Ye can't just cop out like that!" Salisha whined at him. "Ye have t' pick one! And clearly I'm prettier!"

They looked exactly the same to him, but... "How does one choose between the sakura and the wisteria? Both are beautiful, but can they really be compared?" he tried, shrugging. Maybe they would like that.

Desha's eyes narrowed. "Yer hard t' read, wizard, though ye talk pretty." She considered him a moment.

Suddenly, Benjen entered from the deck. "Has anyone seen Marjori, or is she still sulking?" he asked, sounding tired.

Salisha's eyes sharpened, and with an evil grin she grabbed Benjen's arm and hauled him between her and her sister, ignoring the sound of protest he made. "Or maybe Benjen is more yer style?"

"Oh no, not again," Benjen groaned. "Gods, why must you do this with everyone who comes aboard this ship? Can we *not* do this for once?"

"Come on, wizard. Which o' us would ye date, right now, if ye had t' choose?" Desha's grin matched her sister's.

"Unfortunately, my fiancé has died," Takeshi stated, matter-of-fact. "As such, I must wait one year and three days from the date of her funeral before I am free to pursue another relationship."

There was a long pause.

"Was... that a joke?" Salisha whispered, eyes wide.

"It was really dark, if so," Benjen said with a wince.

"I'm trying t' decide if that's amazing or horrifying," Desha added.

Salisha tilted her head to the side, narrowing her eyes at him. "Wait, is that *true*?"

Takeshi kept his expression blank. They could read into it what they wished. It was a good deflection, though he mentally apologized to Hotaru for using her in this way.

A staticky crackle, and Marjori's voice suddenly came from a radio on Benjen's hip. "Oi, we gotta potential mark, Ben. Cap'n wants us on deck."

He raised an eyebrow. "Ah, that's good. Possible resupply." He paused. "Also, Marjori."

The girls had gone still, staring intently at Benjen. "We're coming too, right?"

"Yup; let's go," he said shortly. Then he paused, eying Takeshi. "You might want to stay inside for a while."

Takeshi blinked as they all swept out of the mess. Potential mark? Paired with possible resupply?

Ah. Well, they were pirates.

Takeshi tried to think about what he knew about pirate attacks in the Shae Sea. Unfortunately, as he had been posted to the capital for most of his career, it wasn't much. He knew that it happened, and that it was a problem. He was fairly certain that it was freighters and cargo ships that were hit most often. He had once been subjected to a long rant from the Minister of Commerce about how piracy was evil and ruining supply lines between them and Espon, but he had tuned it out fairly early, as the man had a tendency to go on long rants about anything that annoyed him.

He hummed thoughtfully, giving himself wholeheartedly to the distraction. He really did not have much information to go on, and thus did not know what to expect from this. None of the pirates really seemed like bad people to him. Even the sisters mostly just seemed... aggressively nosy, and a bit overbearing, but not ill-intentioned. The crew was even growing on him a little, so perhaps the best option would be to just observe for now. They didn't seem to expect him to participate anyway, for which he was thankful. He wasn't even sure how he would react, if forced to do something. The pirates were pretty clearly in the wrong, but he was on their ship and he knew them, and for the most part he liked them.

And yet – he was supposed to eventually be making contact with people who were rebelling against the Rose. By their nature, they would be defined as terrorists who broke the law. Would it be easier to make contact if he showed that he was also willing to break the law, and was no longer one of those who upheld it? Quite possibly. It might also be better cover for him as far as the Rose itself went. They saw him as a murderer, but perhaps being a murderer who still tried to be a good citizen would be strange.

He was testing the waters of lawbreaking. Wonderful.

He gave a little internal poke at his reserves. Still not nearly up to full, but enough that he could do something if necessary. He decided to meditate for a while to see if he could replenish a bit more.

He roused quickly, pleased that he had not fallen asleep this time, when Ashi coughed politely to get his attention. She was holding a plate of food. "Dinner is likely t' be... significantly more rowdy than usual," she said apologetically, ears tilted down somewhat. "Ye may wish t' eat by yourself tonight."

Takeshi smiled wryly to himself, eyeing the plate of rice and beef strips. "I understand," he assured the green-haired Avari, taking the plate. "I think I'll turn in early tonight, anyway."

"That's probably for the best." Ashi nodded, ears coming up again slightly.

"Thank you for dinner. I will return my dish in the morning," Takeshi said, already heading to the narrow staircase in the corner of the room. He could hear the voices of the other crew members heading for the mess from above, and swiftly exited.

He made his way back to his room, where he placed his plate down on the chest at the foot of the berth. He waited ten minutes before heading back out, silent. He listened carefully as he slunk through the ship, but it sounded like everyone was in the mess. Slipping into the room below, he counted the voices. Seven. Good. That meant he likely only had to worry about discovery from one direction. He stilled himself and settled into a shadow to listen.

Currently, the sisters were complaining. About him.

"Why'd ye send him away?" one of them asked, clearly put out.

"We know basically nothing about him." That was Marjori. "No need t' bring in an unknown for a job."

"A bigger concern is that he was a Silent One – someone who upheld the law. Even with everything that happened in Ni Fon, there's a pretty good possibility that he does not approve of piracy." Benjen was on the mark as usual, Takeshi noted wryly. "He's been fairly amicable to us so far, but we also haven't really done anything other than save him from drowning in a storm."

"A bigger concern for me is that he just sort of drifts around the ship like a ghost," Ashi pointed out. "I'm not sure he's really 'better' than when he came aboard. He needs more time t' heal, before we spring more things at him."

Takeshi frowned slightly. He thought he'd been doing pretty okay. His reserves were at maybe a third, and movement was no longer extremely painful.

"The wizard be a puzzle for another day," Caron's voice boomed from the room above. "The freighter be the current one. Don, ye sure about the timing?"

Don's voice was significantly quieter. "Aye. We should be within striking range just after midnight. And it's small, Roan class, so crew should be more than manageable."

"It'll be Ben, Don, Desha, and Salisha hitting the freighter." Cheers from the sisters. "Make sure grappling hooks, night visors, and weapons be ready t' go," Caron ordered firmly.

"Aye," Benjen responded.

"Ashi—"

"Everything's good on my end," the Avari interjected calmly. "If there are injuries, I'll be ready."

"Don, how's the new device coming along?"

"It's ready for a go, Captain. I'll bring along my usual methods just in case, but it should work fine."

"Excellent! We should be able t' get in and out quickly, then," one of the sisters piped up.

Takeshi listened a bit longer as they hashed out a few more details, and gleaned that it was likely they were going after the safe on the other ship. Takeshi hadn't known freighters and cargo ships had safes, but he supposed it made sense for dealing with port fees or other expenses, and it could be exchanged for the plastic currency they used on the mainland regardless.

Deciding that he wasn't likely to learn more as the conversation above him drifted to other topics, Takeshi slid back to his room to consider the situation. He had a better idea of what the pirates planned to do, at least, but he suspected he still lacked enough knowledge about shipping vessels to be able to see the whole picture. Certainly, the crew above did not seem overly concerned about the crew on the freighter, for example, and he wasn't sure why. He ate his now-cold dinner, thinking it over pensively.

It was nearly an hour later when the lights went out. Takeshi blinked in surprise, waiting for his eyes to adjust, and held still, listening carefully. After a few moments, he heard someone descend to the sub deck and approach down the hall, then knock quietly on his door.

"Shuurai?" It was Ashi.

Takeshi stood and took the step to get to the door, opening it. "Doctor? Did we lose power?" he asked, eyeing the small, dull emergency lights running the length of the hallway floor.

Her lips twitched into a smile. "We are going t' be running silent for the rest of the night. Lights'll be down until morning, at least."

He nodded. "Thank you for letting me know this is not an emergency. The lights going out did take me by surprise."

Her ears twitched up. "Ye said ye were planning on sleeping early anyway?"

He nodded again. "Sleeping is one of the best ways to recover magical reserves."

He nearly took a step back as her ears swept down in annoyance and her face darkened. "So's eating. The calories are good for ye! I want t' see ye take something more than just a bagel tomorrow, understand?" The look she gave him brooked no argument.

"Aye?" He tried the sea-speak word for yes, hoping it might win him a point or two.

She studied him for a moment longer. "See that ye do," she stated with a tone of finality, before turning to make her way back to the ladder.

Takeshi retreated into his room and glanced at the little clock, squinting at it in the dark. He still had five or so hours before things would get interesting, anyway. Plenty of time for a little extra meditation.

Takeshi listened carefully at his door, but he hadn't heard anyone down below for hours. He considered for a moment and decided to leave his katana. He did not expect to be caught, but he imagined that if he was, having it would only make the situation worse. And as much as it meant to him, leaving it behind did not mean leaving himself defenseless.

Very carefully, he opened the door and confirmed that there was no one on the sub deck. He slid out of the room, shutting the door as quietly as he had opened it. Silent as a shadow in the near dark he glided through the ship. He made his way through the mess to the door to the outside, where he could hear people moving about and talking quietly to each other. He took his time, listening carefully and calculating the crew's positions and movements. He took his chance when he heard a splash to the right, and he silently opened the door and darted into the shadows on deck to observe the proceedings.

Ashi and Caron were standing at the side of the ship, looking down. Takeshi ghosted around the upper decks of the ship to see that the white boat was now in the water, with Benjen, Don, and the sisters in it. The pirates were all armed with pistols and long daggers and were wearing visors. Takeshi's eyes flickered over the water, and he saw a ship much larger than the *Sea Spirit* perhaps half a mile away. Unlike the *Sea Spirit*, it was lit against the dark backdrop of the sea and sky. He carefully tucked himself against the side of the ship, into the sharp shadows cast by the nearly full moon up above. How had the other ship not seen them? Was the *Sea Spirit* utilizing some sort of stealth tech? Or was the other ship just not looking?

Takeshi watched the little boat speed its way silently towards the other vessel, keeping an ear out for Ashi and Caron in case they started to head his way. When they reached the other vessel, Desha and Salisha fired some sort of gun upward, and grappling hooks shot out. The hooks caught on the railing of the ship, and then the girls were climbing up like squirrels. Takeshi was impressed with their speed. When they hit the deck, they appeared to do a quick check around, then stood guard for Don and Benjen as they made their way up.

There was still no alarm from the other ship.

The four slunk their way around the freighter, and Takeshi lost sight of them. He eyed the distance between the two ships. Half a mile was much too far for a shadow step, even if he were in peak condition. He would have to settle for what he could see from here. He waited, patient.

Then he felt it. A flicker of... something. Gone almost immediately.

Takeshi's gaze sharpened as he tried to determine what it was. It had felt like magic. He frowned; no one on the *Sea Spirit* had ever shown any sign of arcane training.

Another flicker–

He felt the pattern bloom into existence as shots rang out on the other vessel. Barely a moment later, the *Sea Spirit* veered to intercept the other ship. Takeshi closed his eyes, trying to focus on the feel of the pattern. It did not feel familiar to him, the way it would if he knew the weaver, and it had not faded either, which suggested... ah, yes. A shield spell. Weakening as more shots were fired. The caster felt small, to Takeshi's senses. Not a very strong mage.

He waited.

He heard a woman shriek, and a splash.

He supposed he had only been deluding himself earlier. His decision had been a foregone conclusion from the start.

Takeshi reached out as the two ships came closer together, looking for somewhere near the weakening spell, and *there...*

He called the pattern he needed to mind easily, wove the foreign shadow with the one he was already in, and stepped into chaos.

Benjen and one of the sisters were firing at the shield spell, an ugly, poorly constructed thing in yellow-green that was fracturing with each hit. Takeshi was surprised it had held up as long as it had; it was poorly balanced. The mage casting it was a plain-looking Human man with messy brown hair and eyes. Behind him on the ground, unmoving, was Don, a metal box lying near him.

This close and he could tell the weaver had almost no reserves left. Takeshi might not have been at his full strength either, but he could certainly deal with this travesty of a mage. The pattern he needed was effortless to envision, one of his favorites, and energy crackled as he wove it to the proper shape.

The small ball of lightning flashed blue-white with his own power and *blasted* the shield apart.

He darted forward, snatching the dagger off Benjen's belt as he passed him, and slammed the other mage against the wall, knife to throat. Takeshi allowed his own power to saturate the air around them, wordlessly letting the other know that he had no chance against the shinobi. He could hear Benjen swearing behind him as he held the mage in place. Brown eyes stared at him, terrified, but they both knew this was already over.

"*Shuurai*, what in the *actual*—"

Benjen was cut off by a female voice sputtering from below. "I'm okay! Just need a line up!"

He could see the other sister staring at him, wide eyed and silent, out of the corner of his eye before she slipped out of his field of vision. He did not look away from the mage.

A crackle of static, and Caron's voice came through the radio. "Did ye say 'Shuurai', Ben? Didn't quite catch that. Status?"

Benjen swore. "Shuurai is *here*, somehow. Got the other mage pinned. Desha is overboard, but responsive; Don's unconscious. Salisha is getting a line. We have the box."

"What do ya mean, Shuurai is *there*?" Marjori's voice sounded shocked.

There was a long pause, during which no one moved, and Takeshi realized he was waiting for an order that wouldn't come. The Empress and her law were far away. The choice to kill, or not to, was his.

"I mean I'm looking at him," Benjen said finally, sounding incredibly vexed. "I mean he is on this ship, not ten feet away from me, and *not* on the *Sea Spirit*." He moved closer to Don, who was beginning to stir. "Don is coming to. Took a nasty blow to the head; make sure Ashi knows before we get there."

Takeshi flipped the dagger and knocked the mage out, letting his body drop to the floor.

"Okay, the mage is now down for the count." Benjen frowned, eyeing Takeshi warily. "Are *you* okay? Gods, I almost shot you."

Takeshi took stock. "I'm fine." A slight headache was beginning to form, but other than that, nothing too bad. He'd sleep well, later, but he hadn't even needed to weave very much. He noticed Salisha helping a wet Desha back onto the deck.

"Great. We need to get out of here, *now*," Benjen snapped, hauling Don up. "Grab the box."

"We'll be ready for ye." Caron sounded almost cheerful.

Takeshi picked the box up and followed after Benjen as he practically carried Don across the ship. The sisters trailed behind, murmuring softly to one another. They reached the speed boat without any more trouble.

Ashi and Caron met them on the main deck as the speed boat was lifted up. Ashi knelt by Don, snapping out, "Desha, Shuurai, get yourselves t' sick bay. I'll be there shortly."

Takeshi's headache was a little worse than it had been, but he was fine. He didn't usually get headaches after weaving, but his body had been under a lot of stress lately. He just needed some extra rest. "Doctor–"

Takeshi wilted almost immediately under the force of the glare she leveled at him.

"Sick. Bay. *Now.*"

Desha gently tugged on his arm. "Not the time, wizard. Let's go before she skins us."

Ashi's pointed gaze followed them until they were out of sight. "She is very scary," Takeshi felt compelled to point out as he and Desha started down the narrow staircase.

Desha snorted. "Yer one t' talk, wizard. I think ye scared Ben and Salisha something awful when ye appeared. Kind o' sad I missed it, being overboard and whatnot."

Takeshi thought about that for a moment, what it would have looked like to someone other than him who was also not familiar with his tactics. "Oh," he murmured softly. "That was not my intention."

She gave him a sympathetic look. "So yer not great at working with other people. We can fix that!"

Takeshi thought sadly that he was good at working with people – *his* people. Satomi, Morita, Hara... he worked very well with other shinobi and kunoichi, none of whom he was likely to work with again.

He sighed to himself as they entered the sick bay to wait for Ashi.

When Takeshi woke up, he was alone with a sleeping Don in the sick bay. He had fallen asleep almost as soon as he had lain down. The remnants of the headache poked at him as he hauled himself up, and he decided to escape before Ashi came back. He wasn't completely sure what she was going to say to him, but her expression had made it very clear he wasn't going to enjoy it.

He crept out of the room and quickly snuck out to the main deck. He paused by the mess, considering acquiring food, but heard Ashi's voice and decided that he could grab some later. Quietly, he found a sunny, out-of-the-way spot on deck to settle in and wait for the rest of his headache to fade.

He was startled out of his doze sometime later by the bulk of the captain settling next to him. "There ye be, wizard!" Caron boomed cheerfully. "Ashi be looking for ye."

Takeshi winced. "Don't tell her I'm here, please."

Caron laughed loudly. "Ye won't be avoiding her forever on a ship like this," he warned gently. "She'll catch up t' ye eventually, and ye'll be worse off for it."

"That," Takeshi drawled slowly, turning his attention to the sky, "is a problem for later."

Caron snorted. "I'll be sure t' remind ye o' that when she finally corners ye."

They sat in silence for a few minutes, before Caron tentatively offered, "Ye know, it seems t' me that going t' Espon be an especially unwise decision for ye at this juncture."

"So you've said," Takeshi stated mildly, watching the fluffy white clouds float by.

Caron shook his head. "That be before last night, wizard. Ye survived in the god storm long enough fer the Twins t' throw ye at us, so ye were clearly something special, but..." His voice trailed off for a moment. "The continent's not friendly t' mages, not anymore. Rumor has it the Blind Ones keep it that way, forbid any knowledge o' it. 'Twould be a shame for ye t' make it there and then be killed 'cause o' what ye are."

Takeshi blinked. "The Truth Seekers? I know of them. I met one, once. Not overly friendly, but then, I suppose he would say the same of me. I don't think they are actually blind." He considered the memory a moment, remembering how strange the other's power had felt. He wished they'd been friendly enough to discuss it. "I don't intend to attract their attention, and if I do, I can handle it."

"Ye seem t' think ye don't have options, wizard, but ye do. We've been talking, the crew and I, ye know? Ye could stay with us, take up piracy. Wizards be prized out here, especially ones capable o' surviving on their own in a god storm and teleporting from ship t' ship."

"You're offering me a place on your ship?" Takeshi asked quietly. "You barely know me. I don't even think all of you like me," he added, thinking of the blue-haired Avari.

"The Twins threw ye t' us for a reason, li'l wizard. It be beyond me ken t' know what that reason be, but it be clear ye be cast adrift, and no matter what Marjori says, most o' this crew be strays I pulled in at one point or another." He clapped a giant hand on Takeshi's shoulder; it covered a good portion of his back as well. "Ye could start over again here. Ye don't have t' answer now. Think on it."

Takeshi's eyes followed Caron as he pulled himself to his feet and strode away. This was quite a surprise. He had seen enough of how the crew interacted with each other to know that they were like a family. Who just... invited people into their family like that? These pirates, apparently, if Caron was to be believed.

The way they worked together reminded him of his squad, before Hotaru's death, and he felt a pang of loneliness and loss for all of it. He allowed himself a moment of weakness to imagine it for a second...

Hotaru's dark eyes stared accusingly at him, as the blood spread...

No. Even if the thought of being part of a group again was horribly tempting, he could never bring himself to disgrace Hotaru's memory like that. She had died to give them this chance. He had to take it.

Rhode watched her study the room through the one-sided glass. Not that the near-featureless white room lent itself to much study, but he was certain she was testing it in other ways, too. She'd find that was useless soon enough.

Rhode checked the holo screens. All systems green. She wouldn't be able to get out. Finally, they had a Romanii agent in their grasp. He checked his tablet for what information they had on her. Frustratingly, it was almost nothing. He flicked the intercom on.

"Who are you?"

He was unnerved by how her eyes immediately tracked to him. He checked the screen readout, and yes, it was set to one-way. Could she see through the tech-infused glass? He supposed that was a possibility, though a disturbing one. This tech was meant to hold mages.

"I've been going by Hel, recently." She shrugged. "Works as well as anything else."

He frowned, but even an alias might give them something. They could work on that more later. "There is absolutely no record of you until you broke out of Greenway Station with the kid. Not even how you got into the station. It's almost like you're a ghost that wandered in."

She smirked at him, violet eyes glinting strangely. "A ghost? I like that." Her ears twitched up slightly. "And there are records of me all over the place, if you know what to look for. Unfortunate, that those in the Empire no longer know what they're looking at."

"Why don't you tell me what I should be looking for, then? You're not a Vampire; we've determined that much."

She shook her head slowly. "No, I don't think I will. It will be a fun puzzle for us, no?"

"Is it fun if one of us knows the answer already?" He paused as Major Cole entered the room silently, handing him another tablet that he glanced at briefly, noting the information presented.

"Who's the kid, Hel?"

She grinned.

Chapter Nine

It was noon by the time they finally reached the Warcross Wall.

From up close, Jamirh could see that the Wall was made of large stone bricks. They were gray and almost unnaturally smooth, but what really gave him pause were the faint lines of multicolored light running through them. They faded in and out of focus as they pulsed, making them hard to get a good look at. But what was more concerning than the strange material was the lack of a door – or any other way into the tower.

"Uh," he started, looking at Jeri, "how do we actually, you know, get in?" He looked up to the top of the tower, trying to judge the distance. "Please don't tell me we have to climb." The Wall itself looked to be at least eighty feet tall, and the tower was higher even than that.

Jeri snorted and rose up to put her front paws on the side of the tower. She looked back at Jamirh and tilted her head towards the Wall.

Jamirh frowned. "You want me to touch the Wall?" Jeri made an exaggerated nodding motion, which looked very strange on her canine body. "Okay then," he said slowly, raising a hand to touch the side of the tower. It felt strangely warm for stone. Jeri's tail wagged once as she looked back towards the large structure.

And then he was no longer outside.

Jamirh looked around in confusion. He and Jeri were now in a large, circular room made of that same gray stone. There were no windows or furniture, but Jamirh had no problem seeing despite the lack of a light source.

"Ah," Jeri said, her form morphing back to Human, "that is much better. Thank you, Morden," she added, glancing up. Jamirh followed her gaze, but all he saw was a high ceiling.

"Are we in the tower?" he asked, baffled. "How did we get in the tower? And isn't Morden dead?" He felt a sense of... amusement? That was strange; he wasn't really finding any of this funny.

"Yes, he is. Technically, he is dead twice over," Jeri replied wryly. "But he remains as the tower regardless, and is responsible for moving people through this part of the Wall." She waved a hand gracefully through the air, indicating the surrounding walls. The veins of light in the walls pulsed in response, turning a dark-gray color before returning to the dim rainbow light as Jamirh realized the walls were the light source. "He's waving at you," she informed him.

Jamirh stared.

The amusement bled into mild concern.

"I know," Jeri sighed, glancing around. "I'm working on it. *She* didn't really help matters."

Mild concern turned to censure.

"Don't give me that, Morden." Jeri's voice cooled as her eyes flashed dangerously. "You don't know what I had to deal with. The novelty wears off very quickly."

"Are you... talking to him?" Jamirh said slowly, looking around. "How?"

And censure turned back to amusement, and a sense of greeting.

Jamirh's brain caught up with the fact that these weren't his feelings *at all*, and his eyes widened. "Oh...!"

Jeri cocked her head to the side, looking at him curiously. "You can sense him, yes? The emotions that are not yours. That is how he communicates – by projecting his feelings and emotions, rather than speech. Empathy, we call it. It is not an uncommon ability among Vampires, in some form or another." Jeri was eyeing him carefully.

Vampires.

Jamirh decided he was too tired to deal with this, and gave up. "Hi," he sighed exhaustedly, his ears drooping low as he reached for his key, the metal offering a sense of familiarity.

There was a distinct sensation of unhappiness and alarm.

"I know!" Jeri repeated, clearly annoyed. "I'm bringing him to Vlad."

Relief.

Jeri rolled her eyes. "Please open the gate, Morden. The sooner we get to Pitesh, the sooner we get to Tarvishte, and I'm starving."

Jamirh absently wondered who this "Vlad" person was. Hel had mentioned him too.

In the center of the room, a series of symbols laid out in concentric circles etched into the floor lit up with a dark-gray light. Jeri glided over to stand in the middle. "Come," she prompted when Jamirh simply watched her. Sighing again, he dragged himself with much less grace to the markings. He stepped over them carefully, not liking the way they were glowing. "They won't bite you," she added dryly as he picked his way over to her.

"What are they, exactly?" he asked wearily.

"Glyphs, arranged into a gate array. Morden is going to send us to Pitesh, so we don't have to walk another thirty or so miles through the Waste to get there." She waited for him to come to a stop beside her, then put her hand on his shoulder. "Thank you, Morden. Farewell."

The walls pulsed again, and light exploded from the array under their feet until Jamirh couldn't see anything else. Jeri's grip on his shoulder tightened as he tried to yank away in panic–

And then they were standing on a slightly raised platform, on which the same symbols as those in Morden's tower had been carved into the white stone. The platform was in a small courtyard, surrounded by white brick walls with a few ornamental trees in the corners. Cut into one wall was a curved archway, under which looked to be a heavy wooden door with brass fittings. Jamirh blinked at the new scenery in confusion as Jeri released him and strode towards the archway. She opened the door briskly, calling another "Come!" at Jamirh over her shoulder, and disappeared inside without waiting.

Jamirh followed slowly, unsure what to expect anymore. It wasn't that he thought Jeri would knowingly lead him into danger, he just felt sort of lost and adrift. He found himself missing Hel's endless optimism.

Through the door was a large room with a glass dome ceiling. There were gray couches, plush-looking chairs, and potted plants scattered around the center area. A sturdy black marble counter stood on the far side of the room, where Jeri was talking to someone seated behind it. There were a few other Humans milling around, and one couch was taken up by a black warg stretched out across it. Jamirh found himself hurrying to catch up to Jeri, eyeing everything suspiciously.

"Really?" Jeri was asking as he approached. "Nothing until tomorrow?"

The Human behind the counter shrugged apologetically. Like Jeri, he was wearing black, and at a closer glance Jamirh realized that their clothing looked very similar. Actually, now that he thought about it, Hel's clothing had looked a lot like Jeri's as well. "They changed the schedule a few weeks ago." He waved a piece of paper through the air absently. "I think it makes less sense, but you know they don't ask us." He glanced at Jamirh, then looked back at Jeri, raising an eyebrow inquisitively. Jeri shook her head ever so slightly, and the man sighed, running a hand through his short black hair. "The best I can do is suggest you book rooms at the Dancer and grab a train tomorrow. Put it on our tab." He shot a wry smile at Jamirh. "Welcome to Pitesh, where the trains never run when you want them to."

Jamirh frowned, ears twitching lower. He wasn't sure what that silent exchange had been about, and he wasn't sure he wanted to know.

"That's just civilization," Jeri pointed out. "Nothing special about Pitesh there. Jamirh, this is Kaeden – he runs the Black Watch in Pitesh. Kaeden, Jamirh."

"And the Black Watch is... a travel service?" Jamirh asked, nodding to Kaeden in greeting.

Jeri's flat "No" was lost in the sound of Kaeden's laughter. "If only! That would actually be easier. But no, the Black Watch is responsible for keeping Romanii safe, inside and out."

The warg on the couch startled at the noise Kaeden was making and turned large blue eyes in their direction.

"Like the Guard?" Jamirh asked, eyeing it warily as it hauled itself off the couch in a slow stretch before wandering over.

"Yeah, more or less like that. Poe, *no–*" Kaeden put a hand out, but the warg ignored it completely, jumping up onto the counter. It eyed them all curiously as Jamirh backed away. "Ah, he won't hurt you. He just likes to be tall, and I've never managed to convince him that he shouldn't be on countertops." Kaeden sighed mournfully. "You can pet him if you want to; he's very friendly. His name is Poe."

"I'll pass, thanks. Is he a person?" Jamirh asked with a pointed look at Jeri, who winced slightly.

"He's like a person? I find most wargs are." Kaeden seemed confused by the question and reached up to scratch Poe's ears.

"No, he's not a transformed person," Jeri clarified, sounding as tired as Jamirh felt.

"Oh, yes, he's definitely a warg. Well, he might be part bird or something, given how much he loves heights, but a warg nonetheless." Kaeden eyed Jeri curiously as Jamirh stared at her. "But yeah, the Guard is a pretty close equivalent, though we do more than they do, I think. Jeri is Black Watch; see the uniform? I'm wearing something similar."

So the clothes did mean something. Jamirh turned to Jeri. "Then Hel is also a member of the Black Watch?"

She winced again, glancing at Kaeden. "Hel... helps the Watch on occasion, but I wouldn't exactly say she's of the Black Watch."

Kaeden's eyebrows rose almost to his hairline, but he said nothing. Poe panted happily, tail wagging, as Kaeden continued to scratch his ears.

"Your version of the Guard just lets people volunteer?" Jamirh was completely lost as to how these people functioned.

Jeri sighed. "It's complicated. Vlad can explain it better than I can. And Ander, perhaps. It will make sense if they are the ones explaining. This is why it is imperative we get to Tarvishte as soon as possible."

Kaeden's eyebrows furrowed as he shook his head slowly. "I don't really think Ander can explain *anything* 'better' than anyone else. I'm usually lost after the first two sentences."

"That's... a good point, actually," Jeri said thoughtfully. "Can't really fault his understanding of theory though, even if it sounds incomprehensible to the rest of us."

"Just have Vlad explain it. Vlad is good at it," Kaeden declared firmly as Jamirh looked back and forth between the two of them, trying to follow the conversation. "But I think the best thing for right now is that you get rooms at the Dancer. Jamirh here looks like a stiff breeze is going to knock him over, and I could fit my wallet in the bags under his eyes. It's poor form to run our charges into the ground, Jeri."

She stared at him, clearly affronted. "It wasn't *me*! *None* of this was my idea!"

Kaeden just shrugged. "Sometimes, the Lady gives us difficult paths to walk. What can you do?"

Jeri glared at him, and Jamirh thought that if looks could kill, Kaeden would be a smear on the wall. "We'll head towards the Dancer, then. Thank you, Kaeden, for your utter lack of aid." She spun on her heel and headed for the large double doors taking up a portion of the wall to the right.

Jamirh gave an awkward wave to a grinning Kaeden, then dashed to catch up to Jeri. "Wait, if he runs this place, what is he doing at the front desk?" he asked her, confused.

She shook her head. "He probably lost a bet, knowing him." She pushed the doors open and stepped into the sunlight, Jamirh following...

...Only to find himself staring at a city the likes of which he had never seen before.

Jamirh had lived his whole life in Lyndiniam, and over the course of his twenty-two years he had thoroughly explored every inch of it he could get to. He was familiar with the clean lines and sterility of white lester and glass that the majority of the city favored, tall buildings shooting into the sky, and well-manicured greenery, as well as the decrepit buildings of Blackfields with their myriad of older materials, crumbling and overgrown.

This was neither of those things. Buildings of white and reddish-white brick were framed with wood and enhanced with ornate copper or brass embellishments and scrollwork. Some buildings shot high into the sky, tower-like; others were only a story tall. Red shingled roofs formed a variety of shapes, from pyramids to cones to rounded shapes. Large pipes traveled up buildings with large circular windows, and there were arches and dormers everywhere. Plants spilled off balconies and filled decorative planters by doors. There was no such thing, from what Jamirh could tell, as a plain building. Avari and Humans both traveled past, greeting and chatting with one another as they went on their way.

Just about the only thing that seemed familiar was that the street was paved. Everywhere else he looked, there was something he had never seen before. Even the clothing here was different. He didn't see any denim, though there was a lot more leather than he was used to, and long coats and belts seemed to be far more prevalent.

Jeri looked back at him when he stopped moving. "Let's go; it's not far from here. You can sleep in a proper bed once we get there. And eat something other than those horrid granola bars."

Well, that was motivating, even if he hadn't thought the granola was that bad.

Jamirh stuck close to Jeri as they navigated the city, which continued to fascinate him. They passed a plaza with wrought iron benches and a strange sculpture of metal and glass, paved with decorative cobble. Street lamps were ornate affairs, with scrollwork decorating both the structure and the casing for the lights themselves, shaped to look like lanterns. Stairways and balconies had decorative metal guardrails.

Strangely, the sky occasionally shimmered high above.

After about ten minutes of walking, they came upon what Jamirh could only assume was their destination due to the large letters proclaiming the building to be The Dark Dancer. Tables surrounded with greenery with large umbrellas sat in front of it around a large fountain with a marble statue. The pair passed through the arched entryway into the foyer, and Jamirh waited close by while Jeri spoke with the Avari at the front desk. Brick archways, balconies, and trailing plants were featured inside the building as well as out. After a few minutes, Jeri returned to him holding a pair of keys, and she led him up two flights of ornate marble stairs and down a hallway.

"Here we are," she stated, handing him one of the keys. She indicated the next door down. "My room is next to yours. If you need anything, knock. They are going to bring up something to eat shortly."

He nodded tiredly. "Thanks. How long until we have to go again?"

Her eyes softened. "Not until tomorrow. I do want to get to Tarvishte as soon as possible, but we are safe here. You can relax. It is going to be a long train ride tomorrow; you could sleep on the train, too, if you want to. The hard part is over."

Jamirh found himself fiddling with his key. He wasn't certain that was the case – just seeing the city outside had really driven home how alien this place was compared to all he had ever known – but at least he was alive. "Sure," he responded, unlocking the door. "Sleep sounds good."

"Sleep well," she murmured, turning to her own door.

The room beyond was just as strange as everything else had been so far. It looked extraordinarily well-furnished to Jamirh, but all he really cared about was the bed, which looked soft and warm and comfortable.

He had barely kicked his shoes off and lain down on the bed before he was asleep.

It was just past dawn when he woke up, the sun peeking in through the sheer curtains coaxing him awake. Jamirh rubbed the sleep from his eyes – he was still tired, and his body still ached from the last five days of intense activity fleeing from Lyndiniam, but he did feel better after a good night and almost half a day of sleep. After a few extra minutes of wallowing in what was probably the most comfortable bed he had ever spent time in, he pulled himself from the soft covers to try to freshen up a bit, taking the time to actually look at the room around him.

It was far nicer and larger than the space he had inhabited back home. Besides the bed, there was a desk, a small round table, and two nightstands, all a polished dark wood. There was a plush armchair by the windows, as well as a leather chair by the desk. A chest of drawers sat nearby. The floor was covered in simple gray carpet. There were framed pictures on the wall and lamps on almost every surface. A small but fancy bathroom was accessible through a sliding door, with a large mirror in an ornate frame above the sink. There was no comparison to how he had lived in Lyndiniam. This was practically luxury, and he found himself wondering what it was costing Jeri for them to stay here.

Jamirh stared at his reflection in the mirror, realizing how bad he actually looked. His hair was an absolute mess, dull ruby strands going every which way, and Kaeden had been right about the dramatic bags under his eyes, which were still present even after having caught up on some sleep. His clothing was also really starting to struggle after five days of walking and sleeping in endless fields.

He wondered what the hell he was going to do now. He hadn't exactly been living the life in Lyndiniam, but at least it had been familiar. Now he was just... lost, and adrift. Hel had clearly had ideas of some sort, which presumably Jeri was carrying out, but Jamirh didn't really know what that meant for him. They were going to a place named Tarvishte, sure, but what then? Was there, like... a place for refugees from the Empire to go? Had he just traded struggling to live in one country for struggling to live in another? Gods, what was he *doing*?

Sighing tiredly as he came up with no answers, Jamirh decided that as long as he was going to be put up in places like this, sticking to Jeri was probably the way to go. It was the path of least resistance. Kind of like when he'd been with Aether... not that they'd lived in or even seen any sort of luxury like this, but Aether had been good about figuring things out. Jamirh would have to pay attention to what

Jeri did and try to start learning about how this place worked. When he inevitably ended up on his own again, he would hopefully have an idea of how to survive.

He spent a bit of time rummaging through the drawers, but only came away with a few paperclips and nine packets of sugar. He'd hoped for something a little more interesting, but at least these things could prove useful later.

Since Jeri had yet to come collect him, he took the opportunity to shower. Without a brush, he ended up running his fingers through his hair to get out the worst of the tangles before returning it to its usual ponytail. As he finished up attempting to look sort of presentable, he noticed a scrap of paper had been slipped under the door.

Meet me at the tables outside for breakfast when you are ready – Jeri.

The elegant letters contrasted with a pretty bad drawing of what might have been a wolf's head.

At the mention of breakfast, Jamirh realized just how hungry he was. He supposed he had slept through whatever opportunity for food Jeri had mentioned the day before, which was probably an unfortunate waste. He wasted no time in leaving the room in search of Jeri and food.

He found her easily, as she was exactly where she'd said she'd be, in front of the building by the fountain. She smiled in greeting when she saw him approach, then cocked her head to the side as she eyed him critically. "Good morning. You look a bit better," she stated mildly after a moment. "Are you hungry? I procured food." She indicated a plate piled high with eggs, a bagel, bacon, sausage, and a cinnamon bun. A glass of orange juice sat next to it.

"*Yes,*" he exclaimed fervently, falling into the chair opposite her and setting himself to devour everything on the plate. Her lips twitched into a smile.

"I wasn't sure what you would prefer, so I got a bit of everything." She watched him as he stuffed himself. "I see this was not the wrong decision."

He shrugged a bit as he swallowed a bite of bagel. It was buttered. "There is no wrong decision when it comes to food," he informed her before taking another bite.

She hummed. "I'm not sure that's true, per se."

Jamirh just shrugged again, glancing around at their surroundings. There were a lot of plants. He wondered how much effort it took to maintain this much greenery. Then again, with the fountain so near, maybe it was actually pretty easy? He eyed the fountain, pondering if it was purely decorative or also utilitarian. His gaze traveled up to the statue that adorned it.

It was a woman in a long, simple, sleeveless dress, holding a long staff with some sort of crystalline structure at the top. Her long hair and gown billowed as though caught in the wind. Her face was carved with little to no detail, save her eyes. She was made entirely of white marble.

"The goddess Hades," Jeri said absently, having seen what had caught his attention. "Our Lady. She is our mother, and our defender. She is much beloved here. We owe much to Her."

Jamirh squinted at the statue as he finished his breakfast. Hades, goddess of death and destruction. He wouldn't have pictured her so... determined?

"There are temples to her here?" He had never actually seen a temple or even a shrine to Hades; most Avari and Humans he knew worshiped the Three, if they worshiped anything. It was considered bad luck to invite the goddess of death into one's life.

"There is one true temple to Her in Tarvishte. Most honor Her with small shrines, and we are very fond of statues," Jeri explained. "She doesn't have a lot of priests in Her service, so it would be difficult to manage the upkeep on a lot of temples."

"If you all worship her, why aren't there a bunch of priests?" That did not make much sense to Jamirh at all.

Jeri sighed, shaking her head. "Very, very few are Called to Her service, and She will not accept anything less than a *true* vocation."

"So she would... object, somehow, if someone tried to be a priest who she didn't think was supposed to be one?" Jamirh tried to clarify.

"Yes," Jeri affirmed. "She absolutely would, and has."

He was confused. "I thought gods wanted to have large followings with lots of priests?"

"She's more of a quality over quantity kind of person," she stated dryly. "And Her bar for quality is quite high. She has plenty of worshipers, She just doesn't really have priests. We don't absolutely need them, I guess; worship of Her is generally considered a very personal thing. There are festivals and celebrations, but they are community-run affairs – the biggest one, the Festival of Night, is actually happening next week." She smiled faintly, seeing the now-empty plate. "Are you ready to go? The train will be leaving soon."

"Yeah, sure. Thanks for breakfast," he added, feeling pleasantly full for the first time in a while. Then he paused. "Are you going to eat?"

Jeri shook her head. "I ate earlier. We should get going." She stood up. "You can leave the plate and utensils on the table."

Jamirh frowned, remembering something Hel had said. "I thought you struggled to be out in the sun as a Human? Are you going to turn back into a warg?"

"The cities in Romanii are safe." She indicated the sky. "Have you noticed that sometimes the air sort of shimmers?"

He blinked in surprise. He hadn't been sure he wasn't seeing things. "Yes?"

"It's a spell that filters out the UV rays. Tricky to set and power, but it makes it so that we can walk around during the day."

As they headed off to find the train station, Jamirh cast a glance back at the statue of Hades, the goddess of death, wondering vaguely who "we" was, and having a sinking feeling he already knew.

Chapter Ten

I took them about ten minutes to walk to the train station. Jamirh wondered at his surroundings, the buildings and the people. Flashes of Avari-bright color mingled with the more somber tones of Humans wherever he looked. It was strange to see the lack of resentment that normally lingered on the fringes of Avari–Human interactions back home. He might as well be in a completely different world.

Jeri seemed completely unbothered as she guided Jamirh through the alien city. Holding himself to his promise to try to pay more attention, he noticed that people tended to be a bit deferential towards her, but she certainly wasn't being treated the way the Guard were at home. People smiled and greeted her. They weren't afraid of her, or what she might do, even as they seemed to acknowledge her as an authority. They clearly understood what her uniform meant.

People even smiled at *him* as they passed on the cobbled sidewalks. Even Humans! And the Avari were only giving him mildly curious looks. Uncomfortable with the attention, he shied behind Jeri, attempting to use her as a buffer. He would *never* make eye contact with someone being escorted by one of the Guard in Lyndiniam; that was asking for trouble. People here didn't seem to think twice about it.

The train station itself was even more ornate than many of the other buildings they passed, with a large, grand entranceway of dark stone decorated with copper-colored ornamentations. Inside was a wide open space with benches all arranged in a circular pattern to go with the metal inlaid design on the marble floor. People were everywhere, sitting, coming, and going. Against the left wall were the ticket counters, made of a dark wood with large glass windows. Jeri headed in that direction, Jamirh trailing behind her. Purchasing tickets from the cheerfully polite Human behind the counter wasn't difficult, and then they were headed for the boarding platform.

They passed through a crowded hallway and onto the large platform. A glass ceiling curved high above, and Jamirh cocked his head to the side, trying to figure out these people's fascination with skylights. Then he saw the train.

Jamirh had never been on a train himself, but he had seen trains in Lyndiniam. Long and sleek, those trains had smoothly pointed noses and painted aluminum bodies, and they used magnets to navigate the track.

The thing in front of him was not that. The front of it was a large, blunt cylinder with a smoking chimney and pipes coming off it. There were metal grates and ladders and rivets and cogs. The cab behind the cylinder looked like a tall box with windows, followed by yet another box with yet more pipes. The long line of cars behind that had plenty of evenly spaced windows and doors where people were getting on. There were small wheels followed by large wheels followed by small wheels again. The whole thing was painted black and brown with gold accents.

The inside of the train was beautiful, Jamirh found as they boarded. Warm wood paneling lined the interior of the car, and fancy lamps hung from the ceiling. The seats, a pair on either side of the aisle, looked comfortably upholstered in a dark maroon fabric, and matching curtains were pulled back from the windows. The luggage compartments above the seats had brassy handles to open them. The floor was covered in a patterned red, brown, and gold carpet.

"Sorry I couldn't get Kaeden to swing first-class," Jeri said apologetically. "It's going to be a long trip, but this was the best he'd pay for."

"This is amazing," Jamirh breathed, looking all around. "How long is this trip supposed to take?"

"Almost seven hours. Tarvishte is on the northern coast, so we have quite a long way to go," she informed him as they found their seats. "Do you want the window seat, or the aisle?"

He considered. "Which is better?"

"Most prefer the window seat." Her lips twitched as she indicated for him to sit first.

He slid in past her and settled into the seat. It was as comfortable as it looked, which was probably for the best if he was going to be in it for such an extended period of time. He ran his fingers over the fabric of the armrest, admiring how soft it felt. Through the window he could see people going back and forth on the platform, carrying on with their business. A little Avari girl with sun-gold hair and drooping ears clung to her mother's leg as the woman kissed a man with short lavender hair. He knelt and gave the little girl a hug and a kiss on the top of her head before grabbing his bag and boarding the train with one last wave. The little girl burst into tears, burying her face in her mother's arms as the woman tried to calm her.

Jamirh looked away. Everyone left eventually.

He glanced around the interior of the train again before turning his attention towards Jeri, who was pulling her long braid over her shoulder as she settled into her seat. "Seven hours is a long time to sit and do nothing."

She winced slightly. "Indeed. Most bring some form of entertainment with them, but we didn't really have that option. It will be a good time to catch up on sleep, if you are so inclined. Or, if you'd prefer, they do rent out novellas for people to read. Though, fair warning – they are not exactly great literature."

He blinked in surprise. "Novellas?"

"Shorter novels, essentially."

"I haven't seen a single tablet since we crossed the Wall, and they just... rent them out, here?" That was interesting.

It was her turn to be surprised. "Oh no, not tablets. We don't use them. I mean that paper books are available to rent."

Jamirh considered that, glancing back out the window. The little girl and the woman were gone. "Why not tablets?" Paper books were all that he had been able to get his hands on back home, but they were definitely not the preferred means of reading in the Empire. Most people liked having a small library of literature on one portable device.

Jeri seemed to consider the question carefully before answering. "We use magic in our society quite extensively. Your kind of technology and magic do not tend to coexist in friendly ways. Often, the presence of one near the other causes unexpected results, or explosive results, or sometimes no results at all. I am not a scholar on such things, so I'm not sure why this occurs, but it is well documented. So we have developed a different kind of technology, one that can coexist with magic. Unfortunately, we've never managed to come up with something like your tablets." She shrugged. "Perhaps it is for the best. I've always preferred paper over a screen."

Jamirh frowned, remembering how he and Hel had broken out of the security station. "Is that why Hel had to scream at the door?"

Jeri stared at him. "Pardon?"

"When she broke me out of jail, we came across a magnetically locked door. She sort of... hissed at it, I think? But it didn't work, so then she screamed at it, and it exploded."

Jeri's expression was slowly changing to one of horror. "She... challenged... a *door*?"

Jamirh shrugged.

"Oh, goddess... she *challenged* a *door*. *Why*?" The last word was practically a wail.

"Is that bad?" Jamirh was confused. Then he remembered. "Oh. I don't think she actually wanted me to tell anyone that," he said with a mental apology to Hel.

"Then at least she had the self-awareness to realize how ridiculous it was to *challenge a door*." Jeri moaned, hiding her face in her hands. "At least it only exploded, I guess."

"Wait, what is a challenge?" Jamirh asked. "Why is it bad that she 'challenged' a door?"

Jeri just sighed. "It is a type of high-level Voice magic. The best way I can describe it is that she needed to light a match, and she decided a firestorm would be the best way to do it. It is just so... *unnecessary,*" she whimpered. "I wish you hadn't told me that. I wish she knew something about restraint."

Jamirh did not understand what the big deal was. So it was overkill. It still got them through the door, and no one got hurt. Though, now that he thought about it, Hel had mentioned a possibility of coughing up blood.

He decided not to mention the second time Hel had used it to get them through the front doors.

"So, what kind of books are available?" he asked, weakly trying to change the subject since Jeri looked physically pained.

She seized the opportunity with relief. "There wasn't an overly large selection last I checked, but most appeared to be geared towards children or, well, a bit trashy. There might be an adventure or two, if that's more your style?"

Jamirh had always liked to read when he could find the opportunity to do so. Paperbacks found their way into the trash occasionally, and stealing from there was child's play. He was used to not having much of a choice in subject matter. Regretfully, he thought back to the books he hadn't had a chance to read back in his home. But any book here was likely to tell him something about this new place he found himself in and how it worked, even if indirectly. "Whatever is fine, I guess."

She gave him a disgruntled look. "Don't you have any preferences about anything?"

He shrugged. Aether had complained about that sometimes, too.

Jeri sighed in disgust. "Very well, then. When we get moving I'll go see what they have available."

They sat in silence for a short time while people finished boarding the train, until finally, with a loud whistle, the train lurched into motion. Jamirh entertained himself by watching first the train station fall behind them, and then the city proper as they picked up speed. He watched the scenery go by with interest, playing a game with himself to note the differences between Lyndiniam and Pitesh. Despite his worries about his future, the complete otherness of the city was in some way reassuring – he was certainly no longer in the Empire. He had escaped.

He found his mind wandering to Hel, and wherever she was now. Whatever her reasons were, she had delivered on her promise to ensure Jamirh got out of the Empire safely. He hoped she was okay, that she had managed to deal with whatever had been following them, maybe even by annoying them to death. The thought brought a smile to his face, imagining her just harassing a Truth Seeker with nonsensical comments until they gave up.

As the scenery began to change to rolling hills, a blond Human man in a black vest and long coat came up to them, asking for tickets in a cheerful voice. Jamirh eyed the gold chain that disappeared into the man's pocket with a critical eye; it looked expensive. But Jeri was between him and the Human. He didn't trust himself to successfully take it without her noticing.

Jeri handed over the two pieces of paper, which the man punched with a small tool and placed on the tops of their seats in a little pocket before moving on. Jeri murmured that she would return shortly before getting up and departing down the aisle towards the front of the train. Jamirh turned his attention back to the window, just in time to see several cows grazing as they sped past.

When Jeri returned she had three thin paperbacks in hand, which she handed over with a dry, "These seemed the least weird. You don't have to read them if you don't want to." She had brought two romances and an adventure, based on the summaries on the backs of the books. He decided the adventure might hit a little too close to home for right now, and the romances seemed fluffy enough, so he settled down to read the first one.

He was thoroughly amused by the time he was done; it had been incredibly lighthearted and hadn't taken itself too seriously. He stretched, glancing over at Jeri, who had a book of her own. She looked mildly concerned by whatever she was reading.

Then his stomach rumbled, and Jeri's head snapped in his direction. "Lunch?" she asked hopefully, shutting her book.

Jamirh blinked at her. "Did we bring lunch?" he asked, ears perking up slightly.

She shook her head. "No, but there is a dining car near the front of the train. We can eat there, or I can bring something back for us?"

He hummed, considering. He didn't like the idea of leaving their seats. Would someone else take them? "Bring something back?"

She nodded. "It shouldn't take too long."

While she was gone, Jamirh noticed that they were once again approaching civilization as hills began to give way to houses. Like Pitesh, the architecture seemed to be mostly brick and metal, though everything seemed a bit more spread out even as they finally came to a stop at the station.

"Current stop: Deva." A cool female voice sounded over an intercom system. "Next stop: Vaslu, heading towards Tarvishte."

Jeri returned, squeezing through the shifting passengers with a tray of food, a bottle of water, and a cup of something red with a straw. She handed him the tray and the bottle of water, keeping the cup for herself. "That timing was unfortunate," she muttered as she sat back down in her seat.

Jamirh was pleased with the large sandwich and bag of chips she had gotten him, but his eyes wandered to her cup warily. "Thanks," he said, tucking into his food. He couldn't remember the last time he had had access to such consistent meals.

"You are welcome," she replied, watching him for a moment. "I feel like you need to eat more, anyway." She sipped at her straw.

After another minute, the train jerked into motion. Jamirh savored his chips, enjoying the crunch they made when he bit into them. His eyes flicked back to Jeri; she had opened the book again and was staring at it like it was a complete mystery to her. She was still holding the cup.

He gathered his courage. "That... isn't something I would like very much, is it?" he asked carefully, indicating the red liquid.

She went very still. "No, I would not recommend it," she replied slowly, closing the book after a minute. "Do... do you want to have this conversation now?"

Jamirh glanced away briefly, touching his key and hoping for courage before looking at her again. "I think I probably should," he said with a resigned sigh. "I'd kind of like to know what I have to look forward to in Tarvishte." He popped the last chip into his mouth.

"Well, I've not been as subtle as I could have been," she admitted. "What conclusions have you come to?"

"You are a Vampire," he answered instantly. "So that's probably blood. Other than that... well, you haven't killed me yet, and Hel seemed to think Romanii was a pretty safe place, so I'm not really sure. You don't really fit what I know about Vampires, but nothing this side of the Wall has matched what I was taught anyway."

"The Empire doesn't like us all that much, and with good reason, I suppose." Jeri sounded amused. "What do they tell you about us? Nothing good, I assume."

Jamirh thought back. "Not a whole lot, actually. Supposedly, the entire area north of the Wall is a barren wasteland. Most Vampires are supposed to have died out, I think, and those that are left are monsters who will do anything to get at fresh blood and flesh." He shrugged. "You eat people, mostly."

"Right. Let me be crystal clear about this," she stated flatly, "I will *never* eat you. Or anyone else. I won't lie – those rumors are not entirely based in myth. The beginning of our race's history was certainly bloody, even though the first Vampires were created directly by the Lady's grace, and... well, there are always individuals who don't follow the law in any society. But the vast majority of Vampires follow the Law as set down by our Lord. There is no taking of blood from any unwilling source. Ever. This," she held up the cup, "comes from donations. We hold blood drives multiple times a year, and cold storage and magic keeps it fresh."

He blinked. "It's against *Vampire* law to attack people?"

She nodded seriously. "There are many more mortals than Vampires, and it just doesn't make good sense to have your food source hate you when they outnumber you. The Law was created so that we could live symbiotically with the people we need to survive, not parasitically. They provide us with food, and we provide them with safety and good health."

"How does that work?" He supposed safety made sense, if they could all do what Jeri could, but "good health"?

"A lot of Vampires – not everyone, but many – choose either a combat profession and enter the Black Watch, as I did, or a healing profession. A properly trained Vampire can tell a lot about an individual's health based on their blood."

That made a weird sort of sense, he guessed, though he had never really put much thought into how blood tasted. He took a sip of water to clear the imaginary taste from his tongue. "Why are those two professions the most popular?"

Jeri was quiet for a while, clearly thinking over her answer. "I suppose," she finally said, "that it has to do with the fact that we *become* Vampires, rather than being born Vampires. I was Human once, and then I died. Thanks to a Vampire who passed to me the Lady's blessing, I was given an opportunity to save others. Most of us, I think, feel like we owe something to Her, and so we try to make Her proud of us. She doesn't tend to look kindly on murderous rampages."

"So, then, you are dead, technically? What does that mean?" Jamirh asked, eyes wide. It was hard to reconcile Jeri with "dead." She certainly didn't seem dead.

She smiled. "Yes, quite dead. I don't need food or drink, aside from the blood of the living. I don't need to breathe. Extreme temperatures don't bother me. I sleep far less."

He stared at her very closely. "You look like you are breathing now?" He liked to think he would have noticed if she hadn't been breathing at all.

"The movement is more of a habit from when I was alive than a necessity. It doesn't actually do anything."

"What about... Hel said something about the sun? And you said that was why there was a shield of some sort over Pitesh?" He was trying to remember the exact wording she had used.

She nodded. "A strange quirk of the magic that brings us back. The sun burns us very badly. Eventually, as we get older, it stops doing so, but it can be quite the hazard for a long time. So we shield the cities for our own safety."

Jamirh nodded in understanding, thinking over all this new information. "The Black Watch is only for Vampires, then? Is that why Hel is not technically a member? Why let her help at all?"

"Yes, the Black Watch is exclusively made up of Vampires, and Hel is not a Vampire. As for why we let her help... well, that situation is a little more complicated than I want to get into right now. Suffice it to say that we can't really tell her 'no' with any guarantee of success."

He stared at her in confusion. "Is she really that much better than you? You looked like the greater threat against that Truth Seeker."

Jeri winced slightly. "Something like that. I'd not have left her, if I thought she couldn't handle the situation."

But the wheels were already turning in Jamirh's head. "Does Hel *outrank* you?"

She pressed her lips together for a moment. "These are questions for Ander. He will be best at explaining. Probably. But I suppose the short answer is yes, she does."

"Who is Ander?" Jamirh asked curiously. "You've mentioned him before."

Jeri hesitated. "Ander is a priest of the Lady. As things stand, he is the only priest currently in Tarvishte."

Jamirh stared at her, ears dropping out of shock. "*One*? There is only one priest of your patron goddess in your capital city?!" He wouldn't call Lyndiniam a religious city by any stretch of the imagination, but he was sure there were at least a hundred temples and shrines of the Three, all fully staffed by clergy.

"Well, when you put it that way, it does sound bad." She looked thoughtful. "I did say Hades was selective, no? And sometimes we even have two or three in the capital at once."

"Does that even count as a religion?" he asked incredulously.

Jeri just shrugged. "It's the people that count; even Ander himself would tell you he's just a trapping. Something nice for Her to have, and something She treasures, but not truly necessary in the end. The gods draw their strength from their believers; they tend to use it through their priests."

Jamirh just shook his head. Romanii was proving to be both interesting and very, very weird. He couldn't imagine one priest trying to serve the entirety of any city, though he supposed that worship of the death goddess was proving to work differently than worship of the other gods. Maybe that was why there were no shrines to her south of the Wall; no one knew *how* to worship such a strange deity.

The yawn took him by surprise.

"Ah, maybe you should rest a bit more." Jeri's expression shifted to concern. "We still have over four hours before we reach Tarvishte. We should arrive right around dinner, so we won't have to eat another train meal."

"If you can't eat food, why do you judge it so harshly?" Jamirh asked wryly.

"I never said I couldn't eat food, just that I do not need to. I enjoy food – good food – as much as the next person," she stated matter-of-factly. "This is merely 'okay' food."

"It's great food where I'm from," he pointed out. "It was a whole sandwich. With meat, and cheese, and lettuce and tomato. The bun wasn't even moldy."

Jeri twitched. "No wonder you are so thin. We need to feed you more."

He paused and considered that statement in the context of everything he had just learned. "That sounds creepy," he said slowly.

She tilted her head to the side. "Does it? Why?"

"Never mind." He settled himself down into the comfortable chair. He was more tired than he had thought, even after getting so much sleep the night before. Surely a nap wouldn't hurt.

Jeri made a soft "hmm" sound and sipped at her straw, turning her attention back to her book. "If you say so."

He must have dozed off, because when he woke up, the hills had been replaced with tall mountains and the sun was lower in the sky. A brown blanket had been laid over him, and Jeri and the food tray were missing. The train car was much more crowded now. He was surprised to find the two women behind him talking animatedly about Shuurai's banishment – apparently he had been officially cast out into the ocean earlier in the day. Jamirh wondered if the entire world was talking about that man and felt a strange surge of pity for him. Hel had said he'd disappear; Jamirh doubted that was possible with how he seemed to be all anyone was talking about.

"Oh, you're up," Jeri stated cheerfully, returning to her seat. "Good timing; we are about half an hour out, now."

Jamirh yawned, stretching as he sat more upright in his seat. He quickly redid his ponytail, which had become slightly lopsided, as he returned his gaze to the mountains. They were beautiful, capped with snow, and he was fascinated by them. He watched them go by as the people around them began to grab bags and luggage.

Suddenly they rounded a curve in the track, and a great, sprawling city came into view. Tall spires shot into the sky alongside thin cylinders from which clouds of steam poured forth. He could see large domed structures and towers and rectangular buildings. Behind it stretched the ocean.

"I always forget how nice the view is from the train," Jeri mused as they sped towards it, mountains bleeding into hills.

"It's incredible," Jamirh whispered, staring at it in wonder.

"That it is," Jeri affirmed, a note of pride in her voice. "And it's home."

As they sped through the suburbs and into the city proper, Jamirh noticed that there were pipes and decorative metalwork everywhere in this city, just like in Pitesh. There seemed to be a great deal more windows and glasswork in many of the buildings, however, and the metalwork looked even more ornate. Finally they rolled to a stop in the station.

"Here we go," Jeri murmured softly as they both stood up. "Tarvishte."

Chapter Eleven

"So now that we're here... where are we going?" Jamirh asked, trying to take everything in as they left the train station. It was a lot more crowded here than it had been in Pitesh. It made his fingers itch.

"Well, Hel wanted me to take you to Vlad, so we are heading in that direction. But first – dinner, I think. How about pasta?"

"Sounds good to me," he replied cheerfully, looking around at the large court-yard they had emerged into. Another statue of Hades – this one with some sort of bladed polearm instead of a staff with a crystal – stood in the center. A group of both Humans and Avari were draping a large piece of black cloth over her while others hung small lights around the area.

"Festival decorations are finally going up, I see," Jeri said dryly. "Late as usual. I wonder what the holdup was this year?"

"What was the holdup in other years?" Jamirh asked as he followed her down a pathway. The trees and iron fencing lining the cobble had already been strung with lights.

"The festival decorations are paid for mostly by the nobles and guilds, but they can be particular about what they want and where," she explained. "You might not think it, but this can lead to all sorts of problems, such as arguing over who gets what spot and which aspect of the Lady they want to represent, and is it too close to a similar representation? The palace has to approve the plans before they are put up and it is a scheduling nightmare, with people fighting over certain spots and activities. Goddess forbid we have two haunted houses within a block of each other, or whatever the issue might be."

"What do activities have to do with it? Or haunted houses?" This sounded interesting.

"On Festival night, the whole city will be set up kind of like a large carnival. There will be vendors and games and activities all over the place, and people will go around dressed in fun or terrifying costumes for a night of entertainment. There will be all sorts of things to do – haunted houses, mazes, races, plays, scavenger hunts, games… and it goes all night, from dusk to dawn."

"That sounds crazy," Jamirh commented. "How much is it to participate?"

She grinned. "That's the best part – it is completely free. Anyone who wants to join in can."

Jamirh stared at her, eyes wide. "Even the food?"

Jeri nodded. "Food and drinks, and that even includes alcohol. The nobles and guilds sponsor everything. It is quite an experience, let me tell you." She led him down a side street.

"And when is this happening, again?"

"Exactly a week from today!" She was clearly excited by it, to Jamirh's amusement. Though to be fair, he was excited too – for the free food.

After they ate, as Jeri led him back to the main road, Jamirh asked, "So where is Vlad, anyway?"

"We are going to the palace," Jeri replied after a moment. "Vlad works there."

To the palace? A hint of unease threaded through Jamirh. He found himself reaching for his key, the feel of the familiar metal beneath his fingers reassuring. "Does Hel also work there?" He thought about that for a second. It was hard to picture her doing anything mundane. "Does Hel actually work?"

Jeri winced. "More or less. She certainly spends a fair amount of time there, when she's not at the Temple. I suppose you could say she works, depending on your definition of the word. She definitely does things."

There were a lot of people out and about in the streets. It almost reminded Jamirh of home, to see so many people in one place. His mind wandered to how a city-wide carnival-like festival would work, when the street opened up into a large cobbled square with yet another statue of Hades standing over a large fountain. He vaguely remembered Hel asking about a statue of Ebryn Stormlight and wondered if she had been interested because she was used to only ever seeing statues of one person. At least Hades was presumably deserving of statues; 'the Hero' certainly was not, in Jamirh's mind. A piece of trash who had condemned his own people to suffer for centuries was not worthy of remembrance.

Things were certainly better now in that regard. He hadn't had to be reminded of the bastard since leaving Lyndiniam.

One side of the square was lined by a tall wrought iron fence, with large, ornate copper and brick posts on either side of the open gates. Beyond the fence was an extremely large building, or perhaps a building complex. The center part was tall and round, roofed with a large greenish dome, surrounded by smaller domed segments of various heights and widths. Tall spires were interspersed among the domes. Balconies and windows of all sizes were everywhere, adorned with metal pipes and embellishments.

"Wow," Jamirh said, staring at the building with wide eyes.

"Impressive, isn't it?" Jeri was watching his reaction with amusement.

"It looks very easy to get lost in," Jamirh said slowly, trying to mentally map out how anything in that building connected to anything else.

Jeri chuckled weakly. "It can be a bit challenging, yes. It helps if you think of it as different zones."

"And people can just walk in?" Jamirh asked, looking around. There were a lot of people entering and exiting through the gate and passing through the excessively large front door.

"It is largely a public space," Jeri explained. "You likely won't see us often, but the Black Watch is present, and does guard the palace, so it is not a complete free-for-all."

She guided Jamirh past the gates and through the grounds, avoiding the main door. They walked across the brick pavers to a much more reasonably sized, less busy door. The inside of the building was as maze-like as Jamirh had feared, and he was lost within a few corridors. Luckily, the same did not seem to be true for Jeri, who confidently led him deeper into the building. They eventually came upon a comfortable-looking office with an older Avari woman seated behind a large desk covered in papers. Her silvery-blue hair was tied in a loose bun at the nape of her neck, and glasses with small rectangular lenses perched at the end of her nose. Jeri knocked on the doorframe politely and stepped in when the woman looked up from the paper in her hands, adjusting her glasses.

"Hello, Gerit," Jeri greeted her. "How have you been?"

"Jeri! It has been a while," the woman responded, smiling warmly at her. "I've been well! Your mission was a success, I hope?" She looked at Jamirh, mauve eyes curious.

He fought not to hide behind Jeri as he held his key tightly.

"It was mostly successful." The Vampire waved an arm in Jamirh's direction. "This is Jamirh. Jamirh, Gerit. She is in charge of housing in the palace."

Gerit smiled kindly at him, ears raising happily. "Greetings, Jamirh. Welcome to the Palace of Dusk."

She wasn't going to say anything? Maybe the Avari here... didn't know? He waved shyly at her. "Hello."

"I have work for you, unfortunately," Jeri said apologetically. "Jamirh needs to be set up in a suite here for the time being, under the Temple's authority. And he is going to need clothing. He didn't have time to pack before coming here."

Now he was going to be *staying* at the palace? Under the Temple's authority? What did that mean? The unease from earlier grew. His grip tightened around the key.

Gerit pursed her lips as she pulled open a drawer of a large filing cabinet behind her and started flipping through papers. "He has at least eaten, I hope?"

Jeri's lips twitched into a smile. "Yes."

Gerit glanced back at Jamirh and waited for his nod. "Good. You look about a size... E5, I would say. I'll have things sent up." She went over to a wall of little drawers, opened one, and pulled out a small brass key that she handed to Jamirh. "Room 401, dear. Jeri can help you find it."

"Thank you," Jamirh murmured, ears twitching slightly. He wasn't sure what to think about this. "But... why am I staying here, exactly?" He looked to Jeri. "I thought we were just going to speak with Vlad."

Gerit snorted. "Vlad?" She glanced at Jeri, who shrugged, looking sheepish. "Well, he's buried underneath preparations for Festival, I'm afraid. It might be some time before he can see you."

Jeri sighed. "It's not surprising. Our timing is atrocious. Or excellent, depending on how you look at it, I suppose. And that is precisely why we are staying here, Jamirh – Hel would want you here until you can talk to Vlad or Ander, and both of them are going to be extremely busy this week."

It made sense when she said it that way, but for some reason, it just wasn't sitting right with Jamirh. It felt like a lot for one random Avari fugitive. Though, these people had proven to be both strange and oddly generous, and the palace was very large, so maybe this was normal for them?

It didn't feel likely. Jamirh wasn't lucky enough for that to be true.

They said their goodbyes to Gerit, and Jeri led him through even more of the palace maze until they reached a long hallway that, to Jamirh, was indistinguishable from the many other hallways they had passed through. Jeri led him to the first door on the left, which had a little brass plate next to it with "401" engraved into the metal.

Jamirh almost expected to see a skylight, even though they weren't on the top floor of the building. Instead, there were four large windows framed by deep-red curtains that stretched nearly from the floor to the ceiling, letting the dying sunlight wash the opulent sitting room in warm tones. A luxurious, cream-colored couch and matching armchairs surrounded a small but ornate wooden coffee table. The center of the hardwood floor was covered by a plush rug boasting an elegant pattern of red, white, and black. A large fireplace of black marble took up most of one wall, and a desk with two lamps and a chair sat against the wall opposite, between two doors. All the dark wooden furniture was gilded with golden swirls and leaves on the legs, and pillows of red, gold, cream, and black sat on the couch and chairs. The walls were covered in a subtly patterned cream paper. A large gold chandelier hung from the center of the ceiling, bulbs coming to life as Jeri flicked a switch by a door.

"Well, these will be your temporary accommodations," Jeri said cheerfully as Jamirh stared at the room. "Feel free to explore them a bit – I'm going to go see how swamped Vlad is, and I need to report back to Prim. Someone should probably be by with new clothes soon, and I'll return to make sure you are settled as soon as I can, okay?"

He nodded speechlessly.

"All right, then. I'll be back." She laughed softly as she swept out of the room, closing the door behind her.

The door closer to the windows opened to a bedroom with three more large windows. A bed at least three – maybe four? – times the size of the one he'd had back home with a headboard upholstered in cream fabric was covered in a rich red bedspread, and a long upholstered bench was placed at the foot. Two nightstands sat on either side of the bed, each with a tall gold-and-cream lamp and long gilded mirrors above each one. There was a bookcase and another desk, as well as a dresser. The patterns and fabrics were the same as in the sitting room. There was a door almost immediately to his right, which opened to an equally ornate bathroom of black-and-white marble with gold decoration, which in turn connected back to the sitting room.

Jamirh looked at the new key and held it up to the one around his neck. They weren't very similar. The new key was larger and rounder, brass to his key's burnished golden hue. The cut teeth on his key were worn down, almost indistinct, and the new key had just one large tooth-like bit at the end of its shaft. But they represented the same thing.

The ability to lock a door. To be safe.

Aether would have been ecstatic.

Jamirh put the new key in his pocket and found himself wandering over to the windows. They were quite a bit higher up than he would have assumed for being on the fourth floor, and he had an excellent view of the city, which was beginning to light up as the day died. He wondered if, because of the UV shield, Vampires preferred to be out during the day, or if they preferred the night. He figured the nightlife must be pretty wild here regardless.

He settled on the couch in the sitting room, wondering what he was supposed to do, and waited for Jeri to return.

"Not that I'm complaining – I would be horribly lost without you – but don't you have better things to do than show me around?" Jamirh asked Jeri the next morning after breakfast. He was wearing his new clothing – a black fitted top with a lot of buttons down the front and a high collar, edged in a dark red, with black slacks tucked into knee-high leather boots – after an excellent night's sleep in the ridiculously comfortable bed. Jeri appeared to be taking a break from her uniform, wearing a double-breasted vest, pants, and boots, all in various shades of brown, olive, and beige.

"It was firmly suggested I take at least a few days off," she said wryly. "I told them I wasn't about to abandon you in a place you've never been before, and it was agreed that showing you around counts as off duty if I want it to – you'll hardly need protecting in the heart of the city."

He was touched. "Thank you," he said, pleased that she would think of him. "Who are 'they'?"

"My superiors in the Watch," she clarified. "Don't worry; I won't leave you until you've spoken to Vlad and been settled more permanently in the city."

"And not that I'm rushing, but any word on when that might happen?" he asked as she led him through the palace grounds towards a large glass-and-metal building.

"Not for a few days, probably, but he is going to try to meet with you before Festival. In the meantime, I thought we could try to help you get more familiar with Tarvishte."

"Will there be maps? I have a feeling that I am going to need maps."

She chuckled. "We'll see what we can find." She gestured towards the building they were heading towards. "On that note, this is the central hospital."

He eyed it curiously, then glanced back towards the palace. "Is it technically on palace grounds?" They were very close together, though there seemed to be a bit of a garden between them.

"Yes; Haven Hospital and the Temple of Night Rising both reside on palace grounds."

Jamirh's eyebrows – and ears – rose. "The Temple of Night Rising? That sounds a bit... dramatic."

"Well, She *is* the goddess of death and destruction." Jeri laughed weakly as they passed by the front doors of the hospital, continuing down a tree-lined path. "And Vampires technically rose for the first time with the night, so there is that."

After having seen almost nothing but oversized buildings, the Temple was a surprise, at a modest two stories tall. Made of a smokey gray marble with black-and-silver trim, there was only one tower to the left of the entrance, and one dome in the back. A large clock sat over the main door, which had been propped open. Two large wargs appeared to be playing tag with each other nearby.

"No statue of the goddess in front of the Temple?" Jamirh teased, eyeing the wargs.

"There's a courtyard in the back," Jeri responded wryly. "The statue is there, usually surrounded by wargs sunning themselves on every available surface."

"Wargs like the Temple? And the Temple doesn't mind their presence?" he asked, curious.

Jeri stopped to watch the two creatures romp. "Wargs are sacred to the Lady," she explained, "and She likes to have them around. You'll see them wandering all over the palace grounds, actually. Sometimes you'll even see them in the palace, but they usually prefer the Temple."

"Do they belong to anyone? Or are they literally just running free all over the place?" That seemed like it could cause problems.

"Wargs don't so much belong to people as people belong to wargs," she mused. "Occasionally one will just start following a person and refuse to leave. It is considered to be something of a blessing if a warg chooses you. And don't let their appearance fool you – they are far more intelligent than the average dog or wolf."

"They don't ever attack anyone?" Jamirh frowned.

Jeri shook her head. "Not once in the entirety of Romanii's history has a warg from a city attacked a citizen or stranger for no reason. They absolutely will defend, if they think it is necessary, but they seem to have an excellent ability to read people. The wild wargs who live in the mountains don't always play by the same rules, mind. You should avoid those to the absolute best of your ability, should you find yourself in the wilderness for some reason." She paused. "Do you want to go in?"

There was a sound like an aborted shout, and a plume of smoke escaped from one of the windows on the second floor of the tower.

Jamirh's ears went down. "No, I think I'm all set," he murmured, looking up at the building.

Jeri just sighed. "Yeah, let's avoid Ander for now."

Jamirh turned to her, brow furrowing. "Do you think he's okay?"

"It would take nothing short of a miracle to kill Ander inside the Temple. He's fine. Possibly singed, but fine." She sighed again. "This happens more often than you might think, honestly. This particular incident is probably related to Festival preparations."

"If you say so," he drawled. The thought of the statue reminded him of what he'd seen the day before. "Why were people covering up the statues? You said they were decorating for the Festival, but why cover them?"

"It's the beginning of the Season of Veils," Jeri explained. "All of the statues will remain veiled until the dawn after the Longest Night, at midwinter."

"The Season of Veils?" Jamirh asked, confused.

Jeri made a soft humming sound. "Yes, the last two months of the year are the Season of Veils. It is a symbol of Her mourning for the dying world as the days get shorter and shorter."

Jamirh snorted. "I didn't pay a lot of attention in science, but I'm pretty sure that's not why the days get shorter."

"It doesn't have to be. Scientific accuracy is not what religion is about." She laughed. "Symbolism is important to people, too – and there is something to be learned from every story."

"If you say so," he said doubtfully.

They spent the rest of the day exploring the palace grounds, and then the palace itself. Despite Jeri's assurances that he would get the hang of it, the building refused to make sense to Jamirh. He supposed it was interesting that there were various public offices and departments built into the palace proper, but he had to wonder what the cost of that was if nothing was laid out according to reason. Not that the illogical layout seemed to bother anyone else – they passed plenty of people who seemed to have no trouble figuring out where they were going.

Perhaps he was just too used to the grid layouts with large, open central areas common in Lyndiniam.

Jeri took him to a small sandwich shop near the palace for dinner, her idea of a "good" sandwich. Jamirh had to admit the sandwich he ate – grilled fish and a slew of greens and veggies covered in a spicy sauce and topped with a fried egg on toasted bread – was an excellent sandwich, but he wasn't sure its existence diminished the quality of the train sandwich.

By the time he curled into bed later that night, he still had no idea what the future held, but he was greatly enjoying the present, and its freedom from the past.

The next day, they explored the downtown area of the city. Preparations for the festival were by now in full fevered swing, and Jamirh was bemused to see that practically the whole city was involved. Everyone they saw was engaged in setting up something, from decorations to structures, and everyone seemed to be having a good time.

They returned to the palace after lunch so Jeri could try again to teach Jamirh how to navigate the labyrinthian halls at least well enough to get to his room.

He asked for a break after the third time they somehow ended up on the wrong floor.

"Maybe a map would actually help?" Jeri mused thoughtfully. "The palace library isn't far; there's usually paper and things for notes and such there."

"Ah, somewhere else to never be able to get to again," Jamirh said tiredly.

Jeri waved a hand at him. "Don't be ridiculous. You will pick up on it eventually," she soothed as she guided him down another hallway.

The library was just as ornate as the rest of the palace, decked out in mostly reds, golds, and blacks. There were large windows on the wall opposite, letting in lots of light, and the rows of bookcases stretched to the far side of the room and covered the walls. There was a large sitting area near the entrance with chairs in groups and some tables scattered around. A few people were sitting in various places or wandering through the stacks.

At a nearby table sat two Vampires, both wearing Watch blacks. The man had long, dark hair in a low ponytail and a goatee, and the woman had bright-red hair pulled up into a high bun. They both perked up upon seeing Jeri.

"Jeri! Welcome back!" the man called out happily. "We've missed you over the past year. And you found him! You must be Ebryn, the long-dead Hero finally returned," he continued, grinning hugely at Jamirh. "It's nice to meet you!"

What?

Jamirh felt himself go cold, ears flattening down, sure he had misheard that.

"That's enough, Frir," Jeri snapped, face paling as she made a sharp gesture with one hand, but it was too late.

The man – Frir? – just looked confused. "But... wasn't–"

"*Enough.*" Jeri's voice drowned out what the man had been trying to say, and he subsided, looking lost.

"Did you just call me Ebryn?" Jamirh asked quietly. One hand came up to touch his key.

Frir was looking quickly back and forth between Jeri and Jamirh. "Perhaps I was mistaken?" he offered after a short pause, beginning to look panicked. The woman, looking equally disturbed, dissolved into shadow.

Jeri knew, he realized numbly, looking at her furiously gesturing at Frir. Somehow, she knew. How? It had been well over a week since he had gone by his birth name – he hadn't dared use it at the casino, and when Hel had asked...

I did not ask what you are called; I asked what your name is, Hel had said to him back in the cells. Had she known then? Was that why she had broken him out of that cell – because he shared a name with some long-dead 'Hero'?

He'd told her Jamirh, thought he was finally escaping the expectations of his name, not running headlong into them. He liked being Jamirh.

"What does 'and you found him' mean, exactly?" he added, feeling an impending sense of dread, replaying the other man's words in his mind carefully. "You were looking for me, specifically? As some sort of... 'long-dead Hero returned'?"

Jeri froze.

Jamirh was getting angry, and was starting to put things together. He didn't like the picture that was emerging. Had they somehow been watching him even before the casino? How? Why? Because they thought he was a replacement or something for an Avari who died a thousand years ago?

"Is that what this – all this, everything I've been through in the past week – has been about?" His voice was very, very quiet.

"Jamirh," Jeri tried after a moment, "maybe we should–"

"Is. That. What. This. Is. About?" He bit off each word, fury practically radiating from each one. "How the hell do you even know what my name is?"

"You are–"

"*Frir, stop talking!*" Jeri all but shrieked, drawing the gaze of the few other people in the library. "You are *not helping!*"

"No, I'm what, exactly?" Jamirh asked coolly. "I want to know."

Frir cringed under Jeri's glare, silent. Jeri looked back to Jamirh but didn't quite meet his eyes. She sighed. "You... look like him," she said finally.

"I know. Red hair, silver eyes. It's why my parents named me after him," Jamirh spat. "But I'm not the only Avari who has these colors."

"No," she said carefully, "you look exactly like him. It's not just your coloring–"

"So what?" he interrupted her, angry and hurt. "How would you even know what he looked like? Unless there are statues of him somewhere I haven't seen yet?"

Jeri rounded on Frir as he opened his mouth. "If you say another word I will remove your head from your shoulders. Get out."

Frir immediately dissolved into shadow and disappeared.

Her expression turned pleading. "I know you are upset, but please, understand – you were in danger there. If the government found out who you were–"

"That doesn't answer the question," he snapped. "How are you so sure I look *exactly* like someone who lived a thousand years ago?"

She looked down. "I met him once, when I was very young. He made an impression."

Jamirh stared at her, trying to process that. "You are a thousand years old?" he asked faintly. "And you *met* him?"

She nodded.

"That's why you were sent," he realized. "Because you would know what to look for. And then you told Hel, didn't you?"

"Jamirh–"

"No," he said quietly, shaking his head. "Both of you have been... you know what, no. I'm done. Leave me alone." Neither of them had helped him for his own sake; they had been trying to help someone who was long gone. He had known there was something strange going on, but he hadn't expected this. This... this hurt. "Just... leave me alone."

He turned on his heel and fled.

Chapter Twelve

amirh ran through the halls, heedless of where he was going. He just wanted to get away. Not that he could escape – he was stuck here, at least until he could figure out where else he could possibly go. But he needed to not be *there*. He needed space.

He ran until he was gasping for each breath. He slowed, then stopped, looking around. He had no idea which indistinguishable hallway he was in, nor was there anyone around to ask, and he had just run from his guide. His guide who had been manipulating him and keeping secrets. Who thought he was some reincarnation or whatever of an Avari who had betrayed his entire people.

He wiped angrily at his eyes. Why couldn't he just be himself?

It had been like this for as long as he could remember – people heard his name was Ebryn and made assumptions, or worse, they made fun of him for it. It didn't help that he had the same hair and eye color as the fabled Hero. He didn't remember his parents very well, but he did vaguely remember them telling him stories about Stormlight – and years later, after their deaths, learning the truth about what their Hero's actions had wrought. He had hated him ever since, and hated the associations that came with being named after him.

Hated that everyone seemed to *expect* things from him.

Miserably, ears low, he wandered on, finding another hallway. The side of this one opened to a balcony overlooking the city and the sea. He was higher up than he'd realized. He drifted outside; the October air was a bit chilly, but the view was pretty. Sighing, he rested his elbows on the thick stone railing, fiddling with his key but finding no comfort in it.

Quiet footsteps sounded on the stone behind him.

"I'm not who you think I am," he snapped angrily. "I am not Ebryn Stormlight, Hero of everything, or whatever."

"Certainly not," a smooth male voice agreed. Jamirh glanced to the side in surprise to see a Human with long, wavy black hair and a well-trimmed beard and mustache approach. He'd expected Jeri.

"If I had to choose one word to describe Ebryn Stormlight, I would choose rage," the man stated thoughtfully as he leaned on the balcony next to him. He was wearing a double-breasted vest of patterned crushed black velvet with pearl buttons over a black silk shirt. "And if I had to choose a second, I would choose grief. You might be angry and upset, but I would hardly define you by those terms."

Jamirh frowned warily, staring back out over the water. "What do you mean?" He had never heard anyone describe the Hero in such a way.

The man sighed. "He hid it well. I met him exactly twice, and neither time did he do anything that one might associate with rage. But it seethed in him, under the surface. He was consumed by the loss of his sister. You look like him, and according to my mother, you were him, but that does not mean you *are* him." The man paused. "That is for the better, probably."

"And your mother is such an authority?" Jamirh said bitterly.

The man inclined his head with a wry smile. "Most would consider Her so, since rebirth is one of Her domains. My mother is Hades."

"I guessed you were a Vampire when you said you met him." Jamirh looked back out over the city. It figured. "I'm not. What gives her the right to run and ruin my life?"

The man hummed softly, tucking a lock of hair back behind an ear. "A good question. One with many answers, few of which are probably satisfactory. Some might say that, as a god, She has, if not the right, then the ability to do so. Others might say you owe Her, since it was on Her orders that we retrieved you from the Rose, and no good would have come from you remaining there." The man's gaze turned to Jamirh, and he noticed that his eyes were blood red. "But perhaps the most unfortunate reason is that Ebryn himself gave Her that right, when She forged the Blade for him."

Jamirh's head snapped towards him. "What do you mean?"

The man hummed thoughtfully. "What do you actually know about Ebryn Stormlight?"

"I know that it was because of him that the Empire was created," he replied, angry.

"But what about his actual journey? About why he did what he did, and how?" The man's voice was curious.

Jamirh thought back to the stories his parents had told him. "He was given a sacred duty by the Three to stop some sort of evil wizard. He traveled all over the world to collect four special crystals, turned them into the Crystal Light Blade, and killed the evil wizard with it. He helped Saran the Rose Queen form the Empire, and then disappeared off the face of the earth, leaving Avari to suffer under Humans for the next thousand years."

"That is a very basic timeline of events, yes." The man considered for a moment. "The wizard was evil because he was summoning demons into the world. To the Lady, who stands for order, it was an expression of Abomination, and so... a serious problem. But do you know how Ebryn forged the Blade?"

Jamirh thought back. "He went to the temple of the Three in Norik, I think, and somehow combined them? I was very little when I heard the story; I don't really remember all the details. I know it went missing from the museum dedicated to Ebryn a few hundred years ago."

"It does make sense that that is what you were told, I suppose, considering that the Rose Empire as it currently stands doesn't particularly like us. But no – he came here, to the Temple, and asked the Lady for help."

Jamirh blinked in surprise, ears twitching up slightly. "Here? Why?"

"Because some Vampires use a technique called soulforging to create weapons, and Ebryn thought it might be applied to the crystal lights to create a weapon of his own. It couldn't really, but Hades made a different suggestion." The man's gaze turned sad as he gazed out over the ocean. "She would use Her power to forge the weapon out of the lights and bind it to him if, in return, Ebryn swore that he and the Blade would forever defend against Abomination."

"What?" Jamirh was getting more and more lost. Certainly no version of the story he had ever heard before had included this.

"As I said earlier, Ebryn was consumed by rage, and grief. He was willing to do just about anything to get revenge for his sister, who was one of the sorcerer's first victims. So he agreed to bind his soul into a contract with the Lady, in return for a sword that would give him the revenge he sought. I don't think he thought very much about the consequences of this decision, and what it would mean for him. I counseled both of them against it, and both of them ignored me."

Jamirh thought this over for a moment. "What exactly is Abomination?"

The man sighed. "The simple answer is that it is something that goes against the natural order of things to the point where it begins to warp the world itself. Summoning demons damages the very fabric of reality, so this is Abomination. A priest of Hades might have a better explanation."

"But what does this have to do with me *now*?" Jamirh cried, frustrated.

"There is Abomination in the world again," the man said quietly. "We don't yet know the form it takes, but my mother has already warned us – something is warping and twisting the world, and it appears to be centered in the Rose Empire. She has been trying to figure out what. Regardless of what the cause may be, since Ebryn Stormlight swore to defend the world against Abomination, She brought him back as per the terms of his contract with Her. You are the manifestation of that soul reborn." The man's voice was oddly gentle as he continued, "And so here you are – caught in a situation of which you have no knowledge and no say, due to the actions of a man a thousand years gone."

"That's not fair," Jamirh protested.

"No, it's not," the man agreed. "It is, however, where things stand."

"So Jeri and Hel both went to get me – specifically me – from the Empire because a thousand years ago Ebryn Stormlight made a deal with your goddess to basically be on call for the rest of eternity in exchange for a magic sword and revenge, and now that the world is unraveling the goddess wants a hand?"

The man's eyebrows raised as he tilted his head to the side. "Basically, yes."

"So you want me to fight demons?" Jamirh's voice was flat.

"I don't want you to do anything, nor do I know that demons are even the problem at hand," the man replied mildly. "It is possible that whatever form the Abomination takes won't require combat, though I will admit that does seem unlikely. I think it is likely that the Abomination will find you regardless of what any of us want." He paused. "Though, if demons do show up, I believe my mother would expect you to fight them."

"So I'm screwed, is what you're saying," Jamirh muttered angrily, running a hand through his hair. "I don't know how to fight. I steal things. And survive."

"Surviving is a good first step in a fight," the man replied wryly. "And we could teach you, if you wanted. Ebryn was extremely skilled with a blade; it is possible you share his aptitude for combat. But while you remain in this city you will be safe. The Black Watch follows the Lady's mandate to defend."

Jamirh laughed bitterly as he turned to fully face the Vampire. "And to keep secrets? To lie?"

The man met his eyes evenly, ruby to silver. "From my understanding of the events told to me by Jeri, Hel figured out very quickly that you were not going to be open to being Ebryn reincarnated. She decided the best course of action would be to remove you from the Rose's influence as quickly as possible and explain things later. Jeri followed Hel's lead. They knew that this conversation would be upsetting, and so wanted you to have it in a safe place. Were mistakes made? Probably. Even I made mistakes in this situation – if I had found time to meet with you earlier, as Jeri kept asking me to, perhaps this" – he gestured vaguely around the balcony – "would not have happened."

Jamirh stared. "*You're* Vlad? The person everyone says I'm supposed to meet?"

"Indeed so." He took a step back and made a dramatic bow. "Vlad, son of Hades, First among the Night Children and Ruler of Romanii, at your service."

Jamirh's brain shorted out. "What?"

Vlad smiled kindly and waited patiently for Jamirh to process that.

"You are" – Jamirh was trying to wrap his mind around this – "the king of the Vampires?"

"Almost no one uses that title, but technically, yes. Most of my subjects use 'Lord', though many Vampires don't use any title unless they are being formal or obnoxious. I prefer the informality, generally, though most of my people seem to prefer the pageantry."

Jamirh looked around, confused. They appeared to be alone. "Is that why there are no guards or anything? Aren't kings supposed to have guards?" He very much doubted that the Emperor was ever left on his own like this; every time he'd caught a glimpse of the man on a vid screen it had been with a robust retinue.

"It is partly that, and partly that I am my own protection." He laughed softly. "I am very difficult to kill."

"Why... why did you come find me, though?" Jamirh looked down. "I expected... Jeri." The anger was beginning to fade into more hurt, but she was still the only person here he really knew. "Why the Vampire king?"

"A few reasons," Vlad said, considering. "For one, it was supposed to be my job to explain the situation in the first place. Just because things did not go as planned doesn't absolve me of that. For another, when four members of the Watch burst into a meeting saying I am needed in the library immediately, I make it a priority. You had already left the library by the time I arrived, but it was not overly difficult for me to find you. As for why it was me chosen to do these things in the first place, that is what my job is, as king – I mediate problems and find solutions. It was thought that I would be best at presenting the situation in the least upsetting way possible. I am also Hades' son, and thus to some degree some of Her responsibility falls to me."

Jamirh was silent, trying to pin down why that still didn't sit right with him. The metal of his key was warm under his fingertips.

"Ah," Vlad said quietly after a few moments. "But perhaps the problem is that you don't want to be important enough to draw the eye of anyone of rank."

Jamirh's head snapped up, eyes wide. He was right. How did he know? "Yes, it's... uncomfortable. I'm not that important. I don't *want* to be that important."

Vlad hummed thoughtfully. "Come with me," he said, turning to head back into the building. "I have something to show you."

Jamirh sighed as he followed. "How did you actually find me, anyway? I can't understand how anyone finds anything in this maze."

The Vampire smiled gently. "I am a fairly powerful empath, and you were radiating anger and hurt. You stood out like a beacon." He cocked his head to the side, curious. "You have been unable to navigate the palace?"

"I don't understand how it's laid out," Jamirh admitted miserably. "Jeri has been trying to show me around, but I just don't get it. We went to the library because we were going to try a map."

"I don't actually know that a map would work," Vlad said wryly. "Maybe. This building has existed for a very long time and has seen many works of magic, both great and small. It has somehow... become more, over time. It tries to be helpful. It doesn't change, per se, but as long as you think you know where you are going and you want to get there, you will."

"What? How does that work?" Jamirh was flabbergasted. "How is that even possible?"

"Magic is capable of many things, even – or perhaps especially – if we don't understand them. One's will is the catalyst, however. If you believe you don't know where you are going in this building, it cannot help you, and you naturally fail."

"Why didn't Jeri mention this?" Jamirh cried.

"Most of the people who live and work around the palace don't actually realize what is happening, because it is what they have always known. The magic is very subtle. And Jeri is much too young to remember the palace before the magic took root."

Jamirh stared at Vlad. "Jeri is a thousand years old."

Vlad smiled. "Precisely. Much too young."

They walked in silence for several minutes, Jamirh chewing that over. He wasn't sure he cared much for what it implied.

As they walked, the halls began to be populated again. People gave respectful nods to Vlad as they passed, but other than that did not seem to give him any more deference than anyone else. Jamirh had never been inside the royal palace in Lyndiniam, but he rather doubted that the Emperor walked through its halls as casually as Vlad walked through his.

"Jeri did not mean – or want – to hurt you." Vlad's voice interrupted his thoughts. "She is quite beside herself right now with worry. Everything she did was to try to prevent this exact outcome."

"She lied," Jamirh said dully, ears drooping. "So did Hel."

Vlad eyed him carefully. "How, exactly, did they lie?"

"Hel told me that your people help people in danger cross the Wall."

"And you have determined this to be false?" Vlad asked, one eyebrow raised.

"Well, it wasn't why they brought *me* across the Wall," he complained. "They went and got me specifically because they think I'm the Hero reborn."

"We do bring people in danger across, though," Vlad countered. "Granted, those we rescue are normally much closer to the Wall and not in the capital of the Empire, but not always. So that is true. And you were potentially in danger in Lyndiniam because of your previous life, so it applies to you, as well. Was it deceptive? Yes, but not a lie."

Jamirh frowned, ears dropping a bit more. Jeri had said something along those lines, too. "Most Avari are 'in danger' in Lyndiniam; I was surviving it pretty decently. What does Ebryn have to do with it?"

Vlad was silent for several long minutes as they continued walking through the palace. "You are not the first reincarnation of Ebryn Stormlight. The Lady tried once before. As best we can tell, your predecessor was murdered twenty-three years ago. We don't have hard proof that it was the government's doing, nor were we able to recover the body, but from what the Lady was able to gather it was not an accident. We don't even really know why he was killed – just that he was."

Jamirh felt a chill travel down his spine. "Okay, that's disturbing."

"It is, yes. Ander tried to query the spirit, but... he wasn't overly interested in cooperating. I was not aware this was happening at the time, but when the Lady decided to try again She asked us for help. She let us know what to look for, and thus we have been looking for you for the past twenty years or so. It was only last year we pinned it down to Lyndiniam, and Hel and Jeri went to go find you."

"The goddess couldn't tell you where I was, if she was responsible for my existence?" Jamirh asked skeptically.

Vlad's face twisted into a grimace. "I have been told that 'It doesn't work that way'. She cannot lie, so I have to assume that if She could, She would have, especially based on how invested She is. Out of curiosity, however – your parents named you Ebryn because of your coloring, no?"

Jamirh nodded.

"Do you know of any other Avari with that name and coloring?"

He thought about it. "It's not a super common name, I guess, and the only other Avari with red and silver that I knew was a girl. Avari come in a lot of color combos, so specific combinations are rare no matter what you're looking for."

"Interesting," Vlad murmured, but he did not elaborate on why that might be so. Instead, he continued, "Regardless, please understand that Jeri and Hel went into Lyndiniam for the sole purpose of saving your life. It was important enough to them that Hel decided to stay behind to ensure you made it here, and Jeri has been trying quite hard to make sure that you are comfortable."

He didn't want to hate Jeri, but still... "It still hurts."

"Of course it does. I am just giving you more information to keep in mind for when she inevitably apologizes. Whether or not you accept that apology is entirely up to you."

They came to a stop by a large pair of ornate doors, decorated with iconography of the eight elemental deities in some sort of blue crystal. "Here we are."

"And... where is that?" Jamirh asked wearily, staring at the door. The anger had mostly burnt out; now he just felt tired on top of the hurt.

Without answering, Vlad pushed the giant doors open and indicated that Jamirh should enter. The doors swung inward to a fair-sized room of gray and white marble, brightly lit by motes of blue-white light hanging in the air. The other end of the room was rounded in a half-circle, with an inlay of black marble forming a long, winged staff topped with a crystal taking up a large portion of the wall. A strange pillar-like structure sat in the semi-circle formed by the far wall; it looked like the blue crystal had grown out of the floor and formed a sort of a resting place for something.

It was a sword.

Jamirh stopped dead in his tracks.

"You know what it is, no?" Vlad asked gently. "We have had it for some time now."

The blade was made of about three feet of pale-blue crystal. The hilt was black, with a silver cross-guard shaped like a spiky but delicate pair of wings. A large, dull violet crystal was set between them, and a smaller crystal decorated the pommel. It lay on a piece of silver silk that had been draped over the crystal stand.

"The Crystal Light Blade," Jamirh breathed in shock. "It's here? How?"

"Ander stole it when he left the Rose Empire some three hundred plus years ago," Vlad stated wryly. "He brought it here, and here it has remained since." He walked briskly past Jamirh and picked it up, examining it. "It's a very nice blade, I must say. An excellent weapon, but completely mundane in my hands. I could use it as a sword, if I wished. Anyone could, really. But the goddess forged it for Ebryn, and so it will only be special for Ebryn. Would you like to hold it?" He held it out to Jamirh.

Jamirh took a hasty step back.

"No," he said shortly, ears lowering, both hands clenched tightly around his key. Everything in him screamed not to touch that sword.

Out of everything that had happened, and everything he had learned, he thought it might be that internal warning that scared him the most.

Vlad merely inclined his head, placing the sword back on its pedestal. "As you wish. This is the most definite answer I can give you – to who you were, and how important you are. But I cannot and will not force it upon you. The Blade will remain here until it is claimed." He tilted his head to the side. "Would you prefer to be called Jamirh, rather than Ebryn?"

Jamirh pulled his eyes away from the Blade lying innocently on its pedestal to look at Vlad. "Does it matter?"

"Of course it does. We will call you Jamirh, if that is the name you prefer. You shouldn't be unhappy here." Vlad guided Jamirh from the room, closing the large doors behind them.

"Everyone expects me to be Ebryn, though, don't they?" Which was discouraging on its own. He didn't want to be Ebryn. He had been trying to escape Ebryn.

Vlad just shrugged. "Only amongst the Vampires, but that is something easily fixed. I hear Jeri has been all but threatening people not to call you by that name for the last few days anyway, so the shift will be quite minor. She must have missed Frir, somehow, to what is sure to be his regret." He gestured for Jamirh to follow him as he turned and began walking.

Jamirh frowned. "She was threatening people?"

"Probably less severely than the word implies. Or perhaps exactly as severely, considering it is Jeri we are talking about. When Hel asked for your name, you very tellingly did not answer with Ebryn. Jeri assumed that you being called Ebryn would upset you, so she tried to head it off. It wasn't entirely that she wanted to keep things from you, but also that she wanted you to be comfortable here."

"Oh." That was... nice of her. At least that part of it. And in truth, he had much preferred being Jamirh. "I want to be Jamirh – I don't want to be Ebryn," he declared.

"As you wish," Vlad stated mildly. "It will be so. I know I've given you a lot to think about today. All I ask is that you do that – think about what you've learned. My people will endeavor to support you whatever you choose to do."

They came to a stop, and Jamirh was surprised to realize they were outside his room.

He did not like this castle.

Vlad attempted to hide a smile, seeing Jamirh's ears flick down in annoyance. "And I will try to talk to the palace's magic and see if anything might be done for you on that account. Would you like anything sent up to you? Food, books? A member of the Black Watch not involved in today's events?"

Jamirh smiled a bit despite himself. "No, I'm fine."

"Someone will be around" – he gestured vaguely – "if you call. Do not hesitate to do so. Until next we meet, I wish you well, Jamirh."

And with one last piercing blood-red glance, he turned and left Jamirh standing in the hallway, trying to comprehend the entirety of the situation he had gotten himself into.

"He has interesting coloring," Rhode stated conversationally, eyeing the picture on the tablet. "Some might even say legendary coloring."

"Are you implying something?" the woman asked with a grin, ears twitching happily. "I certainly hope you don't think me so shallow as to make assumptions based on appearances."

"I don't honestly know you well enough to make that call yet, though I assure you I will by the time we are done," he responded. Blue eyes flicked to a screen showing various readouts. "You should know that I'll be able to tell when you are lying."

She stood up straight, one hand fisted over her heart before she folded in a graceful bow. "I swear on the name of Hades that I speak no falsehood, though you should be well aware – even the absolute truth may still deceive."

"On Hades' name? Why her, and not Selenae?"

She looked up sharply, still grinning, still looking directly at him. "Selenae may be the goddess who stands for truth, but Hades alone of all the gods is bound by it."

Interesting. He made a note indicating religious affiliation.

"And how does one deceive with the absolute truth? With partial truths and half-truths, certainly, but the absolute truth is the truth," he reasoned.

"Because even when truth is spoken, most will only hear what they want to hear."

"Well, not to worry. I prefer to hear the full truth as is," he assured her dryly. "So let's start with why you broke that kid out of Greenway. It wasn't for his looks?" He kept his eyes on the readout.

"Looks are superficial," she purred. "It's what's on the inside that matters."

Rhode snorted. "So I've heard. What's so special about this particular Avari's insides?"

She pouted. "That's not what that means at all."

"But it could mean that, no? But perhaps I am asking the wrong questions already," he mused contemplatively. "Tell me, as a follower of the goddess of death, do you believe in reincarnation?"

She tilted her head to the side curiously. "Of course I do, but do you?"

Chapter Thirteen

T akeshi eyed his reflection in the small mirror in his room. He had thought about it carefully and decided that a disguise would be the best course of action while in the Rose Empire. Everyone on this ship seemed to think that it was a miracle he wasn't dead, so perhaps that was something he could play into, and pretend to be someone else at least until he had a better grasp of the situation. He could approach the rebellion as himself once he had found them. He didn't have any supplies for a mundane disguise, but he could do a very simple, low-power illusion that would be easy to maintain.

And he had to do something. It kept him from thinking about Hotaru, who would have probably been charmed by the pirates. She'd always loved meeting new people, and–

No.

He forced himself to focus on the paper and pencils he had borrowed from Ashi so he could sketch out some ideas for the pattern he was going to need. While he could build it in his head, for something that could potentially be under scrutiny for an extended period of time he preferred to be able to check his work on paper first. He had also borrowed a small spool of thread and a needle – he intended on embroidering the finished pattern onto the inside of one of his gloves so it would be even easier to maintain.

He sketched a basic circle to start, considering the glyphs he was going to need. The subtler the change, the harder the final weave would be to detect. He just needed to look not like himself. Lighter hair and eyes, widen the jaw a bit, shorten the hair... make himself shorter altogether. He sketched in the glyphs as he considered them, making sure to bind them together into a cohesive, balanced whole. He discarded the first few drafts for inefficiency or being too complex. When he was pleased with the final result, he pushed a bit of energy into it to check the results.

He looked like someone who sort of looked like Shuurai Takeshi. Excellent. Most people would now think their first impression was a mistake at a closer look. Maybe when he was in Gallia he could find a pair of glasses to add to the look; those tended to really throw people off. He only needed the bare minimum of energy to keep the pattern active as well, and once it was sewn into the glove he wouldn't have to think of it to keep it up.

He wasn't overly concerned about the Truth Seekers finding him because of it – he was good at staying hidden. Even if they were looking specifically for him, which was a possibility, Takeshi trusted in his abilities to remain out of sight. The Truth Seekers were not generally subtle when they were looking for something, and that would only work to his advantage. Going unnoticed was something he was very good at.

He let the magic fade from the pattern, and the image in the mirror returned to his own. Pleased, he took the needle and thread and his sketch and headed up to the mess. The lighting in his room wasn't great, and he did not want to make any mistakes with the stitching. The mess was for once empty, and Takeshi settled down at one end of the table with his supplies. He took off the left glove, turned it inside out, and got to work making very tiny and exact stitches.

The pattern was about two-thirds complete when Salisha and Desha slunk through the doors from the deck, giggling together about something. Their attention shifted with laser focus as soon as they noticed him, and with a shared glance they danced over to the table.

"Wizard!" one cooed happily in greeting. "What ye be doing?"

"Oooh, actual wizard stuff!" the other cheered as she eyed the pattern sketch on the table.

"Yes," he agreed blandly as he set another stitch. "Wizard stuff."

The first sister hauled herself up to sit on the table next to his supplies. "That's pretty," she commented. "What does it do? And why are ye sewing it inside the glove?"

"It makes me look less like me," he answered without looking up, "and it is inside the glove so no one can see it."

"Yer really planning t' leave us then, eh?" the other asked, pouting. "Why? The ocean be sooo much better than the shore."

"And we're here!" the first added cheerfully. "Why deprive yerself o' our fantastic company?"

Why indeed, though Takeshi would never say that out loud. "I have to go to the continent," he said instead.

"What an obsession with rules," the second complained, draping herself over his shoulders and nearly causing him to stab himself. "Live a little, why don't ye?"

He fought down the urge to throw her off. "Please remove yourself."

She did so with a mildly annoyed huff as her sister giggled, "Touchy."

Takeshi very deliberately made another stitch.

Brushing herself off as though he had been the one to touch her, she said, "Well, at the very least won't ye show us what it does?"

"Do I need to?" he asked, studying that last stitch and deciding to redo it.

"Yes!" they chorused together, excitement entering both voices.

He sighed. Weaving the pattern mentally, he cast it.

"Oh!" exclaimed the one on the table. "It's a disguise!"

Hadn't he explained that just now? "Yes," he said shortly.

The other woman brought one hand up to her chin as she tilted her head to the side. "Not as cute," she declared after a moment. "Can ye make it cuter?"

Takeshi stared at her. "That's not the point?"

"It should be the point," her sister commented. Takeshi let the pattern go as she continued, "Ye should always try t' be as cute as possible."

"Words t' live by," the other added. "See, that's better."

"This is what I always look like," he pointed out, turning his attention back towards his stitching. He was almost done, and he wanted to finish before dinner.

"Exactly," came the cheerful reply. "Cuter."

Takeshi just shook his head in exasperation. Tiredly he added in the last stitch. The headache he'd had yesterday was threatening to return. He pushed a small amount of energy into the pattern and was pleased when the sisters' exclamations indicated success. He carefully finished off the thread before turning the glove right-side out again. He was pleased to see that the pattern did not show on the black fabric, and he began gathering up his supplies to return them to Ashi.

"What are ye going t' do with this?" one of the women asked, pointing at his sketch.

He picked up the piece of paper and considered it carefully. He called another pattern to mind, and the paper burst into white-hot flame, burning itself in a violent dance to ash in a few seconds. The sisters practically shrieked in delight at the display, green eyes sparkling and matching grins on their faces.

Amused, Takeshi went to find Ashi.

Everyone was in the mess for dinner, to Takeshi's surprise. Aside from when they had been planning on robbing the freighter, he had never seen all seven of the crew members in the same place. He didn't think they were planning another job; they were supposed to be making port in Bariza tomorrow, where Takeshi would be disembarking. They were chatting amongst themselves as Takeshi made his way to an open spot by Benjen and Don, who greeted him with nods. Caron was the only person not immediately visible, and Takeshi assumed that was because he was probably finishing dinner.

He was proven correct when to the door to the kitchen was kicked open, and Caron's massive frame could be seen through the opening. He was leaning back so he could peek through the doorway. Takeshi noted he was wearing a powder-blue apron with little cartoon whales on it. "Wizard!" came the booming voice. "Yer sure ye want t' be leaving us on the morrow? Ye can still change yer mind; we'd be more than happy t' keep ye."

"Thank you," Takeshi started politely as everyone looked at him. "You have all been more than kind, but I'm afraid I do have to move on tomorrow."

"We'll be sorry to see you go," Benjen commented with a frown.

"Perhaps if ye just stayed a bit longer?" Ashi piped in, ears twitching slightly. "Do ye have t' go now?"

"In theory, I should have already been there," Takeshi replied.

"In theory, ye should be dead." Ashi's reply was sharp as her ears swept firmly down.

Marjori leaned her elbows on the table in front of her. "Ya don't owe them a thing. Why hold t' their laws?"

Takeshi tilted his head to the side slightly. Of all of them, he had interacted with Marjori the least, and he'd assumed that she was against him joining the crew. Unfortunately, there was no answer he could give that would be satisfactory. Even the real answer probably would still be found wanting. "I have to," he said finally, knowing how weak that sounded. He looked down at the table in front of him. He had already spent too much time on this ship.

"Is it a magic thing?" one of the sisters asked, studying him carefully. "Like are ye – what's that word – compulsed, or something?"

Takeshi blinked at her. "Compulsed? Do you mean under a compulsion?"

Both sisters nodded enthusiastically.

That was... not a bad explanation. It was even almost true. "Of a sort, though probably not in the way you're thinking. No," he cut them off as they opened their mouths to ask, "it is not a sort of thing that can be broken. I must go to the continent."

Their faces radiated disappointment.

"What if ye just went ashore and then came back?" Don asked curiously. "Would that satisfy it?"

Takeshi smiled sadly as he shook his head, amused at the thought. "No. There is something I have to do," he explained. "It will likely take some time."

He was disconcerted by the suddenly intense looks he was getting from everyone at the table.

"What is it?" one sister asked. "And how long will it take?"

"What about after? Can ye come back then?" the other followed quickly.

"I can't say, and I don't know. I'm sorry," he responded quietly, a little taken aback. "But it is something I *must* do. It could take years."

Everyone was silent for several minutes as they mulled that over. Takeshi kept his eyes down, not wanting to meet anyone's gaze. There was a sick feeling building in the pit of his stomach, but he had to do this. Hotaru's death couldn't be for nothing. He had caused it, after all. It was up to him to see it through.

"Can we help in any way?" It was Benjen who asked, looking thoughtful. "You helped us with the freighter; perhaps we could return the favor."

Takeshi's brows furrowed. "I think the balance still weighs in your favor, after all you've done for me. But no, I don't think there is anything you could do to help. Unless..."

Takeshi thought about it. The crew of the *Sea Spirit* had proven that they were not fond of the Rose Empire and had even shown some approval for Hotaru's death. They were pirates and had no respect for the law in general. Though they seemed to work entirely on their own, perhaps they might have an idea of where he could start looking? It probably wouldn't hurt to admit that he was looking for the rebellion, would it? He very much doubted they would turn him in to the authorities regardless. The worst that could happen would be that they throw him off the boat.

"Unless you have any information regarding the rebellion against the Rose Empire?" he finished, hoping this wasn't a mistake.

Utter silence.

Just as Takeshi started to panic internally, Marjori broke the silence. "*That's* ya game, wizard? All this quiet secretiveness, and it's because ya looking fer the rebellion? What did ya think we were going t' do – throw ya overboard, like some sort o' law-abiding citizens?"

Caron broke out into a great booming laugh, joined by the sisters.

Benjen shot his captain a wry glance before turning to Marjori. "You did literally suggest that when he came on board, though I'd like to point out that's probably not the step 'law-abiding citizens' would take."

She rolled her eyes, deliberately tucking a stray lock of bright-blue hair behind a pointed ear. "Aye, but not fer that reason. The murder be a different matter o' concern."

Benjen just shook his head, turning his attention back to a quietly confused Takeshi. "So you are looking for the rebellion, hm? I guess that's not too surprising, considering the reason for your banishment."

"Oh, and that's why ye need t' go undercover with yer special disguise!" one of the sisters squeaked happily.

"Story checks out," the other added with a grin.

"I'm just glad ye seem t' have a goal o' some sort that's not just disappearin' or dyin'," Ashi said, relief clear in her voice.

"Unfortunately, we have no connection to the rebellion, if it even actually exists," Benjen said regretfully, "otherwise we would send you to them directly."

"I see," Takeshi said. The relief that they were not in fact going to throw him off the boat bled into disappointment at the lack of information. At least he was no worse off than he had been. He just had that much more work ahead of him.

But it would all be worth it in the end.

Right?

"There have been some rumors of possible rebellion-like activity happening up by the Warcross Wall, however," Benjen continued. "Things the Empire doesn't want their citizens at large to know about, but can't really squash, either. You'll probably hear more rumors in the Empire than you will from us – we tend to be pretty removed from it all out here on the ocean."

"Which is how we prefer it," Marjori added. "No need t' get mixed up in all that."

Takeshi perked up a bit at the information. It wasn't much to go on, but it was something. "Thank you."

"Ye don't have t' go very far if ye want t' work against the Empire, li'l wizard," Caron interjected. "Ye can do that here. Why go looking for something that may or may not exist?"

Takeshi paused, thinking again of Hotaru. Then he said, as full of conviction as he could muster, "I have to."

"Ah," Caron responded, eyebrows raised. Then he smiled. "Yer welcome here regardless, wizard."

Takeshi bowed his head towards Caron, who was now placing a number of steaming bowls on a cart. "Thank you. Your generosity is greatly appreciated."

Caron pushed the cart into the mess proper. Takeshi looked at it with interest; the meals weren't usually served in individual portions like this. Perhaps that had been the cause of the delay? The captain began placing bowls in front of each crew member – Takeshi was amused by the size of Caron's own portion. He thanked the man quietly for his, looking at it curiously.

It was oyakodon.

He stared at the bowl in complete surprise. In the entire time he had been on the ship, not once had they had a dish native to his home. He hadn't even thought it was an option. But here was a steaming bowl of rice covered in a mixture of cooked chicken, egg, and onion, a dish he had often had at home. He could smell the sweetness of the broth. The egg wasn't even overcooked. Eyes wide, he looked up at Caron, who had been watching his reaction.

"Does it look all right?" the man asked as he continued placing bowls in front of the crew, who were making sounds of delight. "It's been some time since I made food from Ni Fon, but I thought ye might be in the mood for something familiar before ye hit the continent tomorrow. A good way t' send ye off, ye know?"

"It looks – and smells – fantastic," Takeshi assured him, looking back at his bowl. "I don't know what to say, except thank you. It's just..." He really didn't have the words to express what this meant to him. "Thank you." He hoped it sounded as heartfelt as he meant it. Caron was right – who knew when would be the next time he would be able to have proper food from home again.

The captain gave him a big smile. "Glad t' be o' service."

Takeshi pulled his mask down and tucked into the warm bowl of comfort food as the rest of the crew expressed their enjoyment of the dish. It tasted perfect. He let the conversation flow around him, content to enjoy his meal, tucking this memory beside others to look back on fondly later.

If only Hotaru were in it.

The next morning, Takeshi made sure to pack his meager possessions in a backpack Benjen had found for him. He would leave the fishing boat – he certainly wouldn't have any use for that on land – the harpoon, and the net with the pirates. The rope he might be able to use, so that went in the backpack, along with an extra set of clothes and his mask. His katana lay on the bed next to the pack. And... that was it. His first order of business was going to have to be getting funds through any means necessary, because even he could not survive on so little. He considered the katana – that was going to need a decent illusion to get past whatever passed for security or customs here. He was not leaving that behind. He would ask the crew what the customs procedures were before attempting to breach them.

He glanced around the tiny room, making sure it looked exactly as it had before he claimed it. Satisfied, he slung the backpack over one shoulder, picked up his katana, and headed up to the mess.

The breakfast buffet was set up as usual, and Takeshi grabbed a bagel, some scrambled eggs, and some bacon, along with his coffee. Caron waved him over to his place at the window with Ashi, reaching down and grabbing another bag from the floor next to him.

"Li'l wizard!" he called. "We put this together for ye." He handed the bag to Takeshi. "Some foodstuffs that won't go bad for a while – mostly dried stuff. Should buy ye some time t' get yerself settled."

"There's some basic first aid supplies in there too," Ashi said with a smile. "Hopefully ye won't need them, but better safe than sorry."

"Thank you," Takeshi said, pleasantly surprised at the gift. "This will be extremely helpful. Food was one of my main concerns."

"Ye know, it's okay t' ask for help," Ashi pointed out. "Ye don't have t' do everything on yer own. Also, please eat more than that, if what ye goin' t' be eatin' from here on out is dried crap."

"Hey." Caron gave his wife an affronted look.

"Oh please – if he were stayin' on this ship ye'd never dream o' feedin' him whatever's in there," Ashi sniffed, "and don't ye dare tell me otherwise."

"I'm sure it's great," Takeshi tried to interject, charmed despite himself. "It is infinitely better than what I thought I'd be eating in my immediate future, which was nothing."

They both stared at him blankly. After a moment Ashi slowly got up, went over to the main table, fixed another plate, and handed it to Takeshi. "Eat that, too," she said flatly.

He stared at the filled plate in consternation. "Ah, thank you, but this is probably too much–"

"Eat it," she repeated coolly, and Takeshi gave up.

"I'll try," he conceded with a sigh. "Thank you for your concern."

He retreated to his favorite sunny spot on deck to eat. He was surprised to see they were already docked amongst other ships of all shapes and sizes. From his location, he could see a surprising number of trees decorating the tiered harbor area. Beyond, tall buildings shot up in straight, smooth lines. Takeshi considered the city as he ate. It had very little character compared to the cities and towns back home; many of the buildings he could see looked nearly identical in featureless, boring shades of white and gray and glass.

He ran into Caron when he went back to the mess to return his mostly finished plates. "Li'l wizard!" came the now customary greeting as Takeshi put his dishes on the end of the table with the others. "We have just a li'l more for ye before ye go," he said, indicating Don, who had been mostly hidden behind Caron's mass.

The boy stepped forward, handing Takeshi a small plastic card – credits. "This is yer share from the freighter," he declared. "It should be enough to help ye get going, at least. This is the paperwork that goes with it – I made ye an account, so if ye decide to get a job for some reason ye can get paid legit." He thrust a small packet of papers into Takeshi's hands. "Don't lose that. By the way, yer now Yuki Tanaka."

"You're paying me?" Takeshi asked as he took the papers, wondering if Don knew he had said the names backward. "Why?"

"Ye take part during the job, ye get paid," Caron informed him cheerfully. "Would never dream o' shorting someone their due."

Takeshi considered this. "I see," he said after a moment. He wasn't sure he would count what he had done as 'taking part' in the job – he had only done the one thing, and quite late, at that – but he was going to need the money, so he'd take it. "Thank you again. It seems as though every time I think there could not possibly be something more you and your crew could do for me, I am surprised."

All this for someone they barely knew.

His own people had thrown him on a boat with nothing but a sword and a mask.

"Oh, we're not done quite yet," Don said dryly. "Show this" – he handed over a brown, circular piece of plastic with a sword stamped on it – "to anyone who challenges ye over the sword; it gives ye the right to carry it. Not use it, mind, so be careful with that, but ye can have it in the city."

"And finally, if yer looking for a place t' stay, ye can head t' the Dancin' Whale on Flood Street, not far from here." The sisters had come in behind him while Don was talking, and looked quite pleased with themselves at their declaration.

"The owner o' that fine establishment is an old friend o' ours – tell her Desha and Salisha sent ye; she'll make sure yer taken care of," the other finished with a bright grin.

"We're going t' miss ye, wizard!" the first exclaimed dramatically, throwing her arms around his neck. She was joined by her sister almost simultaneously, and Takeshi froze, waiting for them to let go. Mercifully, they did quickly, allowing Takeshi to breathe comfortably again.

"Ye look weird, without yer mask," the second said, staring at him critically. "But I guess ye won't need it with that spell o' yers."

Takeshi looked around and realized the entire crew was present to see him off. He carefully put the papers and credit card into his bag. "No, wearing it would draw more attention, rather than less," he agreed.

"Ya really be heading out there, eh?" Marjori asked with a frown. "Last call fer 'ye don't need t' go.'"

Takeshi just shook his head. Part of him did wish he could stay, but the mere thought of Hotaru drove him forward. "I'm sorry, but I really do. I honestly can't thank all of you enough for everything." He took a step back so he was facing all of them, then folded into a deep bow. "Thank you."

"Yer more than welcome, li'l wizard," Caron said kindly. "Know yer always welcome on the *Sea Spirit*. When ye finish what it is ye feel ye have t' do, we'll be out there. Find us."

"Be careful, Shuurai," Benjen added. "The Blind Ones watch for anything and anyone the Empire doesn't like. People tend to disappear in the Empire when they catch the attention of the Blind Ones. If your goal truly is to find the rebellion, you'll want to avoid them at all costs. You are not Avari, so you will have a layer of protection, but it won't save you if you become their target. Humans disappear too."

"I understand; I will," Takeshi responded. He would take it seriously; it seemed to be what was worrying them the most. "I will take it into account when planning my next steps." He paused, looking them over and burning this last image into his memory. "Thank you again. Farewell."

A chorus of goodbyes answered him. He bowed once more. Then he turned, threading his power into the pattern inside his glove to activate his illusion, and stepped off the boat into Bariza with Hotaru's ghost leading the way.

Chapter Fourteen

Takeshi had already decided to stay in Bariza for a few days to orient himself and learn what he could before heading north to the Warcross Wall. He stopped by the Harbor Office to pick up two maps, one of Bariza and one of the western half of the Rose Empire, to help him plan out his next few steps. He also picked up a newspaper, both to get an idea of what was going on in the city and to check the date. Unfortunately, the paper confirmed what the pirates had said – an entire half of a year had passed without his knowledge.

It was extremely concerning, but he had no idea where to go or what to do with that information. Anyone who had answers was back in Ni Fon, and manufactured reason or not, he could not go back.

He just wished he knew why. He felt like he was floundering, and wished that the Empress had given him a bit more direction, a bit more information. Yes, he was spying on the Rose Empire for her, and trying to connect with this supposed rebellion, but how was he supposed to be passing this intel back home? She had wanted him to make landfall as himself, said that because he had been banished he would be beneath the attention of the authorities, but was this disguise not better to avoid detection? Why not just send him in disguise in the first place? Why was he missing six months of his life? What possible purpose did that serve?

Too many questions.

Do not worry; it is not your concern, they had told him. *Plans have already been set in motion. It will be dealt with.*

It did not feel dealt with.

And on that note, why not tell him, if he was the person being sent? Why was he not allowed to know? Was he supposed to just stumble around the continent and hope for the best?

He considered, for a few moments, just turning around and getting back on the ship. How would Ni Fon even know? Hell, maybe they would think he died in the crossing.

But...

Hotaru had actually died for this. She had hoped for a future for her country where they were free from the power of the Rose, and she had willingly sacrificed herself to see that dream become a reality. It was something he had always admired about her – the strength of her convictions and her will, even when her body failed her. And she had always been so kind, even when she herself was suffering. After their engagement, he had always tried to help when he could, but he could only do so much when the enemy was her own body.

So for her sake, he *had* to try to see this through. Anything less would be a horrible betrayal of her memory.

He walked over to a large screen displaying an interactive map of the area. Ni Fon had only recently begun adopting technologies like this, preferring magic and their own traditions. But the Rose Empire had been pushing hard in recent years for them to adopt the more tech-based systems the mainland utilized and abandon the way they had lived for centuries. As such, there was something of a battle happening between those who wanted the new tech and those who wanted the old ways. Takeshi himself sided with magic, being someone who used it, but he could see why those who weren't particularly gifted would be drawn to tech. It was a strange situation, considering how poorly the two systems seemed to work when they came into contact with each other, though there were some groups trying to find ways to make tech and magic work together. To his knowledge, they had yet to be successful.

He found Flood Street on the map and made a mental note of where it was in relation to the harbor. The sisters had been right; it was close.

He kept an eye out as he headed in that direction, observing his surroundings. Nothing in the city looked organic. Everything felt planned, placed. Streets were perfectly straight and met at right angles. Buildings were all similar, with the main differences being height and width. Whites and grays and glass made up the vast majority of the color palette, though there were some pops of light blue and a beige-pink color. Plain white benches made of lester were evenly spaced from each other on the sidewalks. Even the vegetation looked perfectly placed, each tree and bush trimmed and pruned to look exactly the same as every other tree and bush. At home, signs for businesses would be everywhere – painted, carved, lit up, moving, anything to catch someone's attention – but here, it looked like establishment names were etched into the glass windows of the storefronts almost universally.

In short, everything looked boring. Interesting and novel at first glance perhaps, and they definitely had an aesthetic, but very much the same everywhere he looked.

Maybe it was just this section? At least the streets were well-labeled; otherwise Takeshi could imagine himself getting lost very easily.

The Dancin' Whale was only about a five-minute walk from the harbor. A cartoonish whale dancing on its tail was etched into the glass under the arch of the name. Takeshi pushed the door open.

The inside, he was relieved to see, looked less sterile and more like a place people might actually inhabit. There was a small reception area that opened up to a larger room with several tables, chairs, and couches scattered around in tones of beige, blue, and brown. The large glass window at the front of the building let in plenty of natural light.

An older Avari woman with a bright-pink bob was seated behind the front desk. She looked up from her computer as Takeshi came through the door. "Can I help you?" she asked politely, ears twitching.

"Hello," Takeshi greeted, trying to sound friendly and hoping he was in the right place. "I was told to ask for the owner of this establishment by Salisha and Desha, of the *Sea Spirit*?"

"Ah." Her expression turned amused. "You must be their friend who they have been sailin' with for the past week or so, even though they can't tell me what you look like or what your name is – just that you're male, Human, and lookin' for a place to stay."

Takeshi tried not to cringe. At least he was definitely in the right place. "Tanaka Yuki," he introduced himself with a shallow bow.

"Freja Harkin. Welcome to the Dancin' Whale," she said with a smile. "How long will you be needin' a room, Mr. Tanaka?"

He considered for a moment. "I think two nights should be enough. May I ask the rate?"

She laughed kindly. "The gals put you on their tab – you're covered for up to a week, if you need it."

He blinked. That was extremely generous. "I... thank you." He didn't know what else to say.

"I'll pass that on," she assured him, taking a blue plastic card out from a drawer. She ran it through a small machine as she typed something into her computer. The little machine beeped, and she handed the card over to Takeshi. "That's your room key. Follow me; I'll show you where to go."

She brought him up a narrow flight of stairs tucked into the back of what she explained was the common space for guests. She stopped at the first door at the top of the stairs. "This is your room. Just hold your key against the lock here for a second or two, and the light will turn green and you can head in. The key will also open the front door if you need to get in after I've already locked it. I serve breakfast at eight; please let me know before nine the night before if you would like to skip. There are three other guests currently, so remember to keep the noise down. Everythin' is soundproofed pretty decently; just try to be considerate. Any questions?"

He shook his head mutely.

She smiled at him. "All right hon, I'll leave you to get settled. Let me know if you need anythin'." She turned and went back down the stairs, leaving him in front of the door.

He held the card to the lock as she had said, and the light switched from red to green as the lock made a soft clicking sound. He wondered how the card unlocked the door without having to swipe or interact with it. Inside was a small but comfortable room in soft grays and blues, with a bed, a chest of drawers, and a nightstand with a digital clock and a lamp. A large window looked out over the street, and a door on the left opened to a small bathroom.

Takeshi sat on the bed, putting his backpack down next to him. He took out the bank and ID paperwork, flipping through and scanning the information. He raised an eyebrow at the number of credits to Tanaka Yuki's name – it was a sizable amount. He wondered how much they had made off the freighter in total; piracy was apparently quite lucrative. At least he would be okay for a month or so – longer if he was willing to compromise on some things.

How to go about finding the rebellion? A rebellion that – according to the pirates – might not exist?

Based on what he knew of the Empire, Avari would probably be more likely to know about or be part of a rebellion. Unfortunately, that presented a challenge, since Takeshi himself was Human. Most Avari would be unlikely to talk to him purely due to his race, especially about something they had good reason to keep secret. It was going to take time to convince any Avari that he was legitimately looking for the rebellion in order to seek help, so he would have to consider ways to prove his sincerity. He briefly considered modifying his illusion, but decided the added cost of changing his race might make it too noticeable. It also felt a bit... disrespectful, to pretend to be Avari.

Absently, he unfolded the larger region map, wondering where he should go next. He knew he was going to have to head towards the Warcross Wall. Alenci looked like the closest major city, just a hundred miles or so south of the Wall. Finding a method of travel to get there would be his next major step; perhaps he could take a train?

He considered the thick black line that marked the Wall. Several hundred years ago, before the Rose Empire had taken over Ni Fon, there had been communication with a country ruled by Vampires there. Supposedly, the country had been hit by some sort of plague just before the Wall was built, and Ni Fon lost contact. The Rose held that they had all been wiped out, but scholars in Ni Fon had long theorized that they had used their superior magical ability to separate themselves from their aggressive neighbor and had become insular as a result. Ni Fon had been unable to make any sort of contact with them since then. Ships sent reported fog impossible to sail through, and as far as he knew no one had ever managed to cross the Wall itself.

If the rebellion had the most activity near the Wall, what if that country had a hand in backing it? Perhaps he should plan a trip to the Wall proper to get a look at it; maybe there was a way through that the Rose did not understand due to their reliance on tech. He was certain a mage from Ni Fon had to have come into contact with the Wall at some point over the last five hundred years, but he could not think of any records of such an event. He would have to look for himself.

He was fairly certain the country had been called Romanii, though it had been a long time since he had learned about it. At least this was something he could actively investigate, even if nothing came of it.

He put the map aside and turned to the newspaper. The story on the front page was about some sort of sporting event he had no interest in. He flipped through – last week's local food drive had been a success, a new theater building had opened the night previous, the Guard Commander in Lyndiniam had been forced to resign after a jailbreak that had happened two weeks prior, the Emperor was planning on holding the most expensive party ever for the Harvest Celebration in a few weeks.

A jailbreak had been successful in the capital city? That was interesting, but the article didn't go into any details of the event, instead focusing on the former commander. It did mention that the fugitive was still at large, and anyone with any information should contact the Guard. A picture of a younger Avari with red hair and silver eyes was next to the contact information.

Takeshi snorted to himself. Some kid had broken out of a jail in the capital? And gotten away with it? Such a thing would never happen in Ni Fon.

He folded the newspaper and placed it on the nightstand, and decided to spend the rest of the day looking around Bariza. There were some things he wanted to pick up – a knife or two for when he could not have his katana, more clothes, a wallet, maybe a pair of glasses – and sooner was better than later.

Bariza was strange, he decided.

Takeshi had managed to complete his errands fairly quickly, stopping back at the Dancin' Whale to drop off his purchases. He had been wandering around for several hours since, taking in the sights and sounds of the Rose Empire and trying to get a feel for this new place.

It was interesting to see so many Avari. Ni Fon was fairly homogenous, and Takeshi could count the number of Avari he knew personally back at home on one hand – and he had nearly doubled that number on the *Sea Spirit*. Here, there were wild pops of color everywhere he looked. Depending on where in the city he was, they even sometimes outnumbered the Humans. The Avari back home were extremely skilled in magic; he wondered how much potential was being wasted here with their insistence on tech.

And the tech was another thing. Everywhere he went in the city had far more tech than he was used to. Interactive maps were placed at carefully chosen intersections. Some places had large screens outside the buildings, showcasing the news, a sporting event, or a concert. Several stores he went into had some sort of inventory terminal, where you could check to see if they carried what you were looking for without actually going in. The streetlights and cars were much sleeker and looked more advanced than what he was used to. Even their credits were just plastic cards with tech, rather than actual currency.

He wandered in and out of shops, checking off various sightseeing locations mentioned on his map as though he were a simple tourist. He found a large library where all the books were digital, an ornamental park that looked over-cultivated and artificial, and a temple to the Three that was gorgeous on the inside even if the outside conformed to the generic look of everything else. It reminded Takeshi of his promise to Caron, and after a bit of searching he found a small shrine to the Nyphoren near the docks, where he left an offering of food and wine in thanks for his arrival on the *Sea Spirit*.

He returned to the Dancin' Whale to eat some of the jerky Caron had given him for dinner and take a quick nap, as he intended to be up late. He set out again around eight to see what the city was like at night.

It was surprisingly loud and bright, he discovered quickly. The area where he was staying was thankfully not too bad, but the more central areas were a riot of sound and light. The buildings themselves had a slight glow to them, and many had additional lighting features as well. Loud music spilled from multiple buildings, creating a cacophony of noise. People, both Avari and Humans, were everywhere – it was even busier than it had been during the day.

Many stores were still open alongside the clubs, to his surprise. They were quiet inside, and thus a sanctuary from the assault on his senses. He wasn't sure what the buildings were made of, but even though the music was more than audible in the streets, once inside the buildings it couldn't be heard. To his pleasure, while taking a break from the noise he found a store selling tea, and he happily bought a small tin to add to his meager belongings.

Takeshi wandered around, keeping his eyes and ears open for anything that might be useful, but mostly just watching. It was far more lively at night than he had expected. He wondered if it was something particular to this city, or the Empire in general.

He finally retired to his room very early in the morning to get in a second, longer nap before he had to be up for breakfast. Even though the nightlife still seemed to be in full swing, once in the Dancin' Whale he could thankfully no longer hear it. He drew the curtains, made sure the alarm was set, and was asleep within moments.

Breakfast was a fairly quiet affair. Freja served toast and omelets made with potato and onion alongside juice and coffee. The other guests – who were all Avari, Takeshi noted – were also present, spread throughout the common area.

He received a few strange looks, but no one approached him, and he was left to enjoy his meal in peace.

He spent the majority of the second day much the same as he had the first, exploring different parts of the city while looking for anything that could point him in the right direction. He also stopped by the train station to look up the schedule for the next day, hoping to be able to head up to Alenci soon. Luckily, it seemed he had plenty of options. He took a schedule and returned to looking around.

He returned to the Dancin' Whale for a dinner of more jerky and tea. Then he started trying to plan out his next few moves. He pulled out the schedule and the map and began plotting his route. The train was less expensive than he had expected, but a little more than he had hoped. Still, it would leave him with a decent amount to put towards lodging in Alenci, though he would have to look for some sort of work soon.

Takeshi found himself just staring at the map blankly, wondering what the right course of action truly was. He felt confident that he was doing the best he could with what little information he had to go on; he just hoped the conclusions he was coming to were not mistakes. He didn't want to be wasting time chasing after shadows. He wanted to do what he had to and then be done with the whole mess.

He could feel a headache coming on. His neck and shoulders were beginning to stiffen up, and there was a hint of pressure building behind his eyes. He decided to stay in and rest instead of continuing to explore Bariza; it was early – a glance at the bedside clock told him it was just past eight – but he could afford to get some extra sleep. He grabbed the bottle of painkillers Ashi had given him and took two. Hopefully he could sleep through the worst of it and the headache would be gone in the morning.

He carefully folded and put away the papers and made sure everything was packed for the next day. He wanted to get moving as soon as possible and be on his way to Alenci. He turned off the lights in the room and found himself sighing in relief at the decrease in light. He closed his eyes for a moment and took a deep breath as the pain spiked again, then slowly drew the curtains shut to block out the emerging city lights. He all but fell onto the bed, curling up and pressing his face into the pillow in the hope that the pain would ease.

Suddenly, it got much, much worse.

The pain spiked horribly, almost as if someone were stabbing him in the back of his neck and behind his eyes over and over again, then reaching in and scooping something out. He gasped at the sudden pain, recoiling when even that slight sound caused another wave of agony. He felt dizzy, even though he was lying down and his eyes were closed tight, and with each bout of pain he began to feel more and more nauseous.

Takeshi lost track of time as he lay there, trying not to move and incoherently praying for the pain to go away. He felt chilled, but couldn't bring himself to move under the blankets even though his shivering was itself adding to the misery. The pain came in waves, denying him even the possibility of acclimating to it. All he could do was lie there and wait, trying to fight the nausea and sobbing silently.

It was sometime later when the pain had receded enough for him to think coherently again. He felt completely wrung out and exhausted. His whole body ached, but it was a dull ache compared to the torment of before. He was still shaking, so he tried to maneuver himself beneath the blankets and was mostly successful. He wiped at his eyes, and blearily he blinked them open...

...and immediately shut them again, as the light from the digital clock on the nightstand caused another stab of agony to shoot through his head. His mind shrieked silently, a mental scream of anguish, begging any deity who might be listening to just *make it stop–*

:?:

Once again he found himself trying to hold still, shivering under the blankets, waiting out the pain as fresh tears began to fall.

:I... here.:

Luckily, this time it began to fade to more manageable levels quickly. Still, what *was* this? Never in his entire life had he experienced such a debilitating migraine.

:Abomination.:

What?

That thought... had not been his own. Weakly, his abused mind flailed about in confusion...

There was another presence.

It was not like when the Empress used her telepathy, where she thrust herself into her target's mind. He could sense the presence, but just on the edges of his perception. It felt feminine, and kind, and seemed to be content to let him figure it out as it observed him. It also felt... very *other*. Very much unlike him, somehow. Bigger, or maybe more?

Takeshi did not have the thought processes to deal with that right now.

:Abomination,: it – she? – repeated, gentle as a whisper of wind through leaves, sounding sad. Also very distant, like she was struggling to reach him. *:Little. You hear...:*

He didn't think he was catching all of what she was saying to him. He didn't think he could, right now, with the remnants of agony drifting through his mind. He didn't understand what she meant.

As he struggled to comprehend, the presence seemed to come a little closer, and with it came relief. *Oh*, he thought weakly as the pain receded, *thank you thank you thank you...*

:Better?: The thought whispered through his mind, as though purposefully trying to avoid causing more pain. *:...difficult. Let...:*

Takeshi took a few moments to breathe, feeling his body finally begin to relax as the pain and stress eased. He had no idea how he was going to drag himself out of bed in the morning. He wanted to sleep for the next week, not go traipsing across the country.

:Why... go?: came the soft query. A feeling like she was gathering herself, and then a much firmer thought, *:Rest!:*

He wished he could. He wished a lot of things, actually. He wished Hotaru wasn't dead, and that he hadn't killed her. He wished he were back home among his friends and not banished. He wished he were back on the *Sea Spirit* with people who cared. He wished he wasn't lying on a bed in a strange place trying not to throw up from agony. He wished he had already found the rebellion and helped Ni Fon regain its autonomy, and all of this could be over.

:Rebellion?: The whisper felt intensely interested in that. There was a long pause, during which he felt like he was being assessed somehow, before it breezed through him again. *:Another... Charve.:* The image of some sort of facility flashed through his mind. The architecture was distinctly Empire. *:Aid... insurgent...:*

He tried to untangle that, but his focus was still scattered in a thousand directions. *What?*

:Charve.: An image of a city, as though seen from high up, followed by another of the same building as before. *:Rebellion? Save...:*

The rebellion is in Charve? He was trying to piece it together, but now that the pain was mostly gone exhaustion was stepping in, and he could feel himself fading. *Who are you? Why are you helping me?*

There was a distinct sense of amusement. *:...difficult. Few... speak.:* There was a feeling of warmth, almost like being wrapped in a very soft blanket, and affection. *:Sleep.:*

As Takeshi slid under, he heard one last thought.

:Charve.:

Chapter Fifteen

Takeshi woke up the next morning to the sound of the incessant beeping of the alarm. Miserably, he felt around for the button to shut it off, then lay there basking in the sudden silence. He felt horrible; though the pain in his head was gone, every muscle in his body ached as though he had run a marathon the day before, and he still felt chilled.

He dozed off again, waking to the sound of a knock at the door. Exhaustedly, he pulled himself from the bed and staggered over. Then he staggered back to his bag, grabbing the glove with the illusion stitched into it and activating it, cringing at the pull of energy he barely had. He opened the door, wincing at the light in the hallway, to find Freja standing there, eyebrows raising as she took in his disheveled appearance.

"Mr. Tanaka, is everythin' okay? You slept through breakfast," she explained, eyeing him carefully.

It took him a moment to find the words in the correct language. "I'm... very sorry, Ms. Freja. I'm not feeling well today."

"I see." She paused. "Is there anythin' I can get for you? Water, or medicine? Is there anyone you would like me to call?" Her voice was kind, reminding Takeshi of...

He shook his head carefully. "There is no one. I would be thankful for some water, though. And... I think I would like to stay another night, if that is all right?" The thought of trying to leave today was almost enough to make him nauseous again.

"Of course you can, honey. I wouldn't dream of throwin' you out lookin' like this. Stay as long as you need to. I'll be right up with a pitcher of water for you." She gave him another concerned look, then turned and went back down the stairs.

Takeshi blinked tiredly at the space where she had been, deciding it was less effort to stay in the doorway and wait than to lie down and have to get up again when she returned. He felt himself zoning out a bit as he leaned against the door frame, trying not to fall asleep standing up. Freja's voice had reminded him of something – or maybe someone? Who–

"Mr. Tanaka?"

Takeshi startled at Freja's voice, eyes snapping open as he jerked upright. She was standing in front of him again, this time with a pitcher and a glass.

"Oh," he said lamely as his heartbeat began to return to a normal speed. He tried to rally. "I'm sorry; thank you for the water." He reached out to take the items.

"Are you sure you'll be okay?" she asked, voice full of concern as she hesitantly handed him the pitcher.

He nodded very slowly, regretting it anyway. "Yes, it's just a very bad headache. I have some medicine, and some sleep should help."

She frowned slightly. "Well, you let me know if you need anythin' else, all right?"

"I will; thank you," he murmured, retreating back inside his room. He put the pitcher and the glass down on the nightstand, tossed the glove on his bag, then collapsed back into the bed, curling under the covers.

When he woke up for the third time, the clock read almost noon. He stared at it for several long minutes, watching the numbers change as he lay unmoving without the will to get up. He registered the bottle of pills sitting on the nightstand where he had left them the night before, and finally managed to make himself sit up so he could take two more. He felt a little better than he had earlier, but there was absolutely no way he was going to Charve today.

Wait, Charve? He had been planning on going to Alenci. There was no way he was going to Alenci today. Well, there was no way he was going anywhere today.

Confused, he lay down again, trying to figure out where Charve had come from. Had Freja mentioned Charve at some point? He didn't think so. But... someone had. He felt like someone had definitely mentioned Charve.

He was starting to wake up more as the painkillers kicked in. He poured himself a glass of water and sipped at it, trying to figure out what could possibly have resulted in such an awful migraine. He wasn't generally prone to headaches even when under stress, never mind the monster he had suffered the night before. Where had it come from?

He blinked as the word "abomination" floated through his thoughts. What did that...

Had the pain been causing him to hallucinate last night? He seemed to recall a woman speaking to him, though he could barely remember the words, more just impressions and feelings. A few words did stand out – "abomination," "Charve," and "rebellion." Was that where he had heard Charve mentioned?

He looked around the room carefully, pulling the curtains open to let in more light. Nothing looked disturbed; he was pretty sure he had been the only person actually here. Telepathy, then? It hadn't felt the same as the telepathy he was familiar with, so perhaps it was something his mind had constructed to help him cope with the pain?

But the more he thought about it, the more he thought he had definitely felt *something*, even if he didn't know what. And he was fairly certain that whatever it was had wanted him to go to Charve. He still had no idea what "abomination" meant, but maybe the presence had been trying to tell him that the rebellion was in Charve? Or that he should go to Charve to find the rebellion?

Okay, that sounded a bit crazy even to him.

He tried to remember if there had been anything else to help him determine if it had been real or imagined, but it was hard to think back. Mostly he remembered being in agonizing pain; the memories felt fractured, like he could only see pieces and not the whole.

It was exhausting him to try to think about it. He closed his eyes and took a few deep breaths, then considered his bag. The thought of food made him feel a little sick, and he didn't feel up to staring at maps or timetables, so he decided to lie down again and try to get some more rest.

He felt much more like himself when he woke up later that evening. He managed to eat a little, even though he wasn't particularly hungry, and drank some more water. Looking for a mindless activity, he pulled his entire pack apart and re-packed it, making sure everything fit neatly. He refused to even consider going out into Bariza's very active nightlife, content for now to do nothing instead.

He opened up the map of the Empire again, looking for Charve. It was almost five hundred miles south of the Wall, he realized with dismay, and quite a bit farther east from Bariza than Alenci. It didn't seem to meet any of his criteria for where to go next, except that for some reason, he felt like that was where he needed to go.

No. Alenci was where he needed to go. Most of what he was banking on involved the Wall, and the one piece of information he had stated that there was some sort of activity happening near it. While Charve was certainly closer to the Wall than Bariza, it was still nowhere near it. What did Charve have to offer over Alenci, other than a feeling?

Takeshi rubbed at his eyes tiredly. He was going in circles. He checked the timetables for trains leaving the next day for Alenci, but he nearly threw it down in disgust when he found his eyes wandering to trains headed towards Charve.

He decided he was still having trouble focusing because of his migraine the previous night. Some more sleep would hopefully fix the problem. He had already been forced to waste a whole day due to feeling unwell; he didn't want to have to waste any more time. He would go to Alenci tomorrow, and with any luck, he could put all of this behind him and make some actual progress on finding the rebellion.

He double-checked that everything was packed and ready to go for the next morning, including his katana, which he had wrapped in a piece of fabric and rope, attaching the brown token to it. He wove a very precise fire pattern to heat some water for tea and spent some time meditating to re-center himself after the previous day's misery. When he found himself dozing again, he decided to just go to bed and get plenty of sleep for the next day.

He shut off the lights and wrapped himself up in the blankets, allowing himself to drift off, hoping the next day would be better.

:Let... in.:

The next morning, Takeshi gathered his things and went down to breakfast.

Freja looked overjoyed to see him up and about and greeted him warmly. "Good mornin'! You look much better today! Are you feelin' better?"

He nodded. "Much better, thank you. Some time to rest was really all I needed." He sat at one of the small tables as she brought him a sliced bread roll filled with scrambled eggs and bacon and a cup of juice.

"Are you still wantin' to check out today?" she asked, adding kindly, "You could stay a few days longer, if you wanted."

"Thank you, but I need to be moving on," he replied. "Should I give you my key now?"

She shook her head. "No, you can give it to me after breakfast. Where are you off to in such a rush?"

Takeshi considered her for a moment. "Alenci. I'm interested in the Warcross Wall and was hoping to do some research on the subject. Alenci seemed like a good starting point."

"The Wall?" she asked, looking surprised. "What about the Wall is so interestin'?"

He shrugged. "My interest is purely academic. How was the Wall built? What is it made out of? Things like that."

She frowned. "Be careful, Mr. Tanaka, if you'll take an old lady's word on the subject. Nothin' good comes from the Wall. It kills everythin' for miles around. They say they built the Wall to keep out the plague, but most people think they were tryin' to keep somethin' worse out. Those who see it say there's somethin' wrong with the way it's built, say it feels uncomfortable to look at."

Takeshi felt his eyebrows rise. "Is that so? What were they trying to keep out? Is there anything else you know?"

She paused. "Not specifically, no. Just... *they* don't like it too much when people go sniffin' about the Wall. Be careful up there, you hear?"

He inclined his head gratefully, sensing that she wasn't likely to talk more about it. It clearly made her uncomfortable. "I will be. Thank you." He watched her walk away as he chewed on both his food and the information. So there was something special about the Wall, something that "they" didn't want people to know about. Intriguing. If he assumed "they" were the government or the military, then he might actually be heading in the right direction.

Cheered at the thought, he finished breakfast quickly. He thanked Freja again as he turned in his key and said his goodbyes before stepping out into an absolute downpour. Instantly soaked, he hurried through the city to the train station, glad his bag was made of a waterproof material.

The train station was full of people, though many looked like they were hiding inside waiting for the rain to ease up a bit. Takeshi navigated his way through the noisy crowd, looking for ticket sales. The terminals for buying tickets were all interactive screens with card readers for payment, and while there were a lot of people around, several of them were available. He slid over to a free terminal and began navigating the interface carefully, as he had never done this before. Double-checking the information on the screen against his timetable, he clicked through, but found himself pausing over Alenci.

His eyes strayed to Charve.

:Help?:

He... could go there. For some reason, even though all evidence pointed to Alenci, he felt that the place he needed to go was Charve. He considered the screen for several minutes as he thought it over. Something had happened during his migraine, and it had left him feeling like he was needed in Charve, even though that made no sense whatsoever. But he couldn't shake the feeling that something was calling him. He could always investigate the Wall later.

He paused, remembering Desha or Salisha suggesting he was under a compulsion of some sort. He closed his eyes and did a quick mental check, trying to shut out the conversations happening around him, well aware that this was not really the place, but to his relief he did not find any of the psychic hooks that a compulsion would leave. There was nothing tying him to Charve, magically or otherwise. But he felt more certain than ever that something or someone had contacted him and wanted him to go there.

Even if something had, could he risk that?

:...*choose.*:

With a sigh, he bought the ticket to Charve. He prayed he wasn't making a mistake.

:...*helping!*:

A woman laughed close by and Takeshi frowned, not having realized someone was so close. He glanced around, but whoever it was had already moved away. He started working his way from the terminals, hoping to find somewhere a little less crowded to wait for his train. He paused by the display of maps, but unfortunately there weren't any of Charve. He checked the time; he had about twenty minutes before boarding. He hoped the rain would let up soon so people would go on their way instead of taking shelter here. Honestly, it was just water. He had walked through it just fine; so could they.

As he escaped the central area through a narrow hallway, he thought he saw something like long black fabric flicker out of the corner of his eye. His head snapped to look, but it was only his own – or rather, Tanaka Yuki's – broken reflection in a series of abstractly shaped mirrors lining the wall. He stared at it a moment, then continued on, admonishing himself for being so easily startled by a reflection, and wondering what kind of person would think that was a good decoration for a hallway.

He reached the platforms, taking a deep breath and looking around. There were far fewer people here than in the main area. He found the platform his train was supposed to be arriving at and sat down on a nearby bench. He pulled out his timetables and grimaced when he realized his six-hour, twenty-minute train ride had turned into a nine-hour, fifteen-minute one with a half-hour stop in Mardoba. Why did Charve have to be so far away?

Though to be fair, in Ni Fon a journey of the same distance would take far longer – maybe fifteen hours or so? The trains here went very, very fast. A point in their favor, he supposed.

He looked around at the large tunnel he was sitting in. If he had to pay it a positive compliment, he would say it was clean, but otherwise it was just pale-gray lester and bright lights. There were some posters on the wall near where he had entered for various events coming up – a soccer game, a concert, a science convention. He stared at them without really seeing them, finding himself wondering again why he was heading to Charve as a pair of shrieking children ran past him.

:Rebellion.:

Right, he had the vague idea that someone might have sent him a mental communication saying the rebellion might be in Charve. Excellent. He felt a surge of exasperation. He would go to Charve and see what was there. If it proved to be nothing, then at least he could move on to Alenci knowing he had tried. Maybe that would satisfy this feeling that he was needed there.

Why him, specifically? Was someone looking for him? Why?

Maybe the Empress had been correct after all – by killing Hotaru, he had indicated that he was anti-government, and as a shinobi who was skilled in combat and magic he would thus be quite desirable by anti-government movements, who would then seek him out. Perhaps... this strange plan actually was working out? But then how had they known it was him? He checked his illusion absently; it was working as intended.

He mused over the conundrum until the train streaked into the station, a sleek white shape that turned the area into a wind tunnel. Takeshi noted with surprise that the train did not have visible wheels; he wondered how it moved on the track. There was certainly no magic about it, so it was tech of some sort. He watched as passengers disembarked, some with huge suitcases and others with smaller bags like his own. He waited patiently for boarding to be called, then waited with a sigh for the crowd of people that suddenly formed to get on the train.

He checked his ticket for his car and seat numbers while he waited, hoping to be able to find his spot quickly. When he finally got on the train, he quickly navigated to a spot near the back of the compartment by following the letters and numbers and slid into his seat. A screen set into the back of the seat in front of him lit up and the words "Insert Ticket" appeared. He carefully did so, and the screen changed to a readout of his receipt – where he was getting on, his destination, etc. It asked for confirmation – was this correct?

Sensing this was his last chance to change his mind, Takeshi nevertheless touched the part of the screen that said "Yes." He received a message thanking him for his purchase and noting the estimated time of arrival at seven-fifteen in the evening. It then provided a selection of movies that he could watch, offering a pair of complimentary earbuds he could use if he didn't have any.

Was everything automated? At this point, Takeshi wouldn't be surprised if it turned out the train was driving itself. At least he would have something to occupy his mind other than his own thoughts chasing themselves in circles. He didn't really want to fall asleep here, so he would need to find something that could keep him awake – though he felt he had done enough sleeping the day before to last him the whole week.

He considered putting his bag and katana on the overhead shelf but decided to leave them at his feet. He wanted quick access to his food, and he didn't feel comfortable putting the katana up by itself. He had plenty of floor space for both of them, even if the rest of the row filled.

Idly, he scrolled through the options, finally settling on a science-fiction action movie that he could watch in Nifoni. He settled a little more into his seat as the train began to move, determined to make the best of the long journey.

Takeshi was tired of sitting by the time they reached Charve. He had taken the opportunity to stand up and stretch a bit while they were stopped in Mardoba, but after over nine hours of being mostly stationary he was ready to get off the train and move around. He was also tired, even though all he had done was sit and watch extremely mediocre movies all day.

His ear buds suddenly beeped three times in quick succession. The screen in front of him flashed a warning that they were approaching his stop, and could he please collect any personal items and be ready to disembark when they arrived. Takeshi stood, making sure he had both his bag and katana as he felt the train decrease in speed.

They slowed to a stop, and the screen thanked him for riding the Sunset Extended Line and asked him to disembark. Takeshi exited quickly, emerging onto a platform that looked almost identical to the one he had left from in Bariza. He followed the crowd through yet another hallway with bizarre mirror art to the main station area.

His next goal was to find somewhere to stay. He was likely to be here for a while, so he didn't want anywhere too expensive. He went over to an information terminal to begin his search. Some of the larger cities at home did have these, and he had to admit they were handy – the search feature allowed him to find options within a set of parameters, and before too long he had a few possibilities for lodging.

Before leaving the station, he made sure to pick up a map of the city from the display. He hesitated, then purchased an eighty-page "vacation planner," which looked like an in-depth visitor's guide, from a nearby vending machine. He put it away to look at later, then set out into the city.

Charve shared many physical features with Bariza but was somehow even more gray. The buildings were the same straight, blocky architecture, and everything was laid out neatly on a grid. There appeared to be even less greenery in the city itself, but he could see the nearby snow-capped mountains rising up over the buildings, so the view was not completely devoid of nature. Charve did appear to be smaller, however, which at least made navigating to the first place on his list

easier. The sun had long since set, and the buildings gave off a soft glow in addition
to the streetlights. Unlike Bariza, Charve's nightlife lacked a party atmosphere
– the extreme lights and sounds were absent. There were still people of all sorts
going to and fro, still lights and sounds and things to see, but this seemed far more
like a "normal" city volume to Takeshi. Bariza had just felt wild.

Redguard Suites was a fifteen-minute walk from the station, and Takeshi was
thankful that it wasn't raining like it had that morning. He found it without too
much trouble, and to his relief he was able to procure a room for the next month
easily. He noted that, even as cheap as it was, he was going to have to find a source
of income if he wanted to stay longer than that. The receptionist checked him in
with a bored expression, showing no interest in his customer. This suited Takeshi
quite well; the fewer people who paid attention to him, the better.

He used the elevator to climb to the third floor and used another of the strange
key cards to open his door. It didn't feel quite as nice as his room at the Dancin'
Whale had, but it was certainly bigger, and it came with a small kitchen and a vid
screen on one wall. Takeshi spent a few minutes looking around and putting his
things away, then settled on the bed with the vacation planner. He started to flip
through it, but gave up when he found himself struggling to focus after only a
few pages. He wondered if he was so tired because he was still recovering from the
migraine. Deciding that he could start his research in the morning, he prepared
for bed. He turned out the lights and sat on the bed looking out the window at the
soft lights of the city, just barely able to make out the shapes of the mountains in
the dark. He wondered if whatever had drawn him to Charve would be satisfied
now.

He supposed he would find out soon.

Chapter Sixteen

The next morning, Takeshi found himself sitting with the vacation planner and a cheap blueberry muffin at a table outside a gas station. He was flipping through the booklet idly, looking at ads for exhibits and restaurants in the city and the nearby mountains, when he came across a simplified map of the area around Charve. It showed several attractions and points of interest in the area, such as a zoo, a few hiking trails, and a large park, but two things really caught his eye – Laurent Military Academy and Charve Military Base.

He was in a city with both a military base and a military academy.

Well, that was problematic.

Avoiding the notice of both the Guard and the military was important. The Guard was the lesser threat, and easy to avoid. The military was a different game, however, and the risk factor for discovery was much higher in a city with both a base and an academy. He didn't know what sort of training facility the academy was. It could be general training, or intelligence, or engineering, or Truth Seekers, for all he knew. It made sense that it was in the same city as a base, which he also knew nothing about, but unfortunately for him the presence of both raised the percentage of people associated with the military in the population. That was not what he wanted. He rather doubted that that was what a rebellion would want, either – it now seemed even less likely that he was in the right place.

He sighed, tired and a bit angry, and took another bite of muffin. He was still certain of his ability to handle any Truth Seekers that might be about, but that didn't mean he particularly wanted to. Chances were good that he would run into at least one at some point if he remained in this city. He eyed his glove for a moment, considering, but he had created the pattern with this scenario in mind – it would hold. Illusions weren't his specialty like lightning magic was, but he had faith in his execution of the pattern. He also had the two knives on his person if it came to that.

It would be safe enough to stay for a little bit, he decided. Besides, he had already paid for a month's worth of hotel fees. If nothing else, perhaps he could learn some information about the military installations, as long as he proceeded with caution. He had no interest in tangling with them directly.

He resigned himself to a month of being paranoid. He would have to be both very observant and careful in order to avoid compromising situations. He studied the map in the visitor's guide; while it wasn't a great indicator of the exact location of anything on it, it did give him an idea of where the bases were. He could avoid those areas of the city, though it didn't look like either was in the city proper. He could check his city map for the exact locations when he returned to his room.

Why did everything have to be so complicated?

Though... something about the city did look familiar. He wasn't sure what. Maybe it was just that it looked similar to Bariza?

He finished his muffin morosely, continuing to flip through the vacation planner. It looked like they expected tourists here – the surrounding area apparently boasted trails, rock formations, and other unique geological features that made it a popular place for hikers and people seeking to "reconnect with nature," according to the booklet. It explained the plethora of hotel options he had found, and hopefully it would mean that he wouldn't stand out too much. He had noticed that there seemed to be far fewer Avari here than in Bariza, so at least he would blend in with the mostly Human population.

Though, there being fewer Avari also felt like a sign that there was no rebellion here.

He gathered up his trash and went to throw it in the nearby garbage can. For just a moment, out of the corner of his eye, he thought he saw something draped in black fabric instead of his reflection in the large window. He sighed; maybe he still needed more sleep to get over the last of the migraine, even though he felt pretty good now. It was good to know the paranoia was already setting in, though it was probably just someone inside the gas station overlaying with his reflection briefly in a strange way. There were enough things to be worried about in the real world; it would be nice if he didn't have to worry about things his mind made up.

Similarly to in Bariza, he wanted to spend a few days just scouting the area so he knew what he was dealing with. The visitor's guide was a good starting point, but there was no substitute for seeing with his own eyes and making his own observations. If he found another library, perhaps he could spend some time looking up the military facilities and figure out what he could expect from them.

Ni Fon didn't really have a military unless you counted the shinobi, but it wasn't the same thing. Gifted children were trained from a young age in magic and combat to become shinobi; joining the military here was a career choice, to his understanding. He wasn't actually sure how they produced the Truth Seekers though, now that he thought about it. He supposed they might have a similar method to what the shinobi did, since the Truth Seekers definitely used magic in a country that wanted to pretend magic did not exist, and getting adults to cast magic after being told for years they couldn't was usually a near impossibility regardless of potential.

Believing you could weave spells mattered. It was part of what made the Rose Empire such a tragic waste of potential – most of its citizens would never be able to weave so much as the simplest of patterns even if they did learn of the existence of magic, since they had been told their entire lives that they couldn't. It was incredibly difficult to overcome that sort of entrenched belief. Coming to believe magic existed was one thing; coming to believe you could do it was something else. Doubt was poison to magic.

Takeshi wandered around the downtown area for a while, looking at the brightly colored ads being shown on the large vid screens that were basically everywhere. He supposed that made up a bit for the lack of color in the architecture. There were plenty of restaurants and shops around, as well as a few sadly struggling parks. He noticed several strange, abstract, sculpture-like structures scattered around the area, but after reading the plaque on one he realized they were just that – sculptures. Like the mirrors at the train stations, he found himself wondering at what these people considered art.

He took the opportunity to stock up on some cheap dried and canned food at a small market. He wanted to keep some food in his room in case he didn't want to go out for a meal. After dropping his purchases off at the hotel, he considered finding a trail and doing a hike, if only to be in actual nature for a little while. Everything was so... inorganic, in these cities. Unnatural. It made him uncomfortable. How did people actually live here for long periods of time? Then again, the apparent draw to Charve was the nature around it, so maybe they didn't like their cities much either.

He decided against a full hike but settled on one of the parks that was right outside the city proper. He hoped it was an actual park, and not one of the sad things he had seen inside Charve. Hopefully it would help him re-center and re-focus, and then he could get back to combing the city for any information at all.

A short bus ride later, he arrived at Green Garden Park. Thankfully, it was a real park, with greenery growing everywhere and stone paths and shrubs and flowers and trees. There were even several small creeks that cascaded together into a pond, to his surprise. It was also quite large; Takeshi spent the afternoon exploring the area, feeling himself unwind as he wandered. It did seem to be a popular place, though it never got too crowded. Humans and Avari both strolled around the area, singly, in pairs, or in groups, but Takeshi observed that they never mixed – Avari stayed with Avari and Humans stayed with Humans, and though there was no outright animosity the two races did seem to be avoiding each other.

A number of people had brought their dogs, to Takeshi's delight. He'd always been fond of dogs, large and small. A number of ladies in the Imperial court had kept canines, both as beloved pets and as hunting dogs. Seeing the creatures romping around in the grass made him warm to the place a little more.

He spent some more time looking around. A garden like this in Ni Fon would usually have a shrine to the Patoran somewhere about, but if there was one here, he couldn't find it. He couldn't find any mark of the twin deities of earth and plants, which felt strange. A garden that didn't have their mark to help it grow? This one seemed to be doing fine regardless, though maybe the shrine was not in a public space or he just hadn't found it, but perhaps the "parks" in the city could stand to have a little of the twins' blessing.

Most of the visitors started to leave as the sun began to set, and Takeshi took that as his cue to leave as well. He headed back to the front of the park and settled on a bench to wait for the bus near a group of other people, watching a pack of children running around with a harried-looking woman chasing after them, clearly trying to get them to stop.

"Can you even believe it? In the heart of the Empire, no less."

The words came from behind him, full of bitterness and anger. Takeshi didn't react, continuing to watch the children play.

"It doesn't matter; it will never happen. They can threaten it all they want, but they won't want to deal with the resulting uproar."

Both speakers were male, though the second one seemed far calmer than the first.

"That's their job – to deal with uproars. And protests. They won't think twice about it if this gets nasty," the first voice continued.

"Nah, it won't go that far. They won't want the bad press it'll cause."

"Do you want to bet on it? Fifty credits the curfew goes through before the week is out."

A potential curfew? Takeshi silently cursed himself for forgetting to pick up a newspaper when he arrived at the train station. Or this morning, for that matter. He resolved to get one before returning to his hotel room.

"Why would they even bother, at this point? It's been, like, two weeks since they increased the security at the base, and nothing has happened. Also, tomorrow is Saturday. Not really giving yourself a whole lot of time there."

"I'm telling you, something must have happened. The Seekers have been showing up–"

"We host a base. Seekers are always 'showing up.'"

"*–in greater numbers than before*, if you'd let me finish, and they've been hanging around in weird places. Tania said she saw one in the Old Quarter, and Adisan saw *two* near the zoo–"

"Why in the name of the gods would they be near the zoo? Does that make any sense to you whatsoever?"

Takeshi was listening closely, though he was careful not to show it. He wondered if this increased military activity was good or bad news for him.

"No! That's what I'm trying to say! It's *weird*!" The first man's voice was rising as he tried to make his point. "That's why I think they are going to push the curfew."

"But what would that realistically accomplish, other than making people angry?" the second man pointed out, matter-of-fact despite the first's passion.

"I don't know!" came the exasperated exclamation. "I'm not a Seeker *or* military! I don't know what's going on at the base, but it is definitely something, and it's something that has all the military folks on edge. I don't like it, whatever it is. We've never had a problem like this here."

"Oh, don't be so dramatic. We don't even know for sure that there is a problem. For all we know, it's some new training program."

Takeshi watched the bus pull up as the first man retorted, "Then this is all normal to you? They nearly shut down the east side of the city two weeks ago, there's Truth Seekers everywhere, and there's talk of a curfew, and everything is normal?"

"You are blowing everything way out of proportion," the second responded with a sigh. Takeshi glanced at the two Humans as they came around the bench to get in line for the bus. "They didn't shut down anything, you've listed maybe three Seekers in the city, and the talk of a curfew is mostly rumor based on something one person from the base said in an interview. This is all..."

The voices became hard to follow and then were lost completely as the pair got on the bus. Takeshi was only a few people behind, but he was disappointed to see that there were no free spaces anywhere near the two – now quietly arguing – men.

Still, they had given him quite a lot to think on, he mused as he took a seat. Apparently something had happened here, though what that was appeared up for debate. It was enough for him to look into, at least. Perhaps coming to Charve hadn't been a complete waste of time.

He spent the short bus ride considering what he had learned. It wasn't a lot, but it was certainly something. Not enough to draw conclusions from, or even enough for plausible theories, but now he had something to work with. And if two random people had been talking about it while waiting for the bus, he would bet that other people were talking about it too – he would have to be sure to listen.

Takeshi headed for a nearby convenience store when he got off the bus, hoping to pick up a newspaper. He could also try to find the news on the vid screen back at the hotel and see what they had to say – if there was going to be a curfew, they would certainly announce it. Even if it was a rumor, they might discuss it anyway. As he walked briskly past the large windows, he again thought he saw a flutter of black in his reflection, but when he turned his head to see what it was–

:Danger!:

Takeshi forced himself to keep walking at the same pace as he felt himself nearly panic internally, keeping his eye on the window. In the reflection of the glass, he could see a Truth Seeker in gray across the street. He wasn't looking in Takeshi's direction at all; his attention appeared to be on a nearby street light, waiting for it to turn. The people walking past on the sidewalk were giving the Truth Seeker a large berth, clearly not willing to come very close. Some glared, others skittered away. The Seeker didn't seem to notice or care, though it was hard to tell with the cloth covering his eyes.

Takeshi forced himself to breathe evenly and keep walking, focusing on just being one person in a sea of many. Fear would not help him here. Why was he even panicking? He had known this was a possibility and had prepared for it. The Seeker did not seem to be looking for anything in particular – Takeshi did not feel the pulse of magic that would accompany a search. He slipped into the convenience store, keeping the Truth Seeker just on the edges of his perception in case he started to come closer. He would be fine as long as he remained aware of the situation. Unlike shinobi, Truth Seekers were not subtle when it came to their casting, so he would have a warning if it came to that. Not that he wanted to have an altercation with one in the middle of the street; that would be disastrous for his cover.

Takeshi quickly navigated to the newspaper dispenser, swiping his card and taking the paper as it fell out. He wished he dared try to determine how powerful the Seeker was, but he didn't want to accidentally reveal his presence to the other caster. The one he had met before had been significantly less powerful than Takeshi himself, but that wasn't necessarily true of Seekers as a whole. He folded the newspaper up and grabbed a sandwich from the prepared foods section for dinner. As he paid for it, he felt the Truth Seeker fade out of range.

He analyzed the near encounter carefully as he headed back to Redguard Suites. People had been skittish around the Truth Seeker, so he would remember that if he ended up any closer to one. He did think it was a little strange, that their own people seemed to fear them so. He could understand some unease, but not the outright panic and suspicion he had seen. Were they not supposed to protect their citizens? The pirates had also mentioned something similar, that people tended to disappear because of the Blind Ones. Takeshi had assumed that it was in regard to the rebellion, or perhaps lawbreaking in general, though that seemed harsh. However, the way people had acted around the Seeker today had him wondering if that was the case. But why kidnap their own people?

And on the subject of unreasonable fear, why had *he* panicked? There was no excuse for that sort of sloppiness. Paranoia was one thing; acting on it was another.

:Apologies.:

He had had plenty of warning that this was a possibility, and he had just heard evidence that the Truth Seekers were around in greater numbers than before. He had seen this coming and had thoroughly prepared for it, even. It was amateurish of him to react in that way. He'd been lucky this time, but that sort of reaction in a different situation could get him killed.

He continued chastising himself as he unlocked the door to his room. Unhappily, he tossed the paper and sandwich onto the small table and removed his gloves, dropping the illusion as he tried to untangle his anger from his... shame?

:Hear?:

He froze. That wasn't him. Guard up, he reached out mentally, looking for the source of the foreign emotions.

:Here!:

There was a presence. It felt very distant, and also familiar. He felt his eyes widen – it was *the* presence! The one he'd thought he had imagined during his migraine!

:Difficult... to reach.:

Now that he was paying attention, he could just barely hear the whisper of the voice. *Who are you?* he thought at her, trying to strengthen the connection.

:...friend. Trying... help;...rebellion?: Her "voice" was still fading in and out, but there was a strong sensation of sincerity under the words. He wished he knew exactly what she was asking. But...

You panicked, he accused wryly, *and that made* me *panic.*

:Yes! Mistake.: She sounded honestly apologetic. *:Did not....:* She faded out again.

He frowned. *Are you reading me completely, or in pieces? I'm not catching everything you're sending.*

:Fine!: she reassured. *:Something...:* She trailed off, but it felt more deliberate, like she was thinking about something rather than just not coming through. *:Try... this...:*

It was as if she showed him how to use his mind to reach out in a different fashion, a method of telepathy he had never seen before. Instead of using force, like the Empress did, it was more like politely knocking and being welcomed. It also made his earlier attempts to reach her look like someone stumbling around in the dark. *:Thusly?:* he asked.

:Yes! You send... read you.:

He considered that a moment. :*It's a little better, but not by much. You are still going in and out.*:

He could feel her frustration, and she was silent for several minutes. Takeshi let her think on it, contemplating what this could mean. He needed a better way to communicate with her. He had a lot of questions, and it was going to be torture if he could only understand less than a third of every sentence.

:*Mirror?*: she finally asked.

:*What about a mirror?*: he responded, confused.

:*Mirror!*: she insisted, repeating the word over and over.

:*Okay! I'm going,*: he protested, alarmed by the intensity. He strode to the bathroom, where there was a large mirror over the sink. He looked at the mirror and froze in surprise.

Instead of his own reflection, there was the silhouette of a woman, wearing a long black dress and draped in black veils, opaque to the point that he couldn't understand how she was seeing through them. The only skin he could see was the very pale alabaster of her arms and hands.

"Hello?" he tried, staring at her. It was pretty clear this was an avatar of some sort to hide her identity, but why? It wasn't even very subtle; she had literally just covered herself in black fabric.

:*Greetings!*: came the cheerful reply, as the figure in the mirror inclined her head deeply.

"Why are you hiding?" he asked curiously.

:*Not hiding... of Veils,*: came the prim response, whatever that meant. He did get the impression she was a little offended he thought she was hiding. :*...expected to wear... midwinter.*:

He shook his head. "You are still not coming through well."

She shrugged. :*...tried... some... interference. Most... at all.*:

"Well, at least yes or no questions will be easy enough with the mirror. And I think I'm getting the simple thoughts and emotions just fine. So then..." He paused, thinking of what he wanted to ask, and how to ask it. "You are with the rebellion?"

There was an uncomfortably long pause. *:Define?:* she asked sheepishly.

"Define *rebellion*?" His heart sank. "A group of people working to overthrow a government?"

She raised a hand and tilted it back and forth.

"*Kind of?* How are you 'kind of' with a rebellion?" Wasn't that a binary thing? This was not off to a good start.

She pointed to herself and shook her head no, but then indicated the space around her and nodded. *:...know of others...:*

That was a little better. "So you are not specifically with the rebellion, but you know people who are?"

She hesitated but nodded again.

"All right." He considered that. At least it was something. "But you did want me to come to Charve?"

She nodded enthusiastically.

"Why–" He cut himself off, realizing something. "Does it have to do with something that happened two weeks ago?" He felt as if a picture of what was going on was starting to emerge.

For a third time, she nodded. *:...captured!:*

His eyebrows rose. "Someone related to the rebellion was captured? And is being held here..." His voice trailed off as he dashed back to the kitchen table to grab the map and the newspaper, not waiting for the woman to respond. He brought both back to the bathroom, spreading out the map on the counter and putting the paper aside for the moment. "Here," he repeated, pointing to the Charve Military Base, which had recently increased security and drawn more Truth Seekers than normal.

She clapped, nodding happily.

He stared at the map silently. She seemed content to let him piece things together himself, waiting patiently as he slowly realized what it was that she really wanted. "You want me to rescue this person?" he asked softly after several minutes.

Her head tilted to the side as she nodded once.

"That... sounds like almost certain death," he drawled slowly. "But even if I was willing and able, why do you want me to save this person? You said you are not really with the rebellion."

It was her turn to think. Takeshi watched the veiled shape in the mirror as he waited.

:...important to...: she finally answered. He could sense the effort she was putting in to be understood. *:Rescue... bring you to others... get you in.:*

"I see," he murmured as he stared at the map. Prove himself by saving this person and be brought into the rebellion. Aside from being nearly suicidal, it was a good idea. Risking his life for one of their agents did seem like a pretty solid declaration of intent, and he had been wondering how he would gain their favor.

:Difficult, but... not alone... help!:

"I'm not sure how you could, but thanks for the sentiment," he said dryly. He closed his eyes. He was so very tired. "I am going to need some time to think this over, and to find out if what you are asking me is even feasible," he informed her. "It might not be. I have no idea what kind of security I would be dealing with."

She regarded him silently for a moment. Then she nodded. *:Understandable... I will... here. Call... in the mirror, and... come.:*

The black-draped figure in the mirror faded into his normal reflection.

Takeshi sighed, picking up the map and the newspaper and bringing them back into the main room. He had a lot to think about, and a lot to consider, but he already knew what his answer was likely to be. He was already in much too deep to try to withdraw; he should be happy that a path to his goals had finally revealed itself.

It just felt like a really bad idea.

He sighed. He was certain he would dream of Hotaru tonight, and any doubts he had would be swept to the side by duty.

He missed her. She'd had a way of looking at things that made them seem not so bad. He felt like he needed that positivity right now, but it was long gone.

He settled on the bed with the newspaper, determined to make the best he could of the situation.

"Oh, you're back! I have a question for you!"

Rhode paused upon entering the room. How did she know he was there? For what felt like the hundredth time, he glanced at the screens, but everything still read green.

"Perhaps I have an answer," he offered, determined not to let her throw him, even if violet eyes were already tracking his movements as he put the tablet he had been holding down on a nearby table.

"Have you ever considered... wait, no, let me explain. The Rose Empire has the Truth Seekers, mages who are – in some places – called 'Blind Ones', right?" She sounded far too excited for someone who had been in isolation for the last several days.

"Everyone knows Truth Seekers use tech, not magic," he responded calmly.

"Oh please, you and I both know that isn't true. It might be what you tell your people, but it is a lie." She waved a hand as though it were a minor annoyance, completely dismissing his comment as she continued, "And Ni Fon has the shinobi, mages who are – in some places – called 'Silent Ones'. See where I'm going with this yet?"

"Ni Fon is part of the Empire, so it has both, I suppose," he agreed, not at all sure where this was going, but willing to let it play out. Major Cole entered behind him, tapping at her own tablet.

"So, my question is this. Do you think that there might be some places that call the Black Watch – the mages of Romanii – 'Deaf Ones'?" She stared at him intently, violet eyes glinting as her ears twitched.

Rhode blinked. "Are many members of the Black Watch hard of hearing?"

"What? No! Truth Seekers aren't actually blind, and shinobi aren't actually mute; that's not the point." She pouted.

He waited.

"'See no evil, hear no evil, speak no evil'?" the Avari asked after a moment.

Rhode turned, meeting Cole's confused look with his own. She shrugged.

"The three... wise... you have no idea what I'm talking about, do you?" The disappointment in her voice was palpable.

"The three wise what?" he asked, wondering if he could draw it out of her. Two weeks, and they had frighteningly little to show for it. He wished they dared go in.

"No, never mind. I'll have to save that for later, I'm afraid. Someone back home will get it, I'm sure." The Avari sighed dramatically, flopping into a boneless heap on the floor.

"I thought we were being honest with each other?" Rhode reminded her. "We both know you will never leave this containment unit alive."

She laughed softly. "Then we don't actually understand each other very much at all, do we?"

Chapter Seventeen

J amirh wasn't proud to admit that he spent the next few days hiding in his rooms. He felt awkward and uncertain knowing that the Vampires thought he was the Hero reborn, and he wasn't sure what to do or how to respond to that. He also wasn't on speaking terms with the one person who might have been able to help.

So he did what he did best – avoided the problem completely.

He had a lot of random reading material to distract him, even if some of it was rather dry, and meals were being delivered to his rooms. The circumstances of his arrival and the resulting fallout aside, Jamirh was better off than he had ever been. He had an excellent roof over his head, things to occupy his time with, and plenty of food – all of which was being supplied to him with zero effort on his part. He had always had to work for such things, scavenge and steal and scuffle. Now, meals were brought to his room by servants, and he was left to his own devices. He could do whatever he wanted without fear for survival for the first time ever.

He thought that maybe the people who would care the most about him hiding in his rooms were involved in the preparations for the upcoming festival, so he took full advantage of their distraction to do absolutely nothing. He slept in, took long baths, lazed about on the fancy couches, made sculptures out of the frankly ridiculous number of pillows, flipped through a book made up mostly of drawings of different plants, read a mystery novel. He spent some time gazing out his window at the city, watching people scurry around like ants below, trying to get everything in order before Saturday's festival.

When he wasn't entertaining himself, most of his thoughts were taken up by his conversation with Vlad. He ran through it in his mind over and over again, picking it apart, looking for ways to try to disprove their theories. He thought back to the stories of Ebryn Stormlight that he knew, but it had been a long time and most of his memories on the topic were faded. He was left with very little to prove or disprove his identity. The best thing he had going for him was that he was of a completely different temperament than Ebryn, but that didn't seem to be a concern to the Vampires at all. It certainly didn't seem to bother Vlad.

Jamirh wasn't sure a logical argument would work even if he could construct one – the goddess had spoken, and it wasn't like the Vampires were going to take his word over hers. From what he could tell, her word was *literally* law around here.

He was not going to touch that sword.

Vlad's words about Jeri trying to help him also wouldn't leave him alone. Jamirh didn't usually hold grudges for very long to begin with, and she had been his only anchor in this strange place. He found himself missing her company even though he was still upset at how much she had been keeping from him. Several times, he thought of seeking her out, but he didn't have the slightest idea of how to find her. He didn't even know for sure if she was in the palace anymore, or if she had been sent out to go do Black Watch things.

As his thoughts chased themselves in circles, the self-imposed isolation was slowly beginning to get to him. He had always been around other Avari. Black-fields wasn't exactly the safest part of Lyndiniam, and there was safety in numbers. Homeless Avari often congregated in groups to sleep or to distribute a good haul, if there was enough to share. Jamirh hadn't been especially close with anyone since Aether, but he had floated around several groups and had a few acquaintances he socialized with when he could stand the teasing and the references to the Hero. He was used to being around people, even if he wasn't close to them. Here, he had no one to talk to – even the servants who brought his food exchanged little more than a pleasant greeting before leaving.

After three days of almost no social interaction, Jamirh's growing restlessness convinced him to try to strike out on his own. Vlad and Jeri had both told him that the city was safe, and he wanted to get out and see more of it. The Festival of Night was going to be the next day, and he was curious how the city was being set up. It was midmorning – plenty of time to explore.

Jamirh opened the door to his room and looked out. The hallway was empty. He stepped fully out and closed the door behind him, trying to remember what Vlad had said about navigating the palace. He had to believe he knew where he was going, which was difficult, since he did not in fact know where he was going.

Except... he did know where he wanted to go, which was the palace entrance. He cleared his throat.

"Uh... excuse me? Palace?" he asked out loud, feeling like an idiot. "I would like to leave," he finished quickly, before turning right and hoping for the best, thinking very hard about the large doors that dominated the castle entrance.

Amazingly, after only a few minutes and three flights of stairs, he found himself in the large entryway, people moving about everywhere. "Thank you," he whispered, hoping no one heard him speaking to the air as he scurried out of the building.

No one stopped him, or even seemed to look twice at him, to Jamirh's relief. He looked around at the front courtyard, seeing the statue of Hades draped in black fabric beyond the gate, and decided to head in that direction.

He was determined to have a good time. He didn't have any money, but that had never stopped him before. He swung by a street cart to filch a fried pastry filled with a soft cheese, then strolled through the city munching on his treat.

Vaguely, he wondered what the penalties were for stealing here. Based on what he'd seen so far, they couldn't possibly be worse than back home. He generally preferred to know what he was risking before he risked it, but these people were all so... nice. How bad could it possibly be?

Though Jeri would probably disapprove. And Vlad. And Hel.

This was why he preferred not to become attached to people. Worrying about what other people thought of his behavior got exhausting after a while.

He wandered through the streets, enjoying the festive atmosphere. People were mingling everywhere he looked, cheerfully exchanging greetings as they went about their business. Even Jamirh was wished a happy Festival by several people he passed. Practically every bit of Tarvishte was adorned in lights and decorations. He was interested to see that some sections of the streets and some buildings were blocked off, signs nearby stating to come back during the festival. Or... Festival? Who called a festival "Festival"? It seemed a bit lazy.

He wondered what sorts of events and attractions were going to be held; Jeri had told him a little, but he was very curious how it was all going to play out. Was it really all free? He couldn't imagine the dukes and duchesses of the Empire, or even the Emperor himself, springing for entertainment for the masses back home. There were festivals and events, sure – but you still had to pay for the food and other stuff, sometimes even entry.

He looked down at his last few bites of stolen pastry. Had *this* been free? When did the free stuff start?

He stopped at another veiled statue. This one was draped in white fabric. Jamirh had noticed that the statues that had the staff were covered in white, and those that had the polearm were covered in black. He wondered why – it was clearly deliberate, but what did it mean? Why black and white? What was the symbolism behind the staff and the weapon? He wished he knew a little more about the death goddess, but aside from people occasionally asking her to stay away, no one in the Empire ever really invoked her, never mind worshiped her. Who would?

Well, all of these people, apparently. Had he seen even a single shrine or temple to any other deity since he had crossed the Wall? He wasn't sure.

"Do the lights look even to you?"

Jamirh whipped around. A tall man was standing right behind him, looking critically at the statue. He looked to be in his late thirties. His bright-green eyes and short white messy hair said Avari, but his ears, to Jamirh's confusion, were just barely pointed. Jamirh's gaze flicked between them and the long, prominent scar that ran almost vertically down his face from the center of his hairline to almost his mouth, passing just to the left of his nose. It looked like whatever had caused it had just missed his eye. "The lights?" he asked, ears dropping slightly in confusion as he pulled his gaze away from the man back to the statue.

"Yes, down at the bottom," the man clarified, waving a hand vaguely in the statue's direction. His voice had a strange accent that Jamirh couldn't place.

Jamirh looked down at the circular base of the statue. Sure enough, there were lights strung up around it. "Uh... they look fine to me?"

"Hmm." The man walked past Jamirh over to the statue and tugged very slightly on one of the strands of lights. He turned back to Jamirh, tilting his head to the side curiously. "Is that better?"

Jamirh could not possibly think of how anyone would be able to tell the difference. "It looks the same to me," he admitted honestly.

The man took a step back from the statue and stared at it intensely for a moment. Then he nodded. "Much better," he declared, slipping his hands into the pockets of the long white coat he was wearing. "Thank you for your help," he added, almost like an afterthought.

Okay, sure. "No problem," Jamirh said with a shrug. This man was strange; something about his behavior felt familiar, though Jamirh couldn't place why. His eyes flicked again to the man's ears.

"Something I can help you with?" the man asked pleasantly, still looking at the statue.

Jamirh was not about to be that rude, but he did have the other question. "This might be a stupid thing to ask, but why do the white statues have a staff with a crystal, and the black ones the spear-like weapon?"

Green eyes slid to him briefly before returning to the statue. "The weapon She carries is called a glaive. The Lady draped in black celebrates the aspects of death and destruction: She who is warrior. The Lady draped in white celebrates the aspects of healing and rebirth: She who is guardian."

Jamirh frowned. "She is worshiped as the goddess of healing, too?"

The man chuckled. "Not from around here, are you, kid?" Something in his eyes gleamed knowingly. "The Lady is the Great Healer. When all other healers have failed, it is She who eases the suffering of mortals."

"Oh." Privately, Jamirh wasn't sure that counted, though it did make a twisted sort of sense. "Well, thanks for the info." He turned to walk away.

"By all means. Feel free to ask me anything, anytime."

Jamirh blinked at him, a little weirded out by that response. He tugged at the key around his neck, uncertain. "I'm good; thanks." He paused. "Happy Festival."

"Happy Festival," the man responded, seemingly absorbed in looking at the statue.

Jamirh lengthened his stride to melt back into the throng of people passing by. The encounter had been unsettling in a way he couldn't quite describe. The ears were especially strange, though; they hadn't been the ears of either a Human or an Avari, and Jamirh couldn't think of another race that was described that way.

He continued wandering around the city for a little while longer. He kept an eye out for the strange man, but thankfully did not come across him again. He meandered about, taking note of some places he might want to try to revisit the following night. Finally, he decided that he should return to the palace if he wanted his free dinner, and he began to head back.

Past the gates, he saw a large, white-blonde warg lying just out of the way of the foot traffic. Her tail wagged twice when she saw him looking at her, green eyes not quite meeting his silver.

He sighed, fiddling with his key. It was hard to argue with an overly large dog, which may have been the point. "Come on," he said, waving her over. "We need to talk."

She hauled herself up, looking awfully contrite for a canine, and padded silently behind him as he led the way back into the palace. He paused when they entered, but just long enough to focus on reversing the exact route he had taken that morning to return to his rooms before heading off to the left-most staircase. He was pleased and relieved to find himself by room 401 several minutes later, glad that the palace seemed to be working for him now.

He turned to Jeri, whose form was shifting back into Human. "You've figured out where your rooms are," she said quietly. "I'm glad you are not getting lost anymore."

Jamirh stared at her for a moment before opening the door. "Come in," he said shortly, ignoring her pained expression. He didn't have to make this easy for her. She was in the wrong. He shut the door behind them and sat himself down in the middle of the couch, gesturing towards one of the armchairs.

Jeri sat down carefully on the edge of the chair, looking extremely uncomfortable. She pulled her braid over her shoulder and fidgeted with it for a second before folding her hands deliberately in her lap. "I owe you an apology," she began, "for essentially kidnapping you under misleading pretenses."

Jamirh raised an eyebrow but said nothing.

"Well, for helping Hel kidnap you, since I suppose she set the stage and tone. Which I criticized her for, and then hypocritically continued myself." She paused, then looked down. "It was easier to expect that Vlad would explain things to you than to try to untangle it myself, even when I knew we had the time and the space to discuss it. For that, I am sorry."

"You criticized Hel? When?" He didn't remember that.

"You were unconscious at the time, since she had failed to explain my presence," Jeri explained with a slight wince.

"Oh." He felt his face heat as he remembered that awkward encounter. That hadn't been his best moment. "Got it."

She nodded. "I am also sorry for the distress you suffered, both on the road and while here. It was never my intention to upset you. For what it's worth, I don't think it was Hel's intention, either. We just..." She trailed off, before rallying. "We just wanted you to be safe, and that meant removing you from the Empire. I'm not sorry for that, though perhaps we could have gone about it better."

To be fair to them both, Jamirh himself was pleased he wasn't in the Empire anymore either. He considered her for a moment. "Are we really friends?"

Her head snapped up. "What do you mean?"

"Did you – and Hel, I guess – pretend to like me and be my friend because you think I was Ebryn? Or because you were friends with him?"

Jeri's eyes were wide. "No! That's... not something I would do for a job. I can't really speak for Hel, but she's not the kind of person who pretends to like people either. She'd probably be quite upset that you would think that. And I definitely wasn't friends with Ebryn."

"You said you had met him before," he reminded her.

She nodded. "Once. The encounter was less than pleasant."

Oh? "Tell me about it." He wanted to know.

She blinked at him in surprise, then looked thoughtful. "It was a very long time ago, obviously. I was... maybe about ten? Just a normal Human child at the time. My mother worked in the palace as head housekeeper, so my friends and I were used to playing all over the place. No one minded; we didn't cause any trouble. Kids are always running all around here. We were playing tag one day, and I was trying to escape one of the other children and wasn't paying attention. I accidentally crashed right into Ebryn, nearly fell over." Jeri's voice was wry. "My first thought was that he had very pretty hair and eyes. But he had grabbed my arm to keep me from falling, and he was hurting me. Then he snapped at me to watch where I was going. The Aradian lady he was with told him very disapprovingly that he should be kinder to children, and asked me if I was okay. I remember scurrying back to my friends, feeling like his glare was burning a hole in my back. He scared me quite badly."

"The Aradian was Sukra?" Jamirh asked, thinking of the desert woman who had followed Ebryn on his quest to find the crystal lights. She wasn't often mentioned in the tales, though she had supposedly been present for most of the journey.

"Yes, though I didn't learn either of their names at the time. I watched them leave a few days later from behind a column and thought, 'Good riddance.' I had bruises on my arm for days afterwards where he had gripped me." She shrugged. "In retrospect, it was a little thing, but rather upsetting to me as a child. It stuck

with me. I thought of him as 'the mean red man' for a while, because of his hair –
he wore it in a ponytail too, but kept it longer than yours – and only learned his
name much later, after he had returned to bargain with the Lady for the Blade. So,
please believe me when I say I much prefer you to Ebryn. You are very different
people, from what I can tell."

Jamirh frowned, ears twitching down. "He sounds like kind of a jerk."

Jeri shrugged again. "He does. I don't know that he meant to hurt me; it's
possible he didn't know how tightly he had grabbed me. It did seem to be a
reflexive action. Vlad says that Ebryn had his reasons for being the way he was,
but to child-me, he was definitely harsher than he had any reason to be."

"So, why did you come looking for him... me... whoever, if you didn't like
him?" Jamirh was puzzled by this. "And were there no other Vampires who met
with him who would remember what he looked like? You were a kid who literally
just bumped into him."

"Not liking someone is a poor reason to let them die," she pointed out. "It's
not like I loathed him, or anything. I just... strongly disliked him. As I grew older,
and the rest of the tale came to light, I did feel a little bad for him. In the end,
he disappeared into the ether, and the whole story felt a bit tragic even if he
did technically win. And according to Ander and the Lady, we had already lost
a reincarnation of Ebryn, and had good reason to believe that the same could
happen to you."

She leaned her chin on her hand. "Why me, though? Strangely, my accidental
encounter was one of the few interactions he had with people in Tarvishte. He
wasn't much of a people person and kept to himself. Vlad said he was very focused
on his task, and not interested in anything that did not work directly towards his
goal. There were other Vampires who met him – Vlad, for one – but of all the
current members of the Black Watch, I was the one with the strongest recollection
of him with the skills to infiltrate the Empire and extract you. It was a thousand
years ago, and our memories do fade over time."

That was a lot of information to think about. He hadn't even considered that
Jeri might not have liked Ebryn, or that she had only been a child when she

met him. Before coming here, he hadn't thought anyone would have disliked the Hero. It was a relief to hear from another person that he wasn't like his namesake at all, though the major personality difference still wasn't selling that he wasn't the Hero reborn to the Vampires.

He supposed he didn't actually care if he had legitimately been Ebryn. He wasn't him now, and he didn't want anything to do with him.

"What do you know about this whole 'Abomination' thing?" he asked after several minutes of silence.

She cocked her head to the side. "What do you mean?"

"Vlad said that the whole reason the Hero was supposedly called back to the land of the living was because there was apparently 'Abomination' in the world again, and that the last time it took the form of demons tearing holes in the fabric of reality or something. But what about this time? Do you all really know nothing about it except that it is somehow present?"

Jeri looked sheepish. "Unfortunately, that is true. We would feel much better about the whole situation if we knew what form the current threat is taking. However, despite our efforts, we just don't know."

Jamirh frowned, ears lowering. "What if it is something that can't be fought? Then what would the point have been in bringing back a swordsman?"

She looked confused.

"Like, what if it's something like a plague brewing somewhere, or a discovery someone is going to make? Can the Crystal Light Blade fix problems it can't stab? If none of you can find it, then maybe it's because you are not looking for the right thing. I think we would have noticed demons popping up in this day and age."

"I suppose that's a possibility," Jeri conceded. "But an Abomination has to be something that affects the fabric of reality. A plague or discovery wouldn't do that, as far as I'm aware. Those things could be bad, but they don't go against the laws of existence or nature."

"But demons do?" What was the difference?

Jeri shrugged. "I'm sorry, but I'm not a theologian or a philosopher. Maybe Ander might have a better explanation, but... to be honest, it would likely be incomprehensible. Be prepared for a three-hour-long presentation that leaves you feeling like you know less than when you started."

"You said something along those lines before. Is he really that bad at explaining things?" Jamirh asked quizzically.

"I'm sure he would say everyone else is just bad at understanding him," she said with a sigh, "and the truth is that he is brilliant. Ander is an amazing surgeon and healer, though he generally prefers 'doctor'. But... he's a little too smart, I think. He understands concepts perfectly, and usually does not understand why everyone else doesn't. Then he usually fails at explaining them in a way anyone else can understand."

"Uh huh," Jamirh drawled. "I'm not sure I want to meet this man."

Jeri cringed. "He's likely to find you, eventually. I would bet the only reason he hasn't sought you out already is that he's working on Festival things. He does tend to get very focused on tasks."

"Great," he muttered. "That's what I need – another weird person following me around."

The Vampire smiled weakly. "Hel wasn't that bad, was she?"

He gave her a dry look. "She was pretty crazy." He dropped his gaze. She had been crazy, and she hadn't told the complete truth about why she was saving him, but... she had been saving him, and she'd done a lot to ensure he got to safety. And then they left her behind. "Do you think she's okay? I would have thought she'd have caught up by now."

Jeri's eyes turned sad. "We've received word she was captured and brought to a military base in Charve, unfortunately."

Jamirh's eyes widened as he jerked back in surprise and horror. "What?!"

"There's not much chance of rescue, that deep into the Empire, but we are hoping she'll manage to get herself out," Jeri continued optimistically. "The situation is pretty bad, but Hel is full of all sorts of surprises. The Empire won't know what hit them."

"You're just going to leave her there?" His fingers found his key. That didn't sit right with him at all.

Jeri hesitated. "If there is something we can do, we will do it. But right now... she's rather on her own. Don't worry too much – if anyone could manage it, it's her."

"How can you say that?!" Jamirh exclaimed. "Do you have any idea what those bases are like?"

"Yes," she replied shortly.

He stared at her, a little taken aback.

She sighed and shook her head. "There's nothing we can do about it right now on our end. Trust me, we do not want to leave her there. If there is anything we can do, we will do it. But for right now, all we can do is wait."

Jamirh huffed an annoyed breath. How many lives were going to be ruined over this ridiculous theory that he was Ebryn?

Chapter Eighteen

Jamirh looked down at the little black card in his hand, marked with silver ink. "Lunch? I mean, sure, of course I'll go, but why lunch? I thought dinner was the formal, invite-only meal of the day."

Jeri smiled from where she was leaning against the doorframe. She had come by late in the morning with a pair of black cards, which were apparently invitations to a formal Festival luncheon with the court. "Usually, yes, but dinner is not a real meal today. Most people will be eating all sorts of junk from dusk to dawn, so the court holds a late lunch instead of dinner on the day of Festival." She paused. "Wear something nice for lunch, but you can change into whatever you want for the festivities afterwards."

"How many people are usually at this thing?" he asked curiously, ears twitching. "What are the expectations? Do I have to know what fork to use when?"

"For a formal court meal? Usually around a hundred people or so. This meal won't be as formal as normal court dinners; it's served buffet-style. Guests sit wherever they want as long as there's an open seat and it's not the head table – those seats are assigned. Don't worry," she said with a laugh upon seeing the face he made, "Vlad didn't think you'd enjoy that, so we will be with the majority of the guests in the free-for-all. The atmosphere is usually quite festive, and there won't be much ceremony. No one is likely to notice what cutlery you are using."

"Is there a lot of food? Like, if it's a buffet, how many plates am I allowed to have?"

She rolled her eyes at him. "Yes, there will be a lot of food. One plate at a time is polite, but there's no upper limit."

"Awesome!" he chirped. "Do we have to RSVP, or will they just assume we are coming?"

"It is generally assumed most people will say yes to a formal court invitation," she said dryly. "No need to RSVP. Find something to wear; I'm going to run a few errands, but I'll be back in time for lunch." With a quick wave she was gone, the door swinging shut behind her.

Jamirh sighed, ears drooping slightly. He felt both better and worse after their conversation the previous night – better about Jeri, and worse about Hel. He felt horribly guilty that Hel had been captured because of him. He hadn't asked her to help him leave the Empire, but she had still been trying to help him.

He was glad he had made up with Jeri, at least – he was certain this was going to be a lot more fun with a friend than it would be alone. And she could explain things for him so he wouldn't have to ask any creepy strangers.

He considered his clothing, settling on a sharp-looking outfit of black with red trim as probably the most formal of the few outfits he owned. He changed, eyeing his reflection in the mirror. He barely even recognized himself. Had it really only been two weeks since the party at the Silver Ring Casino? It felt like years.

He ran a brush through his hair quickly and tied it back again. There, now he was ready to go. He didn't have much time, so he settled down with a science-fiction novel to wait.

Jeri returned, wearing a bronze-and-green gown that flared out at the bottom. She handed a black masquerade mask to Jamirh, keeping a gold-and-ivory one for herself.

"A mask? What for?" Jamirh asked curiously, admiring the subtle detailing on the mask.

"To wear at lunch. Everyone will have them on. Originally, worshipers of Hades wore masks for the Festival of Night as a sort of emulation of Her veils – since they both cover the face, and Her first priest is a man who refuses to wear a veil – but over time these small masks have gained in fashion, so now it's more of a suggestion of the idea rather than actually copying it."

"Huh." He flipped it over, examining it. "How does it stay on?"

"The inside is coated with a mild adhesive that sticks to skin. It will peel off with a gentle tug," she informed him. "Shall we?"

They donned their masks as Jamirh let Jeri lead the way. She took him deeper into the palace to a large hall, where very well-dressed people were milling about and talking to each other. The pair threaded their way through the crowd to reach a pair of tall, open doors, which led to an opulent dining room. Tables laden with trays of food lined the walls, and people were eating and chatting at a number of tables in the center. Another table sat empty on a raised dais across the room.

Jamirh didn't know where to begin.

Jeri guided him to one of the buffet tables, and Jamirh wasted no time in filling up a plate before following her to a table to eat. He looked around curiously as they took their seats, wondering how many of the surrounding Humans and Avari were actually Vampires.

"Where is the king?" he asked, glancing back at the raised table. "I'd have thought he would be over there?"

"Vlad's wandering around here somewhere," she assured him, looking around. Jamirh took advantage of her momentary distraction to stealthily grab a shrimp off her plate and pop it in his mouth. "He likes to socialize. The rest of the people who normally sit up there are probably mingling as well."

"Some of us enjoy socializing more than others," came a familiar, strangely accented voice from right behind Jamirh.

He startled, nearly inhaling the shrimp in surprise, and started coughing.

"Please, don't die," the man said mildly, strolling around the table so Jamirh could see him. "That would be extremely counterproductive at this juncture."

Wearing a dark-gray-and-black mask was the strange man with the odd ears from the day before.

Jeri shot an unimpressed look at the white-haired man. "High Priest." The censure dripped from her voice. "Jamirh, this is—"

Jamirh got himself under control and interrupted her. "You!" he accused.

"Me," the man agreed.

Jeri looked between them, expression fading into confusion. "I'm sorry, did you already meet?"

"Not really," Jamirh exclaimed in exasperation, as the other man answered, "He was very helpful in adjusting a string of lights."

Jeri stared at them for a moment, before sighing. "Right. Jamirh," she said, sounding very tired, "this is Ander, one of the Lady's High Priests. Ander, this is Jamirh." Her tone turned warning.

"I know who he is," Ander brushed her off, sounding amused. "Not much has changed since the first time we spoke."

Jeri's expression darkened as Jamirh frowned, trying to figure out why that sounded strange, but before Jeri could say anything another voice cut in. "Ander," Vlad said pleasantly as he and a woman in a deep-red gown approached the table. "Please. Jeri, no murder on Festival night."

Ander inclined his head in Vlad's direction and took a step back. "My apologies," he said smoothly.

"Lord," Jeri murmured in greeting, also inclining her head to Vlad.

Jamirh nodded politely, his eyes skipping to the woman. She had warm brown skin and violet-colored hair pinned up in an intricate style, revealing her round ears. Her burgundy-colored mask did not fully cover the darkly pigmented markings around her eyes, nor did it do anything to hide their blue-green color that flickered and smoldered like cinders behind glass.

An Aradian.

"Lady Miravu, this is Jeri, of the Black Watch, and Jamirh, who is a guest of my House," Vlad introduced them. Jamirh fought to ignore the snort from Ander. "Jamirh, Jeri, this is Lady Miravu, the ambassador from Dalmara."

"Many greetings," she said, the cinders in her eyes flickering into flames as she gazed at Jamirh, "and a happy Festival, yes?" Her voice was heavily accented.

Jamirh had never seen an Aradian in person before; he found the effect of her eyes extremely disconcerting. "H-happy Festival," he stammered, fighting not to cringe back from under her gaze.

"Happy Festival," Jeri repeated calmly, taking a sip from her glass. "And how are you finding the experience, Ambassador?"

"Very interesting, so far, but the true experience is later, no? I have been told I have much to look forward to," she replied, glancing away from Jamirh only briefly. "Things are done here very differently from our celebrations at home. There is joy to be found in the discovery of something new, no?"

Jamirh glanced around, noticing Ander frowning at the ambassador.

"Indeed so," Vlad agreed. "And there will be many things to do later. Right now, why don't we attempt to experience some of the buffet? If you will come with me, Ambassador. Happy Festival, Jeri, Jamirh, Ander."

"May the Fires light your path," Miravu intoned with a shallow bow, moving with Vlad to the buffet after the group had shared their goodbyes.

Jamirh watched them go for a moment before turning back to Jeri and Ander, who was staring at him intensely. "I don't suppose–"

Jeri cut the priest off. "No, you don't, Ander."

He frowned at her. "You're no fun at all."

"I have no idea what's going on," Jamirh stated, turning back to his plate as he eyed the rest of Jeri's shrimp. He really should have grabbed some of those. "But this is really good." Unfortunately, it was also reminding him of Hel and her wish for shrimp and pasta.

Ander laughed at that. "I'm sure the staff will be pleased to hear."

"On a scale of one to ten, how upset is Hel likely to be that she's missing this?" Jamirh asked. "Because this whole thing feels like something she would enjoy."

Jeri winced. "She was rather looking forward to Festival this year."

Ander raised an eyebrow. "Don't worry – she'll be here, she just won't be" – he gestured wildly next to him – "here."

They stared at him.

"Thank you for that clarification, Ander," Jeri muttered after a moment.

Jamirh squinted at him. "Do you mean that she'll be here in spirit?"

"Exactly so," Ander declared with a definitive nod.

Jeri gave a pained sigh, slowly hiding her face in her hands.

"I don't think that's the same thing?" Jamirh asked carefully.

"No?" Ander tilted his head to the side curiously.

"No," Jamirh said, slowly shaking his head.

Ander grinned at him. "As enlightening as this has been, I should be moving on. I meant what I said yesterday, kid – feel free to ask me anything, anytime, though you may wish to lose your guard dog first." He ignored Jeri's affronted exclamation. "You can usually find me in the Temple, or somewhere on palace grounds. Any member of the Watch should be able to locate me if you can't. Have a happy Festival." He raised his hand in a lazy wave and strode off without waiting for a response from either of them.

Jamirh stared after him.

Jeri coughed. "So, that's Ander."

"Wow," he declared. "He's... something. Is he okay?"

"Yeah." Jeri drew the word out. "How did you meet him yesterday? I assume it was when you were out in the city?"

"Yup," he confirmed. "I was looking at one of Hades' statues when he asked me about the lights being uneven or something out of nowhere. It looked fine to me." Jamirh shrugged. His hand fiddled with his key absently. "But the whole encounter was bizarre. I guess I know why, now." Ander had been looking for him, probably. And he had definitely known who Jamirh was. Jamirh looked around, seeing Ander sitting with the king and the ambassador at the high table, and decided it was probably safe to ask. "Why are his ears like that?"

Jeri blinked. "His ears?" She glanced up at the dais. Jamirh stole another shrimp. "Oh, yes. Ander is half-Avari, half-Human."

Jamirh almost spat out his food for the second time. "*What?!* Is that even possible?"

"Clearly," Jeri said dryly, "though it is very rare. I don't pretend to know anything about the genetics involved, but the two species do not breed easily, from my understanding."

"I can't even imagine a Human and an Avari liking each other enough to try. That would never happen in the Empire."

Jeri raised an eyebrow. "Ander is from the Empire, though he was born quite some time ago, before relations between the races really broke down."

That sounded familiar, actually, even if the concept was still utterly alien. "Oh yeah, I think Vlad mentioned something along those lines... that Ander left the Empire, like, three hundred years ago or so? And he took the Crystal Light Blade with him?" Jamirh hadn't considered it before, but... "Is Ander a Vampire? How is he so old?"

Jeri laughed. "No, Ander is not a Vampire. A benefit of being a priest of the goddess of death is not dying. And three hundred years is pretty young, by our count."

"Not by mine, it's not," Jamirh snorted.

"Age is relative," she said with a smile. "A few centuries tends to give you a little extra perspective. And for what it's worth, Ander does not wish you harm. You're right – he did take the Blade from the Empire, and I think it makes the whole situation a little more personal to him." She considered him seriously for a moment. "If – and this is a big, very unlikely if – something were to happen, and you think that you are in danger, *find Ander*. You might not like him personally, but he is the most capable person in this city when it comes to defense."

"What do you mean, 'if something were to happen'?" he asked. "I thought Tarvishte was safe?"

"Oh, it is," she hastened to reassure him. "I certainly don't expect anything to happen; I'm just saying that in the extremely unlikely possibility of danger, Ander is your best bet. Healing and defensive magic are his specialties, and priests of the Lady are capable of some pretty ridiculous things when they feel the situation calls for it."

Jamirh hummed thoughtfully. "Defensive magic? Like shields? Hel said she was very good at that kind of magic, too."

"She is, yes. Most of..." She trailed off, looking down at her plate with a confused frown.

"Is something wrong?" Jamirh asked as he finished off his own plate.

"No, it's just... I could have sworn I had more shrimp."

"Maybe you ate them without paying attention," Jamirh shrugged. "And there's always more, right?" He glanced back over to the buffet tables.

"True," she said slowly, before shaking her head. "Let's finish up; we have fun stuff to do tonight."

Jamirh was not a stranger to city-wide celebrations. Though they didn't celebrate the Festival of Night, Lyndiniam did celebrate the anniversary of the Emperor's ascension to the throne every year as well as various holidays such as the Harvest Celebration and Trinity Day. Widespread partying when a sports team won a championship was also not uncommon.

None of that, not even the anniversary of the Emperor, came even close to what Tarvishte did for the Festival of Night.

Jamirh had thought he'd had an idea of what it was going to look like based on his excursion the day before, but it was clear there were some decorations that had been saved for today. Lanterns had been hung from almost every conceivable spot, and paper cutouts of wargs, bats, and pumpkins were strung together and wrapped around poles or threaded overhead across the streets. Actual pumpkins had been carved to have faces and were lit from within in colors of purple, orange, or yellow. Motes of light hung in the air above people's heads, many of whom wore masks or had painted faces and were dressed as all manner of creatures.

Taken all together, it was one of the coolest things Jamirh had ever seen.

True to Jeri's word, there were plenty of food and drink stands with all manner of treats to try. Most gave out small portions, which Jamirh didn't mind because it meant he could try even more things. His favorite thing so far had been the mini iced pumpkin bread shaped like an actual pumpkin, closely followed by a hot pumpkin-flavored coffee drink.

The first thing Jeri took him to was a haunted house, though she warned him before they went in that nothing inside the building was actually real. The entire building had been set up so visitors walked along a set path through each of the rooms, and a thick fog obscured any ability to see outside the immediate area. People dressed up as various creatures and monsters jumped out at them from around corners and behind furniture, and there were creepy sights and sounds everywhere. The last room even had a ghost that breezed right through Jamirh as he approached the exit. Even though Jeri had said nothing was real, it looked very real to Jamirh and succeeded in disturbing him in a way nothing else in the house had.

They went back to the palace to explore the large maze that had taken over a portion of the gardens. Part hedge and part haybale, it twisted and turned in ways that made Jamirh lose track of where he was in minutes. Jeri taught him a trick of always going left, and said that while it might take longer, you were guaranteed to get out eventually. The center of the maze had a veiled statue of Hades, decorated with lit pumpkins and candles and actual wargs – Jamirh counted fourteen of them lounging around. Occasionally, one would happily wander over to people who had food and give very sad looks, clearly hoping for a treat of their own. The veils on the statue seemed to billow in an unnatural breeze, constantly in motion, making it seem eerily alive. Faint apparitions floated at the edges of the clearing, hazy green mist forming the veiled shapes that drifted around each other.

After that, they went to an area of the city that had been closed off the day before. Games had been set up under tents around the large cobbled square, and children and adults alike were competing for candy prizes. Jamirh handily beat Jeri at climbing a rock wall and scurrying up a suspended rope ladder before losing horribly to her at darts and archery.

As they headed over to a knife-throwing booth, Jamirh found himself commenting, "There's an awful lot of weaponry at this festival." He could see swords and axes a little farther down as well. A group of children ran by. "Isn't it dangerous?"

Jeri shrugged. "No more than the magic contests, and between weapons and magic most citizens are often armed in some way anyway."

Jamirh raised an eyebrow, ears twitching slightly. "There are magic contests?" He paused. "Most citizens are armed?" In Blackfields Avari usually had something on them for defense, but he didn't think the normal Lyndiniam Human walked around with anything dangerous that wasn't purely for show.

"Sure. Usually little things – mage lights, lighting small fires, illusions." She studied her knife for a moment, tossing it into the air once before throwing it straight to the bullseye. "Many people have at least some affinity with magic, so those games tend to be popular. And yes, small weapons like knives are common among the general public, though you occasionally see swords. Carrying a weapon is seen as being fairly traditional according to the old ways, when Humans and Avari were less trusting of Vampires on the whole. And magic is what it is."

Jamirh looked up to the top of the tent, where several brightly colored bats were flying around leaving trails of light behind them. "Illusions seem to be popular. Was the ghost at the end of the haunted house also an illusion?" Citizens here carried weapons because at some point they had feared Vampires. Interesting.

She nodded, following his gaze. "Yes. Things like these, which are anchored in one spot and don't need to actually look real, are fairly easy. A realistic illusion is much more difficult – you'd be surprised what the eye can pick up on without knowing it. You could be tipped off that something is not right without understanding why." She threw another knife, which landed beside the first. "Not impossible, but it takes a skilled mage to build the right array and execute it properly."

Jamirh hummed thoughtfully, watching her technique closely. He didn't want to lose any fingers, and the knives looked sharp. "What about making yourself invisible? Would that be an illusion?"

"Yes, though that is very difficult to pull off. There's a lot of variables to consider for true invisibility." She tossed her third knife, forming a neat cluster. "I guess illusions are something you don't see in the Empire, if there's no magic."

It was his turn to shrug. "They've been messing around with hologram tech for a while; I think it gets used a lot at concerts nowadays for visual effects. Looks pretty similar to what I've seen today. I don't know about invisibility, though. I don't think holograms can be used that way? They create images; they don't erase them." He picked up his first knife, studying it the way she had studied hers without knowing what he was looking for. It was a little heavier than he had expected.

She cocked her head to the side slightly. "The uses for tech increase day by day, it seems. I can see why the Empire leans on it as a substitute for magic. Illusion magic is popular for our concerts as well. It's a shame the two systems don't cooperate with each other; the possibilities would be truly endless."

"I don't really understand how either of them works," Jamirh snorted. He tried to remember what Jeri had done before and threw the knife, glad that the area was large enough that he had no chance of hitting another person.

They both stared as the knife thunked into the center of the target.

"Wow," Jeri stated after a moment. "Good job. Have you been holding out on me?"

He shook his head, wide eyes never leaving the knife. "No, I've never done this before. I mean, I've used knives before, but normal knives or switchblades, not these things. I've never thrown them like this, either. I didn't even expect to hit it, to be honest."

"After the darts, I didn't expect you to either," she agreed.

He threw again, the knife landing a little farther out than the first, but still respectably close to the center. "Well, this is surprisingly easy," he exclaimed happily, ears twitching upward as he threw the third knife to join its friends.

"Except it's really not," Jeri murmured, eyeing Jamirh's cluster.

"Maybe I'm just naturally good at it, which is kind of cool," he suggested with a shrug. "Or maybe it's beginner's luck. Your throws were still better."

"I've been throwing knives for centuries," she pointed out dryly. "You've been throwing knives for two minutes, *if*," she emphasized the word, "you are telling me the truth." She smiled, taking the sting out of her words.

"Really," he protested with a laugh, raising his hands. "I promise I've never done anything like this before."

"If you say so," she mused, collecting her prize of candy from the Avari running the booth. "You said Hel used her Voice to get you out of the Security Station, right?"

Jamirh blinked at the change in topic. "Yes?"

"There's a small concert being held in Faradin Square, if you want to hear how Voice is more often used," she offered. "You haven't heard someone sing until you've heard a proper Bard, and Master Caelessa is very, very good."

"Sure," he agreed readily. "Let's grab something to drink on the way."

She nodded with a wry smile, but Jamirh couldn't help but notice how her eyes lingered on the knives for a moment before she turned and led the way.

Chapter Nineteen

It took Jamirh – and the vast majority of the city – several days to fully recover from the night-long celebration of Festival, starting with sleeping in well past noon the next day. When Jeri finally showed up to drag him out of bed and back to the land of the living, Jamirh found that thirteen hours of trekking around the city participating in various physical challenges had resulted in every muscle in his body protesting his every movement. Gorging himself on candy and other sweet treats probably hadn't helped matters, leaving him feeling almost nauseous even after attempting to sleep it off. Luckily, Jeri came with a tea that eased the aches and his stomach enough for him to attempt some toast and oatmeal while she sipped on a mug of warmed blood, watching him with faint amusement.

Apparently, the Vampires were all fine – the lack of sleep and influx of sugar didn't bother them at all.

After the requisite "Day of Rest," looking for something to do, Jamirh and Jeri joined the palace staff in taking down Festival decorations and cleaning up the grounds. There was a lot of work to do, due to how much had gone up for the celebration. All the garlands and candles had to be taken down and put away, though the pumpkins would apparently be left out as seasonal decorations until they began to rot. As Jeri had mentioned, the statues of Hades all remained veiled, a silent, eerie testament to the goddess they portrayed.

They fell into a steady routine for the next several days, eating meals together and continuing to help return the palace to normal. They were eating a quick lunch in the palace cafeteria when Jeri asked, "So... how *did* you meet Ander?"

Jamirh shrugged. "I was just exploring the city, looking at one of the statues, and he was... uh... adjusting the lights, I think? I asked him about the statues, he answered, and that was the end of it, really." Though... "I guess the way he answered does make sense if he's one of Hades' priests."

Jeri frowned. "You met him in the city? Not on palace grounds?"

"Yeah, definitely in the city. It was before I met you at the palace gates. Why?"

"It's just that he never leaves the palace grounds," she said slowly. "To the point where I don't think he's left once in the three hundred years he's been here."

"That's a long time to be in one place," Jamirh pointed out. "How do you know he never leaves?"

She pursed her lips. "It may not seem like it, but the Black Watch keeps a close eye on who comes and goes from the palace grounds. And Ander, as a priest of the Lady, is an important person. I've been disconnected from the gossip mill since we got back, but if he left palace grounds I'm sure that's been the topic of the hour, unless..." Her voice trailed off, and her eyes flickered away from Jamirh.

He scowled. "Unless I'm more interesting?"

She shrugged. "Hard to say. Ander being all but a shut-in has interested us for centuries at this point; him going out into the city represents a potential for a lot of gossip." She hummed thoughtfully. "Though if I'm the only one who knows he met with you..."

"Where did he get that scar from?" Jamirh asked, trying to shift the conversation away from himself. Absently, he rubbed at his key. He was also an "important person," wasn't he? Did they follow his movements that closely, too?

"His scar?" Jeri blinked at him. "Oh, I don't know. He already had it when he came here."

"It's probably too rude to ask." But Jamirh had to wonder. It didn't look like the kind of injury caused by an accident.

"I wouldn't." Jeri snorted. "And unfortunately, I doubt he'll ever just say what happened. It's not his style."

"What is not my style?"

Both Jamirh and Jeri jumped at the lazy drawl as they twisted to look at Ander, who was standing next to their table. "*Goddess*, Ander, walk up and greet us like a normal person once in a while," Jeri practically snarled.

Ander's brow furrowed in confusion. Without the masquerade mask, the scar running down his face was his prominent feature. "I did. You were both very intent on your conversation."

There was an uncomfortably long pause while they all stared at each other.

Ander cleared his throat, looking at Jamirh. "It's beside the point. Hades has contacted me. There's been a development." Jeri glanced sharply at Jamirh, but Ander continued before she could speak. "Being aware of the situation doesn't make you beholden to it. I'll be honest, kid – being informed is probably your best bet right now, whether you want to stay out of it or not."

That felt true. If he knew what was going on, he could avoid it. Jamirh glanced at Jeri to see her looking at him with a worried expression. He turned back to Ander. "I'm not going to pick up that sword," he stated firmly.

Ander held up his hands in surrender. "I swear, as the eighth High Priest of the goddess Hades, the suggestion will not cross my lips."

Eighth High Priest? Jamirh filed that away to ask Jeri about later. He studied Ander carefully, but the taller man appeared to be sincere, even if Jeri was frowning.

Jamirh shrugged. "Fine. What's the worst that could happen?"

Jamirh found himself sitting at a large table in an ornate room with Vlad, Jeri, Ander, and another Vampire in Watch blacks. She had darker skin, short ashen-pink hair, and the pointed ears of an Avari, and she had been introduced to him as Primrose, Tarvishte's Captain of the Black Watch. She was the "Prim" Jeri had mentioned on their first day in Tarvishte. A pale-gray warg lounged at her feet, forcing her to sit slightly away from the table.

It was, he reflected, a group he didn't particularly feel like he belonged in, even if Vlad greeted him warmly and he was with Jeri all the time.

Prim waited for the servant delivering a tray of small cakes and pastries to leave the room before asking, "What is this about, Ander?"

"If you've brought this group together, I assume something of importance has happened," Vlad stated mildly.

Ander nodded. "For the first time in several weeks, Hades has spoken to me."

Jeri's eyebrows rose. "She's been silent for weeks?"

Jamirh was confused – priests talked all the time about communing with their gods, but he hadn't thought it was a literal conversation, just the priests interpreting what they thought their god would want. Ander actually talked to Hades? And she responded? Sure, it happened in the legends – even Ebryn had spoken with Hades long enough to screw Jamirh over, apparently – but those were things that happened long ago, before the rise of tech made people less reliant on the gods. He fiddled with his key uncertainly.

Ander shrugged, oblivious to Jamirh's internal confusion. "She's been present with me, but Her attention has been elsewhere for the most part. She's been trying to determine the form of the Abomination but has been disappointingly unsuccessful – at least until last night."

Jamirh sat up in his chair, ears perking up, feeling invested despite himself. The others were all studying Ander with intense focus.

"She found something?" Vlad questioned, red eyes intent.

"Last night, by chance," Ander explained. "I want to be clear that She hasn't been very explicit about what She found, and Her communication with me has been distracted at best – She's very excited about it."

"Spit it out, man – what did She tell you?" Prim exclaimed, exasperated.

Ander shot her an unimpressed look but answered: "She heard a Prayer of Agony, and when She investigated, She found residue of Abomination – not enough to get a clear idea of what it was, but enough to know the Human came in contact with it at some point."

Jamirh considered that. It didn't disprove his theory that the Abomination was un-stabbable, he supposed. He eyed the little cakes, sitting untouched in the center of the table.

"Agony." Vlad frowned, leaning his elbows on the table and folding his hands together. "Did whomever She found survive?"

"Yes," Ander said slowly. "And that's where all of Her attention is right now – She's very intent on following him."

Jeri snorted. "She's put a lot of effort into finding out what the Abomination is – it's unsurprising She doesn't want to lose track of the first real lead She's had in forty years."

Ander looked away. "Well, that's where it gets a little complicated, because he can hear Her, apparently."

Dead silence. Jamirh looked around in confusion; apparently talking directly to Hades was not very common. That made sense. He took advantage of everyone staring at Ander to stealthily slide the plate of cakes closer to himself.

"Okay," Vlad said finally, "then the question becomes this – can he hear Her because he is Hers, or is it a result of coming into contact with the Abomination?"

"She is certainly acting like he is Hers." Ander's voice was dry as dust. "So I'm not sure the distinction matters."

Prim cracked a wry smile. "Congratulations then."

He shook his head. "No Choice has been made. It may yet come to nothing. She hasn't been able to reach him since last night, either, though that hasn't stopped Her from trying."

Vlad looked worried. "This feels far too coincidental. It may be a trap of some sort."

"How could it be a trap?" Jeri asked. "How would you artificially induce the ability to hear a god? In the entire history of Romanii, there have been *eleven* priests."

Okay, it wasn't very common at all then. Jamirh was beginning to think that whatever type of communication they were referring to was not what he was picturing.

"You might be able to do it with Hades, but the death toll would be catastrophic before you succeeded," Ander mused. "Not even *we* know the entirety of what it is that calls us to Her, and Her to us. The only similarity has been that each of us is broken in some way."

Jamirh frowned at that as he tried to follow the conversation. Broken? He popped one of the little cakes into his mouth. It had a strawberry filling, to his delight.

Prim looked concerned. "And yet, our instinct when we come across a person with that potential is to bring them here. If they could force or even mimic that ability, it would make an ideal trap, because we can't just leave him there." She paused. "Right?"

Ander suddenly looked off to the side, head cocked slightly.

Vlad sighed like the weight of the world was on his shoulders. "Correct. Even if we had conclusive proof that it was a trap, that fact that he can hear Her means we have to at least try."

"She has already considered this," Ander said suddenly. "Or rather, She's considered that we would consider it. *Her* mind is made up." He rolled his eyes. "She's going to try to convince him to go to Charve." He ignored the exclamations of surprise, eyes glancing quickly in Jamirh's direction as he paused. "Ah... She has decided he should break out Hel and cross the border with her, which should 'negate any surprises.' Her words, not mine."

"That's suicide," Jamirh said flatly, joining the conversation. "There's no way one person could even break into that sort of facility, never mind get someone out of it."

"Agreed. Even with Her help, he'd have to be some sort of magical prodigy to manage that," Prim added, nodding to Jamirh before looking back at the priest. "Could you do it, Ander?"

Vlad looked like he was going to say something, then stopped, a dawning look of realization coming over his face.

Ander shrugged helplessly. "No, but my talents are mainly defensive in nature. It would take a completely different type of mage."

"Yes, I once watched you very 'defensively' cut a Lorn into twenty pieces," Jeri cut in dryly, "but you have a point. Either you need enough offensive firepower to overwhelm everything on that base, or stealth enough to *avoid* everything on that base – tech *and* magic, since there are almost certainly Truth Seekers there."

Vlad was slowly putting his face in his hands. "Ander," he said, sounding horribly pained, "did my mother happen to mention a name?"

Ander looked faintly confused. "No. Why?"

"If you ask Her, will She answer you?"

Ander paused for a moment, eyes flicking down. "No, She says it's not important."

"To Her, it's probably not. She likely didn't even ask," Vlad muttered unhappily. "Very well, I will keep my conclusions to myself for now."

"You don't want to share with the class?" Prim drawled. Then she frowned. "Wait. You don't think...?"

"I can't be sure. It's just a suspicion. I suppose we'll see how it pans out," he answered tiredly, shaking his head.

Jamirh cleared his throat, drawing everyone's attention. "So, just to be clear, we still don't actually know what the Abomination is, just that someone who can hear Hades came into contact with it at some point, and that person is now going to Charve to break Hel out from a high-security military facility?"

Ander grinned wryly. "Yeah, that pretty much covers it."

"Great. Just making sure I didn't miss anything." It wasn't much to go on, in his opinion.

Vlad sighed again. "You have a talent for summarization, Jamirh. For what it's worth, it is more information than we had previously. Ander, please keep us informed with whatever information my mother deems important enough to pass along."

Ander inclined his head. "Of course."

"Then, if no one has any questions...?" Vlad paused. "Hopefully we will know more soon, since it seems things are now fully in motion, and forewarned is forearmed." He stood, Jeri, Prim, and Ander a breath after him, and Jamirh awkwardly a moment after that. "Unfortunately, I now have a completely different situation to look into. Good day, everyone. Prim, if you could come with me?" He swept out of the room, Prim and the warg following.

"I think that went well," Ander declared after a moment.

Jeri just shook her head. "Did it?"

Jamirh kept his thoughts to himself as he took another of the little cakes. He hadn't learned much about the Abomination, but he still had a lot to think about.

"Please? I think it could be fun," Jeri pleaded with him several days later. "You're a natural at it; I can tell. And I'm a very good teacher!"

A week after the Festival of Night and the city was more or less back to normal, according to Jeri. This had left Jamirh feeling a bit adrift without something to occupy his time, which had led to this conversation with Jeri.

She wanted to teach him how to wield daggers.

Jamirh was on the fence about it. On the one hand, it was a weapon, and that felt like a dangerously slippery slope. On the other, it wasn't a sword, and he was beginning to think that being able to defend himself in some capacity other than running away might not be a bad idea. Sure, he could do some hand-to-hand, but a dagger was a whole different game.

He had spent the last few days thinking over what he had learned at the meeting and putting his thoughts in order, but in truth it had raised more questions than it answered. Was the unlucky Human – who had prayed a "Prayer of Agony" and was "broken" – actually bait to draw out the Romanii? Were the Romanii really going to let him try to rescue Hel on his own? Why was Ander's method of talking to a god special? Why had Ander even wanted him to be present for that meeting?

How could you cut a Lorn into twenty pieces? They were evil lizards made of rock.

They were no closer to understanding what the Abomination was. According to Ander, Hades had remained silent. The lack of information was very slowly starting to eat at Jamirh. There was a growing sense of unease, like the calm before the storm, except they had no idea what kind of storm it would be.

Jamirh did not like not knowing.

And so, he found himself seriously considering Jeri's offer.

"I thought you used those two swords?" he hedged, thinking back to when she had beheaded the Truth Seeker. "Actually, where did they go? I only ever saw them in Sturlow."

"Oh yes, my cutlasses." Jeri raised her hands, and in a swirl of dark shadow the two weapons appeared. "These are soulforged; they only exist when I need them."

"What?" he asked, part lost and part exasperated as he stared at the swords. Another question: would these people ever stop dropping world-changing statements casually in conversation?

She smiled. "The ability to soulforge a weapon is a gift from the Lady to Her children and Her priests." She paused, choosing her words carefully. "Every living being has a soul, which in its natural state is without form. But there is a way to make your soul physically manifest, at which point it takes the form of a crystal. It can take a long time before you can do so successfully. Once you get to that point, though, you can use the crystal to forge – magically, not literally – weapons for yourself. Vlad and some of the older Vampires and priests can do full sets of armor in addition to weapons. The resulting artifacts are much stronger than normal weapons and armor, and are literally a part of you. You are never without them."

He stared at her. "I can't even begin to comprehend how dangerous that sounds."

"Yes, it's not for everyone," she agreed wryly.

He thought back to his first conversation with Vlad. "And Ebryn wanted to do this to make the Crystal Light Blade? Was he insane?"

She frowned, and the swords dissipated into the air. "Did he? That doesn't sound like it would work, since the crystals he was using were artifacts of power from the elemental gods and not his soul."

Jamirh shrugged. "Vlad told me that was why he came here to make the damn thing, because he wanted to soulforge it. Instead, Hades made the Crystal Light Blade for him, I think."

Jeri hummed, looking thoughtful. "Yes, Hades forged the Blade for Ebryn. I guess that explains why he came here. He would have had to go to Her if he wanted to attempt a soulforging." She looked back to Jamirh. "But daggers would be good weapons for you! Speed is definitely one of your strengths, and Ebryn never wielded daggers."

"Just swords," Jamirh mused. The ultimate swordsman. Then he had a thought. "What about magic?"

Jeri looked at him in surprise. "What about it?"

"Did Ebryn ever use magic?" he asked curiously. "Like, I know the Blade itself is magic, but did he ever cast spells, like you and Hel?"

"Ah." She was quiet for a long moment. "No, he didn't. Magic can be broken up into two main types – inherent magic, and learned magic. My magic is inherent; it comes from me being a Vampire, though most types of inherents people are just born with, like Voice, or the Aradians' fire-starting. Inherents function more like abilities, and are usually pretty easy for those who have them to use, though practice can make you better at them.

"Learned magic uses the arrays you saw Hel use – the big, glowing purple circle? It encompasses everything considered actual 'spell casting'. But even though we call it learned magic, in order to use the arrays, you still need to have what we call 'mage potential.'"

"Then that still sounds like the ability is inherent, though," Jamirh pointed out.

"The name is a bit misleading, yes," she agreed. "It's just that you can't use that potential without learning the glyphs and how to form the arrays. It takes study to be able to cast anything with learned magic. But if you learn the glyphs and how they form arrays without having the potential, you won't be able to do anything with that knowledge. And while most people have at least a little bit of that potential, Ebryn had none."

Jamirh's eyebrows rose. "None?"

"None. He could use spell crystals – anyone can, since the spell has technically already been cast – and the Crystal Light Blade is a magical artifact made for his use, but he was unable to cast spells like you saw Hel do, and he certainly didn't have any of the inherents I do."

He thought about that and came to the logical conclusion. "I can't cast spells either, can I?"

She shrugged. "I would guess not, but I also have no potential myself, so I have no way to check. Ander would know, or Vlad."

"You can't cast spells?" That surprised him.

"I can't even so much as light a candle," she confirmed.

He thought back to Hel's shield spell. "What about the color of the circle? Does that indicate what the spell does?"

Jeri shook her head. "The glyphs used indicate what the spell does. The color of the array is the color of the caster's magic. Hel's magic is violet, Ander's magic is bright green, Vlad's is wine red, etc. And while mages can have similar colors to each other, a perfectly exact match is extremely rare, so it is possible to tell who is casting a spell if you are familiar with the caster's color of magic."

"So all of Hel's spells would be purple? She created a light in the security station when it lost power, but it was white?"

"All of her *arrays* are purple. The actual spell effects could be any color," Jeri clarified.

That checked out as far as he remembered. "So innate magic is something you can just do, and learned magic you have to study in addition to having the ability?"

She nodded. "Yes."

"Magic is complicated. No wonder the Empire uses tech. At least everyone can use it." He turned his attention back to the original question. Did he want to learn how to use daggers?

If he was being really honest with himself, yes. Yes he did. It sounded cool.

"It would make sense if tech was developed in the beginning as a substitute for magic," Jeri mused. "A way for non-gifted people to do many of the same wonders as mages. I would say it's really only started to catch up recently, though."

"What does learning daggers entail, exactly?" he questioned. If he was going to do this, he wanted to know what he was getting into.

"Hmm?" Jeri seemed a bit thrown by his change of subject, but then she brightened. "Oh! You're going to do it, then?"

He sighed. "Maybe. A definite maybe. How would we go about this?"

"Practice. Lots and lots of practice," she grinned.

He looked at the grin on her face with some concern. It had something of an evil edge to it. What was he getting himself into?

"Colonel, I'm *bored*. Why don't you let me out for a little bit? I promise I'll behave," her voice purred.

Rhode froze, then looked up at the glass. "You've figured out who I am, then?" he asked conversationally, wondering how in the name of the gods she possibly could have done so.

"No, but now I know you're a colonel," she replied cheerfully from where she sat, legs crossed, in the center of her cell. She was still *looking at him*. How?

He took a deep breath, trying to force down his anger with himself. That had been a careless mistake. But still – it was a strange guess for her to make with any sort of accuracy. Intelligence officers existed within all ranks; how had she settled on colonel?

He decided to drop that thread of conversation entirely and switch to another.

"I have to thank you, you know – without you, we might not have noticed him. He had slipped through the cracks of our intelligence for so long. Who knows how much longer he could have remained hidden, if you hadn't drawn our attention to him?"

She shrugged, completely unbothered as she lay back to stare at the ceiling. "Eh, he was already arrested when I got there. You all would have figured it out pretty quick, I bet, if you were on the lookout for red hair and silver eyes."

"Maybe, maybe not." He let a hint of suggestion enter his voice. "It's been over twenty years since those protocols were put into place; you know as well as I do that not every Guard follows such random protocols down to the letter. Ebryn may have slipped through our fingers again, if you hadn't made such a production out of the whole situation."

She was quiet for several minutes, and Rhode started to think that he may have scored a point, when she finally answered, "You know, I don't actually think he likes that name all that much."

He blinked in confusion, then looked back at his tablet for a minute to double check. "You don't think he likes his own name?"

"Is that his legal name? I wasn't sure. But yeah, no, he doesn't go by Ebryn anymore, that's for sure."

His mouth pressed into a thin line at the realization that once again, he had given her something and learned nothing of consequence in return. Why did nothing they said or did phase her? What did she know that they didn't? Perhaps a curfew was a wise move after all; there was already no chance she could be rescued, but better extra safe than sorry.

This Avari was a puzzle, that was for certain. But that was okay, Rhode reminded himself.

He liked puzzles.

Chapter Twenty

"What do you think, Takeshi?"

He smiled at the princess, not that she would see it beneath his mask. He injected a little extra warmth into his tone. "Your composition is lovely, as always."

Hotaru turned back to the flowers she was arranging with a smile as one of her attendants spoke up. "Does not the bold color of the lilies overpower the pussy willow? It seems strange to put two such disparate plants together like that."

Hotaru inclined her head gently. "Not at all; I think the willow brings a softness that balances the bright colors of the lilies. In all things, we must strive for such a balance. Here, we can even bridge the two with this." She placed a white lily in amongst the colored ones. "Bridge and balance, the two tenets of magic. Don't you agree?"

"Then why have you placed so much more of the willow?" asked the other attendant.

"Because balance is not equality," Hotaru murmured, "and that is what makes it dangerous to pursue." She placed a final sprig of momiji to finish off her design.

So the tech integration meeting earlier had not gone well, Takeshi surmised.

One of the attendants took the arrangement to be displayed as the other helped Hotaru to her feet. "Princess, perhaps you should rest before dinner," she suggested, seeing the look of pain that flashed across Hotaru's face.

"No, I'm fine." She shook her head, the decorative pins in her hair chiming gently as she swept in his direction. "Isn't that right, Takeshi?"

He blinked at her in confusion, realizing he was holding her, his katana pinning her to the floor below as the blood pooled out around them. He couldn't look away from the intense look in her dark eyes.

"Promise me we'll be okay?" she whispered as the blood began to pour from her mouth–

Takeshi shot up in bed, heart hammering as he took in his hotel room at Redguard Suites in Charve.

He staggered to the bathroom to splash water on his face, rubbing at his eyes. He shuddered, trying to force the memory away, though her eyes stayed with him. They always did, though the dreams hadn't been so vivid since the sentencing.

Mechanically, Takeshi forced himself to get ready for the day. He tried meditating for an hour or so before he gave up, the usually comforting activity not enough to soothe the shock of the dream. He tried to remind himself that Hotaru herself had chosen to die, but it still didn't seem fair that she had needed to.

Annoyed with himself, he angrily ate a granola bar with his tea while he tried to decide what exactly he was going to do today. He now had a much better grasp of the situation in Charve thanks to the woman in the mirror – a rebel had been captured and imprisoned at the military base two weeks ago, leading to increased security in the city, which implied that whoever had been captured was important. Important enough that the military was still concerned about either possible rescue or escape and could be instituting a curfew and presumably other measures to counteract that. He was going to have to figure out what those other measures were, along with the normal methods taken at the military base for keeping people out.

In short, he had a lot of work to do, and not a lot of time to do it in if he wanted to get the rebel out in one piece. Who knew what had already happened to them in the past two weeks? Takeshi wasn't sure what laws the Rose Empire had for treatment of prisoners, or even if the military would abide by them.

He decided the first and easiest thing to determine would be the increased security measures that were in place now around the city as a whole. Those he should be able to figure out purely through observation and the news, which he had missed again last night. He made a mental note to make sure he watched it when he returned from his scouting mission.

He took the vacation planner with him; if nothing else it made him look like a legitimate tourist. He triple-checked his disguise illusion – now was not the time to get sloppy – and headed out into Charve for some research.

This time, he made sure to pay even more careful attention to the people around him rather than the city itself. Many he pegged as tourists, seemingly unconcerned by recent events, shopping for souvenirs and planning hikes and camping trips. Takeshi himself was doing many of the same activities as a theoretical tourist.

But it was the locals who solidified that something wasn't right. They were easy to separate from the tourists based on the way they hurried from place to place, keeping their heads down and finishing their business quickly. They all seemed on edge. The cashier at one store was short with customers; another's smile was a bit too brittle. A pair of teens folding clothes to put out on a shelf spoke together in low, worried tones about the possibility of a curfew. Their manager kept her eyes on the security cameras. Takeshi stepped into a coffee shop and was served the wrong beverage by a distracted barista.

He saw another Truth Seeker in the Old Quarter as he poked around in various shops. She was merely standing next to a marble statue of some Human on a horse. Her gray uniform and saber set her apart from the rest of the crowd, making her look more like the statue than the people around her. It was hard to tell where or even if she was looking due to the embroidered fabric over her eyes, but Takeshi felt no searching from her, so she was likely here as a deterrent. Which she was doing admirably as people scurried away from her.

Takeshi moved on.

He picked up a newspaper at a convenience store and decided on a small, cheap café for lunch. He settled down at one of the outdoor tables with his sandwich as he started to scan the paper for anything interesting. The potential curfew was one of the big stories. The article cited an "incident" that had happened on the military base two weeks ago that had led to an increase in security about the base, but not what that incident was, or why it should result in a curfew for the city at large. The base itself had since been closed to any but those who were stationed there, and no one else was going in or out.

Takeshi found himself wondering why the rebel had been brought here in the first place, since it seemed – at least on the surface – that this place was not prepared to hold prisoners. Strange that they would take a prisoner to a base connected to a city and then have to shut down that city in order to maintain containment. They also were not telling the civilian population what was going on. Perhaps they were afraid of a panic of sorts? But why? People were imprisoned all over the world all the time without significant difficulties. He supposed there had to be something about this base that led to them choosing it despite the drawbacks; he would have to figure out what that was.

Though, hadn't he read something earlier in the week about there being a jailbreak in Lyndiniam itself? Perhaps... no, that had involved a security station, not a military base. The chances of the two incidents being linked were close to zero. The military wouldn't react more defensively due to a failure on the Guard's part to keep a criminal behind bars, though the timing was oddly coincidental.

He continued flipping through the pages of the newspaper, noting that there was an upcoming concert for a popular singer in Bariza that many people were very excited for, the Emperor's Harvest Celebration party was going to be even more expensive than originally estimated, there was a big soccer game happening tonight, and negotiations with the Aradians had broken down for possibly the two-hundredth time. Takeshi shook his head; there was no way the tech-focused Empire was ever going to mesh well with a culture so tied up in its magic as Dalmara, especially with the Empire's public insistence that magic did not exist.

Then he blinked as he took in another article title: *Shuurai Takeshi – Alive or Dead?*

Well, that was surreal to read.

The article was speculation on whether or not he had died crossing the Shae Sea, noting that he hadn't been seen since he'd been pushed out to sea in a rowboat and that there had been some severe storms that would have hindered his ability to cross safely. Nothing had come ashore so far at either the Nyphoren Islands or the western coast. There hadn't been a formal banishing from Ni Fon in the past century, making it hard to extrapolate if it was even a survivable punishment in this day and age, when magic was gone. The article ended on a disappointed note that if he had died there would never be any evidence, as it would be swallowed by the ocean and lost to time.

This would work to his benefit. If people thought he was dead, they wouldn't be looking for him, and he would be more free to move about undetected. He wondered vaguely if he should try to find a way to indicate to Ni Fon that he was still alive? Probably not, actually; the Empress was not the sort of person to contemplate possible failure in her plans. It likely hadn't even crossed her mind that he *could* die in the ocean, since that would mean her plan had failed, and that Just Did Not Happen.

He took a deep breath and let it out. He had made it to Espon, so he supposed that meant she had been right about that part. He just had to trust that she would be right about the rest of it.

Takeshi gathered up his trash, deciding to see if he could find any information about the Charve Military Base's layout or security. The city was definitely under a soft lockdown even if its citizens and tourists weren't aware, and that was going to make it extremely difficult to get information without being flagged.

He flipped through the vacation planner quickly, looking to see if there were any libraries mentioned he could try, but stopped as one page caught his eye. He thumbed back to the map of the city.

He had an idea.

"The Laurent Military Academy Temple of Faith was completed fifty-eight years ago in 1968 A.G. It took three years to build, during which its design was modified several times due to budgetary constraints," a cool female voice informed him through his earbuds. Takeshi stood in place dutifully while the recording continued its explanation of the temple's origins.

The military base itself might have been under lockdown, but the academy, a mere fifteen minutes away, was not – and it was something of a tourist attraction. The academy boasted a famous temple that drew tourists from all over to see its unique design. The center of the temple was dedicated to the Three Goddesses, but there were large chapels for each of the elemental twin deities branching off at the cardinal directions. Between those were small shrines to four other less-commonly worshiped deities: the Lord God of creation and life, the Silent Goddess of death, the Lord of Tricks, and the Lady of Luck.

The construction was strangely angular to Takeshi's eye considering its circular layout, but he could see the beginnings of the influences that had made their way into the now-common architecture in the city proper. The chapels to the elemental deities had the first real explosion of color he'd seen outside of the park – each one was painted in bold monochromatic color schemes associated with the twins in question. He lingered for a moment in the Nyphoren's room of cool blues, mentally whispering another prayer of thanks to them with a wish that the crew of the *Sea Spirit* was doing well.

He was only half-listening as he followed the self-guided tour, more interested in the visuals of the temple itself. It was thoughtfully done, if minimalistic. He thought Hotaru probably would have liked it – the blend of their smooth, simplistic architecture and style balanced with the usually complicated symbology of the gods.

Balance and bridge.

He blinked at the unintentional reminder of his dream, but he wasn't here to actually sightsee. He was here for research purposes.

Having finished his tour, he returned to the visitor center. There was a drop-off for the little black box that spoke through his earbuds. He looked around and saw a few displays of pamphlets. Browsing through them, he took several that looked promising. Most of them were probably just recruitment propaganda, but he hoped there might be some information in them he could use. He would have to examine the lot when he returned to the hotel.

Curiously, there were quite a few buildings and trails on the campus that were open to tourists, but it was the temple that was the big draw. Takeshi decided he had what he'd come for and went to catch the bus back to the city center.

As he glanced out the window, he noticed with some annoyance that his reflection was once again that of a woman draped in black fabric. He reached out mentally. *:I'm still working on it. Go away.:*

The phantom fluttered and disappeared. He hoped that she wasn't visible to anyone else when she did that – something to ask her later.

:Just you.:

He managed not to jump in surprise, but it was a near thing. *:I told you I needed time to investigate. Now is a bad time.:*

:...curious. No... done, no one...: She felt distinctly amused, whatever she was trying to say.

Takeshi was not. *:Rushing me won't help your friend. I still don't have enough information.:*

There was a thoughtful pause. *:...alone?:*

:Yes, I want to do this alone.: He somehow got the impression of a raised eyebrow. *:Okay, I don't necessarily want to do all the work myself, but there is no one here who can help me.:*

:I... help!:

:How, exactly? You are not actually here. Or are you?: He hadn't actually asked her location before.

He felt like she was debating something, a feeling of uncertainty, and then her presence was gone again.

Takeshi sighed. She was clearly impatient, but these things took time, and her bothering him was not going to make him work faster. This was not something he wanted to rush and end up making mistakes.

The rest of the bus ride was blessedly uneventful, though there was another Truth Seeker nearby when he disembarked. He ignored the gray-clad figure as he crossed the street, intent on returning to the hotel so he could look over the pamphlets. Like the one by the statue that morning, this Truth Seeker was not actively searching for anything.

What were they doing? Just menacing the populace? He was fairly sure every Truth Seeker he'd seen so far was a different person, which combined with what he had overheard from others meant there was a fair number of them in the streets. And based on the way people were acting when they saw them, this was a much higher number in one place than was common.

He unlocked the door to his room and spread the pamphlets out on the little table. He wasn't expecting anything too specific, but even general information could be revealing. Two were recruitment pamphlets, talking about how great it was to get an education through the academy and what one could expect if they attended. He put those aside. Another was for tourists visiting the academy; it listed the places on the campus open to visit as well as the rules for doing so. He put that one to the side as well.

The next was a brochure for the Drenmar Inn, a hotel for members of the military on the Charve Military Base. Takeshi smiled as he flipped it open; one of the pages had a small map of how to get to the hotel on the base. This was exactly what he had been looking for. Some of the buildings were even labeled, though others had numbers indicating that there should be a key. Takeshi figured it was probably a small portion of a much larger map that existed elsewhere. No matter, this was extremely useful as it was. It narrowed down the potential lists of places the prisoner could be held and gave him something to work from should he end up sneaking onto the base. He would have to memorize the layout.

The next pamphlet was also aimed at military visitors, outlining attractions around the academy and base. Not as useful as he had hoped. Another listed a number of facts and features about the Temple of Faith. The last one he had grabbed was yet another recruitment pamphlet. He put it with the first two.

This was a good start. It wasn't enough information to make a decision on whether or not saving the prisoner was possible, but it was a piece of the puzzle he needed to put together. Now it was a matter of finding the remaining pieces to see the picture as a whole.

It was time to try the oldest, most reliable of places in which to gain information – a bar.

The vacation planner had several pages of places to get drinks, but Takeshi wanted a place locals frequented. He had kept an eye out while investigating earlier in the day and had found a couple of options he thought might work.

It was still a little early for the bar crowd, but Takeshi needed to eat anyway. He headed for the first of the places he had noted earlier, but it was closed until six. He decided that would be a good place to go late at night. The second one was open, a seedy little place well off the main streets that had a grand total of three options that barely qualified as food on their menu.

Perfect.

It wasn't very crowded yet, but Takeshi didn't expect it to be. He found a spot in the corner of the room with a good view of one of the vid screens, which was showing the setup for the soccer match he had read about in the paper. He was hoping he would be taken for someone here to watch the game.

He ordered his dinner and a beer and settled in to wait for the crowd.

Less than an hour later, Takeshi was finishing the greasy mess he'd been served while the room filled around him with locals excited for the soccer game. As he'd hoped, the conversations around him were a mix of speculation about the game and speculation about whatever had happened at the base.

The theories were... interesting.

Ranging from plausible to ridiculous, everyone seemed to have their own idea of what had happened two weeks ago. There had been an accident with a slow-acting pathogen and they were trying to contain it. An experimental bionic soldier had malfunctioned and they were afraid of it getting out and murdering civilians. They had opened a wormhole with untested tech that was slowly eating the base. Some sort of tech itself was eating the base. A Truth Seeker had gone rogue. A brand-new classified weapon had been stolen by Aradian spies. A genetically modified bear was on the loose.

What Takeshi was able to gather was that it was believed the base specialized in military research, though what kind was clearly up for debate. It was also interesting that none of the theories involved a captive, indicating that this base was not known for being a prison. That was both good and bad – good, because it meant the security was not normally set up to contain prisoners; bad, because who knew what was actually being done in the base, potentially to the captured rebel.

The game had started, and with it much of the conversation had swung towards points and technique and foul play. Takeshi kept his eyes on the screen as he listened to the voices around him, but there didn't seem to be anything pertinent to his interests anymore. He ordered another beer from the harried-looking girl who came by to take his plate, taking his cues from the crowd for how he should react to the game. It wasn't hard; everyone seemed to be cheering for the team in red, so Takeshi joined in. He'd never had more than a passing interest in the game himself. Still, by the time halftime came about, Takeshi was most of the way to legitimately hoping they would win, swept up in the excitement despite himself.

Suddenly, all the vid screens in the bar switched from the soccer game to the news with a staticky screech. A nervous-looking anchor was sitting at the desk clearing her throat. "If I could have everyone's attention, this is an emergency broadcast," she began as the ticker at the bottom of the screen started scrolling the words, *Emergency Alert. This is not a drill.* "The city of Charve is ordering a curfew from nine p.m. to six a.m. starting immediately. Traveling to and from work, seeking or giving emergency care, and emergency responders are the only exemptions. This curfew will remain in effect nightly until further notice. The Guard requests all non-essential businesses to close during curfew, and all citizens to return to their homes. Failure to follow curfew guidelines will be met with fines or incarceration. If you have any questions, further information can be found at any security station in the city."

The crowd around Takeshi began to angrily proclaim what they thought of that. He kept his eyes on the screen.

"The curfew is for your safety," the anchor was continuing. "The Guard thanks you for your cooperation in this matter. We now return to your original programming."

Takeshi frowned. The curfew had been put into effect, but under the authority of the Guard and not the military? Or was that a smokescreen? If it was, it wasn't doing a good job – many of the people around him were angrily blaming the military for the shutdown, not the Guard. In fact, most of them seemed to be ignoring that part entirely. Luckily, even though they were angry, they didn't seem to be mob angry – he heard mentions of the Truth Seekers and realized their very presence was a deterrent.

He glanced at the clock behind the bar. It was almost eight now; the curfew would go into effect in just over an hour. He had some time to continue observing before he had to leave.

He'd observe from his window tonight, see what he was going to be dealing with. Soon, he'd put his skills to the test.

Chapter Twenty-One

T he city settled into an uneasy routine.

The curfew was loudly protested by civilians and businesses, but the Guard and the military had made up their minds and would not be swayed, presenting a united front against public opinion. "For public safety" became a mantra they repeated every time they were questioned. They refused to explain the reason for the curfew any further, causing speculation to spread like wildfire. The presence of the Truth Seekers, who were suddenly everywhere in the city, was similarly explained. And though the populace was upset, the increased number of Seekers in the city meant no one was willing to riot. The curfew would stand.

Life during the day actually changed very little from what Takeshi could tell, outside of the rumors flying around and the general attitude of discontent. Citizens still went to work and school; tourists still wandered the city and visited the attractions. Though the Seekers were a noticeable difference, they didn't do anything other than be subtly menacing on street corners and unintentionally disrupt the foot traffic around them. Still, they were armed and dangerous besides, so Takeshi avoided them whenever possible. There was no need to invite trouble.

At night, it was a different story. Everything locked down. The streets were deserted save for the Seekers, who appeared to be going out of their way to be as conspicuous as possible. They stood in the centers of intersections, silent sentinels waiting for someone to step out of line and justify their presence.

No one tested them.

Takeshi watched from his window every night, but no one, not even the Guard, stepped out onto the streets once the curfew fell. The city became the domain of the Truth Seekers, unchallenged as they stood watch in the dark.

Blind Ones, the pirates had called them. Takeshi would bet his katana that wasn't true.

He took to visiting several bars around the city in the hours before the curfew went into effect to see if there were any rumors that could be helpful. For all that he knew the reason for the curfew thanks to the veiled woman, he wasn't completely certain if that was the whole story. What was so threatening about one prisoner that the military would start locking down the city in which he or she was held? Or was it that they were afraid of outside interference? Why would they hold a prisoner in a facility that did not seem set up for it in the first place? By all accounts, this military base specialized in research. Were they experimenting on the rebel, or was there some other reason they had been brought here instead of somewhere more suitable? He needed to find out more; there was something important he was missing.

He supposed he could try to ask the veiled woman, but even if she knew the answer he doubted she would be able to communicate it clearly. He also hadn't heard from her at all since the bus back from the Temple of Faith, though he didn't think she was gone, just giving him the space he had asked for. He had no doubt that if he reached out for her she would be there.

Then again, every mission ran the risk of being based on false information. That was why he needed to be prepared for anything, but the problem was that he was having trouble even imagining what "anything" could mean in this place. The Rose Empire clearly had a bias towards tech, but the Truth Seekers used magic. Not that the common people knew this; Takeshi had overheard enough conversations over the past few nights to know that the general populace thought they just used very advanced tech. The question then became how magic and tech were used. As long as they didn't interact they could coexist, but then where was the tech and where was the magic? Was the magic solely used by the Seekers, or were there others? Had they somehow found a way to integrate the two? He didn't think so; he was sure they would have used that knowledge to convince Ni Fon to adopt more tech. There was also the fact that the Empire did seem to want to stomp magic out of existence with the sole exception of the Truth Seekers, so Takeshi doubted they were as interested in combining the two the way Ni Fon was.

Still, if they didn't want anything to do with magic, then why have the Truth Seekers at all? Why not use people equipped with advanced tech instead? If the answer to that was simply that tech hadn't caught up yet to what magic could do, what would happen to the Truth Seekers when it had? Throughout all the conversations in Ni Fon about integrating tech, no one had dared even suggest getting rid of the shinobi. Shinobi were integrated into the fabric of Ni Fon; trying to remove them at this point was risking them going rogue.

So much about this place did not make sense. He needed more information if this mission was to succeed.

The bar he found himself in on the fifth night of curfew was fairly close to the base and had a reputation for being a place the military personnel liked to get drinks. Takeshi was hoping that any information he might overhear here would be both more relevant and more accurate than what he was finding in many of the other bars, so he found himself a table near the counter and settled in with a beer and a plate of mini burgers to watch that night's soccer game while keeping an ear open for any useful conversations.

Unfortunately, as the game began to wrap up, Takeshi found himself disappointed. The bar was full, but nothing he had overheard was useful information. In fact, there had been even less sharing of theories here than there had been in the other bars. Perhaps the Empire's military was more disciplined than he had originally given them credit for, or perhaps they were simply wary of talking about their jobs in a public place. Certainly the patrons here seemed less upset about the curfew in general, joking around with each other about getting home before the Seekers came out in force.

Takeshi glanced at the clock. Forty minutes to go. Time to return to the hotel.

"I mean, maybe now that they know it works they can make others somewhere else, and we can go back to normal," someone muttered at a nearby table. "Charve was never meant for this."

Takeshi kept his eyes on the vid screen above the bar, showing a commercial for a new tablet. They were keeping their voices down, but Takeshi was good at picking conversations out of a cacophony. Returning back to normal? Making "others" somewhere else? That piqued his interest.

"We can only hope," a woman agreed wryly. "This is getting out of hand. I know they told us we supposedly have the only working prototype, but come on."

"What does it even do?" a third voice chimed in. "Does anyone know? Garif says it just looks like a cross between a small room and a large tank."

"No idea. You think they tell me these things?" the first man laughed. "All I know is that they've completely locked that section of the building down. Only the Seekers and top brass are going in or out. No regular base personnel are allowed anywhere near it anymore, and you need orders to enter the building at all."

Takeshi toyed with the last of his beer as the commercial changed to one for an upgraded banking service. A cross between a small room and a tank. A specialized prison of some sort, maybe? Specialized in what way? What were they developing here?

"And everyone's walking on eggshells because of it. Gods only know what they are using that tank for, but I'll be happy when they move it somewhere more suited for this sort of security," the woman murmured.

"I think everyone will be happier," the first man pointed out. "They won't be able to keep this up for too long without some sort of explanation, even with all the Seekers about. The Governor's already chafing that the military is telling him what to do. If he goes to the duchess about it–"

"Duchess Leblanc will back the military. Ever since that breakout a few weeks back in Lyndiniam and that Guard Commander's resignation, the dukes and duchesses have been cozying up to General Nashaat. That's why we have all this funding suddenly, at least according to Asha," the second man offered.

Takeshi blinked. Was the breakout in Lyndiniam linked to this? *How?* For that matter, how were the dukes and duchesses involved? The Empress of Ni Fon was technically the "Duchess of Ni Fon" in the Rose Empire; had she known about the breakout? He was going to have to look into that now as well. He was fairly certain the incident had been a few days before he was officially banished, if he was remembering the dates from the newspaper correctly. She couldn't have given him that information when he left? That would have been so unbelievably helpful! He would have had a direction from the start and could have cut out all this blind stumbling.

He paused and took a deep breath. He was making unfair assumptions. Even if the Empress had known about the breakout in Lyndiniam and linked it to the rebels, that Avari had broken out and fled. It was possible she believed he was no longer reachable – perhaps he had actually fled the Empire entirely. That was assuming the kid was even involved with the rebels in the first place; he might not have been. Also, the situation in Charve had blown up about a week after the breakout in Lyndiniam, so she wouldn't have had any way to tell him about this series of events even if she had made the connection.

Actually... he would have to check, but he was fairly certain the first day the Charve Military Base had shut down had been right around the same day he had set out from Ni Fon in the boat. Still, even if it had happened before he left, it was possible the Empress had received word about it only after he had left her range.

He pushed the annoyance aside – it wouldn't do him any good to dwell on it. He was here now, and he had a lead. He looked around; people were beginning to leave with the curfew looming.

"And yet, here we are, with everyone mad at us," the woman was saying, the conversation having continued while Takeshi had been trying to piece things together. "It doesn't matter that the curfew was instituted under the Guard's authority, everyone knows the military is behind it."

That was true, Takeshi mused to himself as he finished off his beer. The one thing everyone agreed on was that it was the military's fault.

"Well, the Seekers kind of give that away," the first man laughed. "High-tech military personnel? The Guard wishes they had the funding for the tech they use."

"They could be less obnoxious about it," the other man muttered. "There's no reason for them to be so rude to everyone they come into contact with."

"Yeah, the 'I'm so much better than you' attitude could be taken down a notch or two," the woman agreed. "Would it really kill them to work with other people instead of despite them?"

Takeshi stood and made his way to the door. The conversation had moved away from useful information, and he still had a bus to catch to make it back to the hotel. Still, he had gained another piece of the puzzle. There was some sort of special holding cell that was being developed at the base.

The question was, what made it special? He mulled the question over as the bus passed through the steadily emptying streets back to Redguard Suites. Perhaps, he realized, that was the wrong question. What if he looked at it from another angle? What if the question was actually *what are they trying to contain?*

What if the prisoner was a mage?

Most ways of dealing with mage prisoners involved either magic or drugs. As a tech-based society, Takeshi would have assumed the Rose would drug its prisoners, but what if they wanted information out of them? You usually had to drug a mage pretty heavily to successfully keep them from magic, making anything they could tell you questionable at best. If you didn't want to drug them, you needed another mage who was stronger to keep shields up so the prisoner couldn't do anything. For very strong mages, both techniques were often used for additional security – that was how Takeshi himself had been contained while under arrest.

If the Rose Empire had a powerful mage as a prisoner whom they wanted to interrogate rather than kill, they might have problems keeping them constrained if the Truth Seekers weren't powerful enough. Considering the Rose's bias, they might even want to cut out the Truth Seekers and their magic entirely and rely only on their tech. If so, then they would need to develop something that could either cancel or contain a mage's magic. Takeshi didn't have the slightest idea how that would work, but Hotaru had been pretty adamant in her belief that eventually tech would evolve to be able to do everything magic could, and Takeshi was inclined to believe her.

The theory fit. He didn't like it, but it fit. He could try to ask the veiled woman if her friend was a mage, and if she could confirm his theory. If it was indeed the case, then he had a whole different series of problems to deal with. Namely, how was he going to get someone out of a prison made specifically for mages? Would his magic work on it from the outside? If not, he would have to find out how to open it, which probably involved a key of some sort – and knowing the Empire, it was probably a code that needed to be typed into a computer.

Maybe if he just destroyed the computer the tank would open? Or at least the tech preventing the mage from using magic would fail?

He sighed heavily as he entered his room. Every time he learned something new about this mission it got worse and raised more questions. He still had to figure out if it was even possible for him to get into the base in the first place. He sat on the bed and closed his eyes for a minute or two, feeling exhausted. Maybe some meditation would help. And tea, tea was good.

He got up to heat some water and flipped on the news just in time to hear the announcement that the curfew was now in effect. He glanced towards the window reflexively, but it was dark out and all he could see was his own reflection in the glass. He pulled the curtains closed and tugged off his gloves, feeling the relief as the subtle drain on his magic stopped. Though the illusion spell didn't require a lot of power, keeping it up every day was becoming quite taxing. Perhaps he should take a day or two to rest before it became an actual problem? He didn't need any more of those.

While he waited for the tea to brew, he grabbed a piece of paper and a pencil and sketched out a basic calendar to try to figure out the timeline of events. He knew the curfew had started on Saturday; that one was easy. He had the date of the jailbreak in Lyndiniam thanks to the newspaper, which he added with a question mark. That had been on October eighteenth. He had overheard from the two men at the Green Garden Park that security at the military base had first increased two weeks prior – that put the transfer of the prisoner to Charve sometime around the twenty-third. Between then and when he had arrived in Charve on November fifth, Truth Seekers had begun showing up in greater numbers, presumably to help with security. News of a potential curfew had leaked in that time as well.

He looked at it for a moment, then added his sentencing on October twentieth and his leaving Ni Fon on the twenty-fourth. He had made accidental contact on the third of November with the veiled woman whose friend had been captured, and actual contact with her on the sixth. He considered the resulting picture, then added February twelfth above the calendar for the date of Hotaru's death and the start of the Empress's grand plan.

Was it just coincidence that the breakout in Lyndiniam, his sentencing after an unexplained eight-month delay, and the Charve Military Base gaining a special prisoner had all happened in the same week? Or were these events somehow connected? Or was he looking for patterns that weren't there because he wanted to see them?

Add in the veiled woman, and a strange web began to form, though he couldn't see the whole shape of it. Had she been looking for him specifically because he had been banished as a traitor and was therefore more likely to help? Or was there some other reason? It felt too coincidental to have been an accident.

Takeshi cradled the cup of tea in his hands, contemplating what it could all mean, or if it had any meaning at all. He closed his eyes and just breathed in the aroma of the tea for a few moments, allowing the familiar scent to help him relax. The news in the background was talking about improvements being made to the zoo, and he allowed the sound of the voices to wash over him.

When he opened his eyes again, he caught sight of the pamphlets from the Temple of Faith sitting to the side on the table. He sighed. In the end, did it matter? He was here, and he was here to do a job – he couldn't just abandon it, not after all that had been sacrificed to see him this far. Shinobi did not have the luxury of picking their missions, and this one had been chosen for him by the Empress herself. He had to see it through. For Hotaru's sake, if nothing else. He owed her that much.

He put the calendar and its troubling implications aside, deciding to look through the brochures a little more carefully to see if there was any other information he could use. He sipped his tea, keeping an ear out for anything interesting in the news while he read.

He was going through his third one, the pamphlet about the Temple of Faith, when a tidbit of information about the original church the temple had replaced caught his attention: "Because it was too expensive to plow in the case of excessive snow, the utility tunnels that connected the two campuses were sometimes used by instructors to get from the base to the academy, where they would then often stay until the weather improved. The original temple was added to the tunnel network so that students and instructors alike could make offerings even if the paths outside were impassable."

Utility tunnels? Linking the Temple of Faith, the academy, and Charve Military Base? He quickly grabbed for the map of Charve that he had stashed in a drawer and laid it out on the table, looking for the relevant locations. Laurent Military Academy was several miles from the base, so he could see why the instructors of years past wouldn't have wanted to go back and forth by foot every day. But this could be a way into the base for him, if he could find the entrance to the tunnels on the Temple grounds. Tunnel systems that large were ruinously expensive to fill in even if they were no longer being used, so he was confident they were still there even though the evolution of tech had likely rendered them useless. Or maybe it hadn't; Takeshi actually wasn't sure how utilities worked in the Rose Empire.

He would have to go back to the Temple and see if he could find the entrance to the tunnels. The Temple did have a basement, he remembered, though it wasn't open to guests. That was a minor inconvenience at worst for Takeshi – shinobi were very good at getting into places they didn't belong. And from what he had observed a few days ago, the Temple and academy grounds were barely guarded.

The hard part at the Temple was going to be finding the right door. The base on the other side was going to be a different matter entirely, but the perimeter was what would be most heavily guarded – if the tunnels put him on the grounds of the base proper, he would have completely bypassed the larger part of the base's defenses. He could spend one day investigating the church, and one night investigating the tunnels and the base itself before he came to any hard decisions about whether he could rescue the rebel prisoner.

Pleased with this discovery and the resulting plan of action, Takeshi carefully folded the pamphlet in with the map and put them aside for now. He picked up another pamphlet to read through, making a mental note to find something to use as lock picks.

:You... happy?...news?:

He blinked, then sighed. It had probably been too much to hope that she would wait for him to contact her.

:I have found a possible way onto the base.:

:Good news!: The excitement practically radiated off of her.

He supposed that if she was here, he could try to ask her his questions. He tried to keep them as simple as possible so her answers could be simple "yes" or "no." *:Your friend – are they a mage?:*

:...friend...?...a mage.: She sounded curiously thoughtful, but affirmative.

Well, that answered one question definitively at least. He paused, trying to figure out the best way to ask the next question. *:The Charve Military Base specializes in research. Is your friend being held in a new type of prison for mages?:*

There was a moment of stunned silence, then – *:Yes! How... this?:*

:This is usually good information to give to the person you are asking to perform the rescue,: he thought at her disapprovingly. *:Is there anything else you could tell me that would make this task possible?:*

He sensed a feeling of disagreement. *:It... matter. The cage... intact when... arrive.:*

He tried to parse that out, but failed. *:What?:*

:You... don't... worry... about... cage.: She sounded a bit frustrated as she stressed the words so he could understand her.

He was skeptical. *:That is something I feel like I should worry about.:*

Another sensation of disagreement. *:It... dealt with.:*

:It will be dealt with? By whom, the mage?: he asked disbelievingly. He was beginning to hate the phrase "it will be dealt with."

The reply was simple. *:Yes.:*

He considered that, then pointed out, *:If they can free themselves, then what am I doing in this plan?:*

:...only break... cage. ...need you... off the base. ...exhausted.:

If nothing else, that actually simplified matters significantly – if the mage was in fact able to free themself. If not, then it fell back to Takeshi. *:How sure are you of their success?:*

:Completely,: came the confident reply.

Well, that was something, at least. He'd still prepare for that contingency, but hopefully the mage was as competent as the veiled woman claimed. And if he could get onto the base, he should be able to get them off it.

Wait.

:How loud is that likely to be?:

The reply was sheepish. *:Very.:*

Okay, that was not ideal, but it could still be workable now that he knew. *:How do I coordinate with your friend? I don't want them blowing up anything before I'm ready.:*

:Tell me... in place!:

Yes, this method of communication could be quite useful in a variety of situations. The method of mind-to-mind communication he was familiar with was not nearly as easy to utilize and could be disorienting or even painful. This had none of those downsides.

He felt her curiosity. *:It shouldn't... that.:*

He shrugged. *:And yet it is.:* He paused, then decided to ask his other big question. *:Why ask me to help? What about the rest of the rebellion?:*

:You... hear me!: she replied cheerfully.

:Yes,: he drawled slowly. *:But surely there are others who can also hear you?:*

Her reply was a little sad. *:Very few... me. You... special.:*

He wasn't sure how to respond to that.

:You... see. When... Romanii, Ander... explain.:

His eyebrows rose. Romanii? So he had been on the right track with the Wall. *:Who is Ander?:*

:Another...: Her "voice" was fading more and more. He wondered if talking this way tired her, or if trying to reach him through whatever was blocking her did. At least he had some answers now.

:I'm going to search for the tunnels tomorrow,: he informed her. *:Hopefully that method of entry will prove to be viable. I will let you know.:*

:...be near,: she responded, pleased. *:...help...:* She faded out entirely.

He shook his head. He had things to prepare.

Chapter Twenty-Two

The next morning found Takeshi shopping for supplies before catching a bus back to the Laurent Military Academy Temple of Faith. This time he didn't bother with the visitor center; he knew where he was going.

He started in the large central room, dedicated to the Three. For Taijin, goddess of the physical world and the body, he left a small packet of herbs good for healing. At home, he might have gifted her a weapon, but he currently could not afford to give up the few he had. For Gakujin, goddess of the mind, he left a book. For Kijin, goddess of magic and the soul, he was at a bit of a loss – the usual offering back home was a spell crystal, but he didn't think that was a good idea here considering their anti-magic policies. Instead, he left her a monetary donation using the small credit reader set up for that purpose near the altar, mentally apologizing for the lesser offering. The Three had different names here in the Rose Empire – Lanarae, Selenae, and Firilae – but they were still the same deities he worshiped back home.

As he made the offerings and moved around the main room, he made sure to keep an eye out for any doors that might lead elsewhere. The only openings in immediate view led to the elemental chapels, so that was where he headed next, starting in the north with the Espera. For them, he had a small satchel of sage, which he burned to scent the air in their name. For the Nyphoren in the west, he left seashells, and he also offered another prayer on behalf of the *Sea Spirit*. The Patoran in the south received a bouquet of flowers, and the Faleri in the east received a candle, which he lit in their honor. By the time he had made all the offerings, there was a fair number of people about for him to blend into while he searched.

He finally found the door in a small, narrow hallway leading to the shrine of Tadurin, the god of life and creation. He glanced around casually as he tried the doorknob, and was pleased to find it unlocked. He slipped through the door quietly, closing it behind him as he stepped into a poorly lit stairwell leading down into the darkness. He mentally visualized the pattern for a small mage light and called it to his hand before continuing.

At the bottom of the stairwell was another door leading to a dark hallway. Takeshi was considering which direction he should start in when he caught sight of a flutter of black fabric disappearing around the corner of the hallway to the left.

He stared. There was no way.

:Follow,: the voice of the veiled woman whispered through his mind.

:If you are here, why do you not show yourself?: he wondered to her, turning down the left hallway.

:Because I... actually here. But... help you find... looking for. Follow.:

He was surprised to find that she was easier to hear. He still wasn't getting everything, but it felt like he was picking up much more than he usually did, and she sounded a little louder.

:Maybe... made an offering... would hear..., but... we are.: That last thought sounded extremely unhappy and a little hurt, but he didn't know why. He had just made seven offerings as an apology for potentially abusing the temple grounds, what more did she want?

Takeshi followed the scraps of black fabric that disappeared almost as soon as he saw them through the hallways under the church. He passed many doors, which, had he been on his own, he would have had to check, even though many of them were probably just storage. This was far more efficient than what he had planned, he had to give her that. He also made sure to memorize the path they took so he could retrace his steps later.

Finally he came to an unmarked door at the end of a hallway. *:Here,:* she whispered to him. *:I will be... need me.:* Her presence faded.

He tried the doorknob, but unlike the door upstairs this one was locked. He opened his bag and drew out a pair of sturdy paperclips. He preferred actual lock picks, but these would do just fine. He bent them into the proper shapes and made quick work of the lock. The door swung open, revealing a ramp leading down to a second locked door. That lock fared no better than the first, and Takeshi found himself in the utility tunnels.

The tunnel was rectangular and fairly narrow, made of concrete instead of lester. A number of pipes ran the length of the tunnel as far down as he could see in either direction. Only patches of a dingy, gray, peeling paint remained on some of the pipes. He could see an emergency light above the door he had entered through, but it didn't seem to be working. On the wall across from the door was a simple map of the tunnels, labeled with numbers and letters at various exits. He pulled out his city map to compare, deciding exit 4B should be on the military base proper.

He stayed there for about ten minutes in the glow of his mage light, committing the map to memory. He then considered going farther down the tunnels. This was as far as he had expected to go today, but the veiled woman's help had sped up the search process considerably and saved him probably an hour or two of searching. He estimated that the base was about an hour and a half to two hours away, depending on how much the tunnels twisted, though, based on the map, the route should be fairly straight.

He decided to travel down the tunnels at least a little to start to familiarize himself with them. With one last glance at the map, he turned and began walking east. He kept his light close, not that he expected to run into anyone else down here. It was pretty obviously abandoned; he would bet no one had been down here in a long time. The concrete was worn, with reddish streaks of what might have been water damage dripping down from the ceiling, though the tunnel was dry now. He also saw sections that were redder than others, which may at one point have been paint but was now long gone. Some of the pipes clanked ominously every once in a while, indicating that they might still be in use. The tunnels branched off every so often, but Takeshi made sure to follow the map in his head.

After a while, he noticed the ground getting a little damp. He could feel the moisture and warmth in the air and see the condensation on the walls and collecting on the pipes. Up ahead, he could see the tunnel brightening a bit, so he doused his light and continued forward. Here, some of the pipes along the ceiling had been wrapped in a fibrous material that might have been white at some point but was now discolored with brownish tints and looked frayed on the edges. Sounds from above began filtering in – he could make out the sounds of traffic and conversation. He made certain to be as silent as the grave, creeping through as the source of the light came into view – small, narrow windows high up near the ceiling on the left side. He estimated that he was about halfway to his destination, so above was a civilian sector, not either of the bases.

He suddenly froze, staying very, very still, concentrating on being one with the damp concrete as the feeling of a Truth Seeker search swept over him. Literally over him – it felt like they were focusing at street level. He didn't know what had gained their attention – this was the first search he had felt since coming to Charve – and he didn't want to know. Patiently, he waited as another search answered the first, this one farther away. A pair of gray boots walked past the small window above, and the feeling of the Seekers disappeared.

Takeshi waited a few more minutes just in case, considering. Should he continue today? The Seekers were looking for something in the city, and whatever that was did not bode well. This was farther than he had expected to go today anyway, and it was a good start. He now knew how to get into the tunnels, and he knew how to navigate them. He had made good progress, but now it might be time to return above and find out if something had happened that might affect his plans. He knew he wouldn't have any problems returning to this point.

Slowly he backed away from the windows, making sure he was a good distance away and could no longer hear the world above before weaving another mage light. He passed through the tunnels quickly, finding himself back at the Temple without any difficulty. He retraced his steps through the basement and escaped back into the church proper with no one the wiser. Nothing seemed out of the ordinary here; people were still moving around the building, making offerings or following the self-guided tour. Takeshi made one last prayer to the Three, asking them for any aid they could give, before returning back to the city proper.

When he got off the bus, it seemed pretty clear that something must have happened, if not what. He didn't see a single Truth Seeker, and people were gathered around the vid screens in the city, chatting animatedly amongst themselves. Takeshi, both tired and hungry at this point, decided there was nothing wrong with the vid screen in his hotel room, and quickly headed back. He pulled his gloves off almost as soon as he was through the door and turned on the news, finding himself almost stunned.

There had been a bank robbery.

More accurately, there had been an attempted bank robbery. Takeshi had no idea how stupid one had to be to attempt such a thing in a city teeming with Truth Seekers, but then reflected that he was essentially going to try the same thing with a more dangerous target and withdrew his judgement. Then again, he had magic, and it was becoming clear the more he watched that the bank robbers did not. They had actually gotten pretty far, utilizing some fairly basic tech in creative ways, before accidentally tripping an alarm which had brought the entire force of the Truth Seekers swarming down on them.

Takeshi was fairly certain the bank robbers were never going to see the light of day again. He pulled out a can of soup and heated it in the microwave as he followed the unfolding drama. The city seemed desperate for news that was not about the curfew, and this fit the bill. Everyone would be talking about it for days, which was actually unfortunate. It killed his main method of gathering intel; while the attempted robbery was interesting, it wasn't what he was interested in. At least he already had a good amount of information to work with.

He hoped this wouldn't lead to further increased security – the amount they had now was already a pain to have to deal with. More would just be excessively difficult. The Temple would probably be fine; it was the base that concerned him. Trying to infiltrate tonight was definitely out of the question, but he thought he should be able to manage it tomorrow. He could take some time today and a portion of tomorrow to rest and recover some energy, then head to the tunnels.

He sat down with his soup, pulling out the pamphlet with the little map of the base. He needed to make sure he had memorized the layout. Tomorrow he would be putting it to use.

Takeshi made sure everything he would need was packed before he left the hotel room, since he didn't expect to be returning until the next day.

He arrived at the Temple of Faith around four in the afternoon with his bag and slipped into the utility tunnels with the same ease as the day before. He traveled in a little ways before settling down on the ground next to the pipes – he didn't actually want to arrive on the base before nightfall. He was going to need the cover of darkness to pull this off successfully. To mitigate the curfew problem, he had decided to enter the tunnels before it went into effect, and if everything went well he would be leaving them well after it lifted the next morning. He had slept late in expectation of staying up throughout the night and was as ready as he could be. After tonight, he would know for sure if rescuing the veiled woman's friend was a viable endeavor or not.

He removed his gloves and put on a second, non-spelled set and his mask – he would be doing this as himself. It would be easier to infiltrate without an active spell going. He pulled out a granola bar to munch on, as well as a watch he had bought for this purpose, and waited. He allowed himself to doze a little to pass the time.

Finally, the little numbers on the watch switched to ten. Time to go.

Takeshi took a few things from the bag and tucked them into his clothing. He wove a dim mage light, tinting it purple, and tucked the bag away under a nearby pipe before beginning to creep down the tunnel. He didn't make a single sound as he glided through the empty passageways. He dismissed the light when the tunnels began to grow damp, unwilling to risk the possibility of someone seeing the glow through the small windows. He would have to go without light from here on out. He pulled some of his magic into his eyes so he would be able to see in the complete absence of light, and after a few moments to allow his eyes to adjust he was moving again, a silent shadow among other shadows.

He ducked low and stayed as close to the wall and pipes as he could when he came up to the windows, not bothering to look for any of the Truth Seekers in the streets. If he could see them, then they could potentially see him, and that was not something he was interested in courting. He slunk past, picking up his pace a little when the windows disappeared again. He followed the map in his head closely, occasionally checking the marks that remained on the wall, just barely visible in the dark.

Finally, he reached his destination – exit 4B. He pressed close to the door and sent out his senses to the other side. Pleased when he couldn't feel the presence of any people, he turned his attention to the lock. A number pad sat above the mechanism.

Tech. Wonderful. Luckily, though magic and tech did not work well together and attempts to make them interact often ended explosively, sometimes controlled destruction was the goal. Takeshi called a spark of lightning to his fingertips and sent it into the lock, causing the components inside to short out.

The door swung open, revealing a ramp up to another door with a similar keypad. Takeshi wove a quick spell to dry and clean off his boots so he wouldn't be tracking any of the moisture or debris from the tunnels into the building as he examined a faint light creeping in from under the door. He again sent his magic to search for people, but there was no one. He quietly shorted the second lock and edged the door open. No alarm sounded. He pushed it a little further open and glanced around. He appeared to be in a large, dimly lit storage room of some sort, with what looked like medical supplies stacked on shelves everywhere. He was probably in the medical facility, then. He slid inside and quickly shut the door. There was another door directly across from him, though this one did not appear locked.

His next course of action needed to be getting outside.

He slunk around the shelves over to the door. He still couldn't feel the presence of another person, so he eased the door open to find a lit stairwell. He silently climbed the stairs, stopping at the next landing. There were two doors, one labeled "Exit" and the other "Floor 1." Takeshi crept towards the exit, checking for any presences. He frowned; someone was on the other side of the door. They didn't appear to be moving. He would have to find another way.

He checked the other door and found it free of people. He opened it to find a brightly lit corridor ending in a "T" intersection. There were four doors along the corridor, all with frosted glass windows and little copper nameplates. The first door to his left had the name "Dr. Samern" engraved on it. An office, probably. Patients wouldn't have copper engraved nameplates. And windows would work just as well as doors, as far as Takeshi was concerned.

The lights in the room were off, so Takeshi tried the doorknob. It was locked. He pulled out the paperclips and picked it quickly, not wanting to be found standing in the hallway. He slid inside, quietly shutting the door behind him. It was a small office, with a sturdy metal desk and a selection of chairs. A small bookshelf was against the wall to the left, and a number of plants lined the windowsill.

Takeshi unlatched and opened the window, removing the screen and hiding it behind the bookcase. He glanced around outside. He could see people moving along the road in the distance, but there was no one close by. He slid out through the window, making sure to only close it most of the way behind him.

Now, in the night, Takeshi was in his element. One of the first exercises young shinobi were taught was how to hide. Once a week, the children were brought to a place not unlike this, with buildings and greenery and other things to hide behind, and set free. If they could avoid an instructor finding them for twenty minutes, they were allowed to return to bed. If they were found before that time was up, they had to hide again – and again, and again, until they succeeded. If they did not succeed before the sun rose, they had to go without sleep for the day.

Takeshi had fond memories of the game. He had always been rather good at it. This was, quite literally, child's play for him.

He brought up his mental map of the area; the medical facility was on the south side of the base. Based on the conversation he had overheard, he was looking for one of the research and development buildings. There had been two unlabeled buildings north and a little west of the medical facility that Takeshi thought promising, so that was where he needed to go next. He looked up at the sky to orient himself and began heading north-west.

His assumption that most of the security would be around the base rather than on it was quickly proven correct. Though there were some soldiers around the area, they were almost amusingly easy to avoid. By Takeshi's estimate it was nearly midnight, so even though he was heading in the direction of the dining hall and on-base apartments, few people were out and about. He slipped from shadow to shadow towards his target.

It didn't take him long to arrive, and he decided he was definitely in the right place. The more northern of the two buildings had a pair of Truth Seekers standing outside the main entrance, both looking alert. He wouldn't be able to get in that way. He scouted around the building, discovering Seekers at the back entrance as well. He considered it. The building was two stories tall and made of lester, clearly one of the newer buildings he had seen on the premises. There were few windows, further narrowing his options.

:...close enough,: the veiled woman's voice whispered.

He cocked his head to the side as he studied the building. *:Oh?:*

:You... won't want... inside...,: came the quiet affirmation. Her voice was back to being patchy.

:I see,: he drawled.

:...will... time to... array.:

An array? Ah yes, the name for patterns used by non-Nifoni mages. *:How big is it going to be?:* he wondered.

Her response was simple. *:Big.:*

He wondered how the mage was going to pull that off. *:How long to complete it?:*

There was a pause. *:...days.:*

Takeshi nodded. Whatever they were planning, it was going to be spectacular. *:If it fails, we will both die,:* he informed her.

:No!: she replied firmly. Her presence disappeared abruptly.

:Then make sure it works,: he thought grimly. With one last glance at the building, he began to make his way back to the medical facility. Speed would be essential once the mage's spell was cast, so as he flitted from cover to cover he made sure to plan out a path for their retreat. Hopefully he would be able to use the confusion as a smoke screen. He might even be able to plant smaller explosions in other places to add to the chaos. Yes, that was a good idea.

He slid back into the medical facility through the window, carefully replacing the screen and latching the window shut behind him. He then crept back to the stairwell, checking for any possible complications as he went, finally entering the storage room again. There was nothing he could do to fix the locks he had fried; luckily it didn't seem as though the doors were used very often anyway. It was very possible the tampering wouldn't be noticed. And even if it was discovered and fixed, he would be able to deal with it easily.

He glided back into the tunnels, pleased with how the scouting mission had gone overall. The plan was viable if the mage could do what the veiled woman had implied. And it sounded like he had a few days to gather strength himself as well. He began the long trek back through the tunnels to where he had left his supplies; he could rest for a bit while he waited for the curfew to lift and the Temple of Faith to open to the public.

The only way Rhode could describe it was that she seemed distracted, but by what he couldn't fathom. There was nothing in her cell, and for once she wasn't even looking at him through the one-way glass. She seemed to be staring off into space. He cleared his throat.

"Not now," the Avari said airily. "I'm busy."

"Is that so? Anything I can help with?" It was interesting that she thought when they talked was up to her.

"No," came the dismissive response. She closed her eyes.

Maybe he was actually getting to her. He wondered how much longer before she broke. How long had it been since she had eaten? More than two weeks? That had to be doing something. She did seem to be getting thinner.

Patience was key.

He checked the readouts, but they showed nothing of note. For someone who seemed like an active, social individual, she was strangely content to sit by herself and do nothing. He turned to the Truth Seeker on guard by the door.

Madine shook her head. Nothing magical was happening in the cell either.

"I must admit, I had expected a little more from you." He tried to draw the white-haired woman's attention back to him. "But you haven't attempted to escape even once."

She snorted. "You're the one telling me how futile that would be."

"Of course – but you have no interest in testing it even a little?"

"I don't need to test anything," came the mild response. "I already know what I need to."

Rhode considered that. "It seems strange for a woman in your position to take the word of her jailer at face value," he mused. "Not even the strongest mage could escape from here, it's true, but to not even try? There's been no word of a rescue being mounted for you either. They left you here to rot, and you are oddly content with that." He paused. "What kind of a person are you?"

"I am what I am. It's not your fault you're only Human," she murmured.

"Oh? Because the Avari are so much more than that," he chuckled in response, amused at her audacity.

For the first time that day she turned to look at him, certain as ever of his location. "No," she said coolly. "They are the same."

Chapter Twenty-Three

E very muscle in Jamirh's body ached as the alarm went off. He almost whimpered at the thought of dragging himself out of bed for more torture, otherwise known as "Jeri's training."

Every day for the past week Jeri had been bringing him to the palace training grounds. Jamirh wasn't sure what he had been expecting when he agreed to learn how to fight with daggers, but what he got wasn't it. Her first lesson was on how to fall – which meant that he fell many times until he got it right. Jeri explained that since he was likely to end up on the ground often, being able to do so safely and in a somewhat controlled manner was an essential skill. She also explained that Jamirh wasn't built to stand and take hits. Ideally he would dodge them, which meant increasing his reflexes and flexibility, which meant a lot of exercises and stretches. Jamirh had thought he was in pretty good shape, but Jeri was rapidly showing him otherwise.

He hadn't even actually touched a set of daggers yet, not even the fake practice ones he had seen other people training with. They were far from the only people who used the training grounds – Avari, Humans, and Vampires were all present throughout the day and night, practicing in pairs, groups, or even solo. There were all manner of weapons in use. Jamirh had seen daggers, guns, bows, at least five types of swords, staves, spears, even a giant hammer. Some people practiced unarmed combat. There were large outdoor sections as well as indoor and "specialized" rooms you could reserve, whatever that meant. Jeri usually reserved one of the regular indoor rooms for them.

Groaning and ears drooping, he hauled himself up to get ready for the day before Jeri arrived. He might have hated her for it if she didn't bring that tea every morning that did a wondrous job of easing the aches throughout his body. That stuff was amazing. But he was also a bit excited – today he would get to actually use daggers. Not real ones; that would be hazardous to probably both him and Jeri. But it was progress.

He finished washing up and entered into the main sitting area. Strange; Jeri was normally here by now. He stood in place for a minute, trying to make his tired mind decide what to do, before deciding to collapse on the couch to wait for her.

He was startled out of his doze by a knock on the door sometime later. Blinking blearily as he tried to process the knock, it took a moment for him to call for Jeri to come in. She waltzed through the door, carrying a tray with the tea, coffee, and a selection of breakfast foods. She offered a cheerful greeting as she set the tray down on the coffee table.

"Sorry I'm late; there was some sort of strange power outage in Pitesh last night and we were trying to figure out what happened." She smiled wryly as she watched him sit up slowly, trying to avoid making the pain worse. "The more you practice, the less it will hurt," she assured him as he made a beeline for the tea. "Eventually, your body will become accustomed to all the new things you are asking of it."

Jamirh downed the cup. He just had to wait ten minutes for it to kick in. At least it didn't taste bad. Not that it tasted good either; it was sort of medicinal. "So you've been saying. How long does it take?" he complained as he eyed the food, ears starting to perk up. Did he want to start with a muffin, or bacon?

She snorted. "A week is barely anything. Patience; you'll get there eventually. It can vary depending on the person."

He chewed on a piece of bacon, wincing at the pain even that slight movement caused. "Great." He thought back to what she had said about Pitesh. "Is a power outage really a security issue? I thought that's what the Black Watch did, not utilities."

"True, but if the problem is with one of the main boilers it could very rapidly become a security issue. If one of those goes, the resulting explosion would take out a large chunk of the city. The Watch would be in charge of evacuation if we thought that was a possibility. Luckily, whatever was wrong appears to have fixed itself – power came back on about an hour ago. They are going to keep a close eye on it, but everything was checking out last I heard." She selected a croissant from the tray, broke off a piece with her fingers, and popped it into her mouth.

Jamirh chewed thoughtfully. "The boilers can explode?" He didn't think that was a problem with Empire tech.

She nodded. "Yes, though we've never had it happen. Maintenance and upkeep of the boilers is prioritized for that reason, and when they get old enough they are shut down and retired safely."

Huh. Stuff here was strange. Jamirh reached for the cranberry muffin. "So – daggers, today?" he asked hopefully.

She rolled her eyes. "Yes, we'll start with the practice ones – after you've completed your stretches."

He groaned.

"No skipping stretches! They are important. If the pain is bothering you that much, I can acquire a spell crystal that will warm the blankets for you when you go to bed – the heat should help with the muscle ache," she offered. "They are very popular in the winter in general, actually."

"It makes heated blankets? Yes, please," he begged, eyes wide. What he wouldn't have given for something like that during the cold nights back home.

She smiled. "All right, I'll make sure to do that."

By the time they finished breakfast, the tea had worked its magic and Jamirh was moving comfortably again, just in time to go down to the training grounds and do more stretches. Though to be fair, they didn't usually hurt too much while he was doing them; it was after he had stopped moving for a while that he found everything seized up.

Then Jeri handed him a pair of wooden daggers, and they got to work.

Jamirh was going to have a lot of bruises by the time the day was done.

He quickly realized that what he was really good at was following Jeri's movements. If he watched her very intently, all it took to memorize a move was seeing her perform it once or twice. And once he had learned a move, he didn't forget it. He could picture it clearly in his mind, and he could copy the individual actions perfectly when she asked him to. Unfortunately, when it came to actually utilizing what he had learned against Jeri, it felt like his body was in disagreement with his mind over how to execute the actions. The disconnect was leaving him on the ground and sporting new bruises more often than not.

"I kind of thought," Jamirh panted at one point, "that I'd be doing more throwing of daggers, and less direct combat with them."

Jeri tilted her head to the side. "Both techniques are useful, but honestly, this is the better of the two to start off with. Because just so you know, if you throw one of these at me – or any other Vampire over a certain age, or any one of a number of creatures or monsters – and get a perfect heart shot, I'm still standing. Then where would you be? You wouldn't have a weapon anymore, and I'd still be coming at you."

"Uh, if a heart shot doesn't work I think I'm dead either way," Jamirh pointed out dryly. "Whether or not I'm holding a dagger probably doesn't matter." Then he frowned. "What would kill you, if six inches of steel to the heart doesn't?"

"You really have to behead us, or set us on fire. Those are extremely effective methods," she answered easily. "If you have a wooden stake, putting that through the heart will freeze us – we can't move for some reason when pierced through the heart with wood. Steel does not have the same effect. Silver can cause a lot of damage to us as well – it causes a type of chemical burn that can be debilitating. Younger Vampires are also much easier to kill, as we grow more resistant to many forms of damage over time."

"Like the sunlight?" he asked curiously, glancing up at the ceiling as though he could see the slight glimmer in the air high above their heads.

"Yes, like that. With enough blood and time, very old Vampires can put themselves back together from just about anything other than beheading or being burnt to a crisp."

Jamirh's eyebrows rose. "That seems... useful."

"Well, we are technically already dead, so something that would stop a Human or an Avari won't necessarily work against us." She raised her practice daggers again. "Let's keep going."

His head was spinning with the influx of information by the time they finished, uncertain if he had done well or poorly as she ran him through some exercises to help him cool down. It felt like a little of both. Jeri at least was exceptionally pleased with how much they had covered and how he had done, even if Jamirh could already imagine the pain he would be in later that night.

At least Jeri delivered on her promise of the spell crystal. It was a red, diamond-shaped crystal, about three inches long and warm to the touch, that he had to put under the covers at the foot of his bed about fifteen minutes before he planned on turning in. He was initially uncertain how something that small could heat the entirety of the large bed, but his worries quickly proved unfounded – it worked like a charm, and he now had a new favorite thing. Even Jeri's warning that the spell it contained would need to be refreshed at some point midwinter didn't diminish his joy at the little thing and the way it helped him sleep mostly pain-free.

Jeri allowed him to take the next day off from practice to give his body a chance to rest, leading him to declare her his new favorite person ever. They were right back to torture the next day, however, making Jamirh seriously consider revoking that title.

He was panting and sweating, trying to remember everything she had told him to do as he prepared himself to get whacked again, when a cool voice called out from the doorway, "I'd wondered what you were filling your time with. Daggers, really? Not a sword?"

Ander was leaning against the door frame, eyeing them critically.

Jeri sighed. "And what causes a High Priest to grace us with his exalted presence on this day?"

Even Jamirh winced at the bite in her tone, ears dropping, but it didn't seem to bother Ander at all, who bowed in dramatic fashion. "This humble servant of the Goddess has just been wondering what some other humble servants of the

Goddess might be up to lately, since he hasn't seen them in a while." He pulled himself up. "I must say, I'm surprised at the choice of weapon. Wouldn't a sword be better suited?"

Jeri was rearing back to let Ander have it, but Jamirh cut her off, saying quietly, "Jeri says I'm good at them." He brought a hand up to his chest, the familiar metal of his key reassuring.

They all stared at each other for a moment – whatever Ander had expected Jamirh to say, it clearly hadn't been that. The white-haired man cocked his head to the side, sizing Jamirh up, before responding somewhat ominously with, "Is that so?" His eyes slid to Jeri.

Jeri looked uncertain. "He does show an aptitude for them. And any method of self-defense is better than–"

Ander made a circular gesture, and with a swirl of green magic, two wooden daggers appeared in his hands. "Well, then. Show me what you've learned so far."

Jamirh shifted his weight uneasily and looked to Jeri, who shrugged. "Ander is practiced at many forms of combat," she offered with a frown. "Though, we did just start with the actual daggers two days ago, Ander. Keep that in mind."

"What, you don't think me capable of dealing with a novice?" Ander smirked. "What a low opinion of me you must have."

Jeri pressed her lips together in a thin line before answering. "You could always just stop, you know."

"Sorry, but giving up isn't really my thing," he chuckled, before his eyes zeroed back in on Jamirh.

That was all the warning Jamirh got before he found himself on his back on the ground, staring up at the ceiling. "Ow," he said belatedly. He hadn't even seen the other man move.

"Ander..." came Jeri's warning growl.

"What?" came the innocent reply. "I don't think he was ready, actually."

Jamirh sat up. "What the hell was that?"

Ander grinned at him. "Let's try again, shall we?"

"Will I be able to see you this time?" Jamirh asked, mulishly staying in place.

"Sure," Ander shrugged, a strange gleam in his eyes.

"*Yes,*" Jeri snapped, angrily crossing her arms. "Play fair. What would *She* say?"

Ander raised an eyebrow. "Do you really want to go there?"

Jamirh carefully hauled himself up and set himself into the proper stance Jeri had taught him. Ander didn't even seem to be bothering, looking extremely relaxed as he watched Jamirh get into position.

Jamirh managed to deflect the first hit before he was sent spinning away this time. Technically, he had been able to see Ander, but the man was *fast*. Jamirh had no idea how he made himself move that way. At least he was still standing.

Jeri, weirdly, looked pleased. "That was really good, Jamirh!" she praised.

"Thanks?" he asked more than said, uncertain how true that was. It hadn't felt good. And Ander's eyes were still pinning him in place, like a cat about to catch a mouse. Jamirh winced as he took up his stance again.

"Should I add magic? Our opponents might," Ander asked conversationally.

"No!" Jeri exclaimed. "He started learning two days ago! *Two*! Do you know what 'two' means?"

"Fair point, I suppose," he responded as he lunged at Jamirh again.

Jamirh tried to defend, but Ander again scored a kill shot seconds after he engaged. He retreated to give Jamirh a minute to regroup, but Jamirh's mind was replaying what he had just seen. It had been very graceful, the way Ander had almost danced forward on that last move. Pretty, in a deadly way.

Ander came at him again, and Jamirh found himself on stinging knees as he slid four feet back, one of his daggers accidentally flying across the room while Jeri hid her face in her hands. Ander waited patiently while Jamirh retrieved it.

"Are we done showing me how little I know?" Jamirh asked as he mulishly positioned himself yet again, determined not to let Ander discourage him. He was very thankful for Jeri's falling lessons at this point. If he hadn't thought Ander and Jeri strongly disliked each other, he would almost assume she might have put Ander up to it to make Jamirh appreciate her teaching more.

"Yes, are we done?" Jeri sounded tired.

"Once more, I think," Ander said thoughtfully, right before he lunged at Jamirh again, giving him no chance to react–

It happened almost in slow motion for Jamirh. His body moved exactly the way Ander's had earlier, dancing forward and around the other man's attack in order to land his own.

Everyone froze, stunned.

"Damn," Jeri finally said, eyes wide. "That was amazing, Jamirh."

"I– I don't know how I did that," Jamirh stammered, practically falling over himself as he moved away from Ander. "How did I do that?"

"Interesting," Ander said after a moment, slowly straightening up. "Imagine if you put *that* to use with a sword instead of these things." The daggers he had been holding dissolved into green threads of energy. He gave Jamirh a long, searching look, then turned to Jeri. "Can I talk to you for a minute?"

She frowned but nodded. "If we must. Jamirh, why don't you go get cleaned up, and I'll meet you back at your rooms for dinner in a bit, okay? We can talk about this then. Remember to do stretches to cool down!"

He nodded, still a little stunned. He had actually hit Ander. "Ah, sure. See you later, then." He returned his practice daggers to the display against the wall and gave the two a wave before leaving the room, but instead of leaving he stayed close to the doorway, ears twitching, certain that he was going to be the topic of discussion. He wanted to know what they were going to say about him.

"When you and Jamirh broke off and headed towards the Wall, you said it was because something was chasing you?" Ander's voice was quiet, but Jamirh could still hear him clearly.

"Yes, and it felt... strange. It definitely wasn't a Truth Seeker. She said she would deal with it," Jeri responded, sounding a little surprised. "Why?"

Oh. They weren't talking about him at all.

"I think there has been a misunderstanding, and it's at least partially my fault. In the meeting last week, I said – well, I implied – that Hades had finally found some proof that the Abomination is out there."

"And that the residue of it was on that Human She found, yes. You said She was excited," Jeri agreed.

Ander's tone turned slightly annoyed. "That's where I think I erred. I think all of Her excitement was actually about that Human, not the Abomination. She has recently revealed to me that that was actually the second time She had come into contact with it."

"Really?" Jeri sounded shocked. "When was the first time? Why didn't She tell you?" There was a pause that made Jamirh wish he could see them before Jeri said slowly, "Oh. Oh, no. That would explain a lot, unfortunately."

"You said it felt strange. Would you recognize it, if you felt it again?" Ander asked grimly.

"Yes," Jeri murmured. "It was unique enough that I could. Did She give you any more information about what it is?"

"She doesn't seem to have understood it, somehow. She recognized it as Abomination, but couldn't understand why, and has been trying to figure that out *before* telling me. She hasn't succeeded. The good news is that whatever it is, it can be destroyed."

Jeri's voice sounded worried. "Do you have any theories?"

"The fact that She's having trouble comprehending it may mean it has something to do with–"

Jamirh was forced to abruptly pull away at the sound of other voices approaching around the corner. He turned and quickly made for his rooms, not wanting to be caught listening at doorways. He wished he had heard the end of that conversation, though – what did Ander think the Abomination had to do with? He was fairly certain they had been talking about whatever Hel had stayed behind to deal with when he and Jeri had booked it for the Warcross Wall. They thought *that* was the Abomination? That would mean it had been responsible for Hel's capture.

Jamirh frowned as he thought that over. Whatever it was, that meant Hel had fought it and lost. That pretty much killed his hope that it was something that couldn't be stabbed, though he supposed whether or not it *should* be stabbed could still be up in the air. What if it was something that exploded when you stabbed it? He doubted that would be the case. Still, he wasn't sold on the demon idea either – wouldn't Hades have been able to tell if it were demons, since that was something that had happened before? So... it was something new. But what?

Maybe he could just ask Ander? The priest had been fairly upfront with him before. But then, why only direct this information towards Jeri? Why not tell Jamirh too?

They definitely weren't telling him something.

He was also pretty sure that had been the most civil conversation he'd heard yet between Ander and Jeri, which was impressive considering how antagonistic they had just been towards each other.

Jamirh shook his head as he entered his rooms, determined to take a long, hot bath. He could ask Jeri about it when she came by for dinner.

While he was soaking, he came up with another thought – what if they had decided that since he didn't want to be involved, he didn't need to know any more? What if they thought they were doing him a favor? For some reason, that didn't sit well with him either. As much as he did not want to be bound by the choices of an Avari from a thousand years ago, he still found himself wanting to know. He liked to know things. And, if they were going to cut him out of the loop, what was there to say that they wouldn't decide he was unnecessary and send him off on his own again? What if that's what Ander had been doing today – seeing how useless Jamirh actually was as a replacement for their Hero? He could end up losing everything he'd gained by coming to Romanii.

He might not like the threat of having to fight a shadowy danger of some sort, but he liked everything else about being here. He didn't want to have to give that up.

Jamirh was still contemplating this later when there was a knock on the door. He glanced at the clock, seeing that it was dinner time, and called out his permission to enter. Jeri came in with a soft greeting, followed by a palace servant holding a dinner tray. The servant placed the tray on the coffee table and exited, leaving Jamirh with a tired-looking Jeri.

She smiled weakly. "Ander has reason to believe the thing that chased us out of the Empire was at least related to the Abomination, if not a true manifestation."

Jamirh blinked, a little blindsided. She was... actually telling him? Immediately? "What?" he stammered.

"The thing that captured or defeated Hel – that was probably an Abomination," she repeated, folding herself into a chair in the sitting area. She picked up the glass filled with blood and looked into it. "We just barely avoided it, whatever it was."

He frowned at that, though internally he was extremely relieved that Jeri at least wasn't keeping secrets from him. "You don't know?" He thought back to what he had overheard. "How do you even know that?"

She shook her head. "Ander has a partial theory, but that's all it is – a theory. And Hades told him what She could. Apparently whatever it was confused her."

Jamirh did not understand how that could be so. "How does something confuse a goddess with what it is? Did she, like, see it? Or... what even are the other options? How do gods know things?" He was confusing himself with this train of thought. He took the seat opposite Jeri and reached for his own glass of wine.

Jeri smiled faintly. "That sounds a bit like a theological question for Ander, but the short version is that She can sense the corruption inherent in an Abomination. I did as well, it turns out, but I did not recognize it for what it was."

He thought that over as he took his plate. "Did Hel recognize it when she left us?"

"When she left us? Almost certainly." Jeri sighed. "It's probably why she decided to stay behind."

"What is Ander's almost-a-theory?" Jamirh asked after a moment to process that. Hel had known, and still stayed. He didn't know what to think about that. It did make him feel worse.

"Well, it only kind of makes sense, is the problem," she started, pausing to take a sip. "Ander thinks that tech might be involved, since Hades – and deities in general – don't tend to do well with tech, so it would explain the fact that She for some reason does not understand what She sensed. But..." Jeri trailed off.

Jamirh was already shaking his head. "If it were tech, wouldn't the whole Empire be lighting up for the goddess? And we've been using it for over a century at this point – it's a little late if that's the case, isn't it?"

"And that's why the theory doesn't really work." Jeri inclined her head. "He thinks it could be some sort of new tech, but neither of us can fathom what that could be."

Jamirh shrugged. "I have no idea, either. What could cause some tech to alert her, and other tech not to?"

They ate in silence for a few minutes. Jamirh couldn't see how it could be related to any tech he knew about. Ander was right that if it was somehow connected, it had to be something new. Though, thinking of Ander brought up another question that had been gnawing at Jamirh for a while now, though he hadn't really had the opportunity to ask.

"Ander mentioned that he was the eighth High Priest of Hades, or something like that. Is he really only the eighth person to hold that title? How long ago was Hades' religion founded, if that's the case?"

Jeri looked up in surprise. "Oh, no. No, that's not what that means. It means that out of all the priests of Hades currently living, Ander is the eighth oldest. Priests of Hades have been around for thousands of years, just never in large numbers."

Jamirh's ears twitched. "So if one of the older ones were to die, Ander would become the seventh High Priest?"

"Yes, exactly." She nodded. "There are only eight around right now at all – Ander is actually the youngest. In theory, the oldest nine would be 'High Priests', and any others would just be priests, but there's never been more than eight. Actually, there had never been more than seven, until Ander came along and took up residence here."

"Why the oldest nine, if there have never been that many at once?" Jamirh asked curiously.

Jeri shrugged. "Nine is a sacred number."

"Where are the others? Why is Ander the one in charge of the only temple if he is the youngest?" Jamirh had so many questions.

Jeri looked faintly amused. "Ander is the only one who wants to stay. Hades does not tell Her priests how to live their lives, and they have the right to say no to anything She asks of them. Choice is extremely important to Her. So mostly they live in or near the communities they come from, or they travel, and they do what they want, championing whatever causes strike their fancy. Even Ander pretty much does what he wants; he just does it here. I'm sure they are all on the lookout for the Abomination, and if we get a definitive target, some might even show up to help, but they tend to be fairly solitary. Since Ander is here, they will generally assume it will be dealt with one way or the other."

"But then... who would be in charge of the Temple if Ander chose to go live somewhere else?" Jamirh was utterly baffled.

"The state would care for it, as it did before Ander wandered in three hundred years ago and decided to take up residence," she answered easily.

These people were downright bizarre, Jamirh decided. It was like the religion had been created by someone who had no concept of what a religion should look like, and then decided to roll with it.

But one thing stood out – if choice was something that was so important to Hades, why didn't he get one?

Chapter Twenty-Four

J amirh continued training with Jeri, who was more convinced than ever that Jamirh was meant to wield daggers after his performance with Ander.

"I cannot possibly overstate how well you did against him," she was telling Jamirh the next morning. "Ander is very skilled with all kinds of weapons. Even though daggers aren't his specialty, the fact that you managed to get a hit on him at all is nearly miraculous. And you used his own technique against him! It was truly heart-warming to watch."

Jamirh noted that her eyes were practically sparkling as she recalled the event. "I wish I knew how I did it," he said morosely. He remembered the move perfectly, could picture each step and motion, but his body didn't seem to want to cooperate when he tried to duplicate it.

She shrugged. "Could have been beginner's luck, though what a time to pull that out. It's okay; we will work our way up to that sort of technique. Don't get too discouraged! It was amazing you did it at all, and not so surprising that you are struggling to do it again. You've just started learning, and any kind of combat takes practice."

He did appreciate that she was trying to cheer him up, but he just couldn't shake the feeling that he should be able to do it regardless of the logic of what she was saying. Still, his ears perked up a bit. "Yeah, I guess that makes sense." He looked down at the wooden daggers in his hands. "It was really cool, though."

"Oh, that it definitely was." She smirked at the memory. "And Ander could stand to be taken down a peg or two. You've already learned a lot for the short time we've been doing this, you just need more practice to be able to put it... well, into practice, you know? Though if you want a critique, you should have tried dodging more – what did I say about taking hits?"

"I shouldn't be," he repeated dutifully.

"Exactly. Only deflect when you have no choice. Otherwise, your goal is to simply not be where your opponent is aiming," Jeri reminded him.

Jamirh tried to replay some of the exchanges in his head. "Which I might have been able to do if he didn't move so much faster than me. How does he do that?"

"Practice." She smiled wryly. "And exercises. So let us continue."

In the end, even Jamirh had to admit he was learning quickly when Jeri explained where most students were after four days of practice, but it was almost entirely theory. Putting his thoughts into motion was proving to be much more difficult. He was constantly tripping over himself, though Jeri said he just needed to build up the proper muscle memory and then he would be fine.

He was on his way back to his rooms after another day of mixed success when he heard a heavily accented voice say from just behind him, "Well met, Jamirh, guest of the king's house. I had been hoping to speak with you."

It was the Aradian ambassador. Miravu was wearing an off-white gown with gold trim in a much simpler style than what she had worn at the Festival luncheon, and her violet hair was left down, held back only with a simple gold band around her forehead. Without the masquerade mask, the dark markings around her eyes stood out prominently, almost creating the illusion that she still wore a mask. The flames in her eyes flickered blue and green as she approached. She was definitely the most striking person Jamirh had ever seen, and he wondered if all Aradians were as captivating.

"Ambassador," he greeted her, pausing to allow her to catch up. He suddenly felt very self-conscious, having just come back from the training grounds. He was a sweaty mess. Then his brain caught up to what she had said. "You wanted to speak with *me*?"

"Of course." She smiled at him, the flames banking down back to cinders. He wondered if you could use their eyes to read an Aradian's emotions like you could use an Avari's ears. "You are a curious thing, no? I have much desired to speak with you. Have you time now?"

Jamirh had a sudden sinking feeling as his ears started to droop. "Uh…" He fumbled for a moment, deciding on, "I'm not really presentable right now – I just came from the training grounds."

Her head tilted gracefully to the side. "Such a thing does not bother me; ours is a warrior culture. But I understand. Perhaps you would be willing to meet me in the west gardens in an hour? This is enough time, no?"

Jamirh wondered how bad it would be for him to say "no," considering that she wasn't really giving him a choice. Or maybe she was? It was hard to tell with the way she was phrasing things. He played with his key. He wished Jeri were here, but she was going to be busy for the rest of the day with a meeting about the Pitesh power outage, so he was on his own.

He almost smiled, remembering how annoyed she had been that she had to go to the meeting. Unnecessary bureaucratic red tape, she had called it.

Miravu was looking at him hopefully, eyes flickering.

He sighed internally. It wasn't like he had had any other plans for today anyway. "Yeah, sure. The west gardens, right?"

The ambassador smiled and inclined her head. "Indeed so, where the statue of the death goddess is draped in white, yes?"

"Yeah, I'm sure I can find it. I'll see you in a bit, then." He offered a wave as he turned to go.

"We shall meet again," she responded, clearly pleased.

Jamirh scampered to his rooms to clean up. Why was the Aradian ambassador from Dalmara interested in him? What did she mean by "You are a curious thing"? He had a bad feeling he knew where this was going, and he found himself reaching for his key again. He took a deep breath, focusing on the familiar feel of the worn metal. He'd be okay.

Exactly one hour later found him skidding into the west gardens in an attempt to not be late. Luckily, the statue of Hades was right past the arched entrance.

Miravu was already there, sitting on a nearby bench while she waited, looking at the statue.

Jamirh winced. "Ah, I'm sorry. Am I late?" he asked quickly, hoping he was not.

Miravu's eyes left the statue in favor of Jamirh, and she smiled. "Not at all, no. You are just at the right time." She stood in a single fluid motion. "Well met, Jamirh, guest of the king's house."

"Good evening, Ambassador?" he hazarded, not sure what the proper response should be. "And just "Jamirh" is fine, honestly."

"Jamirh, then," she agreed. "And you may call me simply Miravu. I do not believe you play the court games, no? And the court of Romanii is very informal. No offense will be taken at the exclusion of my title."

"If you're sure?" Jamirh found himself hoping he wasn't walking into some sort of diplomatic incident, whatever she said.

"I am, yes. Shall we walk through the gardens? I am always impressed at how much still lives in them, even in this season of fading life."

Jamirh nodded. "Because Dalmara is mostly desert?" he guessed, following her towards one of the paths.

"Yes. All life is hard won in the land of fire and sand," she explained. "You are not from Romanii either, though. How is it in the land from which you hail?"

He had to think about it for a minute. "The Empire has parks and gardens and stuff, yeah. The climate isn't too much different than this, though it is a little warmer, I guess. How did you know I wasn't from here?"

She paused to inspect a bush. "You look out of your depth at all times, a shrakan without sand. It was not difficult to guess."

He winced, but asked, "A shrakan?"

"Hmm." She paused. "A very long snake common to the Dalmaran desert. They love to nest in sand."

"Oh. I see." That made sense.

Miravu turned back to him. "A few days ago, I went down to the training grounds and saw you practicing with daggers. I was surprised, but wished to commend you on your choice to broaden your horizons. Avhad Sukra would have been very, very pleased to see such a thing."

Jamirh was utterly blindsided by how much there was to unpack from those statements. "What?"

"You have been practicing with daggers, no?" she asked kindly, and waited for his confused nod before continuing. "It is a good thing, to use your abilities to their fullest. Avhad Sukra begged Ebryn of Storms and Light to try anything other than the sword."

His stomach dropped. It always came back to Ebryn, didn't it? "I'm sorry, but I have no idea what you are talking about," he said, trying to remain polite.

There was a long silence while she regarded him carefully. Finally, she said, "Let us start at the beginning, yes?"

He dropped his eyes to the ground as his hand sought his key. "If it has to do with Ebryn, I would really rather not."

"No?" She sounded strangely unsurprised. "May I ask why?"

He took a deep breath. He didn't need to yell at the ambassador. "I don't like him," he answered simply.

Jamirh was surprised by her laugh. "So did Avhad Sukra predict. He was apparently not easy to like, and stubborn besides. She claimed he often drove her near to madness." The flames in her eyes danced in amusement.

He frowned. "Did you know her? It sounds like you did." What was one more immortal among all the others?

But Miravu shook her head. "No. I am only twelve decades old, and she died long ago. But I am of the House of Blood, which she created, so her teachings and stories were taught to me with the other children of the House. And Aradians live much longer than Avari – it has been fewer generations for us, no?"

"Only twelve decades?" Jamirh mused before he could stop himself.

Her smile was kind. "Indeed so." She laid a hand on his arm gently. "Allow me then to simply say that I am pleased to see you wield the daggers, no?"

He fought a fierce internal battle with himself, but the need to know won out. "Why?"

She hummed again, resuming her walk down the path. "If you do not like Ebryn, perhaps this is a good thing?" She glanced back at him as he followed her. "You have heard that he was a famous sword-master, yes?"

Jamirh nodded. "That's why I chose daggers, actually."

"Ah, I see. This makes things clearer." She was silent for several minutes while they walked. "He could have been much more than that, but he chose not to be," she finally said.

"What do you mean?" he asked, curious despite himself.

"He of Storms and Light was what we call a Master of Blades," she explained. "It can vary in the specifics, but is generally the ability to learn any bladed fighting style with incredible ease. It is more common among Aradians than the other races, so it is easier for us to identify. Avhad Sukra saw it in Ebryn, but he had no interest in using this ability to its fullest – he had his sword, and that was enough for him."

Jamirh was confused. "And you think that I am a 'Master of Blades' too?"

Miravu inclined her head in agreement. "Certainly. This is why I am pleased to see you with the daggers, yes? To learn many styles is to honor the gift."

He felt himself flush slightly. "I don't actually think that applies to me," he admitted.

"No?" She regarded him curiously.

"I'm not actually that good. And I only just started with daggers – I've never learned how to use any weapon before last week," he explained. "I wasn't even planning on ever using a sword."

"Ah – let me guess. You learn the patterns of movement, but fail at carrying them out, no?" Her eyes were strangely knowing.

He almost took a step back. "How did you...?"

"As I said, the ability is more common among Aradians. This is not uncommon for a fledgling Master of Blades. You are thinking too much. Your body will have learned the proper movement. Do not allow your mind to stop your body. This is how a Master of Blades fights. Instinct, you might call it."

Jamirh thought back to the bout against Ander. Ander had been moving too fast to allow him to think, and his body had just acted. It made sense, even if it sounded unbelievable. How could he have some ridiculous fighting ability?

Who else knew about this?

"As far as not wishing to learn the sword, this is because of he of Storms and Light, no?" she asked gently.

He eyed her warily as he nodded.

"You should not fear," Miravu reassured. "There are many styles associated with all manner of blades, and he chose to keep to the one style and the one blade. If ever you should wish to learn, there are many paths you might take. Just because you wield the same weapon does not mean you must fight the same way. Already, you are one step better by learning the daggers. Once you learn how you learn, you will be able to absorb whatever you wish, and fight however you wish to." Her smile turned amused. "I do not believe it will take you very long to find your feet."

Jamirh rubbed at his key, not sure how this conversation was making him feel. On one hand, she was saying that he was like Ebryn, but on the other, he wasn't. He wasn't even sure how he felt about being something called a "Master of Blades," other than uncomfortable. It implied things he wasn't sure he liked. Yes, he was learning how to use daggers, but ideally he wouldn't have to use them in real combat. It was just a precaution, and it was kind of fun, if also a little frustrating. Being called a Master of Blades made him think that he was going to be using weapons a lot, which meant being in situations he was sure he wasn't going to want to be in.

"Having to fight solely on instinct sounds risky," Jamirh noted.

"Eventually, this" – she pointed to his head – "and this" – she pointed to his chest – "will learn to work in concert, so that you may control the ability, and it does not control you. But for now, trust instinct. You must learn to listen before you learn to communicate, no?"

"I guess?" he asked hesitantly.

"All I ask is that you continue to train your ability," she said kindly. "Nothing more. It is a shame to see such a thing wither."

Jamirh's ears twitched. "How common are Masters of Blades in your society?" he asked curiously. "Like, how rare is it?"

Miravu looked thoughtful. "It is a rare ability, but not incredibly so. I know of four right now in my capital. I do not know how many others there might be among the sands – perhaps another fifty or so?" She shrugged gracefully. "I could not even guess as to how many there might be among the other races, save that it is certainly fewer."

That seemed very rare to Jamirh, but at least he wasn't unique if it were true. There were fewer priests of Hades, for what that was worth. And was this even something he wanted to pursue?

He supposed he might be able to find out soon.

"So I guess I was just wondering if you knew anything about this?" Jamirh finished his explanation to Jeri breathlessly.

They were sitting in his rooms. Jeri had swung by after her meeting finally let out, and Jamirh had all but pulled her into the sitting room to tell her what he had heard from Miravu. Jeri had listened with a thoughtful look on her face, saying nothing while Jamirh stumbled over the foreign terms and ideas.

But she answered Jamirh's question directly. "No. I have never even heard of a 'Master of Blades,' though it sounds from your description a little like an inherent magic. I always understood that Ebryn had no magic at all – this is completely new to me." She frowned. "It does make sense. You pick up the concepts far, far quicker than I have ever seen anyone do before. And you surprised Ander, which is no mean feat."

Jamirh cocked his head to the side. "I thought you knew about inherent magic?"

She snorted. "Yes, I know about it, and I understand my own very well, but you have to understand – there are hundreds of inherents across all the races. I don't know anyone who knows them all. Well, the Lady might, but she's a goddess. I promise, Jamirh, I had no idea that you could have had an inherent. I honestly just thought you had natural talent, kind of like Ander, actually. The ambassador said this applies to all bladed weapons?"

Jamirh nodded.

"Then that is... something," Jeri said slowly.

"Would anyone else have known about it?" he asked her, a little concerned about the answer.

"I have no idea. It sounds like Ebryn didn't particularly care to utilize it to its full potential, so I'm not sure anyone did. Everyone knows how skilled he was with a sword, but it is possible to be that skilled without magic. It just takes a lot of practice and dedication. I suppose Ander could have known, but I think he would have mentioned it when you beat him." She looked at him worriedly. "You seem to be taking this news well?"

He shrugged. "I don't know that it's really hit me yet. It just seems so unreal, that I could in theory be some sort of supernaturally good combat expert, I guess. And to be honest, I don't know if it's something I want, even if not using it makes me more like *him*."

Jeri winced slightly. "I suppose that's fair. For what it's worth, this is something we can test for, now that you know the theory behind using it."

"I thought you said people with inherent magic just know how to use it?" he asked. "Why have I been having so much trouble then?"

"Well, I think you probably were using it subconsciously – you threw the daggers at Festival perfectly, after all, after watching me throw them. And you landed that hit on Ander. The ambassador is likely the closest thing we have to an expert on the subject, and if she thinks it's instinctual, then you thinking too much about it could have a detrimental effect. Some inherents also need more practice than others to utilize it effectively. It's a wide range, and I was very much generalizing when I told you about them. I didn't think the distinction mattered."

His ears twitched downward. "I think it matters now."

She sighed. "Yes, I think you're right. Unfortunately, we won't be able to test it for a few days."

He sat up, surprised. "What do you mean?"

"They may have found something in Pitesh connected to the power outage. I'm being sent to check it out – I'll be gone for two, maybe three days." Her expression was apologetic. "That's actually why I wanted to see you before you went to bed – I leave in a few hours."

"Why are *you* being sent?" Jamirh was confused.

She looked concerned. "Because Ander has identified a possible connection between tech and the Abomination, and our power does technically work on tech, just a different kind than what the Empire uses. There are concerns that something we use might have corrupted. I'm the only one who has sensed the modern incarnation of Abomination, so I am going to rule it out as a possible cause of failure." She paused. "Things are a little tense right now, due to our lack of information. Anything is possible at this point, and we cannot afford to have a boiler blow up for any reason. The destruction and loss of life would be catastrophic."

"Do they really think the Abomination might have been involved?" Jamirh was horrified that that could be the case. For some reason, he had thought that he personally would be the first target – not an entire city full of innocent people. He gripped his key tightly.

"I think it's extremely unlikely, but that's why I'm going – to rule it out. Don't worry," she added, seeing the look on his face, "I won't be gone too long. You'll be fine here on your own for a few days. Hide from Ander or go pester him with questions. Have dinner with the pretty ambassador, harass Vlad if you get too bored. He loves it when we do that."

"Does he?" Jamirh asked doubtfully. That didn't sound like something the king of a country would enjoy.

"Well, he doesn't know he enjoys it, but he does," she admitted. "You can also go explore the city. If you stop by Gerit's office – do you remember her? She's the head of housing and guest management – and ask, I believe Vlad authorized her to give you an allowance. If not, definitely go find Vlad and ask for some spending money; if he's sponsoring you, he gets to pay."

He blinked at her. "Why am I just finding out about this now?"

She opened her mouth to respond, but then paused, looking confused. "I don't think it came up before? Maybe we should have a sit-down and really talk about what you have access to here as Vlad's guest–"

She was cut off by a knock at the door. Jamirh glanced at the clock; it was nearly midnight. Who would come by his rooms now? Jeri might, but she was already here, and she was usually very respectful of his sleep schedule.

The knock came again, impatient.

"Coming," Jamirh called as he shared a bemused look with Jeri. "Can I help you?" he asked as he opened the door.

He was surprised to find Ander, who looked like he hadn't slept in days if the bags under his eyes and rumpled clothing were anything to go by. "Are you okay?" he couldn't help but ask.

Ander brushed his concern off with a wave. "Hades – and the Human – have had a second brush with the Abomination."

She was still ignoring him, and he still had no idea what had triggered this new behavior.

For days now, the Avari had given limited responses or had refused to respond at all to Rhode's inquiries. He had increased the number of Truth Seekers watching her to two, but they assured him she wasn't doing anything. The readouts confirmed this, but Rhode couldn't help but begin to feel paranoid that something was happening that he was missing.

He considered shutting off the air in the cell briefly to see if that caused a reaction, but decided to keep that in reserve for now. Perhaps it was just the lack of food getting to her? Was she trying to conserve energy? For what purpose?

Rhode almost threw his tablet down onto a nearby table in anger. She was going to die in that cell, and they would have gotten nothing from her. So much effort and resources wasted on some death-cult fanatic, including one of the new assets. They hadn't been able to salvage all that much from the wreckage, which was unfortunate. Those things were expensive to replace.

"Everything dies."

His head snapped towards the Avari to see her staring at him coolly. He stayed silent, wondering if she would continue.

"And that which dies cannot be replaced," she finished, violet eyes closing.

He felt a chill go down his spine. That was unsettlingly close to what he had been thinking of. He glanced at Madine, but she and the other Seeker were both watching the prisoner calmly. Then the Truth Seeker's head tilted, and she stepped forward, to Rhode's surprise.

"And yet, that which is destroyed can be," she replied with no real inflection.

"Only if it was not living in the first place, for the living can both die and be destroyed," the Avari countered. "Unless you are making the distinction that only that which lives can die, and only that which does not live can be destroyed?"

"Destroyed is dead for the living. They mean the same thing. To denote the separation, use 'die' only with the living, and 'destroy' with that which doesn't," the Truth Seeker responded as Rhode watched the exchange.

"Then you argue that what I killed was not living." The white-haired woman's voice was curious. "I'm not sure I would say the same."

Rhode wondered if that was all he was going to get from her now – strange ramblings related to her religion. Maybe he should revisit shutting off the air.

Wait – was she referring to the asset?

Suddenly, the Avari's head snapped to the right, as though something had grabbed her attention, and she cried out. Rhode thought at first that something must have startled her, but he realized his mistake almost immediately – she wasn't surprised, she was *furious*.

"Where?!?" she snarled, eyes flashing. "Where is it?!"

Chapter Twenty-Five

Tomorrow, Takeshi was going to rescue the veiled woman's friend and finally make contact with the rebellion. He didn't know what was going to happen after that, but he was pleased at having such a tangible goal in reach. It would mark a major success for his mission as a whole and move Ni Fon one step closer to freedom from the Rose Empire.

He had spent the days after scouting the tunnels resting, gathering his strength, and preparing for the breakout. He hoped the mage was doing the same, since so much hinged on their success. To support their endeavor, he had acquired paper and cut it into squares, keying them to his magic through a lengthy saturation process that had taken the better part of a day. He had then drawn the patterns for fire bombs on them. He would place them in various locations around the base, and when the mage destroyed their cell he could set these off to add to the chaos. The fire bombs wouldn't have the same power as what the veiled woman had implied the mage was going to do, but they would hopefully help buy him time to get the mage to safety.

Well, relative safety. He knew they were going to have to flee north to the Warcross Wall as fast as possible, since the Truth Seekers would be after them. If they couldn't find a form of transportation, it was going to be a rough two-and-a-half-week journey, and he didn't know exactly what shape the mage was going to be in. The veiled woman had told him that he was needed to get the mage off the base since they would be exhausted, but that didn't take into account what they may have suffered at the hands of the military. At bare minimum, after an explosion like that, the mage was going to need food to help regain their strength, and also rest. Circumstances being what they were, they were not going to be able to afford the latter for some time, so they would have to make do with whatever nourishment Takeshi managed to bring with him.

He wasn't actually sure if the tunnels were going to be their best bet to escape – if they could get to them unnoticed, then yes, but if they were spotted entering them then that could become problematic. Rather than use the temple exit, Takeshi intended to go north through the tunnels and resurface on the outskirts of Charve, but the tunnels had not been twisting enough that he was certain he could lose any pursuers if they were followed. He hadn't ruled out collapsing part of the tunnels to prevent pursuit. He would keep one of the fire bomb patterns in reserve just in case, and a few other spells besides. Illusions could also come in handy if it came to it.

He hadn't left the hotel room since returning from the tunnels, taking the opportunity to recuperate from the slow drain of the illusion spell. Today had been especially relaxing. It was storming hard outside, and Takeshi was enjoying meditating to the sound of the rain on the glass windows, and the beauty of nature's wrath as he watched sheets of water fall from the sky. He thought it might even thunder later, though the soundproofing the Rose Empire utilized in its buildings meant he would never hear it. At least it did not silence the rain.

The news was still covering the fallout from the bank robbery for the most part. Though the curfew was still being enforced, the conversation surrounding it on the news had died down significantly. Takeshi wondered if that was because there was nothing else to say and they had given up, or if they had been forced to stop questioning it. He glanced outside at the rain again, not envying the Truth Seekers who were going to have to stand in the deluge all night long.

And that was another thing – he had started to suspect that there were fewer Truth Seekers here than there appeared to be at first. For one, he was fairly certain there were only a few thousand of them in the Empire as a whole, and a large number of those being here would leave other places vulnerable. For another, watching the news carefully had led him to believe only about five Truth Seekers had responded to the bank robbery, yet no one had seen any others around the city for the rest of that day and eyewitness reports had described some as "almost disappearing" with how fast they had left their posts. Takeshi suspected they were using illusions to make it seem like more of them were here than there actually were. It would explain why they did nothing but stand around and look menacing, and since no one was willing to go near Seekers anyway they didn't have to worry about someone walking into the illusion and shattering it. He had certainly not gotten close enough to sense such a subtle spell's presence, since he was trying to preserve his own illusion. He estimated that there were probably only around ten Truth Seekers actually present both in Charve and on the base, a far more manageable number than the perceived thirty or forty.

The veiled woman herself had not contacted him since the night in the tunnels other than to inform him that her friend would be ready tomorrow. In some ways, working with her and the mage was almost like working with other shinobi to pull off impossible missions, even if the communication was lacking. He did wish he knew a little more about what they were capable of rather than having to rely solely on the veiled woman's words, but she had been very confident and had yet to come across as false. The nature of their communication, mind to mind as it was, made him doubt she could even lie to him if she wanted to.

He was sitting in one of the semi-comfortable chairs near the large window with a cup of tea, watching something inane that had come on after the news, when he felt the first bit of pressure building behind his eyes. Takeshi sighed; he got up to get the bottle of painkillers from his first aid kit. He glanced at the clock as he swallowed two of them. It was early, just about eight o'clock, but he decided it might be worth it to turn in and sleep off the headache before it got the chance to properly form. With any luck, this would not turn into a monster migraine like he had suffered two weeks ago in Bariza.

Unfortunately, as he got ready for bed and his neck began to stiffen and the pain intensify, it was definitely beginning to look like this was going to be a repeat of that night. He made sure all the lights were turned off and the curtains drawn, remembering how any hint of light had been agony. Why was he suddenly getting these horribly debilitating migraines? He was going to be in no shape to help anyone tomorrow, as much as he hated to admit it. He was going to need to be able to make quick decisions when he helped the mage break out. Having to sift through each thought like sludge was almost certainly going to lead to failure, not that he would ever jeopardize a mission like that. As he settled under the covers, pressing his head to his pillow, he managed to reach out mentally, hoping to let the veiled woman know that they were going to have to delay a day or two.

He sensed her respond to his call, curious and pleased, and then—

Fury, like he'd never felt before.

:Where?!?: came the furious shriek in his mind. *:Where is it!?:*

Takeshi had no idea how to respond to that, and he didn't have a chance to anyway – the pain spiked at that moment, causing him to recoil in instant misery. He gasped as the stabbing sensation increased, and he buried his head under the pillow at the agonizing sensation, trying to escape from the pain. It was impossible for him to focus on anything other than the feeling of something trying to remove his brain from his head with a rusty spoon. Chills gripped him, even though he was under several blankets. His body felt so cold that the shivering began to hurt. Distantly, he could feel the woman gathering power to herself as though she were going to strike at something, but then she faltered.

The sensation of being stabbed abruptly stopped, the sudden relief almost as dizzying as the agony had been. There was still a pounding feeling behind his eyes and in his temples, and he felt nauseous and cold, but coherent thought was a possibility again. He took a few minutes to just breathe, trying to relax as his body shuddered weakly with the aftershock. Everything ached, but at least it was a much more manageable ache. He could feel the veiled woman's presence all around him, almost like she was shielding him.

:Sleep,: she whispered quietly to him. *:We... about this... wake, but... sleep.:*

He tried to gather his scattered thoughts to respond to her, but suddenly it felt like his mind had been wrapped in soft, fluffy cotton, and he wanted nothing more than to sleep for the next week.

:Sleep.:

He slept.

Takeshi woke slowly the next morning, easing back into the land of the living. He was pleased to find that his head no longer felt as though it were being removed. He still felt a bit chilled and achy all over, even curled under the blankets, so he decided to stay in bed, content to simply doze for a while. Though he had probably slept for some time, he still felt tired, and didn't see any harm in continuing to rest. He didn't feel great, but he remembered feeling much, much worse the morning after the previous migraine. Perhaps the room being quiet as well as dark was helping – he had been awoken by his alarm last time, and the sound had hurt his head horribly.

He had been drifting in and out of sleep for an indeterminate amount of time when he felt the veiled woman's presence nearby. She felt unhappy and worried.

:...awake?: The whisper was even more whispery than usual, as though she were trying to be quiet.

He managed a sort of mental wave at her and began the process of trying to rouse himself from the lethargy to more properly speak with her.

:How... feeling?: she asked, the worry intensifying.

:Not horrible, but not good, either,: he admitted as he sat up slowly, keeping the comforter wrapped around his shoulders. He wasn't willing to give up the warmth just yet.

There was a long pause followed by, *:Did... medicine... night?:*

Takeshi closed his eyes again while he tried to piece that together. His mind still felt sluggish, but yes, he had taken medicine before the worst of the migraine had hit. *:Two pills.:* He pictured the bottle for her.

There was another long pause. *:Ander... two more.:*

He considered that. *:I should take two more?:* he tried to clarify.

:Yes.:

That didn't sound like a bad idea. He forced himself to leave his cocoon and maneuver to the counter where he had left the pill bottle.

:...drink... water!: she added as he stared blankly at the container for a moment, trying to remember how to open it. He grabbed a glass and filled it with water from the sink, then took the suggested two capsules before sitting back down on the bed to slowly sip at the water.

:I'm sorry,: he offered apologetically as he finally got his thoughts in order. *:I'm not going to be of much use today. Tomorrow I should be well enough,:* he added, recalling how he had felt after the first migraine. If he was this much better now, he was sure he would be fine tomorrow.

There was an immediate sense of alarm. *:No! ...abandon this. ...north... Wall when... well... help you cross.:*

:What?: he asked, struggling to find the energy to decipher what she was saying.

:You... to Romanii,: she insisted, the whisper rustling a little louder in his mind.

:Right, after we break out the mage,: he agreed. *:I just can't do it today. Tomorrow night, I promise.:* Takeshi lay down again, wrapping himself in the blankets to wait for the medicine to work.

There was a frustrated silence. *:No... should abandon... north immediately. You need... give you.:*

He turned that over as he slowly tried to make sense of it. *:You want me to give up? Now?:*

A very brief pause before she replied simply, *:Yes.:*

He felt a flash of hurt that she no longer thought he could succeed. It was a migraine, not the loss of a limb or something that would impact his immediate ability to function. It was impacting him now, yes, but he already felt much better. Based on how he had felt at this point with the previous migraine, he was sure he would be perfectly fine in time to rescue the mage tomorrow night. He could even meditate tonight for a little bit to help his recovery. There was no reason to call off the mission on account of a bad headache. He pulled himself together a little more to reassure her. *:There's no reason for that. Surely the pattern – the array – can hold until tomorrow?:*

Exasperation. *:Yes, but... issue.:*

:Then I will be ready and in place tomorrow,: he replied firmly.

:I... not think... good idea. Ander... with me,: she insisted.

Takeshi still did not know who this Ander was, but he was clearly able to communicate with the veiled woman. *:Is Ander able to help free your friend?:*

There was a sense of confusion. *:No... far away.:*

:Then I'm afraid his opinion doesn't apply to this situation,: he explained calmly. *:I can't even communicate with him the way I can communicate with you.:*

He lay in silence for several minutes before she responded. *:He... you.:* She sounded troubled.

Takeshi sighed, mentally dismissing the other man. There was no point in dwelling on something so removed from the situation. *:I promise – tomorrow, your friend goes free, and I will see them safely north to Romanii. I just need today to rest. I'm sorry I can't help them today.:*

:If... you... be okay?: she asked finally, voice quiet.

:Yes. It's just a migraine. They pass,: he assured her. He wasn't sure why he was getting them, but there was nothing strange about migraines in general. Many people suffered from them. Then again, he had lost six months of time, during which he had been drugged nearly comatose. It was possible that the migraines were related to that. Perhaps a delayed form of withdrawal from whatever they had been giving him? That felt plausible.

:Abomination,: she insisted unhappily.

His lips twitched into a wry smile. *:There's no need to be that dramatic about it.:* No, what had been an abomination was what Hotaru had sometimes suffered. This was nothing in comparison. The princess had often spent days resting after an episode.

Ni Fon had access to both magic and tech, and neither had been able to do anything for Hotaru in the end.

He could tell that the veiled woman was giving in, though she wasn't happy about it. *:You really... to Tarvishte.:*

He simply hummed in response. Tarvishte? Romanii's capital? Then it would make sense that Romanii was sponsoring the rebellion against its southern neighbor. Interesting. He would draw more conclusions from that later, when he wasn't trying not to think.

Takeshi could almost feel her sigh. *:Very well... choose. Rest. You... for tomorrow.:* Her presence faded.

He curled up a little more under the blankets, determined to bask in the silence and do just that, but found his mind wandering tiredly in circles instead. It stung, that the veiled woman thought he was no longer capable of saving her friend because of one headache. Had it really changed her opinion of him so drastically? Why? Did people not get sick occasionally in Romanii? But he'd met her during the first one, if he was remembering that series of events correctly. He thought she might have called that headache an abomination too, now that he thought about it. Maybe she really hated headaches? He'd done everything she had asked of him so far, or so he thought. Had he missed something?

And on that note, who was Ander? Why try to bring in another party now? And one that couldn't actually participate, at that. The veiled woman didn't seem to be able to physically engage in the plan either, but her ability to act as a liaison between him and the mage was invaluable. What was Ander's purpose? Takeshi wasn't sure what the veiled woman hoped to gain by this. He vaguely recalled her mentioning the name Ander before, but couldn't dredge up the context for it. Maybe Ander was the mage he was breaking out? No, she had said he was far away and could not help, so that didn't make sense either.

Was it just that she was upset about the delay? He quickly decided against that; the pieces didn't fit. Surely a delay was preferable to not doing it at all and leaving the mage in the Empire's hands. Unless it would be too late to rescue the mage if they waited? No, he definitely hadn't gotten that impression, and she had explicitly said the mage could hold the pattern for a day. Timing wasn't the reason either.

Why, why, why? All he had were questions, and no answers. Maybe the mage would be able to clarify what was going on after he rescued them, since he would be able to have a full conversation with them and not just the broken phrases he got with the veiled woman.

His thoughts chased him into fitful dreams for a while as he slept off the remainder of the aftereffects of the migraine. When he woke in the afternoon, he was pleased to find that he felt almost Human again. Takeshi still felt a little chilled, but that was all that remained of the misery of the previous night. He took a hot shower and made a mug of tea to help warm himself up, content to take it easy for the rest of the day. He pulled the curtains open partway to let in some natural light, then turned on the vid screen and scrolled until he found a movie to watch while he picked at a few pieces of jerky. He was disappointed to see that his supply of food was pretty meager at this point, and realized that he would need to get more before he descended into the tunnels again. The mage was going to need food, and it was easier to buy supplies in advance of being on the run rather than during.

Well, that was something he could do tomorrow morning. He didn't feel up to going out today and pushing himself too fast. Today was for resting so that he could push tomorrow.

He flipped to the news after dinner, curious to see if anything interesting had happened during the day. The bank robbery news was dying out – all the robbers had been apprehended, and every move they made had already been over-analyzed by everyone with a platform. The Guard and the military had both made statements. Takeshi was interested to see that one of the Truth Seekers had made a brief statement concerning their involvement as well. Her report had been concise and brief, delivered in an almost monotone voice that had mildly disturbed Takeshi. The one he had met in Ni Fon had been similar, he recalled. He was also fairly certain they used a type of telepathy to communicate with each other; what one knew, they all seemed to.

While the Truth Seeker was talking, Takeshi realized that he had a clear view of the embroidered cloth that covered her eyes. The base fabric was gray, covered in fine red, blue, and gray embroidery. He had seen the blindfolds before, though he'd never paid them much attention. He'd dismissed them as a scare tactic. But it dawned on him looking at it now that the stitches looked like they might be abstracted glyphs. Was the blindfold... a non-circular pattern? How would that work? What did it do? He could assume it probably helped them see without their eyes, but in what way? Did it enhance their vision? He had always assumed the blindfolds were a psychological technique meant to scare or disturb their enemies, but if there were glyphs embroidered onto them then he had to conclude they had another purpose. Unfortunately, the brevity of the Seeker's statement meant he didn't get a lot of time to examine it further, as she left before he could determine which glyphs were being used.

He had never really asked any questions about the Seekers before. They held an equivalent position in the Rose to shinobi in Ni Fon, but they tended to be very secretive and withdrawn... actually, that was also like shinobi, Takeshi reflected wryly. It made sense. No major power wanted the specifics of their top-tier combatants to be easily available to other countries. Even though technically Ni Fon was part of the Rose, many of their systems were separate, such as Seekers and shinobi. Ni Fon had never been *well* absorbed by the Rose.

There was also the fact that mages of different groups didn't often share with each other in the best of circumstances. Everyone had their own way of using magic, and everyone thought their way was best. In truth, some schools were better than others at specific things, but Takeshi had yet to see a style or philosophy of casting that was better at everything. That was just how magic worked.

Hotaru had once mourned that magic lacked the clear rules of science, and perhaps that was why they clashed. Takeshi disagreed; magic had its rules, there were just far, far more of them than one person could ever hope to know, causing many to appear contradictory. If all the schools of magic came together, perhaps their combined knowledge might lead to universal understanding of how magic worked, but he couldn't see that ever happening.

Still, it did make him wish he had observed the Truth Seekers a little more closely. Foreign schools of magic had always interested him, and the idea of a non-circular pattern was fascinating. Ironically, he had spent far too much time trying to avoid them to actually learn about them, though avoiding them had served his mission far better. He supposed he would have the chance to observe them in action tomorrow night, but it wouldn't be the same thing. There was only so much he could learn on a philosophical level while in battle against them.

The rest of the news was fairly mundane, mentioning another soccer game that was happening tomorrow as well as a concert by some pop star that was being livestreamed everywhere in support of Avari interest groups, or something like that. They would be taking donations and trying to broaden awareness of the prejudices Avari suffered in the Empire. Takeshi turned the vid screen off. How effective would that be in the end? He wasn't sure. It seemed to him through casual observation that most people were aware that the two groups were treated differently; Humans just didn't care, and Avari lacked the power to do anything about it.

He shook his head, deciding to meditate for an hour or so and then go to bed. He had to be ready for tomorrow.

Chapter Twenty-Six

Takeshi dressed warmly the next day; there was a chill in the air even after the storm cleared. He went out in search of a convenience store from which to buy snacks he could easily store in his pack. More jerky would be good. That stuff stayed edible practically forever. Granola bars were also something to look into, and maybe some of those frosted pastries you were supposed to toast? They tasted just fine if you didn't toast them, and they were sealed into convenient portions. He'd browse around to see if there was anything else he could bring with them, but he did have limited space and funds. What he could bring with them was only going to stretch so far, but he would have to worry about acquiring more food when it actually became a problem.

He was eyeing some options, considering how much money he had left in the account Don had set up for him, when he felt the veiled woman's presence. She still felt unhappy, but there was also curiosity about what he was doing.

:What... looking for?: came the whispery inquiry.

:Food. Your friend is going to need it after they destroy their cage,: he informed her, debating whether to go for quality or quantity with fruit-and-nut bars or granola bars. Some mages preferred more food, others better food.

:...quality,: she suggested, and he had the strangest feeling she was looking at the display through him, though she didn't specify any particular product.

Takeshi hummed thoughtfully, looking at the high-protein options. That usually meant more expensive.

:...money a problem? ...help...!:

He blinked in surprise. Was there a way for her to give him money? That would be helpful. *:How?:*

:There's... trick the card... is a different... access funds... south of the Wall... I can help... them.:

He winced. That had been a lot of information, and he was sure he had missed most of it because he didn't know how any of that went together, other than that she thought she could help him somehow.

:Ah....: There was a sense of apology. *:I can... for you... pay as normal.:*

Pay as normal? Well, that he could do. He had the feeling she was going to do something, and wished yet again that he could understand her better. He was looking forward to speaking with her friend to fill in the gaps.

Soon. He just had to wait until tonight, then one way or the other this leg of his mission would be over.

He chose several packages of jerky, two boxes of high-protein fruit-and-nut bars, and one large box of the frosted pastries. After a moment's contemplation, he grabbed another box of the snack bars. He wanted to have at least several days' worth of food ready to go. A week would be preferable, but he didn't think he would have enough physical space for that in his bag.

He brought his purchases up to the counter and dug out his card as the cashier began to ring him out. He received a brief warning of *:Don't panic,:* from the veiled woman before the strangest sensation came over him, almost like he was now sharing his hands with someone else. He watched as his hands, without any input from him, slid the card into the reader backward, then punched a long string of numbers into the keypad. *:Actually,... very difficult... accurately,:* the veiled woman murmured as she worked. Instead of rejecting the transaction, the reader authorized it, and he found himself walking out of the store with a receipt and two bags of goods.

:Okay,: he said slowly as the sensation of another in his body faded. *:As useful as that was, please never do it again without my explicit permission.:* That had been one of the most horribly disturbing experiences in his life. Though he realized she

probably had tried to warn him, he had not had the slightest clue that she could or would take over his body like that. Still, he wasn't angry, just very disconcerted.

:Apologies,: came the contrite response immediately. *:I... not.:*

He took a deep breath to re-center himself and started to head back to the hotel. *:Thank you, though. I'm surprised that that worked, with the card in backward.:* He thought back to what she had said before, realizing she had "accessed funds" for people "south of the Wall." Perhaps they were even set aside for agents specifically. This was something the rebellion had set up, then? It seemed like a good sign she was willing to let him utilize them.

It felt like she shrugged. *:Tech... fooled, if... how.:*

He raised an eyebrow. *:You are very skilled with tech then?:* he asked. A mage who was good at tech?

:Oh, no!: Her laugh rustled like falling leaves all around him. *:...notoriously bad... memorized the steps... particular trick.:*

:I see.: He looked around briefly while he waited to cross the road at a light. A nearby vid screen showed a Human girl in a short white lace dress singing and dancing on a stage, all sorts of lights and effects going on around her. Ah yes, the Avari fundraiser concert. Takeshi could just barely make out the audio over the sounds of traffic. The music was very upbeat and high energy. Pop music. It was a little early in the day for a concert in his opinion, but then he didn't know where it was airing from. Maybe it was evening wherever she was.

As he passed by a department store with glass windows, he noticed in the reflection that the veiled woman was dancing to the tune as well. Her movements were graceful and skilled, and as she moved Takeshi could see flashes of long white hair under the excessively long veil. Perhaps she was an Avari? He hid an amused smile, feeling her delight. *:You enjoy this sort of music, then?:*

:I love... music,: came the happy reply. *:...everywhere, in all... wonderful... communication... emotion... convey so much... speaking. This is... have prayers... songs.:*

In her excitement, she seemed to have forgotten how little he heard of what she said. At least this was not vital information, and she was happier than she had been since his migraine. She was clearly having fun as she followed him past various storefronts and hotels, form whirling gracefully from glass pane to glass pane. *:I really hope I'm the only one who can see you,:* he murmured wryly as he glanced around, but no one else on the street seemed to notice anything strange in the windows.

:You are.: The figure paused, then started dancing again, this time to a different tempo. The song must have changed. He wasn't sure how she was hearing it, though maybe she was watching it wherever she actually was. *:I... dance, and... very catchy. ...like the music?:*

:It is very catchy, from the little of it I heard,: he agreed. *:I don't think I know enough to say whether I like it or not. I'm not familiar with this artist.:*

The veiled woman sounded pleased as she leapt to a different window. *:A Bard... better performance... but I... heart.:*

There was a Truth Seeker at the next intersection, and Takeshi was careful to observe him while the veiled woman continued to dance nearby, seemingly unconcerned. People were giving the Seeker a wide berth as they passed, and he was standing eerily still in the shadow of one of the large abstract statues. In fact... yes, that was a little too still, on closer examination. The man wasn't breathing. That was an illusion, not the real thing, and sort of a sloppy one at that if it wasn't even breathing. They were definitely counting on no one wanting to look too closely. Still, illusion or not, Takeshi wasn't willing to risk setting off some sort of alarm, though he wished he could get a good look at the blindfold.

It was good news, though. That meant there were in fact fewer Truth Seekers in the city than people thought. The four he had seen on the military base were probably real, with at least one or two inside the building. Then maybe five more in the city proper, based on the bank robbery response. That meant ten or eleven Seekers to contend with, though based on the size of the explosion the mage was planning that number might end up being lower. It would also take time for the Seekers in the city to return to the base.

Takeshi shivered as he waited for the light to turn, and he could feel the veiled woman's attention zero in on him. *:...cold?:*

:A little. It's fine,: he assured her. *:The weather has been fairly mild, but winter will be here soon.:* He had never particularly enjoyed cold weather, but he would have to get used to it. He was going north. Everything was going to be colder.

Hotaru hadn't liked the cold either, though she had always enjoyed looking at the snow when it fell.

:...okay? ...sure you... freeing... tonight?: the veiled woman asked gently, worry creeping back into her tone.

Takeshi sighed, trying not to feel annoyed at her concern. Was it for him, or for her friend? He couldn't tell. *:I am perfectly fine now. Completely recovered, as I said I would be. We move forward with the plan.:* He had felt much better when he woke up that morning, as he had expected. *:Your friend will be ready with their pattern, correct?:*

:The array... ready,: she confirmed. *:Just... know when... in position. I... this is over.:* She resumed her dancing, flickering into another window across the street when the signal changed. He wondered how she was doing that. She wasn't nearly as clear as she had been in the mirror, but he could still see her shadowy figure turn to music he couldn't hear, veils and skirts billowing.

Another large vid screen came into view, and he could see the plea to donate money to the cause plastered across the bottom of it. He looked around, wondering what the Avari thought of this, when he realized there weren't any in sight. Takeshi frowned, trying to think back to the last few days. Yes, there had been more of them out and about before the curfew; he remembered the pops of color. Their absence hadn't registered to him, since he was used to a small Avari presence in Ni Fon.

He was wondering why they would all be missing when he remembered Benjen's warning. *"People tend to disappear in the Empire when they catch the attention of the Blind Ones... You are not Avari, so you will have a layer of protection... Humans disappear too."*

In his desire to move forward with his mission, he hadn't given the phrasing of that the attention it was due. "Humans disappear too" implied that it was mostly Avari who went missing, and Benjen had tied that directly to the Seekers. Takeshi liked to think he would have heard if large numbers of people were disappearing from the city, so perhaps it was just that the Avari were keeping their heads down and staying indoors? He hoped that was the case and they weren't being rounded up somewhere for nefarious reasons. He glanced up at the vid screen again, wondering what exactly "Avari interest groups" entailed. They didn't have those in Ni Fon. It was a little ironic that the Avari in Charve felt like they had to hide while a concert was being held for their benefit. It didn't say anything good about the current state of affairs here.

The veiled woman finally disappeared in a swirl of shadowy skirts as he approached the doors of the hotel. Back in his room, he made sure everything was packed tightly and neatly in the backpack, putting his mask and non-spelled gloves easily accessible near the top. He wouldn't be coming back here again if everything went well, so everything had to come with him or be destroyed. He burned the pamphlets and other random paraphernalia he had acquired, then used magic to erase the remnants of his presence. He didn't want to leave any trace of himself behind, in case they eventually backtracked him to this hotel. Truth Seekers were known for finding things, but shinobi were known for hiding. Which would win out? He wanted to make their job as difficult as possible if it came to that.

He pulled on the gloves with the illusion stitched into them and made sure his katana was tightly wrapped in fabric. Knowing that most of the Truth Seekers in the city were fake made him feel confident enough to cast a weak illusion spell on the sword to make it invisible. It wouldn't hold up if he was confronted by an actual Seeker, but he was confident it would fool the average citizen of the Rose. He just needed it to last until he got into the tunnels under the Temple of Faith, since he doubted the Temple would let him bring the weapon inside.

He made one last check, looking around to make sure he hadn't missed anything, and left the hotel behind.

The bus ride was blessedly uneventful. Takeshi kept his senses open for any Truth Seekers, but he didn't even see any of the illusions. Perhaps they had pulled back slightly for some reason, or were just in different parts of town. The temple was just as busy as it had been on his previous trips, and he had no trouble slipping into the basement, casting a mage light, and navigating to the tunnels. He took a minute to drop his illusions, switch gloves, and put on his mask. He closed his eyes and took a deep breath, reveling in just being *himself* again for a moment, before he was on his way.

It was just as cold down in the tunnels as it had been up above, but he didn't let it bother him. He had completed missions in worse conditions than this. He felt the veiled woman's presence join him before he was even halfway, though she didn't say anything other than to impress upon him a feeling of welcome. He sent her his own greeting as he silently glided through the abandoned tunnels, shadows twisting eerily away from the light in a manner reminiscent of how the woman's dress had moved in the glass.

He dismissed the light when the tunnel grew damp, continuing to navigate in the dark. He passed by the windowed section without any trouble, noting that the sun was beginning to go down. He still had plenty of time; he didn't intend to do anything until quite late.

He wasn't very far away from the exit for the base when he reached the intersection he had mentally marked as the one they would use to escape north. He traveled down it a ways before finding another intersection. That was good; more branches would help confuse any pursuers. He had a few blank squares of the keyed paper; he sketched a quick pattern on one and put it in the bag before hiding it behind some pipes. Now, if things went poorly and he couldn't return here to retrieve it for some reason, he would be able to summon the pack with another spell as long as he was within a mile or two from it.

He unwrapped the katana from its fabric prison and attached it to his belt where it belonged. It would come with him. He was very likely to need it before the night was out.

He paused suddenly. He felt... complete, in a way he hadn't since Hotaru's death. Yes, he had been able to be himself on the pirate ship, but aside from the very brief altercation with the travesty of a mage on the freighter, he hadn't been able to *be* shinobi. The ridiculous missions that most other mages would scoff at and turn down... these were what shinobi were meant to do. This was life or death. This was what he was *made* for.

His mood much improved, he checked his watch. It was a little after six. He had about four-and-a-half hours before he started sabotaging the base. He settled down to wait, closing his eyes and sinking into a light meditation, ignoring the uncomfortable chill in the air. He might as well use the time to continue shoring up his strength.

His eyes snapped open when the watch struck ten thirty. He double-checked that his pack was out of sight, then started back towards the base entrance, pulling magic into his eyes to help him see. The veiled woman's presence was still with him, but it felt like her attention was elsewhere for the time being. It didn't worry him; there was no need for her to watch him meditate and slink through abandoned utility tunnels as long as she and the mage were ready at the proper time. He reviewed the plan once again, remembering an old adage one of the shinobi instructors he had once had was fond of saying: Plan for every eventuality, then go with the flow.

He slowed his pace as he approached exit 4B, but there was nothing alive in the tunnels in a large radius around him as far as he could tell. He approached the door and examined it visually and with his magic. It didn't look like anyone had been here in the past few days since he had broken in. The door opened easily. He crept up the ramp to the second door and found that it too had been left untouched. That meant his first visit had gone entirely unnoticed. He cast a cleaning spell on his feet and slid into the store room quickly, reaching out with his senses, but he was alone. He passed through the store room into the stairwell and retraced his steps through the medical facility, exiting through the office window. Now, under the cover of darkness, he had free rein of the base.

He had made eight fire bombs to distribute around the base for maximum chaos, and one to hold on to. Sticking to the shadows, he glided from building to building, easily avoiding the few people who were outside. This time, he traveled all over, carefully choosing his targets. He wanted the bombs to be fairly evenly spread out. He hid the little squares of paper wherever he thought they would go unnoticed – in trash cans, tucked under window sills, slipped into vehicles. They wouldn't do a large amount of damage, but they didn't need to. They just needed to add to the confusion of the mage's explosion, hopefully causing the Seekers to split up to investigate the multiple incidents. He left the medical center alone, since he still planned on exiting through there. He also avoided the building where the mage was being kept; that one was already covered.

It was a little after eleven thirty when he finished, and he turned his attention back to the veiled woman's presence. He was surprised to find her upset and a little angry, her attention still elsewhere. He gave her a mental poke.

:Apologies,: came the quiet response. *:There has... incident in....:*

He frowned. *:Does it affect us?:*

:No,: she replied firmly, her tone hardening like steel. *:...going to... place down.:*

Okay, she was actually very angry about whatever had transpired. Luckily, Takeshi did not have to worry about that if it didn't affect them. *:I'm ready, and everything is in place. I think we should wait a half hour, though. How is your friend doing?:*

He could feel how conflicted she was. Takeshi revised his earlier thought – whatever events had transpired might end up affecting this if she couldn't focus.

:After midnight is usually a good time for explosions, as most people will be asleep by then,: he explained. *:Trust me – in a half hour, we go. The mage?:*

One last mental flurry of indecision, and then she settled, though he could tell she was still seething. *:Ready. We... your mark.:*

Takeshi quickly scaled one of the taller buildings, settling in next to one of the large structures on it to hide. Thirty minutes to go.

"We've done what we can. There is nothing else to do but wait and see if the asset succeeds," Rhode tried to explain. The expression on Duke Belian's face indicated that it still wasn't enough.

"What the hell have we been funding you for, if you can't even tell us how likely it is to succeed?" the red-haired man snarled as he slammed his hands down on the table. Leblanc shot him an annoyed look from where she lay on her couch near the windows but said nothing. "It's not just this – you've had that Avari mage for weeks at this point, and you have nothing to show for it. At this point, just drag her out and torture her the old-fashioned way. You might actually get somewhere."

"And as I've told you in the past, taking her out of the prism sphere would be incredibly dangerous," Rhode argued back. "The Truth Seekers we have watching her say she is very powerful. I don't think we could contain her outside the prism."

She hadn't done anything after that strange outburst. She had gone from looking like she was going to murder something to stricken, then had promptly stopped interacting with them altogether. Rhode had not liked that look in her eyes, though. She was definitely the most dangerous thing they had ever tried to contain. He supposed he should be thankful the prism sphere worked so well.

"You won't be containing anything if we withdraw our funding," Belian warned darkly. "The boy needs to die. Permanently, this time."

"If you have any suggestions as to how to accomplish that–" He was cut off as a Truth Seeker entered the room.

"Colonel. You are required outside," she informed him. He was suddenly reminded of the Avari prisoner with how the Seeker had no problems turning to look at him, even though she could not use her eyes.

Belian sputtered furiously. "We are in the middle of–"

"Immediately, Colonel," she added calmly over the duke's outraged protest.

"We will finish this conversation later," Leblanc said airily from where she lay. "Go deal with whatever has come up, Colonel, and hurry back to us."

Rhode sketched a tight bow as Belian turned on his peer, and quickly left the room with the Truth Seeker. Major Cole was waiting for him right outside the door, looking extremely concerned.

"You need to see this," she said without preamble. She handed him the tablet she was carrying. It showed a recording of the feed watching the Avari from earlier in the day. She was dancing. And singing, it looked like, though there was no audio.

"Well," he said slowly, "that's new."

"It was very strange. At first, Madine and Teuri thought she was trying to taunt them – the song includes lyrics such as 'no damsel in distress,' 'don't need to save me,' and also something about a sword?" Cole informed him, still seeming far more worried about this than he thought it warranted. Unless...

"Was there magic involved? Was she trying to cast?"

The major paused, looking a little thrown off. "Well, no–"

Rhode sighed, disappointed. It was very hard to conclusively prove the prism sphere worked as intended when its inhabitant refused to try any magic. "Then why was it necessary to interrupt my meeting with this? I hope Madine and Teuri enjoyed their impromptu concert. Surely they weren't bothered by it." It was hard to imagine the Seekers being bothered by much of anything.

"But that's the thing!" Cole exclaimed. "The song she's singing – it's the same song that was being sung by Eve Ferline in her pro-Avari concert *at that moment.*" She moved the recording a few minutes ahead. "Second song – the same." She moved it forward again. "*The same* as what Eve was singing."

Rhode's face went blank. That would mean...

"She still has some sort of connection to outside the sphere," he breathed as he processed that. He spun on his heel; he needed to get back to the base immediately. He knew it; he knew there was some reason she had been acting so strange ever since they had captured her. Everyone on that base was in danger. "Contact Integrations – I need an asset on base, now!"

Chapter Twenty-Seven

J amirh sighed, looking out over Tarvishte from one of the palace balconies. It was pretty at night, all lit up and sparkling. Maybe he should go out and explore the city? He needed to do something to distract himself from Ander's words.

Something was wrong with the Human Hades had found, and that something was related to the Abomination.

Ander had looked utterly exhausted; apparently he had tried to reach out to the Human himself using Hades as a sort of mental relay, but all he had heard was static. Neither he nor Hades knew what could be causing it. They had tried to convince the Human to abandon saving Hel and come north to Romanii to get help – Ander was sure he could figure it out if he could examine the Human personally – but the man had refused. He was determined to try to save Hel. Even though they had never met, it made Jamirh warm up to him a little, as it was starting to look like this random Human was the only one who really wanted to save her. Even her goddess seemed okay with abandoning her.

Shortly after Ander had left, probably to get some sleep, Jeri had also said her goodbyes. The new information did not change anything about what had happened in Pitesh, and they still needed someone who knew what they were looking for to check into the situation. She had reassured him it would only be for a couple of days and reminded him to keep up with his stretches.

So he had gotten today off from intense physical workout, at least. Tomorrow too, and maybe the next day, depending on what Jeri found. He'd decided to take a walk after dinner to try to distract himself, but it wasn't working very well. It was very late, almost ten, and he was still restless.

He decided to explore the palace a little before turning in for the night. Exploring was fun, and maybe that could distract him from all the things he couldn't do anything about. He was pretty sure he had only seen a small fraction of the palace; maybe he would find somewhere interesting? He wasn't sure how to go about asking for that, but he had managed to get lost just fine before he had started asking the palace to take him places. He would just wander, and see where he ended up.

He wasn't sure if trying to wander had worked or not, because the first place he found was exactly what he had been looking for. It was a series of halls and rooms dedicated to various artifacts and items from Romanii's history. There were little plaques next to each exhibit that explained what it was and why it was important, and Jamirh found himself fascinated. Some of the items, such as a carefully preserved document written in a language he didn't recognize and a series of weapons made from onyx, were nearly four thousand years old. Others were more recent – a set of jewelry made of gold and ruby that had been gifted from Dalmara was only a hundred years old. He was impressed by how the Vampires did not shy away from the bloody past Jeri had alluded to. A whole section was dedicated to the very beginnings of Vampire culture, a time when Vampires had stalked and killed Humans, Avari, and any of the other living races they could get their hands on for blood.

Jamirh was pretty sure the Empire lied like a rug when it came to covering up their own atrocities. It was just another example of how much better life was here.

He exited the last room and was surprised to find himself in front of the large doors that led to the room the Crystal Light Blade rested in. He frowned, looking around, and almost blamed the palace for taking him there before he realized that it was a powerful artifact in its own right – it may have had its own room, but it made sense it would be near the other artifacts.

He was glad there weren't too many other people around to watch him stare at the doors as he fiddled with his key. What about the sword made it special, anyway? Yes, Hades had made it, but what did it do, exactly? Since it was meant to fight the Abomination, something about it must be different from a normal sword. Normal swords could stab things. What did this one do that was extra?

He sighed deeply. He would have to remember to ask Jeri these questions when she returned from Pitesh. Hopefully she would know. Or maybe he could ask Vlad? The Vampire king had appeared to be quite knowledgeable about the sword and its history. He hadn't had many occasions to speak with the dark-haired man, but he had been extraordinarily understanding to Jamirh's point of view each time. But he was the king, and Jamirh was sure he had better things to do with his time than speak to one lost Avari. Then again, Jeri had indicated before she left that he would be welcome to seek out Vlad for any reason.

Conflicted, Jamirh started to make his way back to his room. It was late, and even though he hadn't had practice today he was still sore and tired. His bed and that wonderful heating crystal were calling for him. A little voice that sounded like Jeri whispered to him that he should do his stretches, but he decided to ignore it – this was a day off.

The corridors were mostly empty this late at night. The Vampires might not need much sleep, but the Humans and Avari they lived with did, so things tended to quiet down after a certain point. The walk back to his rooms was easy, now that he sort of understood the trick of it, and before long he found himself climbing the last flight of stairs to the wing he was housed in.

He stopped, confused. There was a large pile of ash in the middle of the hallway.

Jamirh approached it, ears twitching – was one of the servants doing some sort of cleaning? That would be strange for this time of night. And it was a lot of ash. He crouched down to make sure, running his fingers through it, but that was definitely what it was. Maybe someone had dropped a bag of it, or something? But it looked a little too neat to have just been dropped. And why would they have made no attempt to clean it up?

He stared at the ash quizzically. How bizarre, for someone to have been so careless. The people who worked here took a lot of pride in their work; all the servants he had met so far would be very upset to see this in the middle of the floor. He would go down and let housekeeping know.

Suddenly, there was a strange whirring and clicking sound, and the lights went out.

Mouth gone dry, Jamirh sat for a moment in the dark, waiting for his eyes to adjust. There had never been a power outage in the entire time he had been here. Jeri had said they were dangerous. Something was wrong. What had that sound been? He listened hard, but it was silent in the pitch-black hallway.

Suddenly, every instinct he had screamed at him. Jamirh threw himself to the side, feeling the displacement of air as something passed close by.

:Jamirh!: It sounded like Ander, but kind of echoey, and in Jamirh's head. *:Jamirh, where are you!?:*

Jamirh scrambled back, eyes wide as he tried to see what that had been. He didn't dare answer as something metal thudded hollowly into the wall where he had just been. Terror closed his throat as a red light suddenly lit up, looking like some sort of orb set into something larger. It swung around, stopping when it faced his direction. Whatever it was, *it was looking at him.*

:Jamirh, run!: Ander's voice cried out.

Jamirh wasted no time in regaining his feet, dashing down the hallway away from the light. The ground was suddenly missing beneath him and he tumbled down the stairs, crying out in surprise. He hit the railing and lay there for a second, stunned, but there was another whirring and clicking sound above him. His body moved without his input and he found himself rolling down the next section of stairs as something thumped heavily on the landing he had just been on.

:I'm coming!:

An eerie howl arose from somewhere distant in the palace, almost like an alarm, as what sounded like every warg on palace grounds joined in, making the sound multiply. The power flickered back on and he blinked rapidly, trying to cover his eyes as the light temporarily blinded him. He found himself dodging again blindly, grateful for Jeri's training. He rubbed at his eyes to clear them, trying to see what was attacking him.

:Goddess damn it all, Jamirh, get out of there!: Ander begged.

Jamirh was frozen, staring in horror at the thing facing him. It might have been a person at one point, as most of its head, neck, and right shoulder and upper arm were flesh, but the rest of it was like something out of a nightmare. Metal plates made up its upper chest, looking like they had been stitched or stapled to the pale, almost translucent skin. Below the upper torso was an exposed metal spine leading to a metal structure where the hips should be. The legs were unnaturally long and thin, a combination of plates, wires, and rods, and the feet were weirdly jointed structures. Its left arm was completely metal, ending in a grotesquely elongated hand. The right arm was metal from the elbow down, and a long thin blade extended from where the hand should have been. The red light he had seen was an orb set into a metal plate etched with symbols covering the right side of the thing's face opposite one dull maroon eye. Its mouth was stitched closed.

One long, pointed ear remained intact on the left side of its head. Jamirh fought down the urge to vomit, suddenly very, very certain he knew what the word "Abomination" meant.

It was staring directly at him.

:Jamirh!:

The long blade retracted into its arm with a soft clink of metal tapping metal, and a gun took its place. Jamirh felt the blood drain from his face as it pointed it at him, the red orb turning with jerky motions in its socket, accompanied by quiet whirring sounds.

We need to move, or we die. Again, a soft voice whispered from somewhere inside him. His vision blurred, and he saw a construct not unlike this one but with more organic parts and less metal bearing down on him in almost the same way, and saw it shoot. *If we move like this...* the voice suggested, and he was reminded of Ander's almost unnatural speed.

Jamirh moved. He moved so fast he couldn't even control his own momentum, and he went crashing into a wall. The three shots the thing fired missed, but it was already turning to face him again, a disturbing lack of expression on what remained of its face. Jamirh forced himself to roll to his feet, adrenaline giving him the boost he needed, and prepared to dodge again as the thing took aim. Then it cocked its head to the side in a sharp movement.

Here it comes!

It skittered towards him, equally fast, as two more metal arms unfolded from where they had hidden along its spine. The movement made Jamirh's head hurt to look at – nothing should be able to move like that – and he dodged out of the way again, but he knew he wouldn't be able to keep this up. He was tiring fast, and he wasn't sure the monster in front of him could even get tired. If it came to a contest of stamina, he would lose. He needed a weapon, *yes, a weapon, a sword? We are good with swords.*

Gods, he was going to die here, he realized in an almost detached manner as the construct turned towards him again, red eye beginning to spin. From the extra arms another pair of blades extended out, which a slightly hysterical part of Jamirh pointed out was a little excessive. For the first time, he realized why a sword might have an advantage over the daggers, though at this point he'd take either. He glared at the thing, suddenly angry that it had managed what no one else had – he itched to have a sword in hand, even though he had never held one before in his life.

Gods all damn it, stand and fight!

With what? There's nothing at hand.

He threw himself backward and to the side as the construct charged him again. He still didn't have complete control over the speed, and he tumbled to the floor as his limbs tripped over themselves. The monster switched directions in a flash, giving him no time to recover–

A bolt of bright-green light slammed into the thing's chest, sending it flying away from Jamirh.

He chanced a glance away from the monster to see Ander, eyes glowing bright green. The priest stalked towards them, his clothing changing in flashes of green threads, morphing into a longer white coat that flared behind and around him over a black turtleneck. He was wielding the same glaive the statues of Hades held, and as he came to a stop just in front of Jamirh arrays of bright-green magic burst into existence, lines of power weaving themselves into a sphere around them both.

Ander's cold gaze did not leave the monstrosity as it regained its feet. "Jamirh, are you okay?"

Jamirh swallowed hard, struggling to regain his voice. "Yeah, I-I think s-so?"

A quiet clicking sound came from the thing, and it raised its left hand, the strangely elongated one, to reveal a strange, purple-colored light in its palm. Confusingly, it just stood there, shining the light at them.

Ander's expression darkened with fury, and to Jamirh's surprise, the green of Ander's magic slowly began to bleed into violet. "How dare you?" he snarled, except it didn't sound just like him anymore. Another voice, female, angry and echoing, overlaid his as though they were speaking at the same time. It sounded familiar. "I destroyed you in a foreign place when I was unable to bring my full power to bear, and you still dare come here? To my home? Kill *my* children? I warned you what would happen if I ever came across another."

What was Ander talking about? Jamirh cast a glance up at the priest. The white hair and now violet eyes, the violet sphere of magic, the female voice overlaying the man's – it all reminded him of that day in Sturlow, when Hel had defended him from the Truth Seeker. Jeri had said the color of magic was bound to the caster. If that was really so, how was Ander using Hel's magic? What was going on?

Ander slammed the bottom of the glaive against the floor, and the light in the thing's hand shattered. The blank expression on its face did not change, and it swung the gun up immediately, aiming at Ander.

A rope of shadow grabbed at the arm from behind the monster, wrapping around it and squeezing. The metal made a sound of protest, then broke in two, the gun and the lower arm both falling to the floor. The thing turned to face the new threat. A mass of moving shadows with hundreds of blood-red eyes took up the hallway beyond it. Another pair of shadows sprung out from the horde and ripped the construct's remaining two usable arms off, sending them flying to opposite sides of the hall. The eyes began to close until just two remained, and then Vlad stepped out of the shadows, expression furious. He was wearing silver armor with a dark-red-and-black cape, and he held a thin silver sword in his right hand.

The monstrosity took a step back, then just disappeared.

"Oh, no. Not here. Not in a place of my power," Ander hissed, voice still strangely doubled, and he raised his left hand, palm up. As he did so, a dark, shadowy version of the floor rose with it, revealing the construct from the bottom up as it passed. It hadn't moved.

Vlad stepped forward and swiftly beheaded it in a screech of metal.

The thing's body jerked, as though confused, then collapsed slowly to the floor. The red light in its head continued to jerk around for a few moments before going dim, finally coming to rest. The maroon eye stared blankly into space.

Vlad slammed his sword into its chest, pinning the body to the floor. "Is this a good enough sample for you, Ander?" His voice was tight with rage.

The violet began to bleed away, leaving Ander's green in its place before the array dissolved entirely into green sparks. "How many did we lose?" the priest asked grimly, voice normal again, walking forward towards the remains.

"At least seven of the Black Watch, maybe more." Prim appeared in a swirl of shadow next to Vlad, eyeing the body with distaste. "No civilian bodies have been found yet, thankfully, though we are going to have to do a thorough sweep. For now, it just looks like it took out anything it saw as a threat."

"It was using UV rays," Ander spat. "Death would have been instantaneous for most of them. They didn't even have a chance to alert us."

Red eyes found Jamirh, still frozen on the floor. Vlad's expression softened. "Jamirh?"

Jamirh was still staring at the body. "I-I know what it is," he whispered faintly.

He had everyone's attention immediately. "You do?" Ander asked, sounding confused.

"There h-have been... rumors, for a long time," Jamirh managed, still trying to reconcile what he was seeing. He was gripping his key so tightly his hand was beginning to ache. "Bionics. A person, combined with... cybernetic implants t-to create some sort of... super soldier. I-I thought Hel was... was one of them, when

I first met her. I didn't know they were actually th-this." He could still see the pointed ear on its head. Avari had been going missing for years. Was this really what had become of them?

It was too much. He turned to the side and vomited.

A hand touched his back, gentle, and a soothing sensation traveled through his body, easing the nausea. He looked up to see Ander, green eyes uncharacteristically sympathetic. "That is the nature of Abomination," he explained. "Something so horrible, so unnatural that the living world rejects it, causing tears in the fabric of reality. The world itself begins to sicken and die as a result."

"But what about that makes it an Abomination?" Vlad asked. "It is undeniably horrifying, but that is not enough. I don't understand how this qualifies, though I agree it *feels* like it does."

Ander looked back at the remains, still pinned to the floor. "If I had to guess, I would say that was a mage – or at least, an Avari with mage potential. Magic is the way by which we interact with the natural world on a spiritual and metaphysical level. Magic is life. To supersede that with tech, and strip their will and agency from them, creating this...? Yes, I can see why the living world itself might reject its existence. I will have to study the body to learn more." He closed his eyes, looking exhausted.

Prim looked as horrified as Jamirh felt. "But magic and tech don't work together. The margin for error to avoid killing the subject must be extremely thin. Who would even try to combine them inside of a living body?" She paused, then added, "Was it even alive?"

Ander shuddered. "Yes," he said shortly.

Jamirh fought down another wave of nausea. He took a few deep breaths, trying to get himself back under control, and squeezed his key tighter.

"We need to come up with a way to search for them," Vlad stated grimly. "I will not have such things coming into my country and killing my people with such ease. I assume it was using hologram tech to appear invisible?"

"That is most likely the case," Ander answered.

"I have some ideas," Prim added. "Some of the others might, too. I'll ask around, and put together a plan."

Jamirh looked up at Ander. "How did you use Hel's magic?" he asked quietly.

Ander opened his eyes to look at Jamirh. "What?"

"Your magic – it was the same color as Hel's," Jamirh clarified. "Jeri told me the color of magic is dependent on the caster. How were you using Hel's magic? You kind of sounded like her, too."

Ander stared at him blankly, before looking at Vlad. Vlad looked back, completely unsympathetic. The priest sighed, turning back to Jamirh. "I didn't use Hel's magic," he said gently. "I used Hades'. As Her priest, that is something I can do – use Her power to supplement mine."

Jamirh was confused, ears twitching lower. "But, but the color–"

"Is the color of Hades' magic," Ander clarified.

"But..." That didn't make any sense. Jeri had even said Hel's color was violet.

Ander just looked tired. "For what it's worth, I disagreed with this," he sighed. "But She wanted to be the one to tell you. She thought She owed you that much."

"Tell me what?" Jamirh asked, looking around. No one would meet his eyes.

"Jamirh–" Ander started, then cut himself off, shaking his head. He tried again. "Jamirh, Hel *is* Hades."

Rhode stormed into the room the prism sphere was being kept in, glancing at Madine and Teuri. The sphere itself was covered in a fine web of yellow and indigo lines of power, telling him they had shielded the sphere. Everything was still as it should be. The Avari was standing calmly in the center of her prison. She raised her head to look at him through the glass, her gaze faintly amused.

"We will only meet once more, you and I."

Rhode frowned. "We will meet as many times as I want. You don't get to dictate that."

"Oh, I think you'll find that in this case, I do." She laughed softly and looked around her, taking in her prison.

Rhode felt disturbed, but couldn't put his finger on why. He looked to Madine.

"She has still performed no magic," the Seeker murmured softly.

But how could that be true?

"You know, there were once others who tried to hold me this way." Ears twitching, the Avari looked back to him, voice cold. Something... something was wrong with her eyes. The violet pinned him, unnerved him. Shadows shifted around her, forming shapes hinting at another place, other people, but were gone before he could do more than acknowledge their existence.

Out of the corner of his eye, he saw Madine stiffen, though she still didn't signal.

"The difference is that I don't love you the way I loved her. You are not one of mine, and I owe you nothing." Hel paused, head tilted slightly to the side. "But he is."

"You aren't here because you owe us, you are here because we captured you." Rhode frowned, eyes flickering to the screens nearby. All systems were normal, though the Truth Seekers behind him were alert. Could he even trust the readouts anymore? What had he just seen? What was the Avari rambling on about? Where was that asset he had asked for?

She grinned sharply, dancing backward away from the glass, but there was something wrong with the movement, abnormal, like her body shouldn't have been able to make the motion. For all that she was Avari, for all her strange coloring, she had never looked so... unnatural to him as she did now.

"This is goodbye for now, Colonel," she laughed, that disturbing smile never leaving her face. Alarm shot through him; something was wrong, horribly wrong. "But don't worry – we will see each other again."

Her eyes were *glowing*.

And that's when he realized that the inside walls of the sphere were also glowing. No, not the walls, lines threaded through the walls.

His eyes widened. She had turned the whole prism sphere into an array.

He started to bark out the alarm–

The sound she made then could not have come from that throat. It was the sound of something much, much larger, shrieking its challenge and fury to the sky–

He felt Madine grab him. And everything exploded.

Chapter Twenty-Eight

There had been a flurry of activity on the base starting about ten minutes ago, centering around the building the mage was being held in, but the veiled woman assured Takeshi that it made no difference. He'd watched from his spot on the roof of the nearby building, counting down, when she had suddenly whispered to him, *:Be ready.:*

Well, being a little early wouldn't matter too much. He readied his magic, searching for the threads of the fire bombs he had placed earlier. *:Ready.:*

A scream tore through the night, causing Takeshi to stagger back and reflexively cover his ears, almost losing his hold on the threads he had gathered. The entire city probably heard that, soundproofing or no soundproofing. He felt his own magic trying to answer the call, even as disciplined as it was. That was a Queen's Challenge – an extremely high-level Voice magic, especially at that volume. Anyone with magic *potential* was going to find themselves trying to respond to that.

Then the building exploded.

Takeshi sent a flare of power down each of his threads and felt each of the patterns light up. Vortexes of fire exploded around the base, destroying anything they had been attached to and lighting anything nearby on fire. He fed them for a few moments, letting them grow, before cutting the connection. They would burn themselves out now, but the damage was done. Shouts were going up all around the base as the soldiers realized they were under attack.

He kept an eye on the building the mage had been in. People and debris had been thrown back by the blast. He could see the gray uniforms of two Seekers among the rubble, neither of which were moving. The building itself had suffered heavy damage, especially on the northern side. A large chunk of the building was missing, which gave him a starting point. He leapt down to the ground, reaching out to the veiled woman mentally.

:Come,: she whispered, sounding strangely tired.

Glass was scattered everywhere; none of the windows had survived the shock-wave of power. Takeshi ran to the northern side of the building. He stuck to the shadows as much as possible, something made easier by the fact that the building no longer had any lights and was a faintly smoking ruin. A loud alarm finally began to sound across the base as people began to respond to the chaos and destruction. He quickly entered the building through a missing chunk of wall, looking for the epicenter of the explosion. It wasn't difficult to find; few of the interior walls had survived. There were bodies everywhere among the wreckage.

A woman with long white hair and the pointed ears of an Avari was standing amidst the rubble, head lowered. Her left arm hung at her side as she grasped it with her right. As he got closer, Takeshi knew instantly something was wrong – the skin below the elbow looked fractured into large chunks, and a pale white light seeped out from between the cracks.

What in the names of all the gods would cause *that*?

She looked up at him as he approached, violet eyes tired. She smiled, ears twitching up slightly. "Thanks for coming to get me. We should get going, before this" – she indicated her arm – "gets any worse. Ander is going to be so upset."

He stared at her. "It was *you*?"

The veiled woman's smile grew. "I tried to tell you, but I was never sure what you were hearing and what you weren't. But yes; it's me! Surprise!" Exhaustion made her tone fall a little flat. "I'm going by Hel right now," she introduced herself, before her expression fell. "Kind of, anyway."

He supposed that it didn't matter; they still had to leave. In some ways it even improved the situation, since she already knew where they were going. "Shuurai Takeshi, if you didn't already know. Are you in any immediate danger from that?" he asked, indicating her arm. He wasn't sure what that injury was, or how it would impact their escape. What had they been doing to her in this place?

She shook her head. "No, though the faster we get to Tarvishte and Ander, the better."

Again with this Ander, though they didn't have time for him to ask for an explanation. They could discuss it when they weren't standing in the middle of a mostly destroyed military base. "Do you have any way to cover it up, then?" he asked. "The light will almost certainly draw attention to us."

She raised her other hand above the arm, murmuring softly in a language he didn't recognize, and shadows seeped up from the ruins around them to settle over the cracks, darkening them. "This will have to do for now," she said.

He nodded. The cracks in the skin were still visible, but at least they were no longer glowing. "Come on, then. We need to get out of here."

He kept an eye on her as they headed back towards the medical facility. She was managing very well, considering her injury and the power she had just expended in the explosion. Given what she had said to him before about needing him to get her off base, she was doing better than he had expected. He matched his pace to hers. Takeshi kept them to the shadows and smoke, avoiding the lights that were now beginning to turn on. People were rushing all over the base by this point, trying to put out the fires and get the injured to safety, and the confusion made it easy to slip by unnoticed. But he knew every second they remained the danger rose exponentially. He kept his senses open but felt nothing from any of the Truth Seekers. Had they all died in the explosion? That seemed too convenient, and he hadn't seen that many bodies. He was sure time was running out before those that had been in the city returned to the base.

They were almost at their goal when something skittered in the dark. Takeshi and Hel both froze, Hel's eyes flashing with power. She hissed in a breath between her teeth. "So many, today," she murmured darkly. *:Danger,:* she warned silently, showing him an image of what was coming.

Takeshi drew his katana, feeling slightly ill, and readied a shield pattern in his mind. Who would think it was a good idea to create such a monstrosity? *:Weaknesses? Strengths?:* he asked, trying to decide where it was. Something about it was confusing his senses, making it difficult to pin down.

:It's fast, and uses guns and blades. Has something just for Vampires, but that won't affect you other than possibly a sunburn. It is extremely strong,: she replied instantly. *:Magic is... tricky around it; it seems to be resistant, though more powerful spells can overcome the effect. Don't hold back. It can use holograms to cloak itself. I once exploded one successfully, and dismembering also seems to work. Its spine is metal so make sure you strengthen your sword. I don't know how much I can contribute without literally falling apart at this point, but if I see an opening I'll take it.:*

He could hear her clearly for the first time. Perhaps the physical distance mattered. *:Understood. Take this.:* He passed her one of the daggers so she would have something to defend herself with if it came to it, and closed his eyes.

The first shots bounced off his shield pattern, glowing blue-white in the semi-darkness. He swept out a hand in that direction, sending lightning into the darkness in an arc, searching for a target.

There!

The lightning had disrupted the hologram it was using to stay hidden. He sent two mage bolts back at it, but it dodged. It was very fast, limbs moving unnaturally. He was capable of ridiculous speeds too, but at least he didn't look like *that* while moving. It almost reminded him of a spider.

Hel backed away, eyes still glowing violet in the darkness, and Takeshi charged forward, making sure to keep himself between them. It blocked each of his strikes in an impressive display of coordination for three blades, and he sprung away, not willing to draw out the engagement. He had gotten a good look at its face, and wished he hadn't. The complete lack of expression was very disconcerting and reminded him of the Truth Seekers. At least their mouths weren't stitched shut.

One of the blades retracted and was replaced by a gun, and it shot at him again. His shield bloomed into existence in front of him, catching each of the bullets in the air as they tried to pass. He charged them with electricity and sent them flying back at the construct. It dodged again, the red light in its head twitching around, though he couldn't help but feel like it was studying him intensely. Its normal eye almost looked dead, though it was hard to tell in the dim lighting.

He felt Hel hum thoughtfully in his mind. *:Here, let's try this,:* she suggested, and the blade of his katana took on a violet tinge. *:I won't be able to hold that for long. Make it count!:*

Takeshi threw himself back at the machine, telegraphing a high attack before dropping to the ground and sliding past. His blade sliced straight through one of the knee joints, causing it to lose its balance and fall to the ground. He didn't hesitate to strike from behind, taking one of the extra arms off as well. He danced away quickly at the strange whining sound that came from its chest, as though something were building up inside it.

Hel knelt next to him, adding her power to his shield in a brilliant blend of violet and blue as the whine gained in volume and pitch. It suddenly cut out with no warning, and Takeshi's shield shattered and he nearly lost consciousness as something disrupted the core of his magic. He heard Hel cry out next to him, and the buildings and street lights nearby suddenly went dark. There was a screech of metal from the construct. Trusting his instincts, he grabbed the woman and rolled them both to the side as shots rang out again.

He needed to do something about that gun. It hadn't revealed another one, so hopefully that was the only one it had. He reached inside himself, but where normally there was a calm pool of power to draw from there was now a painful, disorganized mess that was slowly trying to piece itself back together. He shuddered at the feeling, but he couldn't afford to linger on it. He took his remaining dagger and rolled to his knees. He stared the thing down just long enough to aim and throw, adding what meager power he could to the weapon's flight.

The dagger slammed into the construct's palm, shattering along with the gun. Takeshi staggered to his feet, gripping his katana tightly. Hel was slowly pushing herself to her knees, though Takeshi noticed the cracks of light had spread upward along her arm. They had to end this; he didn't know how much longer she could last, and he wouldn't be able to carry her and fight.

"That was new," she coughed as she found her feet, gripping her arm again. "Let's hope it can't do that again. That hurt."

Takeshi frowned at that, though he kept his eyes on the construct. The attack itself hadn't really *hurt*, per se, though his magic felt sore and abused. Maybe that was a sign she was nearing her limit.

The construct's upper leg suddenly unfolded, creating a rudimentary replacement for the limb Takeshi had removed. It heaved itself up again, shaking out the remains of the gun and the dagger from its hand.

Takeshi pulled power from his core, ignoring the ache as lightning spread down the length of his katana, pale blue and crackling. Whatever the thing had done to disrupt his magic, it wasn't permanent – he could feel his magic coming back together again, recovering quickly even though it still felt bruised. That was a minor inconvenience Takeshi wasn't willing to die over.

The red eye twitched in his direction and it turned to face him, another blade extending out of the hand the gun had been in. It took a step towards him, and Takeshi was pleased to see that even if it had replaced the leg, it didn't seem to be able to move nearly as fast on it. It seemed to be testing its weight, and Takeshi rushed forward, trying to catch it off guard.

It swung at him with both of its remaining blades, but this time he pushed magic into his legs and leapt over it, spearing it through from behind. The electricity coating the blade traveled through the circuits in the thing's body, frying them. It jerked for a few moments before crashing to the ground.

He pulled his katana from the body and, just to be sure, beheaded it. He didn't want to find out it could reboot the fried systems, or had secondary systems, or whatever. *:We need to go!:* he called, sending Hel a mental picture of the medical facility. His magic was still recovering from that disruption, but they needed to move. He turned to look at the Avari, who was looking up at a nearby building with a worried frown. He followed her gaze.

Truth Seeker.

He took a step back towards her and realized they had been surrounded while he fought the cybernetic monstrosity. He could sense six in the immediate vicinity, all coming closer, centered on their position.

That was almost catastrophically bad, but he still had a few tricks left. They weren't completely doomed yet.

"What are you?"

Takeshi turned around to see another Truth Seeker emerge from the shadows. He quickly moved to put himself between the two women, though this Seeker looked like she had seen better days. Her uniform was scorched and torn in places, she was missing her gun, and her hair was a mess, free from the usual severe hairstyles they preferred. Her blindfold was still in perfect condition, he noted.

"What are you?" the Seeker repeated. Takeshi got the impression he was being ignored completely, and that the question was being directed towards Hel.

"I am what I have always been," Hel answered from behind him. "You already know. Why didn't you tell him?"

If they were going to talk anyway... :*Stall. I need as many of them here as possible*,: he informed Hel quietly. He sensed a feeling of agreement from her.

"Magic." For once, Takeshi heard an emotion in a Seeker's voice – scorn, though her expression did not change. "You take me for a fool."

Takeshi started planning how he was going to cast a flash bang and a smoke bomb for maximum effect, and how he could use the cover to break away. Once he got himself and Hel out of the Seekers' direct line of sight, he could keep them hidden long enough to escape, but that meant he would actually need most of them to be here. A series of short shadow steps would further confuse their trail.

"Do you think so?" Hel asked politely. "I think not. Not even your commander is a fool; he just lacked any information that could have helped. It wasn't his fault. Though he does lack anything even remotely like faith, or belief."

"You said others had tried to hold you in a prism sphere before. Where? Is that how you knew how to break it?" the Seeker pressed, a hint of frustration entering her tone.

Hel just sounded amused, though waiting for the right moment was making Takeshi twitchy. "Is that what you call it? I never knew its name. There is precious little that can hold me against my will. And if I told you where the first one was, you would never believe me."

The other Seekers were coming closer, but they needed to be closer still. Takeshi waited.

"You break many of the rules as we know them," the Seeker responded. "What would one more be, but further proof– *NO!*"

Takeshi felt it too, saw the hint of a shadow skitter across the ground, and spun, but he wasn't fast enough. Hel shrieked as the blade pierced her through the chest. The now-visible construct released the blade, leaving it pinning her to the ground, and turned to face him.

Takeshi re-wove the patterns he had been planning and struck in an explosion of lightning that threw the Seekers away from them. It was far more powerful than he had expected, more powerful than he had even thought he was capable of. The construct exploded, sending him several paces back. He forced himself to recover quickly, scrambling back to Hel...

...A woman bleeding out, pinned to the floor, blood pooling everywhere...

Takeshi froze. Hotaru was dying, Hotaru was dying and he had killed her, had stabbed her, he had had to, she had asked him to, the Empress had asked him to–

:Takeshi!: The veiled woman's voice cut through him. *:I am* not *her! This is not the same! Listen to me!:*

She pressed something into his hands, a flash of violet – a spell crystal?

:You need to take this north. Present it to any of the towers along the Warcross Wall; it will grant you passage into Romanii. Go to Tarvishte, find Ander. He knows to look for you. He can help you.:

There was so much blood. He felt pinned along with her.

:There is not that much blood, actually look! *Here, in the present! This body doesn't bleed that much.:*

He didn't understand what she was saying. But she was dying like Hotaru had died and it was *his fault* all over again.

Her eyes closed. *:Promise me you will go to Tarvishte. Ander can help you. Ander can explain. I'm going to be okay! This is not the end.:*

"*Promise me we'll be okay?*" Hotaru had asked him, and he had tried, he had really tried–

:Takeshi!: She was begging him now. *:This body wasn't real to begin with. You'll still hear me, okay? You just have to* believe *you'll hear me!:*

North. He had to go north. Romanii, Tarvishte, Ander.

:Yes! And I'll be with you. We don't have much time. I can feel this body dying all around me.: Her breathing was coming in labored gasps. Cracks were beginning to spread out from where the blade pierced her, growing faster and faster. *:Hold on, I'm going to try to shield you from the worst of this.:*

The world whited out around him.

When his vision cleared, he was alone in a large crater. Everything around him had been vaporized. He felt numb, stunned at the turn of events, and felt himself struggle to understand what had just happened. There wasn't even a trace of the body left.

She was gone. How could she just be gone?

:Takeshi?:

North. Romanii. Tarvishte. Ander.

Right, he had to go north. She... she had wanted him to go north. He shakily pushed himself to his feet.

:Takeshi! Can you hear me?:

Around him, outside the blast radius, he could see several of the Seekers slowly recovering as well. His eyes met the blindfold of the one that had been speaking, and they both froze.

"Go," she whispered quietly.

:Takeshi!:

Takeshi fled, the echo of the veiled woman's voice calling him and the sound of weeping following him into the night.

Rhode was furious.

He was resting in an off-base hospital, as everything on base was a complete disaster right now. He had Madine's quick thinking to thank for his life, as she had managed to teleport them out fast enough to avoid any life-threatening injuries from the Avari's explosive escape, though both had suffered minor injuries.

He would get to the bottom of why no one had been able to tell the Avari had been doing magic. He would get to the bottom of how she had been able to do magic at all. They had tested the prism sphere on other subjects – none had been able to so much as light a candle while under its influence.

How had things gone so horribly wrong?

Not only had they lost the only working prism sphere prototype, but multiple sections of the Charve base had been damaged by explosions of fire that had been nearly impossible to put out until they ran out of material to burn. The entire R&D building had to be condemned; they were still trying to figure out what could be salvaged from the wreckage.

There had been some sort of uproar in the city itself, which had prevented multiple Truth Seekers from returning to the base. People had poured out of buildings into the streets, but later they seemed unable to explain why they had done it – only that they had felt they had to.

And now, the news that they had lost three assets! The one they had sent into Romanii had been destroyed shortly before the Avari had freed herself based on when they had stopped receiving transmissions from it, and worse, it had failed to kill Ebryn. Then they lost *two* to the Avari and some random shinobi who had appeared out of nowhere to help her break out. One asset had set off a short-range EMP in its attempt to neutralize the mages, which had knocked out systems everywhere on the base. An explosion later, and both of the insurgents were missing, not a trace of them to be found.

Duchess Kobayashi had better have a very good explanation as to why one of hers had been found so far into Gallia, and why they appeared to be helping one of Romanii's agents.

And three Truth Seekers had died. What a waste of resources all around.

He picked up a tablet to read the latest reports, but his vision blurred, and he had to put it down. That was the last of the lingering effects of the Avari's magic from what the doctors could tell, and he had been assured it was temporary.

Unfortunately, it made it difficult to do his job now. He knew it was only a matter of time before he was called before the dukes and duchesses for a reckoning of what exactly had happened, and he would like to be prepared with both an explanation and a plan of how he was going to proceed from this point forward.

At least one thing he knew. He was going to hunt that Avari witch down if it was the last thing he did.

Epilogue

J amirh stared at the sword.

"Will you take it?"

He didn't turn at the sound of Hel's voice. "Do I have to?"

There was a long silence, followed by a sigh. "The answer to that question is more complicated than you might think." There was another long pause. "It would be... helpful, if you were to take it up." She sounded like she was picking her words very carefully.

"Why?" Jamirh studied the sword. It continued to lay innocently on its pedestal. "Ander and Vlad seemed to have no trouble killing that thing. What does the Blade do that's special?"

"Nothing, I suppose, if you are comparing it to them. Ander is my priest and can wield my power directly. Vlad is my son and was... reborn through my power, and so his own works quite similarly to mine. Realize, however, that they are the exception, not the rule. Most others will struggle far more than they did, and will likely fail."

Jamirh considered that. "Then the Blade channels your power, somehow?"

"Death, destruction, healing, and rebirth... it is over these domains I hold sway. The Blade has the ability to burn out the Abomination on a metaphysical level. Simply bringing the Blade into contact with the bionic constructs should be enough to destroy them," she replied. "It was an extremely efficient tool against the demons, since all it had to do was make contact. The same will be true here. Reality screams in agony at their existence, and the Blade rectifies that."

Jamirh had also felt like screaming when he'd seen it. "And it has to be me? Vlad or Ander can't wield it?"

A soft laugh. "There is nothing stopping them from doing so, but it will only ever be an excellent weapon in their hands. Ebryn asked me specifically for a sword *for him*. He wanted a soulforged weapon. I could not forge a sword out of his soul crystal on his behalf, but I was able to create a weapon tied to his soul meant explicitly to deal with the problem at hand. Only when wielded by its rightful owner can it reach its full potential. So it is better for Vlad and Ander to use their own soulforged weapons than to try to use this one."

Jamirh turned. A figure draped all in black stood behind him, almost exactly like the statues that were all over the city. This one, however, was slightly transparent. "You aren't really here, then? Are you still in the Empire?"

The shape of the head tilted slightly to one side. "I am as here as I am anywhere, but the avatar is not. Ander made it for me so I could more directly influence things. As a god, I am usually confined to working through my priests, or strong believers. The avatar had some drawbacks – I was limited in power, for example – but I was able to interact in ways I normally can't."

Jamirh frowned. "'Was'?"

"Unfortunately, that avatar has been lost. Certain types of tech disrupt magic, and that body was made of magic. I was already cannibalizing it for the power it was made from, but it was overwhelmed in a battle against an Abomination, and it failed."

Jamirh's ears wilted. "The Human failed to rescue you, then?"

"Not for lack of trying. He managed to kill the first Abomination, but the second one got through." She sounded pained. "It was a difficult battle, one that I had a limited ability to participate in due to the constraints of the avatar and how much magic I had used before that point. And he was already fighting a different battle internally, though he doesn't realize it." Her tone turned sad.

"Will Ander make you a new body?" Jamirh asked.

She shrugged. "He has plans to, I think. It took him almost twenty years to make the first one, though, so I doubt it will be completed anytime soon."

He had been wondering how it worked. "Is Hel dead, then? If he makes another body, will it be the same?"

"Hel and Hades are me," came the firm response. "I used a different name, but it was always *me* you were speaking to. There was never a separate entity named Hel; I alone inhabited that body."

"It's really hard to reconcile 'Hel,' the woman who broke me out of jail, and 'Hades,' the goddess of death," he admitted quietly. "Would it bother you if I just kept calling you 'Hel'?"

Her voice was kind. "Not at all. 'Hel' is even a name mortals called me a long, long, long time ago. I've gone by many names over the ages; all deities have. It is mortals who name us. You will be following an ancient tradition."

"And I am Jamirh," he said forcefully.

"And you are Jamirh," she conceded gracefully. "Even if you fulfil Ebryn's contract and take up the Blade, you will still be Jamirh." She paused. "Contrary to what you might think, I can't just reincarnate anyone. There has to be a specific set of circumstances."

"I really don't care." He already knew Ebryn had made that deal, and now he was here. Though, on that note... "I heard a voice, when the Abomination was chasing me," he informed her.

She nodded. "Yes, Ander was trying to reach you telepathically. He was trying to figure out where you were."

"No, not Ander," Jamirh disagreed. "There was another voice, speaking to me. It sounded like me, but it wasn't saying things I would say." *"We are good with swords,"* the voice had said. It was certainly not a thought he had ever had. "It helped me avoid being killed."

"I see," she said slowly.

"Was it... him?" he asked. *"Can* it be him?"

She regarded him silently for several minutes. "It is possible for previous personalities to communicate to a new one since they all share the same soul, especially under stressful conditions, though it would be... out of character, I think, for Ebryn to help you." He wished he could see her expression. "Have you heard it since then?"

Jamirh shook his head.

"Perhaps that is to be expected. If you hear it again... it may be worth it to listen. We are not the selves of our pasts, but that does not mean we should leave them behind completely."

He laughed, a little bitterly. "What does a god know about being bound by others' choices?"

"More than you might think," she answered, voice unexpectedly grave. "We are all bound by the choices others make – immortals and mortals alike."

He blinked at her in surprise, but she didn't elaborate further. He turned back to the Blade, eyeing the pale-blue crystal. The metal of his key was warm between his fingers. "I feel like I have no choice, here."

"There is always a choice. Just because you don't like the options presented or the consequences of those options doesn't mean a choice doesn't exist. If you choose to walk away right now I will not stop you, but you will be in danger still, and you will be unable to defend yourself. And many, many people are likely to die, who did not have to."

His mouth twisted into a wry smile. "You call that a choice."

"It is one," she agreed seriously. "Do not think the answer is so cut and dry – there are those who would choose to walk away in a heartbeat, if presented with those options, and those who would choose to stand and fight. I am what I am. I have seen this play out both ways time and time again since the beginning of all things. It is easy to look at the options and say, 'I have no choice,' but we are not as bound to one path as we think we are. Which will you choose?"

Jamirh stepped forward and wrapped his hand around the hilt.

Takeshi was cold.

He'd spent hours in the tunnels, fleeing north after the veiled woman's death had rendered his mission a failure. As far as he could tell, no one had even attempted to follow him.

North. Romanii.

"Go."

Numbly, he followed the directions she had left behind. He'd emerged from the tunnels a little before sunrise, just on the outskirts of Charve, and had taken a few minutes to disguise himself again. He had decided it was worth the risk to cast another illusion on his katana – he didn't want to draw any attention to himself. Then he had just started walking north until he came to a small town. There had been a train station; he'd used some of his dwindling funds to purchase passage to a city as far north as he could go. For once, he appreciated that the Empire's reliance on tech meant he didn't have to try to speak with another person.

His failures haunted him the whole way, Hotaru and the veiled woman's words bleeding into each other until he could no longer tell them apart.

"Promise me..."

And he was so very cold, even once he got on the train. He wished he had been able to buy some warmer clothing. It was only going to get colder.

Every time he closed his eyes, all he could see was the body, pinned to the ground, and so much blood...

"...be okay."

So he just didn't close them, powering through the exhaustion that was trying to catch up with him. It didn't stop their words from haunting him, but at least he didn't have to see them.

Neither of them should have had to die. Why had they died? It was his fault, his fault both of them were dead, even though a voice that sounded suspiciously like the veiled woman's kept trying to tell him that wasn't true.

Hel? Her name had been Hel. Hel, and Hotaru. And they were both dead because of him.

Go north.

He gripped the crystal she had given him tightly. Unlike most spell crystals, which were diamond-shaped, this one was shaped like an abstracted hound in an all-out run. It was the same violet as her magic. He wondered what it did.

"Present it to any of the towers..."

Right, he had to find one of the towers. None of the maps he had seen had any of them marked.

"Nine, equidistant... Warcross Wall."

Though, if that were true, he should be able to get a fairly close approximation just by estimating. He found himself missing the veiled woman's words in his head, even if he hadn't heard everything she was saying. He had been, for a short period of time, not alone. Now all he had were echoes that wouldn't leave him, constantly reminding him of his failure.

"...still here."

Takeshi got off the train when they called the final stop, and went to find a map. He finally found a pamphlet with a map of the continent and decided the nearest tower was probably a little over fifty miles west of where he was. He bought a bus ticket to the town of Demes, which looked to be as close as he could get, and sought out a quiet place nearby to wait for boarding.

North. Romanii. Then...

"Go to Tarvishte. Find Ander."

Right. Find Ander. Avoid killing him if at all possible.

It was cold here, too, though he supposed that made sense. He was farther north, after all. Still, he would have thought the Empire would have better heating for their buildings. He wished he had a heating crystal. He tried to cast a warming spell, but it made no difference against the constant chill and he dismissed it. Fire spells weren't his specialty, especially if they weren't supposed to explode, and he wondered why he had even bothered.

He looked up as the bus pulled into the station and people began to disembark. Had it really been two hours already? He glanced at the clock to find that it had. Strange; it didn't feel like it.

He waited patiently for the bus to empty before approaching with his ticket. The conductor waved him on, barely even glancing at the piece of paper. He slid into a seat near the back, hoping this was not a popular route.

"This is not the end."

Right, he had to hold onto that, had to focus on his original goal. Hel might be gone, but she had given him the way forward, had made sure he would make it to the rebellion. Though... was it actually a 'rebellion' if it was coming out of another country? He wasn't sure. Did it matter to his overall mission, to help free Ni Fon from the Rose Empire's control? Probably not.

Vaguely, he wondered what was happening in Charve. He wondered if the curfew was going to be extended even longer now, or if there would be even harsher methods of control put into place while they cleaned up. Though, the military no longer had their prisoner. Hopefully that meant the city would go back to normal soon.

What about the Truth Seekers? They had just... let him go. Why?

"That... good question."

The bus jerked to a stop. Takeshi started, not having realized the bus was even moving. People were getting up, collecting their things, and leaving. Were they already in Demes? The display at the front of the bus said they were. Wasn't it supposed to be an hour's ride?

Something was wrong.

"Ander... Find Ander."

Right. North, Romanii, Tarvishte, Ander.

He gathered his things and exited the bus, irrationally annoyed that it was just as cold here as it had been in the previous city. He looked around. This station was very small, but it still had maps. Tiredly, he calculated that the nearest tower was probably thirty or forty miles north-west of here. Half-forgotten words rose to mind. *"The Wall... kills everythin' for miles around."* Freja had told him that back at the Dancin' Whale.

"The Waste."

So he could expect miles of desolation before he came to the Wall. That was good. At least he had plenty of food.

Mechanically, he navigated his way through the little town, making sure to head north-west. It wasn't long before houses and roads gave way to undeveloped land, rolling hills with a few struggling trees scattered about.

He kept walking, focusing on each step in the right direction. If he did that, he wouldn't have to think about *them*.

And then there was... nothing in front of him. A perfectly flat plain, completely devoid of life, gray and uninviting.

"Speak... me."

Shivering, he headed into the Waste, followed by the voices of his ghosts.

Vlad stormed into the Temple of Night Rising. Ander took one look at him and made himself scarce, disappearing into his lab and quietly shutting the door behind him. Vlad let him be; he had a different target.

He planted himself firmly in the center of the sanctuary, angrily demanding, "Well?"

There was a delicate cough from behind him. He turned to see his mother standing there, draped all in black as the season demanded. Here, in Her temple with a priest nearby, She almost wasn't even transparent.

"You are angry with me," She murmured softly.

"You risk much, with very little to gain," he warned. "One day, you will push too hard, and something you cherish will break."

"Everything that is mine is already broken. Thus it has always been," She countered quietly. "Are you angry about Jamirh?"

"You know where I stand on Jamirh. What about this Human you are courting? Shuurai Takeshi?" he asked pointedly.

She didn't so much as twitch. "Ah. That."

"Yes, *that*," he repeated. "You must know how the Nifoni princess died."

Silence.

"How many months did they keep him in prison for, before they banished him? Does that not seem strange?" he demanded. This always happened. Why did She seem incapable of making good decisions where Her priests were concerned?

"He is called to me," came the quiet reply.

"I am not denying that," he agreed. If they were called to Her, they were called to Her; there was no changing that. "But if you knew, you should have tried to convince him to come here immediately, not wasted time on some ridiculous rescue scheme that only ever had the slightest chance for success."

She turned away from him slightly. "It almost worked. If the second Abomination hadn't irreparably disrupted the arrays keeping the avatar together, it would have."

Vlad kept his voice cool. "And tell me, how has communication been going since he saw you die in front of him?"

"He is still coming here. He is almost at the Wall. Titus will grant him entry."

"Of all the gods, you cannot afford to damage your priests' belief in you," he argued bitterly. "You already have so few. How could you ever risk one that way? Tell me, are you happy now?"

She said nothing but slowly turned to face him again. Deliberately, She raised Her veils, something he had not seen Her do during the Season for centuries.

He was stunned to see tear tracks on Her face.

"I grieve for them," She whispered. "I grieve for them both."

Her form disappeared into the ether, leaving Vlad standing alone in the center of Her temple. He closed his eyes for a moment and took a deep breath before heading back to the palace. There was much work to be done, if they were going to succeed in defeating the Abomination.

Losing was not an option.

Glossary

Abomination: A malevolent force that has haunted the world since the beginning of time. Taking different forms, it returns again and again, seeking to destroy all life and magic.

Agale: The main province of the Rose Empire. Was originally the country of Agale, but in the time of Queen Saran over a thousand years ago it joined together with Elbe, Hispa, and Gallia to form the Empire.

Aradian: A race formed by the Faleri, Aradians hail from the eastern desert continent of Falin. They generally have darker or tan skin, pink, orange, or red hair, and eyes that look like flames flickering behind glass. They live for three hundred years, and all are able to magically create fire. They have a matriarchal, warrior culture.

Ardwick: A town in the north of Agale.

Array: The term used by northern mages to describe the arrangement of glyphs and bridging lines that is used to cast spells.

Avari: A race formed by the Three Goddesses. They have long, pointed ears, brightly colored hair and eyes, and are strongly inclined towards magical ability.

Bariza: A city in Gallia, located on the coast. Something of a party city. Where the Dancin' Whale is located.

Blackfields: A poor district in Lyndiniam where many of the city's Avari live.

Black Watch, the: A peace-keeping force in Romanii comprised entirely of Vampires.

Blind Ones: A term for Truth Seekers, used mostly by those not in the Rose Empire. References the blindfolds all Truth Seekers wear.

Bridging Lines: A part of spell crafting; bridging lines connect and balance glyphs in an array so that the spell is able to be cast.

Cartago-Mir: A province of the Rose Empire, south of Agale and on the Patoran continent.

Charve: A city in Gallia; it is home to the Carve Military Base.

Crystal Lights, the: Powerful magical artifacts created by the elemental deities long ago.

Crystal Light Blade: The sword created by Hades specifically for Ebryn Stormlight a thousand years ago after he collected the crystal lights from the various elemental deities. It is meant to destroy Abomination, but will not work for anyone other than Ebryn.

Dales: A town in northern Agale.

Dalmara: The main country on the continent of Falin, comprised mostly of Aradians.

Demons: The expression of Abomination Ebryn Stormlight fought a thousand years ago.

Deva: A town in northern Romanii.

Edo: The capital of Ni Fon.

Elbe: The easternmost province of the Rose Empire. Was originally the country of Elbe, and chose to join with Agale, Hispa, and Gallia to form the Rose Empire.

Emerald Shores: The southernmost province of the Rose Empire; situated on the continent of Vien.

Espera, the: The elemental twin deities of air, lightning, and storms. Their names are Esper and Espra.

Espon: The continent named for the Espera. Where the Rose Empire is based, as well as Romanii.

Faleri, the: The elemental twin deities of fire. Their names are Falare and Falera.

Festival of Night: The largest celebration in Hades' religion, Festival begins the Season of Veils and takes place on October 31. It begins at dust and goes until dawn in a large, city-wide carnival.

Firilae: Goddess of magic, soul, emotion, and trickery. See also: The Three Goddesses.

Gakujin: Nifoni name for Selenae.

Gallia: A province of the Rose Empire situated on the western coast of Espon. Was originally the separate countries of Hispa and Gallia, but were combined early on in the Empire's history.

Gini: A race formed by the Espera, the Gini are few in number a live primarily in the norther mountains of Espon. They have six wings, feathered ears, and talons for feet. They value education, learning, art, and divination – many of them are Graeae, and able to see the future.

Glowlights: A type of flashlight found in the Rose Empire.

Glyph: The basic symbols used to create spells. There are over fifty of them, and the way they are combined is what creates the spell's effect.

Hades: The goddess of death, destruction, healing, and rebirth. She is primarily worshiped in Romanii, as she created the Vampires and they see her as their mother. She is also very active in attempting to destroy Abomination. Called "The Silent Goddess" in Ni Fon.

Holo screen: A type of Empire tech where a screen is digitally projected and may be interacted with.

Human: One of the oldest races on Gaia, and the most numerous. Currently ruling the Rose Empire.

Inherents: A type of magical ability that a person can be born with. Some examples include Master of Blades, Voice magic, and Shadow Walkers.

Kijin: Nifoni name for Firilae.

Lanarae: Goddess of healing, war, fighting, the body and physicality. See also: The Three Goddesses.

Learned Magic: The type of magic that allows a caster to cast spells; learned magic is so named because one must learn how to use the glyphs and bridging lines in order tosuccessfully cast spells. A caster must still have enough magical ability in order to activate the array. It is the most common magical ability.

Lester: A type of building material popular in the Empire; it can be white, gray, or black and tends to have a sheen to it. It is stronger than concrete and has a longer life-expectancy.

Lyndiniam: The capital of the Rose Empire and Agale.

Master of Blades: A type of inherent magic most common in Aradians, this ability allows its user to pick up various combat styles by fighting against them.

Med-berth: A piece of Empire tech that provides a readout of a patient's vitals while they are laying on it.

Ni Fon: One of the provinces of the Rose Empire, Ni Fon is located across the Shae Sea from the heart of the Empire. Ni Fon was brought into the Empire only about two hundred years ago, and they have no interest in remaining a province. They call their duchess Empress, and they actively seek to break free from the Empire. They are also interested in trying to make magic and tech work together.

Night Children: An older, more formal term for Vampires.

Norik: A town in northern Agale. The Crystal Light Blade was housed in a museum here until three hundred years ago, when it was stolen.

Nyphoren, the: The elemental twin deities of water, the ocean, and storms. Their names are Nyphora and Nyphore. Created the Veren.

Nyphoren Islands, the: A province of the Rose Empire located in the center of the Shae Sea. They were brought into the Empire almost seven hundred years ago. Originally the home of the Veren, who now live mostly in the deep ocean nearby.

Palace of Dusk: Located in Tarvishte, the seat of power of Romanii. The palace itself has been so steeped in magic over the centuries that it has become somewhat aware, and attempts to help people find their way.

Patoran, the: The elemental twin deities of plants and the earth. Their names are Patori and Patera.

Pattern: The term for an array used by Nifoni mages.

Pitesh: A city in the south of Romanii. It is the closest city to the Tower of Morden.

Romanii: A country in the north of Espon. Ruled by Vampires, when they saw what the Rose Empire was becoming five hundred years ago, they cut themselves off by creating the Warcross Wall.

(Rose) Empire, the: Created a thousand years ago when the countries of Agale, Hispa, Gallia, and Elbe came together under the rule of Queen Saran shortly after Ebryn Stormlight ended the threat of Abomination. Originally under Avari rule, it is now ruled by Humans, and consists of seven provinces: Agale, Gallia, Elbe, the Nyphoren Islands, Ni Fon, Cartago-Mir, and Emerald Shores. Each province is ruled by a duke or duchess, who wield the true power of the Empire.

Season of Veils: The period of time between the Festival of Night on October 31 and the Longest Night on the winter solstice, celebrated in Romanii. All statues of Hades are draped in fabric to imitate the veils the goddess herself wears.

Sea-speak: A dialect spoken mostly by pirates on the Shae Sea.

Selenae: Goddess of knowledge, learning, the mind, and reason. See also: The Three Goddesses.

Shae Sea: The sea to the west on the Rose Empire proper, though the Empire controls much land around and in the sea.

Shinobi: A specialized force of mages utilized by Ni Fon. Shinobi candidates are chosen early, and are raised to be shinobi, known for their loyalty to the ruling power of Ni Fon. Wear a mask over the bottom half of their face. Often specialize in stealth.

Silent Ones: A term foreigners sometimes use for shinobi, referencing both the mask they wear and they fact that they can be eerily silent when they want to be.

Soulforging: A type of magic used by Vampires and priests of Hades. Allows the user to manifest their soul in the form of a crystal, which can then be manipulated into powerful weapons or armor.

Spell Crystal: A way to store spells for future use. Anyone can activate a spell crystal, one does not have to be a mage. A common use is to create a crystal that can warm the bed at night.

Sturlow: A town in northern Agale.

Tadurin: The god of life, chaos, and creation. In theory, equal in power and status to Hades.

Taijin: Nifoni name for Lanarae.

Tarvishte: The capital city of Romanii. On the northern coast.

Temple of Night Rising: Temple to the goddess Hades in Tarvishte.

Three Goddesses, the: Common term for the three sister goddesses, often shortened to just "The Three". Comprised ofLanarae, Selenae, and Firilae. Responsible for the creation of the Avari. They have many names across the globe.

Tower of Morden: The tower of the Warcross Wall where the Vampire mage Morden died casting the spell to create the Wall. Morden remains as a part of the tower as an empathic presence and guard.

Truth Seekers: Specialized, highly trained troops in the Rose Empire. They all wear a blindfold, and use advanced tech. Feared throughout the Empire.

Twins, the: Common way of referring to any of the elemental deities. Context usually makes clear which set is being referred to.

Vampire: A member of any race who has died and been bitten by another Vampire to transfer Hades' gift, gaining immortality. Vampires require blood to live, and will burn in the sun until they are well over a thousand years old. Struggle to cross large bodies of water.

Vaslu: Town in Romanii.

Voice: A type of inherent magic that allows its user to cast magic using their voice. Often become entertainers called Bards.

Warg: Large, wolf-like creatures sacred to the goddess Hades. Are far more intelligent than normal dogs or wolves.

Warcross Wall, the: A magical barrier that separates Romanii and the Rose Empire. Was created about five hundred years ago in a ritual where nine Romanii mages sacrificed themselves to bring it into being. Each mage became one of the towers along the Wall.

Waste, the: A devastated fifty-mile section of land on either side of the Warcross Wall created when the Wall was.

Weave: The Nifoni term for casting spells; also occasionally refers to the spells themselves.

Acknowledgments

Wow, what a journey this has been! When I started writing *Lost Blades* in 2011 I never could have foreseen what the project would become over the next decade. It wouldn't have been possible without the support of many people along the way. Here are some of them.

Thank you:

To Jessy Jacobs, Lydia Troiano, Angel Moisés Cruz, and Bill Millette, who gave me so. Much. Feedback that I sorely needed, got excited with me over plot revelations, and helped me discover new things about my characters and my world. To Josh Hornoff, Ashley MaKhan, Joe Millette, and Andrew LaFontaine, whose enjoyment of the book means everything to me and helped me keep going. To Jade Sisti, without whom this book probably would have continued to languish after I put it down in 2012. To my brother John Sauco, who did not care one whit about spoilers and helped me figure out where the plot was going. To Sarah LaFontaine, who is always willing to listen to me talk and who always has advice whenever I need it.

To my editorial team, Breyonna Jordan, Naomi Munts, and Jane Spencer. Your advice was crucial to the final shape of the book, and I apologize for my excessive love for commas.

To Jessy (again) and Jen Jacobs, who did an amazing job on the audio for my book, giving my characters a literal voice.

And finally, to my parents, from whom I inherited my love of reading and fantasy, and without whose support this never could have been written.

About the Author

Liz Sauco is an author from Rhode Island who enjoys a host of nerdy pastimes, such as crocheting cute animal plushies and playing video games. After graduation from the University of Rhode Island with a degree in Classics, she spent several years teaching Latin to high school students while working on her first manuscript. You can find her on Facebook, Discord, and Tiktok, and read her blog at lizsauco.com.

Free Short Story

Want to stay up to date on the latest news?

Join my newsletter, and receive a free short story "Another Beginning", set twenty years before *Lost Blades*. Be among the first to get news about new releases, giveaways, events, and promotions!

Also By Liz Sauco

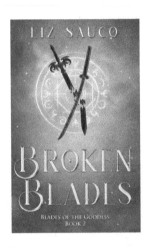

Abomination has returned.
The Goddess must strike back before all is lost –
but are her chosen ready?

Blades of the Goddess book 2, *Broken Blades,* is available now for preorder, and will release on January 12, 2024.

Broken Blades Preview

Jamirh turned on the television and sat down in one of the chairs. A pair of Human women were sitting behind a news desk, images of a mostly destroyed compound of sorts cycling to the side of them. He was about to change the channel to find something more entertaining when he saw the ticker at the bottom read "Aftermath of the Charve Military Base Explosion."

Jamirh blinked. "Hey, that's where Ander said Hel was being held, isn't it?"

Jeri studied the images. "That sounds correct. Wow, She did *not* go down quietly."

"You think she did all that?" Jamirh asked, aghast as he stared at the damage. Multiple buildings had been condemned, whole sections of them having been destroyed. "It looks like there were multiple explosions all across the base."

"Well, She *is* a goddess," Jeri said slowly as the anchors discussed rescue efforts. "And destruction is one of Her domains, so I wouldn't say it's beyond Her abilities, even if She was in a form that limited what She could do." Her voice sounded troubled, almost as though she was trying to convince both of them that was the case.

"I guess we could ask Ander?" Jamirh suggested hesitantly. "Would he be able to ask her?"

"Anyone can ask Her; Ander's just the most likely to hear the answer." She shrugged. "And then he might relay that answer. It honestly might be better to go to the Temple and try to ask Her yourself. He doesn't like to be treated like a phone."

"Maybe that Human did some of it," he theorized, looking at the debris. "Wasn't he supposed to be helping her escape?"

"True," she agreed. "I guess we would have to ask to be sure, though."

"I wonder what happened to him," Jamirh mused. "Did he die with Hel's body? Or did he escape? I didn't think to ask her when we talked about it."

Jeri hesitated. "It doesn't look good from these pictures, but maybe he made it out?"

"–and hundreds of people found themselves trying to get on the base just after the explosion, but when questioned, none seem to remember why," one of the anchors was saying. "The military is still looking into the strange phenomenon."

Jamirh looked at Jeri, who shrugged. "Could be any number of things, honestly, though it sounds like a Queen's Challenge."

He cocked his head to the side. "That shriek-thing she did to the door when we broke out of jail?"

Jeri winced. "Yes. Please don't remind me."

"I would say when you have a hammer, everything looks like a nail, but as a goddess, isn't she technically the hammer?" he mused thoughtfully.

The Vampire twitched. "There's no excuse for using that sort of magic on a door."

The first anchor cut herself off mid-sentence, looking as though she were listening to something through her ear piece. "This is breaking news; we have just been informed that the massive amount of destruction at the Charve Military Base was caused by a gas line explosion," she explained. "One of the old lines runs under the base and exploded at various points due to corrosion–"

Jeri turned very slowly to look at Jamirh, who just shrugged. "What can I say? A lot of our gas lines are apparently faulty."